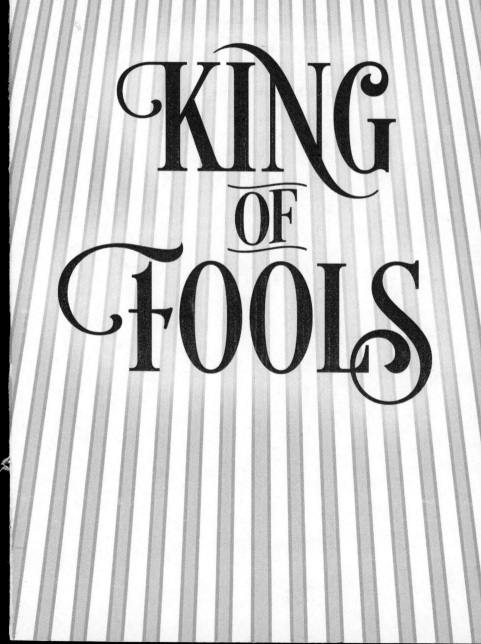

KING OF FOOLS

Books by Amanda Foody

Daughter of the Burning City

The Shadow Game Series

Ace of Shades
King of Fools
Queen of Volts

AMANDA FOOD

KING
OF
FOOLS

inkyard
PRESS

ISBN-13: 978-1-335-04001-5

King of Fools

Copyright © 2019 by Amanda Foody

This edition published by arrangement with Harlequin Books S.A.

For questions and comments about the quality of this book, please contact us at
CustomerService@Harlequin.com.

Inkyard Press
22 Adelaide St. West, 41st Floor
Toronto, Ontario M5H 4E3, Canada
www.InkyardPress.com

Printed in Italy by Grafica Veneta

To Dad, for encouraging all my games, stories and schemes.

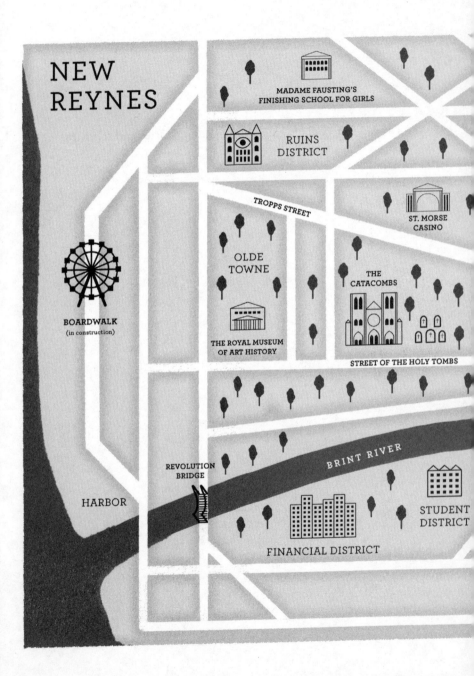

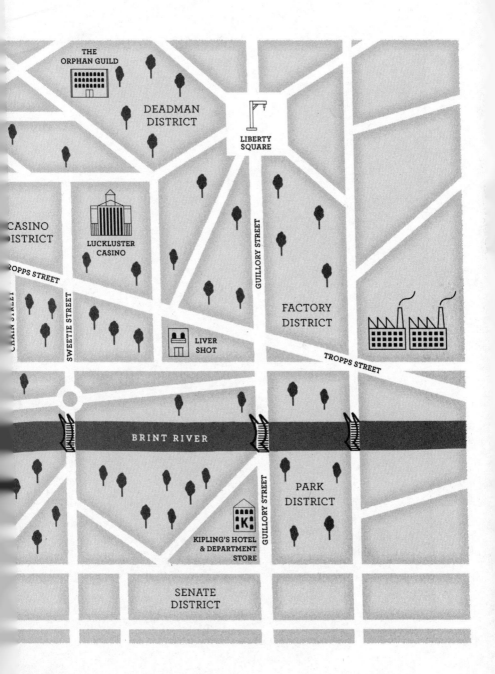

PART I
RISK

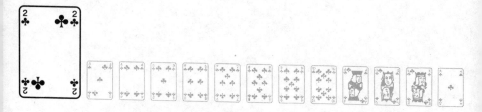

"After the executioner lowered Veil's body from the gallows, he claimed he couldn't remove the wrappings covering Veil's face. He used to wear that black gauze all around his head, you know? Well, the executioner said he couldn't take it off. That it was part of Veil's face like his own skin."

—*A legend of the North Side*

LEVI

Ten hours after escaping the Shadow Game, Levi Glaisyer found his destiny slapped onto the side of a dumpster behind St. Morse Casino.

Criminal Wanted Dead or Alive
Accomplice in the Assassination of the Chancellor

If asked, Levi would deny believing in destiny. Five years on the streets of the City of Sin had taught him that destiny and luck were for the desperate and the thickheaded. As a card dealer, he'd often encountered believers bemoaning the mirrors they'd shattered or the white cats they'd passed. They'd rub lucky coins between their fingers or kiss the shriveled remains of a rabbit's foot, praying for divine intervention in a game that Levi had already rigged.

For Levi, when the cards no longer ran in his favor, he cheated—simple as that. Luck was a mechanism to be devised, and luck and destiny were merely two sides of the same coin.

Yet as he stared at the wanted poster, sirens wailing across New Reynes in search of him, he couldn't deny that something felt inevitable about this moment. The thought made his heart pound, even with the Augustine bodyguard looming beside him. Everything in Levi's life, all his dreams and follies and tragedies, had led to this afternoon, to this alley, to this poster, to this single flip of destiny's coin.

Dead?

Or alive?

Maybe he was meant for more, the feeling of inevitability whispered to him. Maybe this was his new beginning.

He checked his watch. His new beginning was late.

At half past noon, the Casino District was unusually vacant. Gone were the unlucky gamblers, the slovenly drunks, the outrageous street performers, the wandering tourists. The honest and the crooked, the naïve and the wicked had all found their ways home to sleep off whiskey hangovers and mourn empty purses, leaving backwash-filled bottles and half-smoked cigars clustered in the gutters. Despite the lack of patrons, the street's neon signs continued to flash, the ragtime music continued to hum, and the shows continued to play. No matter who you were, what you'd done, or how little you had, Tropps Street was open for your business.

It was remarkably hot in New Reynes today, even for the mid-June afternoon. Levi's bodyguard wiped the sweat collecting from his brow and aired out his reeking shirt.

Levi didn't know or trust this man. But anyone who worked for Vianca Augustine—the owner of St. Morse Casino and the donna of the notorious Augustine crime Family—knew better than to cross her. Regardless of the three-thousand-volt bounty on Levi's head, this man would follow Vianca's orders and protect him. Greed always answered to fear.

Again, Levi checked his watch. He'd pace if he weren't so

exhausted and achy from his collection of injuries: two broken ribs, a black eye, several bruises, and a bandaged knife wound. The City of Sin hadn't been merciful to him these past few days.

After he and Enne had escaped from the Shadow Game and returned to St. Morse, he'd managed a mere five hours of shut-eye before the bodyguard had knocked on Enne's apartment door and informed Levi that his ride to Zula Slyk's safe house would soon arrive. Zula owned an illegal monarchist newspaper in Olde Town and, several days prior, had been the one to coldly inform Enne that her mother was dead. If Levi had a choice, he'd never see that heartless woman again. But thanks to Vianca's unbreakable omerta, Levi never had a choice. Zula's was safe. What mattered right now was moving from here to there without meeting trouble along the way.

But Zula Slyk was the least of his problems.

For the past two years, Levi had been running an investment scam, which was how he'd earned the enemies who'd invited him to the Shadow Game. Once the scam started to crumble, all he'd wanted was to clean it up so he could focus on his gang, the Irons.

He still wanted that. To build his empire, just as he'd always dreamed.

But Levi was in a predicament. The lords of the other two gangs were wanted criminals as well, but Ivory and Scavenger could count on the loyalty and protection of their associates for their safety, whereas half the Irons would probably sell Levi out simply to watch him hang. If Levi was spending all his time trapped under Zula's watch, he'd have no shot at rebuilding his gang. He'd broken out of one cage only to stumble into another.

He tore the wanted poster from the dumpster and crumpled it in his fist.

Maybe he was meant for nothing.

A swanky Amberlite motorcar appeared at the mouth of the alley, painted black and matte as if coated in gunpowder. Levi ducked closer to his bodyguard. Vianca had scheduled his ride, and Vianca didn't do inconspicuous. The car had no metallic fixtures or studded bumpers to be seen. It could be a trap.

Once the car eased deeper into the alley, the driver's window rolled down and a gloved hand beckoned Levi inside. Beside him, the bodyguard nodded for Levi to depart. Apparently this was his scheduled ride after all.

Wanted men don't do flashy, Levi reminded himself oh, so tragically.

He groaned in pain as he slid onto the plush leather of the back seat and shut the door. The motorcar lurched forward, leaving the St. Morse escort behind.

Inside was utter darkness.

As his eyes adjusted, he took in a shape in the seat across from him and realized, breath catching, that his private getaway wasn't so private.

He snapped the fingers of one hand, sparking a faint flame that offered a pinch of light—one of the few useful tricks his orb-making blood talent provided him.

His other hand instinctively felt for his pistol.

The man looked nearly forty. A patch concealed his left eye, but there was no hiding the ugly pink scar that snaked across his brow into his receding copper hairline. His skin was fair, his gray trench coat designed by Ulani Maxirello, and his teeth whiter than a tooth-polish advertisement.

"It was time we met," the man said, as if assuming Levi already knew his identity.

Levi never forgot a face, and although he'd never seen this man before, there *was* something familiar about him. Perhaps in the reptilian green of his remaining eye. In the sharp slant of his nose, the narrow shape of his jawline. Even if his individual features were neither unattractive nor unsettling, collectively and without explanation, his appearance made Levi's skin crawl.

Maybe this wasn't his scheduled ride after all.

"Let's not have any trouble," Levi warned, clicking the safety off his gun loud enough for his companion to hear.

Rather than reacting to Levi's threat, the man tossed him that day's copy of *The Crimes & The Times*. Levi's heart skipped several beats as he examined the matching wanted posters on the front page: him and Séance, whom he knew better as Enne Salta. She'd arrived in New Reynes only ten days ago, but since then, she'd managed to earn a more noteworthy reputation than Levi had in five years. In the portrait, Enne had on the same silk mask she'd worn during the Shadow Game, obscuring all but her black lips.

Her bounty is five hundred volts more than mine, he noted sourly.

Still, they made quite a handsome duo on the front page. Looking at them, that same feeling of inevitability stirred inside him. For a moment, he let himself fantasize about destiny, about how his and Enne's were intertwined, about how badly he wished to intertwine them further. He knew he shouldn't—couldn't. Falling for Enne held its own dangers.

Levi eased his grip on the gun. If this man was an assailant, he wouldn't be updating Levi on today's current events. Still, Levi didn't let go of the weapon. Not yet.

"We've never met, Pup, but I know your reputation," the man started. Levi quietly seethed. He hated that nickname. It came from his split talent—his weaker talent—for sensing auras, but he hardly smelled auras like a dog, like everyone assumed. The nickname was just another way to belittle him. The North Side had always viewed him as a kid playing gangster. "I didn't think you'd be the quiet type."

"I'm still guessing at your name." Still guessing at why a stranger had hijacked Levi's getaway, if not to collect the reward.

"How quickly the city's forgotten." The man pouted, a rather strange look for someone his age. He didn't seem to wear his years comfortably. "But I should think you, of all people, would see the family resemblance. Why do you think it was so easy for me to intercept your car?" He inspected Levi. "I'm told you're my mother's favorite."

Harrison Augustine. Vianca's estranged only child and the Augustine Family prince. It was easy now to spot the resemblance. They carried the same serious, noble features, the same paleness that revealed the green of their veins snaking across their foreheads and necks. He even spoke like his mother, purring names as if he owned them.

If he was anything like Vianca, then he couldn't be trusted.

"I know who you are now," Levi said. "But I still don't know why you're here."

Harrison tapped the newspaper's front page. "You and this Séance character, escaping the impossible Shadow Game and killing both the Chancellor and Sedric Torren in a single night. You're the talk of the town. As soon as I heard what happened, I knew I had to meet you."

Levi stared at the man and reflected on his words. Even without his inheritance or his mother's empire, Harrison was powerful. The Augustine and Torren crime Families were notorious in New Reynes, and Harrison, in his eighteen years of absence, had graduated from prince to mystery. No one knew why he'd left or what he'd been doing since.

Yet here he sat, claiming he needed to meet Levi, of all people. If he was after the bounty, then this seemed a roundabout way of acquiring it. But he'd made a mistake if he thought Levi had anything to offer him. Levi had nothing but the stolen clothes on his back.

"They used to say this city is a game," Harrison mused, drawing a cigar from his pocket. He offered one to Levi, but Levi shook his head. He hated smoking. "Do they still say that?"

"They do."

"Even so, New Reynes must've changed a lot." Harrison lit the cigar, and the car filled with its musky odor. "A seventeen-year-old street lord. I'm impressed you've survived this long."

Levi stiffened, even though he was used to this sort of condescension. "I survived the Shadow Game. The Chancellor is *dead*—"

"Yes, yes." Harrison blew a cloud of smoke in Levi's face, making his eyes water as he scrunched his nose and held in the urge to cough. "And street lords who kill chancellors don't live long. So tell me—why should I bet on you? Even though *you* were the one who killed the Chancellor?"

Levi narrowed his eyes. Was Harrison trying to test him? "I don't know where you got such an idea, but—"

"Don't play coy. The papers say that Séance killed him, but I know the truth. I have friends in the House of Shadows." Yet another reason not to trust him. Maybe this was death coming for Levi after all. He kept his hand on his gun. "They're embarrassed. Chancellor Semper, the revered Father of the Revolution, killed by some scrappy card dealer? But this Séance character... Well, she's a more impressive villain."

Levi's moral compass didn't point north past the North Side, but if it was Séance's identity that Harrison wanted, he would never give that up. Besides, Levi felt he was an impressive enough character in his own right.

"I'm sorry the wigheads feel that way," Levi answered, unable to resist the empty boast. "I'm sure they'll find me a formidable enemy."

"That's what I'm hoping."

Levi's spirits lifted at those words. No one ever saw potential in him. Right now he could barely see potential in himself.

Harrison turned the page of the newspaper.

SENATE CALLS FOR WAR ON THE GANGS

"*War* is a strong word," Levi murmured.

"It's been said before," Harrison replied. "And it's why I'm here."

Before the Great Street War eighteen years ago, two street lords, Veil and Havoc, had ruled the city like kings. It was the golden age of New Reynes crime. But then the wigheads had forced the North Side to its knees, and both of the lords were hanged in Liberty Square in a spectacle of justice and judgment. Ever since then, gangs like the Irons, the Scarhands, and the Doves had attempted to replicate those empires of old. But no one had succeeded, in part because the North Side had never truly recovered from the war, or from the Revolution seven years before it.

"They've talked about clearing out the gangs for years," Levi said.

"The Chancellor was assassinated by—as the city dubs you both—two street lords," Harrison said. "This isn't just talk. It's a promise. And the war has already begun."

Nerves quivered in Levi's chest, and he had the urge to raise his hand to his throat to assure himself there was no noose knotted around it. New Reynes had raised him on its legends; he knew the Great Street War's bloodbath as if he'd lived it.

He scanned the rest of the article, which included the bounties not just of Levi and Séance, but the other lords and seconds, as well. It was the most informative write-up of the gangs he'd encountered since Enne's unusual and questionable tourist guidebook.

KNOWN STREET LORDS

THE DOVES
Leader: "Ivory"
Second: "Scythe"

THE SCARHANDS
Leader: Jonas
"Scavenger" Maccabees
Second: Unknown

THE ORPHAN GUILD
Leader: Bryce
"the Guildmaster" Balfour
Second: "Rebecca"

THE IRONS
Leader: Levi "Pup" Glaisyer
Second: Jac Mardlin

FIFTH GANG: NAME UNKOWN
Leader: "Séance"
Second: Unknown

Levi grinned. His bounty was the same as Scavenger's and Ivory's. Even so, he had a few grievances with the article. For one, the Orphan Guild wasn't a gang—it was an enterprise. Second, breaking the law once hardly made Enne a criminal mastermind. And last, his title wasn't Pup; it was the Iron Lord.

To his shock, each of those named also had a wanted poster—other than Ivory, of course, as no one alive had ever glimpsed her face. Levi's pulse hammered as he studied each of them. In comparison to their fairer features, like those of the majority in New Reynes, Levi's brown skin stuck out. He would be easier to spot, and more at risk.

Then his eyes fell on the detailed sketch of his best friend, Jac Mardlin, with his messy gray-blond hair and lazy grin. He was the only one depicted smiling.

AMANDA FOODY

Jac was likely still sleeping on Enne's floor where Levi had left him. Jac always knew his association with Levi would cause him trouble, but he probably had no idea his wanted posters were already plastered across the city. Before he'd departed, Levi had shaken him awake and asked to meet with him this afternoon. He hoped Jac hadn't ventured outside yet. The sirens were searching for him, too.

"They should put these posters on trading cards." Levi faked a laugh, trying to lighten the mood.

"You're rather cavalier about all of this." Harrison slapped the paper. "This is a death sentence." That, too, he said like a purr.

"So was the Shadow Game," Levi countered. "Now tell me—why are you here?"

Harrison drummed his fingers on the window ledge. On his middle finger, he wore the Augustine emerald ring, same as Vianca.

"I've returned to destroy my mother," he said.

For the second time that morning, Levi had come face-to-face with his destiny. The sirens outside grew quieter, and the nerves knotting in his chest began to unravel. It was a second sign. Too blatant for Levi not to pay attention.

A New Reynes without Vianca—*that* he'd risk nearly anything for.

Maybe this was a new beginning after all.

"You know I can't help you." The omerta, an unbreakable oath Vianca had trapped him into taking, prevented Levi from hurting her. Harrison's blood name was Augustine, which meant he'd inherited his mother's talent for omertas, so he knew their rules better than anyone. And, of course, all of New Reynes—and certainly Harrison—knew that Levi was at Vianca's mercy.

"But you wouldn't be here if you didn't have a plan," Levi added.

22

"I know my way around omertas. You can't directly hurt her, but you can do almost anything else so long as she doesn't expressly forbid it," Harrison explained. "The Senate election for the New Reynes representative seat is in November. It's one of the most influential positions in politics. Sedric Torren was the First Party's candidate, but now that he's been so conveniently removed, *I'll* be taking his place."

Levi's breath hitched. It was no secret that Vianca supported the monarchist party, the First Party's only opposition. However, despite radical measures, the monarchists had never once won an election, and they likely never would. Politics was Vianca's crusade, and she would view Harrison's campaign as the ultimate betrayal.

"You're certain you'll replace Sedric?" Levi asked. The city hadn't seen Harrison in eighteen years. He seemed like a dark horse candidate taken to a new extreme.

"The new chancellor herself asked me to. You see, unlike previous years, the monarchist party has a growing amount of support—primarily here, in the North Side. Being from the North Side and with his Family's connections, Sedric provided votes that are now crucial to whoever wins this election. So she gave me a call."

"But you've been gone for years," Levi said, furrowing his eyebrows. "What do you know about anything that's been happening here?"

Harrison leaned forward. In the darkness of the car, all Levi saw was the glow of Harrison's cigar and the outline of his once-broken nose. Nervously, Levi wondered if he'd offended him.

"That's exactly why I need you to work for me in the North Side. I *don't* have friends here anymore, but you do. We could become powerful together."

That was almost funny enough to be a joke. The whole

city was after Levi. His own gang had betrayed him. Even if the Shadow Game had given him a slight boost in reputation, he'd always been the boy in way over his head.

Before Levi could correct him, Harrison said, "In return, I'll kill my mother. It will have to be after the election, after I win. I won't let her be hailed by the monarchist party as some sort of martyr."

Not only would Harrison see his Family's empire destroyed, but he'd end Vianca along with it.

Levi was struck speechless.

"I realize, with the headlines, you're in a tough spot," Harrison added, "so if you do agree to help me, I'm willing to leverage my own assets to ensure you won't need to worry about the bounty."

It was too good to be true—of course it was. And Harrison had expectations Levi would certainly fail to meet.

But even with his heart racing in warning, all Levi asked was, "How?"

"I know the whiteboot captain," Harrison answered, his voice slick as a businessman's, even as they discussed murder and war. "He can be convinced to ignore Iron Territory, if given enough voltage. I'll purchase local property to make it seem like my interests in Olde Town are purely financial. It should provide you some safety. But while I pay him off, you'll still need to do your own work increasing your personal protection. You might be safe from the whiteboots, but you'll be vulnerable to betrayal. I hear you know a thing or two about that."

Harrison Augustine hears a lot of things.

He was referring to Chez Phillips, Levi's previous third in the Irons. A few days ago, Chez had turned the Irons against Levi and challenged him for lordship—nearly killing him. In the end, Levi had overpowered him, but he'd gone further than he'd meant to. Chez would bear those scars for life, and he'd never be back.

If Harrison knew about Chez, then he knew Levi's friends were few. Yet still he saw potential in him.

It made Levi want to prove him right.

Harrison rolled down the window to let out the smoke building in the back seat. The noise of sirens filled the car, but Levi stayed focused on Harrison's words. "Visit the Catacombs. Ask for Narinder Basra. He's on the Street of the Holy Tombs in Olde Town, and he's well connected. He'll find you a replacement for your third. Maybe even a new reputation."

Hesitance pinched the back of Levi's mind. This was too simple. If Harrison was offering him the world, then what would Levi need to sacrifice in return?

"You've thought of everything. This would solve all my problems," Levi conceded. "So what would you have me do for you?"

"I'm nervous that any violence between the North and South Sides will only fuel the monarchist cause. They believe the First Party has taken advantage of the system to keep themselves in power, to keep the North Side weak. I'm not sure either of us can stop the conflict from escalating, but what I need is information. You were friends with Eight Fingers— become friends with the other lords. I need to know about everyone who matters in the North Side. I want to know the plans before they happen."

Though it was true Levi had been friends with Reymond— Eight Fingers, the previous lord of the Scarhands—he had no reason to be friends with the other lords. Despite what *The Crimes & The Times* reported, Levi barely *was* a lord anymore. And if he was going to cultivate any relationship or influence with them, at the very least he needed to have the Irons back. The Irons might have betrayed him, but they were the slickest, most cunning tricksters in the city, and Levi had spent years scouting his gangsters and building their clientele. He wouldn't turn his back on them yet. But regaining their trust would mean taking deadly risks, rising up when he should be lying low. Even with the protection Harrison offered, it was a dangerous gamble.

It was lucky for Harrison that what Levi wanted, more than anything, was to have the Irons back.

Lucky for Harrison that Levi was a gambling man.

"That could be arranged," Levi said. Even as he tried to keep his voice steady and professional, his own excitement betrayed him. This was truly an offer he couldn't refuse.

Harrison smiled. "I like your confidence."

"It won't be easy," Levi admitted. "But it can be done."

"There's one job in particular, though, that my entire plan absolutely hinges upon. What Sedric Torren was providing that I cannot," Harrison continued, and Levi leaned closer. "The gangs might have monopolies on certain crimes, but the Augustine and Torren Families control almost the entirety of the North Side. If they don't directly employ someone, they own their building. They provided them a loan. They did them a favor. With the monarchist support growing, the votes that Sedric would have provided for the First Party are pivotal to the whole election. Without them, as things stand now, I would lose by a landslide."

Levi's eyes widened. He always thought the monarchists were a radical minority. He had no idea they wielded that much power. Maybe he should've paid more attention to Vianca's political lectures.

"It seems Chancellor Fenice should've just tapped Sedric's Family successor, then, rather than you," Levi said.

"That's true, but the Torren Family is likely to be without a don for a long time—maybe months. Neither Charles nor Delia—Sedric's cousins, brother and sister and equally bloodthirsty—will relinquish their claim without a fight. I could help one of them win, but I can't ensure it. So I need to know who to sponsor. I *need* the next don of the Family to be in my debt, otherwise my election and *your* freedom are off the table."

"You're asking me to call the winner," Levi said slowly. "I don't have the means to do that. I still owe the Torren Family ten thousand volts that I have no intention or ability to repay. I can't give you more than fifty-fifty odds."

"Well, it wouldn't be *you*. You'll send someone inside the Torren empire, someone you trust."

Levi could count the number of people he trusted on two fingers: Enne and Jac. Vianca was certainly already concocting her own plans for Enne as Séance.

Which left Jac.

Levi's stomach churned. There was no way he could send his best friend, barely two years clean, into the very narcotics empire that had nearly destroyed him.

Levi couldn't manage even a smile of false confidence. "Surely you have someone *you* trust?"

"I don't want this traced back to me," Harrison answered. "The monarchists—somewhat correctly—believe the First Party is corrupt. The other advantage I offer as a candidate is my blank slate. I might be able to bribe some whiteboots for what appear to be business ventures, but I can't be caught rigging power struggles in crime Families or making deals with the person who killed the Chancellor, can I?" His smile looked uncomfortably wide.

Levi took a deep breath and swallowed his nausea. He knew what Jac would say, of course. That Harrison was too great of an opportunity to lose. That Levi always had too little faith in him. That Jac was ready for it.

Levi wasn't so sure.

"These are my terms," Harrison told him. "Will you accept?"

"Can I think on it?" Even if this opportunity meant every-thing and then some to Levi, it meant asking a lot of Jac—Levi needed to speak to him first.

"There's no time for that. I have campaign strategy meet-ings in a few hours. I need your decision now."

The car was coming to a stop. Harrison flicked what re-mained of his cigar out the window.

What Harrison was offering Levi was invaluable. A chance to escape Vianca. A level of protection while Levi built his empire. An opportunity to ally with power instead of merely playing with it.

Harrison was offering Levi his destiny.

But it meant throwing Jac into an assignment that could set him back years—or worse. It meant lying to Vianca for how-ever long it took Harrison to carry out his plans. Those were dangerous risks. Levi preferred gambling with volts—not his best friend's life, not his own.

Harrison peeked out the crack in the window. "You don't have much time. The whiteboots are all over Olde Town." His lips curled into a smile. "But give me the word and a few hours. They'll be gone before this evening."

Everything Levi had ever dreamed of versus throwing Jac into a dangerous assignment. He knew exactly what he wanted, of course: to play the game. He wanted it so badly he ached.

A relapse would be Jac's fault, not Levi's, but that didn't mean Levi wouldn't blame himself if it happened.

He knew he wasn't being fair to Jac. If his friend were here, he'd be furious that Levi thought so little of him. Jac would tell him to worry about making them rich, and Jac would worry about himself.

Jac would tell him to take the offer.

At least he hoped that was the case, and not just his own selfishness swaying him.

"I accept," Levi said, nearly choking on the words.

Harrison opened the door for him and handed him a business card. The only thing written on it was a phone number. "Contact me when you have something."

Levi nodded, adjusted his felt homburg hat, and painfully climbed out of the car. Outside, the Street of the Holy Tombs was a grim lane of gothic cathedrals, sharpened spires, and ghostly remnants of the Faith. They'd traveled to the quiet eastern quarter of Olde Town, the most historic neighborhood of the city, where even the shadows were prickly, and where darkness reigned over the day.

It was home.

"I'm glad we met, Levi," Harrison said. With that, he closed the door and the car sped off.

Collar popped, hat shielding his face, Levi ducked into Zula's quaint shop front of *Her Forgotten Histories*, humming a ragtime tune and drowning out his nerves. He'd made his decision, and whatever dangers he faced as a result, from this moment on, his life was changed.

Yesterday he was Levi Glaisyer, a card dealer famous in niche circles.

Today he was Levi Glaisyer, accomplice in the greatest political assassination since the Revolution, survivor of a notorious execution game, and ally with a soon-to-be powerful force on the South Side.

Yesterday he was vulnerable. Today he would become untouchable.

His destiny was upon him.

ENNE

♥ ♠ ♦ ♣

In her dream, she wore a gown. The sleeves were sheer, the color of meringue cream, and as delicate as moth wings. A lilac ribbon cinched her waist and fluttered down her skirts, lost amid the scalloped tiers and cascading chiffon ruffles. As she descended the grand staircase, the others in the hall watched her join them with approving smiles, and the chandeliers of Bellamy had never glowed so brightly.

Enne Salta woke with a gun tucked beneath her pillow, her tokens clutched in her fist, and volts humming in her blood.

For a sweet moment, Enne lingered in the dream and forgot the events of the past ten days. Forgot that she'd abandoned all she knew to find her mother, Lourdes, in the City of Sin. That she was trapped within an unbreakable oath to a despicable Mafia donna. That she'd killed two men. That her mother was dead. That her old life—the life of that dream—was gone, and her innocence and identity along with it.

Then she rolled over to see Lola Sanguick—reluctant criminal, blood gazer for the Orphan Guild, and collector of pointy objects—drooling on the other pillow, and Enne's reveries vanished. Lola looked just as unnerving asleep as she did awake, her white hair tangled and greasy, her canines bared, her arms resting at her sides like a corpse. If you asked Lola, she was Enne's second. If you asked Enne, she was her friend.

Across the room, Jac Mardlin loomed in the bedroom doorway. Whether consciously or not, he always stood like a soldier—shoulders back, expression serious, fists clenched and braced for battle. Every inch of his upper body was covered in intricate tattoos—all black, except for the red *J* on the underside of his right arm, and the matching diamond on the left. Like Lola, he was intimidating at first glance—until his single dimple betrayed his stern exterior, or until he opened his mouth...to say anything at all, really.

Enne scrambled to cover herself. She was wearing only a nightdress. "Barging into a lady's bedroom, are you?"

Jac cocked an eyebrow. "Is that how you're going to refer to yourself? As a street *lady?*"

Admittedly, it did sound like a more fitting title to Enne than street *lord.*

"Where's Levi?" she asked. Last night, she and Levi had returned to St. Morse in the hour after sunrise, and all four of them had slept through the morning in her apartment.

"He already left," Jac answered.

Enne fought off a troublesome pinch of disappointment. Thinking about Levi brought back a rush of painful memories from the Shadow Game. The panic that had washed over her when she'd first glimpsed the House of Shadows. How dreadful Levi had looked as she gambled for his life. The surge of power she'd felt as she fired the gun and the Shadow Game's timer shattered into a hundred pieces.

By now, the news of what had happened in the House of Shadows had surely traveled across the city. Although Enne's true identity was unknown, Levi's wasn't. She hoped he'd left St. Morse without trouble. She didn't even know when they'd next see each other. Levi had become something like a lifeline for her since she'd arrived in New Reynes, and he'd always been merely an elevator ride away.

She caught herself. Her emotions were stormy and twisted in her stomach, as they lately were whenever she thought about Levi. But she wasn't a fool; Levi was being hunted by the law, and due to her Mizer heritage and persona as Séance, she was only one mistake away from exposure and execution. Romance was hardly worth that risk.

"I'm gonna meet him in a few hours," Jac told her. He walked to the window on the far side of the room and peeked out the curtain. There was a faint sounding of sirens. "Listen to this. It hasn't stopped for a second—not all night. I'm surprised Levi slept at all."

"Did you?" Enne asked.

He ran his fingers nervously through his dull blond hair. He was already fair, but right now he looked especially pale. "I never sleep well."

Enne's hand trembled as she squeezed her two tokens. The pair of coins were similar in many ways: both brass, both old, both depicting a cameo of a Mizer—a member of the families who had once ruled the world's many kingdoms, until revolutionaries overthrew their thrones and killed every Mizer left alive. The smaller coin—the queen's token—was a gift from Lourdes, a trinket Enne always kept with her to remind her of her mother. Lola was the one who'd recognized the uneven ridge patterns on its side as a key, and together, they'd opened up Lourdes' secret bank account, where an impossible fortune had once been stored.

By the time they got there, it was nearly empty. One of the objects that remained was the king's token, larger and purely a coin. Although the metal always hummed with an inexplicable warmth, last night, the king's eye had turned purple. But only Enne could see that.

Likely because she'd awakened her dormant Mizer blood talent during the Shadow Game. Even now, she could feel the volts, warm and buzzing within her skin—faint, but there. Maybe the color of the king's eyes was something only a Mizer could see.

Or maybe she was simply going shatz. The City of Sin had changed Enne in many ways, but she was far too practical to start thinking like a superstitious Faithful.

She closed her eyes and squeezed the coins again, tuning out the sirens searching for her and Levi. The more she listened to them, the more she could hear something else in their sounds—a phantom *tick, tick, tick*, like the timer from the Shadow Game. She could still picture the gray, unfeeling faces of the other players from the Phoenix Club. It haunted her that somewhere in New Reynes, they went about their own lives, despite how they had tried to end hers.

Lourdes was dead at their hands, and Enne's birth mother had suffered the same fate.

Yet still the perpetrators lived.

Before Enne's thoughts could continue down this unsettling path, Jac choked out, "They won't stop looking for Levi." He looked up through the space between the curtains, as if searching for gathering storm clouds in a clear sky.

His words did nothing to calm her nerves. The *tick, tick, tick* grew louder. She shot an anxious glance at her night table to assure herself the clockwork timer wasn't actually beside her. Her free hand instinctively felt for the gun underneath her pillow.

She'd destroyed the timer once. She'd escaped.

She could do it again.

Lola stirred and pulled the blankets over her head. "Sounds like doom."

"You could see doom in the burn markings on your toast," Enne snapped. She wasn't in the mood to deal with Lola's constant pessimism.

Lola clicked her tongue and rolled over, her back to both of them.

Enne carefully set both the tokens and her revolver on the nightstand before standing up. Once she did, she realized how tired she was—tired all the way down to her bones. The stains on her bedsheets betrayed how terribly she'd slept the past few nights; they were gray from sweat and grief-stricken tears.

Three days ago, Enne had learned that her mother was dead. And despite all that had happened, and all the mystery still clouding Lourdes' double life, three days was hardly enough time to mourn.

Especially when there were other emotions layered within her grief, complicating it, twisting it. There was the frustration at never truly knowing Lourdes. Guilt that Enne had unwittingly foiled her mother's efforts to protect her. Hurt that Lourdes had used her talents to keep Enne isolated her entire life.

Even worse than realizing she'd been wrong about Lourdes was realizing she'd been wrong about herself. Talents were more than simply abilities—they were a part of a person's identity. Every person possessed two. The stronger one was called the blood talent, and the weaker one, the split talent. All of Enne's life, she'd believed she was a Salta, that she came from a common, mundane dancing family. In Bellamy, she'd struggled and wept trying to keep up with the illustrious dancing talents of her classmates. That was who she had been—the person always reaching for next to last. The person never truly belonging. The person who couldn't help but fail.

Because Lourdes had let her believe it.

It would take a long time to untangle those emotions. For now, all she understood was how deeply she missed her mother.

"Vianca will want to see you," Jac said warily, once again

interrupting Enne's thoughts. He was right—last night, Vianca had instructed Enne to find her as soon as she woke up. *I have excellent plans for you, my dear,* Vianca had purred.

An acidic mixture of fear and hatred rose in her throat when she thought about Vianca. Whatever Vianca had planned for her, it had little to do with Enne's well-being and all to do with the donna's games with her enemies across the city. Enne's only value was her usefulness. Even though Vianca couldn't remove her omerta even if she wanted to, there were other ways to dispose of Enne...if Enne no longer impressed.

Enne refused to let that happen. She'd lost too much to the City of Sin to lose her life, as well. No matter what it took, she *would* survive this city.

She rose, pushing her concerns away. "I'll go see Vianca now. Both of you, wait here until I come back."

"I didn't realize I was taking orders from you now, missy," Jac said, smirking.

Enne didn't rise to his provocation. "It's past noon. Vianca will have news about what's happened while we slept. You shouldn't go outside unaware."

"And what will we do while we wait?" Lola asked, yanking the blankets from her face. "Play cards?"

"You look like a sore loser, Dove," Jac teased.

"I don't gamble away my voltage."

He shot her a sly smile. "Oh, there's more you can bet than volts."

Lola sat up, her expression unamused. "I've killed men twice as big as you."

Enne knew better than to believe her. Lola was all talk, like when she'd claimed she could drive and then nearly flipped their hot-wired motorcar, or when she'd threatened Enne's life but could barely hold her own ground under attack. Jac would best her within seconds in a fight.

But still, her glare cut sharper than any of her knives. Jac averted his eyes and rubbed the back of his head sheepishly.

Enne grabbed a dress out of her closet and walked to the bathroom. She stared at her strange violet eyes in the mirror, eyes that had been brown until last night. Her hand trembled as she reached for the trick contact lenses Levi had given her. It would be easier if he were here. If she didn't have to face the donna—and the consequences of what they had done—alone.

She wondered if he'd woken thinking the same.

On her way out the door, Enne called back to Lola, "Don't scare Jac too much while I'm gone."

One thing Enne missed desperately about Bellamy was the decor. There, upholstery was floral, curtains were frilled, and everything was the color of macarons—cantaloupe orange, pistachio green, and rose pink. Enne's bedroom had resembled a patisserie, and for her, serenity was curling up on her bed amid cream-colored blankets, with a plate of cucumber sandwiches, a scandalous romance novel by her favorite author, and a beeswax candle scenting her room with lavender.

If Enne's aesthetic was a bakery, then Vianca's was a very expensive grotto. All of St. Morse Casino was decorated in emerald and sapphire, with dark wood and velvet fabric and whatever else devoured the light. There was something sinister in its details. The way the legs of tables curled like coiled snakes. The way it smelled of vinegar, like something pickled and preserved. The way the portraits of executed Mizer families lined each of the hallways, staring at unsettled patrons as they passed.

And Vianca, her long fingernails clacking against her desk, her reptilian green eyes narrowed and fixed on Enne's throat, was exactly the sort of monster that slithered out of grottos.

"Come here," Vianca cooed as Enne shut the office door. The pale skin around her forehead and lips sagged in the dim fluorescent light. "Let me look at you."

Enne gulped and walked to Vianca's desk. The old woman wrapped her bony, ring-covered fingers around Enne's chin and pulled her down to examine her face. Her breath smelled of tea and vermouth.

Startled at the close inspection, Enne swallowed as her stomach leaped into her throat, and she prayed the purple of her eyes didn't show through the contacts. Keeping secrets from Vianca Augustine was dangerous. She kept enough portraits of Mizers in her casino to recognize when one was trembling right in front of her, even if the world believed every Mizer to be dead.

Don't let them see your fear. She mentally recited one of Lourdes's rules, which her mother had always told her were for proper behavior. She'd learned last week that they were actually the street rules of New Reynes. Apparently behaving like a lady or like a criminal wasn't so different.

"You'd never know, looking at you," Vianca mused. "You must have fangs hidden beneath your cupid's bow. Or shadows lurking in those doe eyes."

Those words didn't sit well with Enne. Vianca was the only monster in this room.

Vianca let her go. "I gained more than I'd imagined with you, my dear. And I reward those who please me."

She reached into her desk drawer and pulled out a leather pouch. She opened it and removed a glass orb, sparking with volts. It glowed bright enough to light the room, and Enne guessed there were at least a hundred inside. A small fortune on its own, and there looked to be several orbs in the pouch.

"I've put up with interviews about Mr. Glaisyer all morning for this voltage, and here I am, giving it to you." Vianca patted Enne's hand. "Remember this. Remember how well I treat you."

"Thank you, Madame," Enne managed. Volts were hardly enough to forgive how Vianca had quite literally delivered

Enne to Sedric Torren, wrapped in a bow and all, but Enne wasn't so proud that she wouldn't take them—nor so unintelligent as not to thank the donna of the Augustine Family for such a generous gift.

"Buy yourself whatever you need. And Mr. Glaisyer and Mr. Mardlin, as well. Now take a seat."

Enne did so, laying the pouch on her lap. Of course she hadn't come here only to be doted on. Vianca always wanted something. She might give occasionally, but she would always take twice as much.

Vianca slid Enne that morning's edition of *The Crimes & The Times*. Enne stared in horror at the wanted sketch of herself below the headline. Séance's black mask covered most of her features, and although Enne *knew* it was supposed to be her, it wasn't an exact match. Her jawline wasn't wide enough, and her forehead was much too high. No one would pass her on the street and look twice.

Unlike hers, Levi's adjacent sketch was entirely recognizable. He wore his signature smirk, like he wasn't the least bit surprised to find himself on the front page.

SENATE CALLS FOR WAR ON THE GANGS

Enne's stomach dropped as she scanned the article. There were portraits of the lord and second of every gang, as well as the Orphan Guild. She held her breath as she examined Jac's easy smile and the warrant for his arrest and execution below it. She really hoped he'd listened to her and stayed in her room.

"Have you heard of Worner Prescott?" Vianca asked.

Enne skimmed the page, in case she'd missed his name. He wasn't mentioned. "No, Madame."

"And that is precisely the problem." Vianca sighed and poured herself a refill of her tea, though the drink looked long cold. "There's an election this November for the seat of the New Reynes representative—one of the most influential positions in the Senate. Worner Prescott is the monarchist party's candidate."

Enne knew little of politics. Because Bellamy was only a territory, not a state of the Republic, they didn't have voting or representation rights. The rivalry of the First and monarchist parties was no concern to them. Most found politics a beastly discussion at salons and parties.

Still, she knew the reputation of the monarchists: violent radicals. Lourdes had devoted her life to their cause, but Enne didn't know why. She wasn't sure if this meant Lourdes, too, had been a violent radical, or if the monarchist party was less despicable than she'd always believed. It unnerved her that Lourdes and Vianca had something so fundamental in common.

Malcolm Semper, the late Chancellor of the Republic, had been the father of the First Party. Josephine Fenice, his successor, was another First Party politician, another soulless member of the Phoenix Club. Enne might hesitate to call herself a monarchist, but she did know if the Phoenix Club was on one side, then she was on the other.

"Sedric Torren was running against Prescott," Vianca continued. "Now that he's dead—much thanks to you, my dear— the First Party will need to scramble for a new candidate and campaign. For once, we have the advantage."

The Augustine and Torren Families had rival casino and drug empires, and so Enne had always assumed Vianca had wanted Sedric gone because he was a business competitor. But clearly Vianca had also had political motives since the beginning.

"On top of this, we have this supposed war," Vianca continued. "Do you know anything about the Great Street War?"

Enne shook her head. She only vaguely remembered it from Levi's stories and from her guidebook.

"For the South Side, it wasn't noteworthy. It barely touched them," Vianca explained. "But for the North, it was blood-baths and chaos." Her tongue lingered on those last few words, as if savoring their taste. "We can only hope for history to re-peat itself. The monarchist party thrives on troubled times."

Bloodbaths and chaos. Would that happen again? What must that have meant, by New Reynes's standards?

"You've thoroughly impressed me, Miss Salta. But this new assignment is long-term, and you'll need more than luck and charm to manage it," Vianca told her, as if Enne had escaped the Shadow Game solely on her superficial qualities. "Because of it, I'm terminating your role with the acrobatics troupe."

Enne gaped. "But...but—"

"It's decided. The troupe takes up too much of your time. And I would prefer our working relationship to remain out-side of public knowledge...unlike my relationship with Mr. Glaisyer."

Acrobatics was the only thing in New Reynes Enne had actually enjoyed. She might not have had her cucumber sand-wiches, but at least she had her work as a release. Enne had spent her entire life fighting to achieve mediocrity, and for the first time, she'd discovered that she was naturally talented at something. For once, she could compete. She could *excel.* And just like that, after only a week and a half, Vianca was taking it from her.

"What is this new assignment?" Enne gritted out between her teeth.

"You're going to embrace Séance's newfound infamy and fashion yourself into a proper street lord." The donna let out an unnatural giggle and sipped her tea.

"You can't be serious," Enne whispered. The streets of the North Side had always been dangerous, and now they were even more so, according to the article right in front of her. And Enne might've been friends with Levi, but she didn't know the first thing about being a successful street lord—as if Levi really served as any example.

"Am I ever not serious?" Vianca poured a second cup of stale tea and slid it to her. Enne took it only to have something to fiddle with to soothe her nerves. "I need someone influencing the North Side from the streets, and who better than the famous Séance?"

"The Iron Lord?" Enne suggested.

Vianca scoffed. "Levi's ridiculous dreams of becoming a street lord are over. Will he be managing a gambling enterprise from Zula's basement? He doesn't have the volts or the connections, and with the Scar Lord dead and Mr. Mardlin now an equally wanted man, who will be Levi's face?" She shook her head, the corners of her lips tilting into a smile. Enne didn't understand how Vianca could pretend to care about Levi, yet take such pleasure in the mutilation of his desires. "That boy has always had delusions of grandeur. Besides, I intend for Levi to help you. As a consultant, if you will. You're a more promising criminal than he ever was."

It was a compliment Enne neither wanted nor appreciated. Lola might've called Enne a lord, but Enne wasn't someone who could command a *real* gang. She'd hoped that, in a few months' time, Séance's name would slowly fade from notoriety to memory. If she had to embrace Séance's persona and live the life of Enne Scordata, a born criminal, then how much of Enne Salta—the dancer, the lady, the romantic—would remain? She had so little left to surrender to New Reynes.

"This is what you will do. Now listen closely." Vianca leaned forward and lowered her voice. "First, you must pay a visit to dear Bryce."

Enne frowned in confusion. "Bryce?"

"The Guildmaster," Vianca said impatiently. "He'll help you recruit others. Use the remaining volts I gave you to purchase members."

The Guildmaster referred to the Orphan Guild. Enne didn't know much about them. She knew Lola worked for them as a blood gazer—she could read the talents of those who didn't know their ancestry. Enne remembered Harvey Gabbiano, their salesman, who had used his Chaining blood talent to try to ensnare Enne at a cabaret. She also knew from Reymond that Levi opposed the practices of the Orphan Guild on some sort of moral high ground.

"I have a busy schedule these next few months supporting the campaign," Vianca continued. "I cannot be everywhere at once. I need someone to insert themselves into Worner Prescott's inner circle. I'm investing a fortune into this candidate, so I want to know what he's doing at all times—who he speaks with, where he goes. That information is invaluable. The First Party has already succumbed to corruption, and we can't afford to do the same."

Enne gaped. Anyone operating in Prescott's inner circle would need to be wealthy, refined... Goodness knew how Enne could locate such a person in the North Side. She imagined herself attempting to teach etiquette to Jac or Lola, who would probably question the purpose of a butter knife if you couldn't stab anything with it.

"I'm not sure the Orphan Guild will be able to supply such a person," Enne said slowly.

Vianca raised her eyebrows. "I was referring to *you*. We'll see if that finishing school of yours paid off, won't we?"

Enne caught her breath. The South Side might've been the closest place to Bellamy in New Reynes, but it was also the place the Phoenix Club called home.

When she had last looked a member of the Phoenix Club in the eyes, she'd been wearing a mask. Would they recognize her if she did so wearing pearls?

Before Enne could formulate a response, Vianca continued. It seemed as though, despite Enne's and Levi's actions making front-page news, Vianca had barely penciled in fifteen minutes for this meeting.

"Keeping tabs on Prescott will hardly be a full-time commitment. You'll have plenty of time to find and train your associates. You'll perform tasks as I suggest them, and of course, you can improvise on your own as you find appropriate. Whatever benefits Prescott and the monarchist party."

Vianca was right—this wasn't like poisoning Sedric or stopping the Shadow Game. This was four months of organization until the election in November. It was complex and all-consuming, just like Levi's investment scam had been. And if not for Enne, that scam would've gotten Levi killed.

In the span of minutes, without Enne being able to interject a word edgewise, Vianca was sealing Enne's fate for her.

But Enne knew what it would mean to object. Vianca's omerta held a terrible power over her. Twice now, Enne's past refusals had resulted in her suffocating and groveling on the donna's carpet, and she had no intention of doing so again. Her only option to save herself was to convince Vianca her plan wouldn't work.

"Levi won't want to be a consultant while I'm the one playing lord." That, at least, Enne knew was true.

Vianca raised her tea to her lips and looked at Enne pointedly. "That's not my concern."

"He'll be difficult."

"He knows by now not to make me impatient."

The already dark room seemed to grow darker still. She was running out of options.

"If I'm not an acrobat, how will I earn income?" Enne asked, as though she were being strategic rather than desperate. "I'll need to pay these associates."

As if in answer to her own question, her fingertips suddenly tingled with the static of the volts pulsing inside her skin. The Mizer blood talent was to create volts. Now that she'd awakened hers, there was no limit to her potential for wealth. All it would take was an orb-maker, and she happened to know one very well.

She quickly dismissed the thought. If her ancestry was discovered, she would be killed. There was no quicker path to death than using her talent.

Vianca set down her empty teacup. "Miss Salta, this is the City of Sin. Opportunity is only a flip of the card or roll of the dice away. I'm sure even you can think of something. Besides, you can still live here on my generosity, and you're quite welcome for that." She tossed *The Crimes & The Times* into her waste bin. "You're dismissed."

Thirty minutes later, the bells above the door chimed as Enne slipped into a Tropps Street clothing boutique. The store's floral perfume filled the air, and Enne inhaled it deeply, willing it to soothe her the way such comforts once had. The more she reflected on her conversation with Vianca, the more helpless she felt.

The Casino District, ordinarily so crowded with ruckus and filth, was quiet. In the wake of the headlines, the citizens of New Reynes had stayed indoors. The sirens had gradually stopped. The city felt like the hush before a stage curtain lifted, but what the city waited for was war.

Enne fingered the lace details on a dress sleeve. She liked it. She liked the beads embedded in its neckline. She liked the creamy white canvas boots on display in the window.

She liked the feeling of a gun in her hand.

And it was that thought, that last thought, that made her hand falter as she examined the dress. It didn't feel right that she could like all of these things without contradiction. Somewhere, there was a lie. *She* was a lie. How could she pretend to be her old self after all of the horrible things she had done?

Enne had never been someone to feel apologetic about herself. She hadn't been sorry that she always trailed behind her classmates—they'd hardly noticed her enough to claim she got in their way. She never apologized to Levi when she demanded courtesy, or cried, or wanted for things she knew meant less than nothing to him. So the weight of this shame that she carried for who she was felt wrong. It felt ugly. And she was apologizing to no one but herself.

She had been a lost, naïve, spoiled girl overwhelmed by the City of Sin. And she wasn't sorry for that.

Now she was no longer lost, or naïve, or spoiled. She was hardened, and strong, and heartbroken. She had made terrible, difficult choices—including *murder*—but she had survived. She wouldn't apologize for that.

Vianca would force her to make more terrible, difficult choices, and if Enne ever hesitated to apologize for herself, then she would fail—just like Levi had failed. If someone wanted to call her naïve, then they would. If someone wanted to call her heartless, then they would. It didn't matter whether she decked herself in knives or pearls. The world would always demand that a girl apologize for herself, but she would apologize for nothing.

And so Enne filled her arms with as many frilled, beaded, silly clothes that she could carry, and she paid with the volts she'd earned through blood.

"You know what would look splendid with this?" the cashier asked her, with the first genuine smile Enne had seen in a while. She reached for the basket behind her and retrieved a pair of white satin gloves. They were delicate, ladylike, and indeed splendid.

Enne pursed her lips, images of the Irons' signature card tattoos and the Scarhands' marked palms coming to mind. Vianca had instructed Enne to form a gang, but had "no concern" for how Enne would lead it.

"You're exactly right," Enne answered. "But let's make it two pairs."

JAC

♥ ♠ ♦ ♣

Last night, Jac Mardlin dreamed of his own death.

It started with a bad decision; he jumped into the driver's seat of the flashiest motorcar he'd ever seen—white leather seats and a black racing stripe streaking across the hood. He hadn't intended to steal it; all he wanted was to lean back, close his eyes, and fantasize about owning something so luxurious. But suddenly, the locks on the doors bolted, the keys twisted in the ignition, and the car raced forward at a stomach-lurching speed.

He cursed and fought against the steering wheel. The wind rushed at him so fast his eyes watered, and everything he passed became a blur. Even as he slammed his foot on the brakes and tugged the clutch so hard it snapped, the car still sped on.

Until it drove straight off Revolution Bridge.

Many hours later, in the waking world, Jac eyed his hand of cards and chewed his bottom lip, mentally tallying every foggy detail of the dream. The white from the car's seat leather made him think he should pick an even-numbered card. But there'd been that black racing stripe, and black always symbolized an odd number, a contrast.

He settled on the four of hearts and threw it down. "Better save your luck, Dove, because—"

Lola let out a wild cackle of victory and snatched a switchblade from the pot of weapons. "You muckhead." She threw down her own pair of fours on the table.

He scowled. "I don't like Pilfer. It's a kids' game."

"Then deal a game of Tropps. You don't have much else to lose." She shrugged and slipped what had once been his best switchblade into the pocket of her jacket. The nightdress she wore underneath, borrowed from Enne, was clearly several sizes too small and made her look bone-skinny and vaguely feral. Jac had encountered stray cats who looked more charming than Lola did in the morning.

She rested her feet on the table, and he crinkled his nose as he yanked the pile of cards out from under them. "I thought Irons were supposed to be good at these sort of games," she said.

Strictly speaking, Jac wasn't half lousy at cards. But the sirens that had blared all through the night in search of his best friend had suddenly gone silent. He twitched his leg restlessly. "I'm gonna open a window."

"It's hotter outside," Lola warned. Both of their foreheads dripped with sweat. It was officially a New Reynes summer.

"I need a smoke." He stood up and slid the window open. Twelve years he'd lived in New Reynes, and he'd never heard Tropps Street so quiet. Not after One-One-Six, a long dead street lord, shot up every last soul in a private auction house. Not after the casket of Sedric's father, Garth Torren, had been solemnly paraded outside his casino, as though he'd died some kind of saint.

It was hard to scandalize a city built on sin, a city that had seen it all. But today—more than any other day—the city was shaken to its core.

Jac struck a match and watched it burn like a votive candle.

"I can turn on the radio, if you want," Lola offered. "But Levi's probably fine."

"I'd rather you didn't."

"Afraid you'll hear *your* name?"

He inhaled his cigarette deeply. It was no secret that he worked with Levi; that he lived on 125 Genever Street in Olde Town, apartment 4C; that he covered the Wednesday through Saturday shifts at the Hound's Tooth tavern. The whiteboots had probably already interviewed his boss, already rummaged through his home and what little he had. He tried to imagine what conclusion they could've drawn from his possessions. *A loner, this one*, they'd say. *No decorations. No sentimentals.* Jac had lived there for two years and still treated his place like it was temporary—a side effect of someone who'd never really had a home.

"I wasn't in a good place not that long ago, but I have been lately, or at least in a better one," he explained. He didn't normally share these details with anyone, even ones so vague. But he needed to unload his thoughts on someone other than Levi, someone who could feel sympathetic without also feeling responsible. "I guess that's gone now."

Levi and Enne had made sure of that last night.

He squeezed his hand into a fist. He knew Levi hadn't wanted to start that shatz investment scheme that got him invited to the Shadow Game. And Levi had looked out for Jac time and time again, so Jac didn't feel he had a right to be angry. Hell, he was angry at himself for *feeling* angry.

But Jac also knew Levi and his reckless dreams. And if Levi *was* safe right now, then Jac would swear some part of his friend was mucking pleased—even if Levi had put everyone around him in danger.

But he didn't say that. Instead, he bitterly spat out, "I hate this casino."

Lola pursed her lips, and Jac waited for her to say something about how, while he'd sworn his allegiance to Levi willingly, *she'd* been forced to give Enne her oath with a knife at her throat. Or how good people did bad things, and bad things happened to good people, and neither they nor their friends could really call themselves good people anyway. She was annoying and wise like that.

But all she said was, "Deal the cards. You're clearly very vulnerable right now, and I intend to take advantage of that."

Jac snorted and tapped his cigarette ashes into the rim of a teacup as he slid back into his seat.

"Enne will hate that, you know," Lola told him. The teacup was porcelain, covered in some floral design that Enne would find pretty. Jac realized Enne, who'd only lived here for ten days, probably didn't possess much she could call her own, so he retrieved his cigarette guiltily and pushed the cup away.

Lola leaned over and slid it back toward him. "But *fuck* them." The corner of her lips slid into a smile.

Jac barked out a surprised laugh, and the knots in his shoulders loosened. Over the next ten minutes of Tropps, the teacup's bottom steadily grew coated in ash.

Then the apartment's front door swung open, and Enne marched inside wearing an outrageous floppy hat, a floor-length jacket she definitely didn't have on when she left, and at least a dozen bags hanging off of each arm. "I'm back," she chirped. She set the bags down in a heap by the couch.

"Why are you dressed like you've suddenly become a rich widow?" Lola asked.

"I went shopping. Levi doesn't exactly own anything anymore, does he?" she huffed, collapsing into an armchair as though she'd just finished back to back gloves-off matches in the ring.

Jac raised an eyebrow. "Dressing him now, are you?"

Enne ignored him and gestured aimlessly to all the bags. "I also bought him some medication, since he looked terrible last night. There's stuff for you, too, Jac. I guessed at your measurements."

Jac stood up and examined the pile skeptically. "I'm almost afraid to look. What do *gentlemen* wear in Bellamy? White ribbon boater hats and daisy cufflinks?"

"As if that soiled newsboy cap you wear every day is such a deliberate fashion choice?" Enne countered. Jac cleared his throat, prepared to defend his beloved, patched-up hat to his grave, when Enne furrowed her eyebrows and sniffed the air. "What's that smell?"

"Jac's been using one of your prized teacups as an ashtray," Lola said quickly.

Jac glared at her and muttered, "You traitor."

Enne waved her hand dismissively. "I don't care. And I didn't just go shopping. There's something I want to talk to you both about." She reached into the closest bag and pulled out a copy of today's *The Crimes & The Times*. She tossed it at Jac, who caught and unfurled it. He squinted at the headline for a moment, untangling the words he recognized, but he didn't need to read them to understand the significance of the two wanted posters on the front.

Lola's chair screeched as she stood up. She studied the paper from over Jac's shoulder.

"Three thousand volts," Lola read under Levi's sketch. Instantly, all Jac's resentment from earlier vanished like a puff of cigarette smoke.

His best friend was a dead man walking.

"I'm getting out of here," Jac breathed. It was still several hours before Levi had asked to meet, but he didn't care. If Levi *was* in danger, then Jac would find a way to save him.

Because that was what they did for each other. There was no line they wouldn't cross. Not even a line of fire.

"Wait," Enne said sharply. "Turn the page."

He did, though a part of him already knew what he would find.

"One thousand volts," Lola murmured, reading his own bounty.

Jac stared at his face with the feeling like there'd been some terrible mistake. Levi was hardly a notorious political assassin, and Jac was barely a second-string bouncer at a third-rate pub. Not that long ago, the two of them had sat on street corners in the Casino District, goading passersby with games of coins and cards in the hopes of conning at least enough for a meal.

"Vianca said there could be a repeat of the Great Street War," Enne told him, which was the last thing she could've said to make him feel better. He supposed she wasn't trying to comfort him. The clothes she'd bought weren't gifts—they were necessities. And if daisy cufflinks were what it took to make him unrecognizable now, then he'd happily strut around town like a dandy. "If you want a motorcar to Olde Town, I can call you one."

Enne's voice was level, calm, all practicality. For the first time, Jac wasn't at all surprised that he was looking into the eyes of the person who'd killed Sedric Torren. If she was afraid, she was damn good at hiding it.

"How did you pay for all this?" he asked her, eyeing the shopping bags with suspicion.

"Vianca gave me the voltage."

"And you took it?" It was Vianca's fault that they were in this scramble to begin with. And if they all hanged for it to-morrow, the donna would hardly deign to host their funerals.

Enne stood up and held out two more of the bags. "Of course I did. Just like you're going to take these."

He hesitated. He wanted nothing to do with Vianca, but that was impossible. So long as he was friends with Levi, so long as Levi was infatuated with Enne and they were both prisoners of the donna's omertas… They would all be in bed with Vianca Augustine.

"I'm really, really sorry, Jac." Enne said it like she meant it. Then she shoved the bags into his hands. "But don't be thick."

Jac took them with a weary sigh.

"I'm going to call you a motorcar," she told him. It wasn't a suggestion. She walked to the other room to find the telephone, leaving him alone with Lola.

"Bossy," he grumbled.

"No, she's just the boss." Lola clicked her tongue. "I guess I wasn't deserving enough to be showered with expensive gifts."

Jac reached into one of the bags and fished out the first thing he noticed—a scrap of yellow silk with polka dots. "Here. Take this…"

"Cravat," Lola finished for him. "And I think I'll leave that for you. It'll match your wanted poster. They made you look very dapper, for some reason. Doesn't suit that terrible scrape you've given yourself across your eyebrow."

Jac sheepishly brushed his finger over the stitches on his browbone, a souvenir from a boxing match he'd lost the other night at Dead at Dawn. His skin was still swollen and tender.

Lola instead pulled out a black felt case and opened it to reveal a leather wristwatch. "Excellent." She tossed the box on the armchair and buckled the watch around her bony wrist. It hung ridiculously.

"I actually like that one," he muttered.

"Keep the cravat, Polka Dots."

Enne returned from the other room. "Jac, the car is waiting

for you downstairs. It'll take you straight to Zula's. When you get there, can you tell Levi…" She flushed, and Jac had half a mind to crack a very lewd joke, but the other half of him wanted to roll his eyes and stalk out. They might've had the good sense not to let anything more happen between them, but he didn't know why they made things so dramatic for themselves. "Tell him if he so much as opens a *window* before all of this has died down, I will personally turn him in and collect his bounty. Which, please remind him, is five hundred volts less than mine."

Jac had braced himself for something sweet and nauseating, so he wound up laughing so hard he wheezed. "With pleasure."

Then, without warning, Enne wrapped her arms around him in a fierce hug. "Be careful," she told him.

"Always am," he managed. But Enne still looked skeptical. "No, you're not."

He shot Lola a smile. "Now's your chance, Dove."

"I don't do hugs," she said flatly. "Just don't die."

"Words I'll cherish forever."

After Enne let him go, he grabbed the bags, exchanged good-byes, and left. He found his driver waiting for him in the alley out back. Before climbing in the car, Jac took a deep gulp of air—his first full breath since he'd entered St. Morse Casino the night before. It didn't matter how many gifts he received or how much protection he was given; he could never bring himself to think of Vianca Augustine as anything less than despicable.

"I'd like to make a detour," Jac told the driver, and he gave him the address to his apartment.

Olde Town, much like the Casino District, was quiet and still. Jac peeked from behind his window screen at the streets they passed, at the barred windows and chipped paint. The sunlight came and went as they drove, disappearing behind spires and church towers and reappearing for fleeting moments in the too-narrow alleys.

Jac lived on a large residential street. His building was too old to have central heating or electricity, and on a day like this, he would shove his bed close to the window, drenched in sweat, and listen to his neighbors fighting down the hall while he waited for his shift to start. It wasn't a great place, but it was far better than his last. There were no bad memories there.

Now, his entire block was cut off with bright yellow signs, informing Olde Town residents that Genever Street was a crime scene. The car came to a slow halt, and Jac stared at the whiteboots standing outside his front steps, speaking to a neighbor of his whom he only dimly recognized. They held wanted posters in their hands.

Have you seen this man before? they probably asked.

Jac fiddled with his necklace. It was a Creed, a symbol of the old Faith. Jac was more superstitious than he was reverent, but it was nice, now and again, to pray for something.

When a priest had first taught Jac to pray, he told him the prayers of a sinful conscience would go unanswered. Jac thought of the volts he'd helped Levi scam—both from the rich and from the Irons. He thought of the wounds he'd left on Chez Phillips to save Levi's life. He thought of his own anger and resentment and desires, and the ashes left in the bottom of Enne's teacup.

He tried very hard to feel sorry.

But as he stared at those yellow signs, at what all of this had led up to, he knew he wouldn't pray for forgiveness. They could all pray for forgiveness when they escaped to a place far, far away from here, where there were no bounties on their heads, where no one knew their faces at all. A place he doubted Levi would ever willingly go.

Or they could pray for forgiveness when they all hanged. That seemed a more likely scenario.

But because Jac Mardlin was an unrepentant sinner who didn't want to die, all he had left to pray for was mercy.

LEVI

Levi hadn't forgiven Zula Slyk. Three days ago, he and Enne had arrived at *Her Forgotten Histories*, Zula's monarchist newspaper, grasping at their last threads of hope and searching for answers about Lourdes Alfero. Bad news hurt no matter how gently you dealt it, but Zula had crafted knives out of her words, designed to bleed and infect and scar.

And all for what? For Enne to flee to the safety of her old life in Bellamy? She bore Vianca's omerta. She was a prisoner of the City of Sin, just like him.

As he stepped into *Her Forgotten Histories* and found Zula sitting at her desk, he glared at the journalist's serious, unfriendly face and decided he hated her.

"Your shades are darker since you were last here," Zula said as a form of greeting—though Levi still had no idea what that meant. She had short, curly hair, fair skin, and wore far too much jewelry—most notably a large wooden Creed that hung down past her navel. The black tattoos of eyes over her eyelids sent a shiver down Levi's spine. "You've killed."

He felt no guilt over killing Chancellor Semper, just as Semper had undoubtedly felt no guilt over almost killing him.

"I've survived," Levi said darkly.

She glanced over him. "Barely, by the looks of you."

Her Forgotten Histories resembled a typical office, filled with unoccupied desks, an old printing press, and a gnarled gray carpet. It looked like it belonged on the South Side, where middle-aged men carrying briefcases and toiling over paperwork could earn the wages they'd later gamble away on Tropps Street. But unlike those places, bits of Faith merchandise were tucked discreetly around the room—ancient etchings in wind chimes, paintings with Creeds hidden in their background, prayer tokens scattered on countertops. Those would never be spotted below the Brint River; the Faith reminded the wigheads too much of the Mizer kings, who had used the Faith's lore to gain more political power for themselves. It was technically banned after the Revolution.

"Vianca didn't give me much of a choice in letting you stay here," Zula huffed. "I don't want any trouble. Not from the whiteboots. Not from that gang of yours."

"There won't be trouble. I'm an excellent houseguest."

Zula *hmph*ed like she didn't believe him, then stood up and slid aside the carpet to reveal a trapdoor. "You'll be down there."

As she pulled it open and ushered Levi down the wooden steps, excitement stirred in his stomach. He was a person of interest now. Living a life of whispers and mystery, raising empires out of shadows. Now that he wasn't bemoaning his future, he could see the glamor in his situation.

Until he smelled the sewage.

Zula pulled the string on a dangling light bulb, illuminating an unfinished cellar filled with dusty, forbidden books; a cot; and, in the corner, a sink and a toilet. The stench wafted from behind a door that Levi guessed led to the sewers—probably to serve as a less conspicuous exit.

It took all Levi had not to retch. Even hooch kept down here would sour.

"Not exactly your penthouse in St. Morse, is it?" Zula asked smugly.

He clicked his tongue. "It was never mine. It was always Vianca's."

"It was comfort all the same."

Levi ignored that comment. "I'm expecting company," he told her. Jac would meet him here this evening, assuming his friend found a means of safely venturing outside of St. Morse.

"I don't host playdates."

"We won't be trouble. Just let him inside when he comes."

Zula clicked her tongue and walked up the stairs. Before she closed the trapdoor behind her, she added, "And the girl? Is she this Séance character in all the newspapers?"

"It's none of your business." Zula had made it clear she'd rather criticize Enne than help her, and Levi didn't care that Zula had been Lourdes's friend. She didn't deserve to know anything about Enne.

"This will end badly," Zula snapped, echoing her words from their last meeting, and slammed the trapdoor.

Two hours later, footsteps creaked upstairs. Levi lay on the rigid cot, attempting to sleep, but he suspected Zula was slamming her drawers and clacking her pens against her desk just to irritate him.

"How long are you staying? This isn't a hostel," he heard Zula snap. "And look at you. All those burdens on your soul. They'll devour you, if you let them."

"Um… Yeah, well, the bags are actually for Levi." That sounded like Jac. He was early.

The trapdoor opened, and Jac's calming aura mingled with the unpleasant odors of the cellar. It wafted in wisps and ribbons and smelled like linen and the color gray. Everything about Jac was gray. His blond hair was more colorless than golden. His irises, his skin…even the ever-present dark circles drooping beneath his eyes. During a bright afternoon, with the sun reflecting off his fair features, you'd almost mistake him for a trick of the light.

Jac thumped down the steps, shopping bags from several ritzy Tropps Street boutiques hoisted over his shoulders. He dropped them on the bed and crossed his heart, as gangsters did for their lord.

"That woman's spooky," Jac said, coughing. "And it smells like muck down here." His face twisted in disgust as he lit a match and waved it around the room.

"You might as well light the whole building on fire," Levi grumbled.

Jac sighed and resigned himself to breathing through his shirt. "You look terrible."

"I'll heal," Levi responded blandly, even though it seemed like the more time that passed, the more he ached.

"I know you'll say no, but I'm offering anyway." Jac gave him a pointed look.

Jac's split name was Dorner, from a family capable of manipulating pain. Because it was his split talent, his abilities were weaker—he could take pain away, but when he did, he held onto the pain himself. Jac claimed his strength blood talent made him more resistant, that he could heal faster, hurt less, and take more, but Levi didn't believe that.

Besides, this pain should be his and his alone.

"I've never been better," Levi lied.

Jac pursed his lips. "Well, I brought meds. And clothes."

"I don't want any more of Vianca's clothes."

"They're from Enne."

Levi sat up and eyed the bags with curiosity. He couldn't

believe she'd had time to go shopping, especially on his behalf, but he was surprised to find a full new wardrobe inside. The clothes weren't exactly his style—all pinstripes and subtle and black—but that was probably the point. Levi needed to be less recognizable.

As if he'd heard his thoughts, Jac handed Levi a tube of something. "Hair dye," he explained. "It's for both of us."

Levi snorted as he popped open the bottle of pain medication. "Do we have matching outfits, as well?"

"Don't be thick. You look terrible in plaid." Indeed, Jac pulled out a blazer identical to Levi's in every way except for the print. The color was burgundy, the stitches silky and light-catching—something flashy that Reymond would've worn. The thought hit Levi with a wave of grief. If Reymond were alive, Levi would've been hiding with *him*, not with a woman he detested and barely knew.

The raven black hair dye would suit Levi's dark complexion, but he was hesitant to lose his natural hair. The coloring—copper at the roots and black at the ends—was the mark of an orb-maker, and it was as much a part of his identity as his brown skin, as the Iron ace and spade tattoos on his arms, as the memories of every boy and every girl he'd kissed. Even though Levi didn't make orbs, his talent, his family, and his past still defined him. The dye felt like an erasure.

But that was exactly why he needed it. His hair was too recognizable, especially when orb-makers were so scarce. A bounty hunter wouldn't even need to know his face to guess his identity.

As they washed their hair out in the sink, Jac quietly asked, "Have you seen the papers?"

"I have," he answered, not meeting his friend's eyes. He'd hoped for a little more time before telling Jac about Harrison. Maybe it was unfair to stall, under the circumstances, but Levi had just dyed over centuries of Glaisyer history and pride in his hair, and he could use some extra time to pretend at least one part of his life was still normal.

"Do you think it really will be like last time? The war?" Jac asked.

A thrill danced in Levi's chest—a dangerous, irrational thrill. Because Levi might have raised himself on the legends of the Great Street War and made heroes out of masterminds like Veil and Havoc, but all of those stories had ended in ruin.

The only thing he should've felt was fear.

"I doubt it will be like last time," Levi answered, even if a small part of him hoped that wasn't true. Despite his many recent and frightening brushes with death, the thought of failure scared him more. He would rather die a legend than end his life in anonymity. Jac would probably punch him if he heard him say that, though.

Once Levi finished rinsing out the dye, he nervously checked his reflection in the mirror. It was silly to claim he looked drastically different, but he felt like he did. He wondered what his father would say to see him like this. He'd probably grunt that, because Levi's two talents clashed with one another, Levi had never been much of an orb-maker, anyway.

Without the mark of his blood talent, Levi's head of tight, short curls resembled those of most people from Caroko, the city where his parents had been born. Levi was actually pleased with his new look. He'd never noticed how closely he resembled his mother.

Jac, meanwhile, appeared nearly unrecognizable. The black hair contrasted harshly against the pallor of his skin, as did the new pair of thick-rimmed glasses. Apparently Enne had provided them with a full dress-up set. The plaid burgundy suit, the bow-tie, the hint of his tattoos beneath his collar— Jac was remade. Something slicker and more wicked.

"How do I look?" he asked, grinning wide enough to show his dimples.

"You look sharp. What about me?"

Jac examined his all-black ensemble. "Like a menace."

Levi smugly rubbed some hair grease through his curls, then straightened his jacket. He didn't normally wear this much black, and the platforms on his shoes made him unusually tall, but he did feel good. Fresh. A new look for a new beginning.

Zula's voice echoed above them. "I wasn't expecting you," she said, sounding annoyed. "You're asking quite a lot of my hospitality."

"I thought we were in agreement about Mr. Glaisyer," the intruder responded.

Levi and Jac warily met each other's eyes. Levi would recognize that voice anywhere, and sure enough, he sensed the faint wisps of the donna's green, acidic aura from upstairs. Jac turned a similar shade of green himself.

"He's downstairs," Zula told her.

Levi's skin prickled as the trapdoor swung open and Vianca Augustine descended into the grimy cellar. She scanned the room, narrowing her green eyes—an exact match of her son's, he realized. She passed over Jac with disinterest, as if he might as well have been wallpaper. Her gaze, instead, fell on Levi, and his stomach clenched.

"You've changed your hair." Vianca pouted. "You used to be so striking."

Levi rolled his eyes. Dyeing his hair had been a hard decision, but it had nothing to do with his vanity.

"How have you found your accommodations here?" Vianca asked. She ran a finger along one of the liquor shelves and inspected the dust.

"Who wouldn't want to live in a cellar that smells like muck?" he said flatly.

"Missing St. Morse already?"

Levi would gladly inhale the odors of sewage every night if it meant avoiding her casino. Even if he could barely breathe, he was still breathing somewhat free. And if he had his way, he'd find a more suitable place in Olde Town as soon as possible. Maybe even tonight. As long as Vianca had a means of contacting him, what did she care where he lived? She and Zula didn't exactly seem like friends.

"Why are you here?" he asked. He didn't like the idea of Vianca paying him visits whenever she wished, or Jac witnessing exactly how helpless Levi was in the donna's presence.

"Because I'm in need of you, of course."

She twisted the emerald ring around her fourth finger, identical to the one Harrison also wore. Levi resisted the urge to wipe his sweaty hands on his jacket; his betrayal was probably written plain on his face.

"I spoke with Miss Salta this morning. Since you're already so close..." Vianca looked at him pointedly, as though accusing the two of them of something. Perhaps she assumed their relationship was more than a casual acquaintance. The thought didn't sit well with Levi. All of his weaknesses and desires were Vianca's to exploit, and he didn't want Enne to face Vianca's torment more than she already did. "I thought a joint assignment would be appropriate."

"I'm surprised you didn't drag her with you, then," he responded, even though he wasn't truly surprised. In Vianca's opinion, fear was best felt while alone. Having Enne here would have been too much of a comfort.

"I need your undivided attention," she said slyly.

And then she launched into one of Levi's most loathed subjects—politics. He was accustomed to her radical monologues, and he was typically well-skilled at zoning out while appearing to listen. Whoever wore the wigs in the South Side had no effect on him.

But since his deal with Harrison, he could no longer ignore news from below the Brint. So he listened. And very quickly, Vianca's words made his blood run cold.

"Whoever is running against Worner Prescott won't matter," she said dismissively. "Séance is going to win him the election, and you're going to help her do it."

Harrison Augustine had not yet announced his candidacy, so Vianca didn't know that the person running against her party was her own son. Levi needed Harrison to win the election, otherwise the hopes he harbored for his freedom were futile.

He was powerless to defy Vianca's direct orders, but he had no idea how he could follow them and help Harrison at the same time. He swallowed down an urge to throw up. The expression of glee on Vianca's face and the look of horror on Jac's hardly helped.

On top of this dilemma, if Vianca forced Enne to become a lord, then Enne would spend more time in the city's spotlight. She couldn't afford to risk exposure.

If she were here, if they'd faced the donna together, maybe they could have found a way out of this situation. They'd escaped the Shadow Game after all.

But she was somewhere else, and he was here.

"And what will I be doing to help her?" he managed.

"You had that little gang of yours." Vianca waved her hand dismissively, and Levi caught her use of the past tense. His stomach sank further. Without the Irons, without the power of being a lord, Levi would have no means of providing information to Harrison. He was running out of loopholes. "You'll be her consultant."

"But the Irons—"

"Are a distraction. It's time to abandon these fantasies and turn your attention to your true strengths."

"My *true* strengths?" he gritted out between his teeth. Was she trying to flatter him by taking away everything he'd ever wanted?

"You're a businessman, not a lord. There's more than one way to achieve grandeur."

"If that's what you think, then why bother making me Enne's consultant?" Nothing good had ever come to him by angering Vianca Augustine, but he couldn't swallow down his sarcasm. "If I'm so lousy at what I do, what could I *possibly* have to offer her?"

"You look unhappy, my dear," Vianca said, feigning maternal concern. "I thought you'd be thrilled for something to fill your time, as you'll be spending so much of it in Zula's basement." She spoke with delight, as though she loved the picture of Levi locked away somewhere only she could reach him.

"But you wouldn't have dyed your hair if you intended to stay here, would you?" She leaned forward and smiled, accentuating the harshness of her frown lines. Levi dug his nails into his thighs. He was playing a dangerous game, keeping secrets from her. "Tell me—what have you been planning?"

She coaxed her finger, forcing Levi to speak. He frantically searched for some kind of excuse, anything that wouldn't give away what he'd planned with Harrison. Pressure from the omerta built around his neck, forcing the air out.

"I'm rebuilding the Irons," he rasped. It wasn't the full truth, but it was *a* truth, and that was enough for the omerta.

"The what?" Vianca asked coolly.

He ground his teeth. He hadn't seen her investment scheme through and escaped the Shadow Game to remain her plaything. He hadn't made a reckless bargain with her son only to see it collapse that very same day. She was ripping away his ambitions one by one. She was humiliating him in front of his best friend. After all, she knew all the ways to make him hurt.

But he knew her weaknesses, too.

Even if he couldn't resist her orders, if he was truly a moment away from the omerta killing him, Vianca would relent. The donna wasn't interested in seeing him dead. She wanted to see him tormented.

So Levi mustered up his willpower and declared, "I won't."

The grip around his throat tightened, and tears sprang from his eyes. Across the room, Jac stood up, as though he'd charge Vianca. But even Jac would know that a small army of Vianca's henchmen undoubtedly waited outside Zula's door, should Vianca fail to return. "You're making a mistake," Levi sputtered.

"The matter is decided," she said firmly.

"Would you care to place a wager?" he asked with the little breath he had left.

Vianca eyed him coolly for several moments. He strained his neck, gasping for air. Even as black spots darkened around his vision, even as doubt and fear crept into his mind, he refused to lift a hand to his throat.

"You're killing him," Jac croaked. He lunged for one of the bags and pulled out his pistol. He pointed it at her head, his chest heaving.

"If you don't lower the gun," Vianca snapped, "I *will*."

Levi sputtered and waved his arm, trying to call Jac off.

She wouldn't let him die.

She wouldn't let him die.

She wouldn't let him die.

Jac grimaced and laid the gun on the bed. Suddenly, the grip on Levi's neck slackened, and he gulped in air.

"What sort of wager?" Vianca asked impatiently.

Levi grimaced and wiped the spit off his chin with his shirt. "You think Enne should be the lord over me. I'm telling you we both can—and with greater success."

She laughed. "And what do you have to bet? Your dignity?"

"You know I want this," he said. "You know I won't stop trying. Enne, a lord? Instead of me?" He forced a laugh. "I was the one who killed the Chancellor. I'm the one who knows this city. I'm the one who already has the connections, the resources, the associates."

Jac paled at Levi's words, and even Levi could agree the Irons wasn't worth dying for.

But his freedom was.

"Give me two months," Levi told Vianca, "and I will prove to you that the Irons are worth keeping. That you won't even need Enne to do this."

"How selfless of you," Vianca purred. "But though it might be difficult to imagine, Enne possesses certain skills that you lack. Why should I let you waste your time on a pointless wager when you could be helping her?"

He didn't mean to deny Enne aid; he would still gladly assist her—whatever she needed. But, he quickly decided, under no circumstances could he tell Enne about his deal with Harrison. Even if Vianca's death would free her, too, telling her would give Vianca another opportunity to discover the truth. This risk was his and his alone to take.

"Three thousand volts," Levi said. "That's what the city placed on my head, what they think my gang and my reputation are worth. It might be less than hers, but it's the same as Scavenger, the same as Ivory. And as far as I can tell, six and a half thousand combined is a far better value than what Enne could offer alone."

Vianca licked her lips. "I'll give you six weeks."

"Six weeks," he echoed, his voice high-pitched with relief.

Levi knew this plan wasn't foolproof. Even if he did manage to rebuild the Irons in so little time, once the wager was over, the gang would only become another tool at Vianca's disposal. So when the time came, he'd find another loophole, another desperate solution. He'd wager everything, over and over again, if that was what it took.

"If you fail, then you will abandon the Irons and your fantasies about them forever. Including *that* one." She nodded at Jac.

Levi inhaled sharply. He had bet his dreams, his *freedom* on this wager, but now his best friend was at stake. Levi tried to imagine a future where he never saw Jac again. There was so little that the donna could take from him that would still hurt, but sure enough, she had found the only remaining good in his life and seized it.

No, not Jac. Not for this. The risk was too great.

But hadn't he risked worse for Jac already with Harrison?

"Don't look so frazzled, Levi," she said, turning to go up the stairs. "I'm the one who should be disappointed. I was looking forward to a partnership between you and Miss Salta. I thought you would have, as well. Unless you think now you'll get both things you want. The gang...and the girl."

Levi didn't give Vianca the satisfaction of seeing him grimace. If Vianca could dangle his friendship with Jac as bait, he hated to think what she could do with him and Enne. No wonder she was so keen to play matchmaker. Jac must have agreed with him, because his aura was prickly with warning.

"It's not like that between us," Levi said quickly.

Vianca shot him back an icy smile. "I suppose we'll see, won't we?" And then she climbed up to the top floor and shut the trapdoor behind her.

Levi and Jac didn't speak until the sound of her footsteps disappeared. Levi sat down on the cot, heart pounding. He didn't know if he'd managed to save or damn himself. It felt like he'd done both at the same time.

Levi took a deep breath, ready to come clean to Jac on all of the events of this morning, every detail of his deal with Harrison. But then Jac stood up, seething.

"Is that what I'm worth to you?" he demanded. "Muck, Levi. I'm not just another thing for you to gamble away."

He made toward the stairs, and Levi shot up after him.

"Jac, wait! I had a reason for this. A *good* reason—"

"Yeah, I bet you did." Jac threw open the trapdoor.

Levi winced as he raced to follow him. His broken ribs made it agonizing to move, let alone run. "Where are you going?" he called. Jac couldn't go home—not with a bounty on his head.

"Like you care," Jac snapped.

Before he made it to the door, Zula let out a shrill shriek. "You—boy—don't you *dare* go outside. Both of you, be quiet."

They whipped toward her. Zula was seated at her desk, a beaded shawl wrapped around her shoulders and a mug of tea in her hand. She hunched over the radio and turned up the volume.

"The most recent reports are confirming eight casualties," the newscaster spoke. "Several of the injured have been rushed to New Reynes North General Hospital. Although Captain Hector declined to comment, we were able to get in touch with Sergeant Roy Pritchard, who personally participated in the operation. Sergeant, what information can you give us about tonight's events?"

"After the tragic assassination of Chancellor Semper, the precincts across the city have been working around the clock to bring the perpetrators—Levi Glaisyer and this so-called Séance—to justice. But as far as we see it, these are two individuals who make up part of a much larger problem. We fully intend to purge organized crime from the North Side, and the success of today's operation sends a clear message to criminals: We will show no tolerance…and no mercy."

Levi and Jac crowded around the radio together, their fight momentarily forgotten. "What happened? What does he mean?" Levi asked, his mouth dry. He wasn't exactly used to hearing his name on the radio.

"Eight people are dead?" Jac murmured. "Who did they say—?"

"If you'd both be quiet, you'd have your answers," Zula hissed.

The newscaster continued, "Many have already called our station expressing outrage at the age of the victims. The Orphan Guild—"

"Is a misleading title," the Sergeant said quickly. "They are an organization comprised of people of all ages, feeding agents directly into gangs such as the Scarhands and the Doves. It's little better than human trafficking. Although we were unable to apprehend the Guildmaster, Bryce Balfour—"

"Lola works for the Orphan Guild," Jac squeaked.

"She couldn't have been there," Levi said, even though he didn't know if that was true. Eight casualties at the Orphan Guild wasn't just an operation—it was a massacre.

It was war.

Zula switched the radio off and glared at them. "*This* is how it began last time. Already, people are dead." Her gaze fell on Jac's fingers, clamped around his Creed. "*Your* prayers are worth nothing, boy. You're the ones who started all this."

But Levi wasn't in the mood to swallow Zula's pointless judgment. He shot Jac a desperate look. "Please don't leave." Without Jac, he had no means of securing the information Harrison needed about the Torren empire. Without Jac, Levi was without a second, without a best friend, with the entire world in flames around him.

Jac averted his gaze. "I won't. Yet."

Levi realized this was the best he could hope for until he explained the truth. But there wasn't time for that now.

He spotted Zula's telephone against the wall and limped toward it. His fingers trembled as he turned the dial. "Operator? I need you to connect me to St. Morse Casino. I need to speak to Erienne Salta."

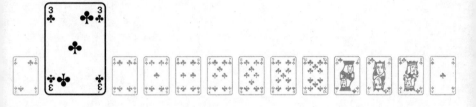

"They say the Bargainer wanders the world, approaching those desperate enough to strike a deal. But everyone knows that the Bargainer is from New Reynes. The most fearsome legend ever told, and it started *here*.

"And one day...the Bargainer will come back."

—*A legend of the North Side*

ENNE

♥ ♠ ♦ ♣

Enne sat on her bathroom counter, gingerly examining her bloodshot eyes in the foggy mirror. The contacts Levi had given her were uncomfortable and, she suspected, deeply unsanitary. She'd managed to find better ones at a costume shop, colored a warm brown as opposed to the unnatural blue of the old ones. She prayed Vianca didn't notice her eye color changing every other day. Thankfully, the donna had other things on her mind.

"It looks like a crime scene in here," Lola said from behind the shower curtain.

"Pleasant," Enne muttered.

"I still resent this. I want you to know that."

Enne rolled her eyes and unscrewed the bottle of eyedrops. "You can't keep your white hair. You look like a killer."

"That's why I liked it."

Enne cringed as the cold liquid touched her eye. The redness still looked no better.

Lola turned off the water and drew back the curtain. She

looked gangly and awkward in Enne's short towel, her newly red hair plastered across her shoulders and dripping on the floor.

Despite Lola's jokes, Enne knew her old hair meant far more to her than just the intimidation factor. Lola had originally bleached it because her brother had joined the Doves, and white hair was their trademark. Years had passed since then, but she still kindled the hope of finding him. And though her disguise had gotten her nowhere but trouble—which Lola herself acknowledged—Enne knew it couldn't have been easy to let her past go.

Lola glanced at herself in the mirror. "Wow. I hate it."

"You can't keep looking like a Dove," Enne told her. "Not when we're supposed to..."

Enne trailed off and bit her lip. She'd recounted her conversation with Vianca to Lola earlier, and Lola hadn't taken it well. Since then, all she'd done was order them the most expensive room service on St. Morse's menu and pick at her food in stony silence. Enne had waited for her to say something—anything—all day, but Lola's cold shoulder treatment meant Enne just wound up reading one of her favorite Sadie Knightley romance novels and brooding for six hours.

When Lola didn't respond and walked back to the bedroom to change, Enne jumped off the counter and called after her, "Are we going to talk about this?"

Lola whipped around. "Talk about what, Enne?" Still clutching her towel, she marched over to the bags of clothes from Enne's shopping trip. She grabbed the top item—a simple blouse with a lacy collar. "What are you supposed to wear? This?" Lola threw the shirt on the couch. "What are you supposed to say? With your posh, South Sider accent?"

She stormed back to Enne and loomed over her. "You're going to march into the Orphan Guild and...and *what*? No

one there went to finishing school. They're thieves and killers and liars, and all you look like is a target. Bryce Balfour
will eat you alive."

Enne blinked back tears. She'd already made the decision
not to apologize for who she was, and besides, there was
nothing Lola said that Enne hadn't already considered herself.
She didn't know anything about organized crime, how she'd
find the volts to pay for associates, how she'd ever convince
anyone to follow a clueless schoolgirl from Bellamy. It didn't
matter that the world thought she'd assassinated the Chancellor. Within minutes of meeting her, anyone would know
she was a fraud.

"I thought you wanted this! Isn't that what you said at Scrap
Market? That I could be a—"

"That was before I knew about you and Vianca."

"So did you mean anything that you said about me, then?"
Enne asked, her voice shaking. Lola once saw a potential in
her when no one else did, but it seemed like now she only
saw her as a pawn.

Lola crossed her arms and looked away. "Of course I meant
what I said. You're a *Mizer*, Enne. And the world doesn't know
that—the world *can't* know that—but regardless of Vianca, you
have real power. And you don't want it. That's what makes
you different from the other lords, different from everyone
in New Reynes. You don't want it, and so, maybe, you could
do *good* with it."

Enne went silent. Of course, Lola was right. Enne didn't
want this, hadn't asked for this.

"You…" Enne said carefully. "You think I can do this?"

"I wouldn't be here if I thought otherwise."

Lola was bony and uncomfortably wet, but Enne threw her
arms around her, anyway. "Thank you," she whispered, her
mind whirling with Lola's words.

Did she have real power?

And if so, what could she do with it?

"You're welcome. Now please let go of me." Lola writhed out of Enne's grip, smirking. "I'm going to get dressed, and then we can talk about making an appointment with the Guildmaster."

The telephone rang.

Enne froze. Only two people would have any reason to call her: Vianca or Levi. She moved to answer it and prayed it was the latter.

"'Lo?" whispered the voice on the other line.

Enne sucked in her breath. "It's you. Are you all right? Are you safe?" she asked.

"Have you heard the news?" Levi asked.

She pursed her lips. *Yes, I'm fine. I suppose you must be, too.* "No."

"We need to meet—now. Write down this address." He read off the name of a place Enne didn't recognize. "Leave as soon as possible."

"Is something wrong?" she asked, voice hitched.

"Yes, it's…we'll talk about it there." He paused, and the sound of voices bickering around him almost muffled Levi's next words. "Please be careful." He hung up.

Enne set down the phone, worry knotting in her chest. She grabbed her tourist guidebook off the dining table and flipped to the map. "Lola," she called. "Turn on the radio and get dressed. We're going to the Deadman District."

By the time they exited the Mole Station, the sun had set. The streetlights of the Deadman District shone through shattered glass, and the metallic mortar between the white stone of the buildings glinted in the darkness, so bright that Enne squinted and shaded her eyes as she walked. Everywhere she turned, she saw a chain, a gun barrel, a blade—her mind playing deadly tricks.

While frantically getting dressed, she and Lola had managed to catch enough of the newscast to understand what had happened. Armed brutally with automatics, the whiteboots had executed an attack on the Orphan Guild, killing eight and injuring many others. Their meeting point was only a few blocks from the Orphan Guild's now-abandoned hideout, and as they approached, Enne had the distinct sensation she was walking into a battleground. The silence around her could be *felt*, like its presence haunted these streets—like death itself lurked in every shadow.

The last time she'd roamed the streets of New Reynes at night, she and Levi had been fleeing for their lives. Now, the reflection she passed in the dirt-crusted windows was no longer her own. Instead, she saw *them*. The sallow-skinned, lifeless faces of the Phoenix Club.

She felt for the gun in her pocket, seeking reassurance, seeking the power that Lola had seen in her—that she couldn't seem to find herself.

At their destination, a long vertical gash stretched across the door, as though someone had dragged a knife down the wood. Lola and Enne exchanged a grim look before Lola knocked, and Jac swung the door open with a pistol pointed at eye level. Enne let out an unladylike curse and grabbed her second's arm.

Once he saw who they were, he lowered it. "'Lo, missies."

"Call me missy again," Lola growled, "and you can be the new Eight Fingers."

Jac laughed, and despite his familiar dimples and easy demeanor, he looked different. Sleeker. His black hair, greased back and glossy, made his gray eyes look more like steel than dust. *He* might've been hesitant about Enne choosing his wardrobe, but, she noted smugly, he looked great. She clearly had excellent taste.

They climbed the stairwell to the first landing. Behind the door, Levi sat stiffly in a leather office chair. His curls had been dyed black, and his shirt and jacket were colored to match. However, his new ensemble did nothing to hide how terrible he looked. Every time he shifted his posture, he winced in silent pain.

Levi's gaze moved from the window and met hers, and his breath hitched.

Enne went to sleep last night reminding herself of all the reasons she couldn't fall for Levi Glaisyer. But her heart still stuttered seeing him look at her like he was now—like he'd felt their separation every bit as acutely as she had.

"Did anyone see you?" Levi asked.

"I don't think so," Enne answered.

The room was filled with desks and toppled chairs, each coated in a thick layer of grime. Enne grimaced as she sat down at the one beside him and tried her best not to touch anything. Jac perched on top of her desk without concern for his new clothes, and Lola resorted to standing. Everyone shared the same grim expression.

"I assume you've spoken with Vianca," Levi said to Enne.

"I did this morning," she replied. "I told her you're the one who should be doing this, not me."

"Well…" His gaze flickered to Jac, who avoided his stare. In fact, Jac was faced away from Levi, like he had no intention of looking at him at all. "I convinced her that we should *both* be doing this, that we'd be better off as allies."

"I thought the Irons hated you," Lola said.

Levi pursed his lips. "They have mixed feelings."

"Your third tried to kill you."

"I said mixed."

Enne felt a pinch of resentment. Levi had argued against Vianca exactly as Enne had warned her he would, yet still Vianca had acquiesced to his requests and therefore left Enne without a consultant. It paid to be the donna's favorite.

"Were you able to catch the news?" Levi asked Lola.

"Yes," she answered darkly.

"You know far more about the Orphan Guild than we do. What do you think of this?"

"I..." Her voice was unusually high-pitched. Enne knew she must have recognized at least a few of the names on the list of casualties. "I'm shocked. Bryce keeps the location private, known only to Scavenger, Ivory, and the members of the Guild. There must have been a mole—someone who knew where it was and how to cause the most damage."

"But *you* know the location," Levi said. "Has Bryce made any effort to contact you? He must suspect you."

Lola stiffened. "I doubt he suspects me."

"Why is that?" Levi asked.

"Because he made it very clear that he'd kill me if I ever betrayed him." Enne flinched at Lola's coldness. Was that how the Guildmaster treated all his associates? "And he knows I'm not thick. Or a killer."

Levi's forehead creased with worry. "I'm nervous about this. The Irons is the only gang that doesn't hire from the Orphan Guild, but this attack was directly prompted by events Enne and I caused."

Enne shivered. "Which means the other lords might blame us."

The notion of becoming enemies with Ivory, Scavenger, *and* Bryce left Enne ill. Even if she needed to call herself a street lord, she wasn't like them. They were...dangerous.

You killed Sedric, she reminded herself. *You wanted to. He was despicable. He was a predator.*

79

She remembered the sweetness of the drugged Lollipop Lick on her lips, the pity in the bartender's eyes. How many girls had Sedric targeted? How many people around him had been complicit in the suffering he'd caused?

You watched Semper die, and you were glad he did.

Enne was just as dangerous.

You killed the whiteboot. You didn't even hesitate.

She was just as deadly.

You're not like the other lords. You don't want this.

It was true that Enne didn't have a cause to drive her, like Vianca. Or ambition to motivate her, like Levi. But she did have her anger, her grief, her frustration. She felt it all unfurling and writhing inside of her, like a snake rising from its slumber. *You do have power,* it whispered as it curled around the broken cavities of her heart.

"Enne?" Levi asked, drawing her out of her thoughts. "Do you mind if we speak in private?"

"Of course," she said, and she cringed watching Levi shakily get to his feet. They walked back into the stairwell, keeping the door propped to let in a sliver of light. Levi leaned against the wall to support himself.

"I want you to know that I'll still help you," he told her seriously. "In any way I can."

Her resentment waning but not quite gone, she said, "You assume I want your help. Last time you called yourself lord, *I* had to rescue *you*."

He put his hand to his heart as though she'd wounded him more than he was already hurt. "I'm offended you don't think higher of my consulting skills."

"Then tell me: how will I pay for these associates? Where will they stay? How will I convince them I'm not a fraud?"

He gave her a weak smile. "Just give me some time and a bottle of whiskey, and I'll find you a few clever ideas."

She frowned. She didn't want to hear about his confidence in himself—she'd suffered through enough of that already. She needed to hear that he had confidence in *her*.

"That life philosophy is why you look like you do now," she grumbled.

"Like what?" He smoothed the front of his blazer. "I think I look rather dashing. You know, you're pretty observant, if you guessed my measurements." He smirked. "*Very* observant, even—"

"You look terrible," she said quickly, before he could embarrass her further.

His laugh was followed by a wince. "I mean it, though. I'm sorry I don't have solutions yet, but I will—I promise. I've spent all day trying to figure out how to piece my life back together, and it feels like every time I think I've gotten ahead, there's some other problem, some other risk." His voice grew gradually more heated. "You saved me yesterday, and I don't have it figured out yet, but give me a chance to think and—" he angrily hit the side of his wounded leg "—and put myself back together, so I can save you, too."

As touching as his feelings might have been, Enne didn't want a savior. She wanted a partner.

She looked away and changed the subject. "I noticed Jac... Did something happen between you two?"

He took a shaky breath. "Jac witnessed my conversation with Vianca."

Levi didn't need to say anything else; Enne could already imagine how that must've gone. In her conversations with Vianca, Enne could do nothing more than beg. She'd never want someone else to witness that, especially not someone she cared about. Despite being Vianca's victim, there was a shame tied to the omerta she couldn't describe. She didn't deserve it—it defied her own logic—but she felt it all the same.

"I'm sorry," she murmured, reaching for his hand. It was meant to be for comfort, so she was surprised when Levi took her hand and laced her fingers with his. She flushed, thankful for the darkness.

"I'm sorry, too," he breathed. "I know becoming a street lord is the last thing you'd ever want. It's the last thing you *need*. The more famous you are, the more you become a target. And you can't afford for the world to realize what you are."

The last thing you'd ever want.

A feeling of wrongness rumbled in Enne's stomach, heavy and low like the toll of an iron bell. She was a Bellamy schoolgirl. She wore white lace and patent leather and had a sweet tooth. She wasn't allowed to want this.

To want the danger of being a street lord.

To want the boy who stood in front of her.

To want power.

But who was there to stop her?

In the darkened stairwell, Levi was silent, as though holding his breath and waiting for her to answer. Enne could tell him about how the Shadow Game's timer still haunted her, and that she hated it. She could tell him about how she *was* dangerous, that maybe it was the only thing in her life she'd ever been good at. She could tell him how badly she wanted to feel powerful.

Instead, she reached up and brushed her fingers against his chin, her thumb resting only inches from his lips. He froze in surprise. They had touched before—he had held her before—but they had always left a line uncrossed.

She drew that line now, her fingertip trailing goose bumps across his neck and tracing down his abdomen. Each one of her heartbeats sounded as loud to her as gunshots, but she could still hear the sigh he breathed as he leaned into her, wanting her.

This was how she'd tell him.

Suddenly, the door swung open, and they sprang apart. Jac raised the lantern, wearing a serious expression.

"I heard something outside," Jac grunted.

"Are you sure?" Levi asked, his voice higher than usual.

Jac's gaze dropped to their hands, and Enne quickly lowered hers and made to smooth out her skirts. Whatever had happened between Levi and Jac, she didn't want to make it worse.

"Sure enough that we should check," Jac answered.

Enne's mood sobered. Anyone could be lurking outside—a bounty hunter, a whiteboot, a Dove. Which was why, once Jac was angrily thumping down the stairs and out of earshot, Enne stood on her tiptoes and kissed Levi on the cheek. He opened his mouth to say something, but for once, he looked at a loss for words. Enne grinned, pleased with her own daring.

"I wish I hadn't seen that," Lola muttered as she pushed past them.

"Oh, shut up," Enne grumbled, flushing deeper as Levi shot her a wry smile. "I—I was just..." she stammered at him, her confidence dissipating after being so awkwardly interrupted. "I was just going to tell you..." Below them, Jac and Lola reached the bottom of the stairwell.

"And I intend to be the most attentive listener..." He cleared his throat. "Later. After this."

They descended down the stairs and paused beside their seconds at the exit. Each brandished a gun, except for Lola, who hated firearms and pitifully wielded her favored scalpel.

"No confrontation," Levi whispered. "If we see someone, we run. Don't shoot—"

A gunshot rang out, and they all jolted back. The bullet lodged in the wall in front of them.

"Muck," Lola squeaked.

"Who's there?" their assailant called out into the night.

"Is it just one person?" Levi hissed.

Jac craned his head to look, but as soon as he did, another shot fired. He cursed and pulled back. "If we go back inside, we could find another exit."

"Come out!" the other person shouted.

Levi cleared his throat and called out, "We don't want trouble."

There was a strange *thump* on the ground, and after several moments of silence, Jac nodded and charged out from behind the wall, pistol raised. He blanched and immediately lowered it. "Come look," he croaked.

The three of them did, and Enne gasped when she saw a young man lying face-down on the pavement, gun still clutched in his hand. His sleeve was stained with blood.

"I know him," Lola gasped, rushing toward him. With Jac's help, they turned the body over. He'd been shot in the chest—quite a while ago, judging by how much he'd bled. His eyes were closed.

"Is he dead?" Levi asked.

Lola felt for a pulse, then her eyes widened and she slapped him lightly on the cheek. "No. And he's from the Guild."

His eyes fluttered open, then he grasped wildly at Lola's hands. He coughed, spewing blood on her front. "I can't go back," he rasped. "I can't go back."

Jac pressed against the man's chest to stem the bleeding, but the man writhed in agony. He rolled onto his side, revealing a heinous exit wound. Lola tried to pin him down, but his face only filled with more panic.

"It's me," Lola told him. "You're going to be—"

"I can't go back!"

Enne cringed and squeezed Levi's hand as Lola tried to calm the man. Gradually, he stopped fighting and stilled. It happened so suddenly that Enne could scarcely believe what she was looking at—that a stranger had gone from a man to a corpse right in front of her.

A siren sounded in the distance, frighteningly close.

"The whiteboots heard the gunshots," Levi said. "Get up. We need to go."

"So we just leave him here?" Lola snapped.

"It's that or get caught," he answered.

Levi pulled Enne away, but even as they ran down the street, she turned once more to look at the body. It seemed insignificant in comparison to the death she'd witnessed the previous night, but she needed to see it and remember it. These were the terms of the assignment Vianca had given her. This—not a stolen kiss—was the price to pay in New Reynes for something you wanted.

Enne pictured each of the faces of the Phoenix Club, as quickly and deftly as she'd so often recited her mother's rules.

Her reason for wanting power seemed so clear now. She saw it in the body bleeding out in the alley. In the bruises covering Levi's skin. In the memory of her mother. In the anger steeping inside of her, hot and quiet and simmering.

Vianca wanted righteousness.

Levi wanted glory.

And she, Enne realized, wanted revenge.

JAC

♥   ♠   ♦   ♣

"Ah." Levi grimaced as Jac opened the trapdoor to Zula's basement. "There's that smell." The office of *Her Forgotten Histories* was cloaked in darkness, the only light source the faint flame above Levi's fingers.

Jac watched the way Levi winced with each step as he descended. It was hard to tell exactly what was hurting him, other than everything. Jac still had a few sore spots from his boxing match at Dead at Dawn, but he had the Mardlin strength talent—he was made of stronger stuff than his friend.

But Jac didn't have it in him to both hate Levi and feel sorry for him. So as he waited at the top of the stairs, pinching his nose, he settled on the former.

"What are you doing?" Levi asked.

"I'm not staying here."

Levi and Jac had a lot in common. They both liked to gamble. They had mastered the art of hungover mornings, of sneaking into variety shows, of wandering the streets at moonlight hours searching for food or beds or both. Levi had helped Jac clear his debt at his One-Way House. Jac had sworn Levi that oath he'd always wanted. Their first jobs, first romances, first troubles—they'd seen each other through them side by side.

But there were differences that separated them, and to Jac, that gap had grown much wider in the past few days.

It went like this.

I only need four hundred more volts. Then I'll be out, Jac had said. They were thirteen years old and sitting on a stoop in Olde Town they'd claimed because nobody else wanted it. Back then, his big dream was finding a way out of that One-Way House, one of the many "schools" that shipped in kids from across the Republic for "educational relocation." Jac hadn't learned to read, but he knew his way around a factory.

Reymond offered to make me his third today, Levi had confided in him. He'd said it like it was no big deal, like he'd been expecting it. Jac had laughed because he didn't know what else to say. He was trying to pay out an indenture, and Levi was being offered everything.

I didn't take it, Levi had said.

Not quite a year later, Jac got his first job as a dishboy at a tavern, and Levi was being recruited by the best casinos in the North Side.

And after that, when Jac's job started paying him with Lullaby under the table, when it started to go bad—it didn't compare. Jac had made the wrong choices. Levi hadn't gotten a choice with Vianca.

Whatever Jac dreamed of, Levi dreamed bigger. Whatever Jac's problems, Levi's were worse. It wasn't something that Levi had done intentionally, but it was plain all the same. Ever since the beginning, Levi was going to be a legend, and Jac—at best—was going to be a cautionary tale.

"Just give me a chance to explain," Levi pleaded, shaking Jac out of his dark thoughts.

"I don't want you to. I know how these wagers of yours

work—you always think you'll win. And you probably will. But I'm not a bargaining chip." Though a pathetic part of him wondered if he always had been.

"Where will you go?"

Three Bells Church was always open. "I'll be fine. Go decorate your room with your wanted posters."

"You think I'm happy about this?" he asked, voice rising. If they weren't careful, they would wake Zula sleeping in the apartment above them.

"Aren't you?" Jac demanded. Levi had gotten everything he'd always wanted—a chance to rebuild the Irons, the repeat of his glorified Great Street War...and Enne, or so it seemed from earlier.

"Muck no," Levi snapped. "But if you come down, if you give me ten minutes..." He let out an unnerving laugh. "You'll probably hate me even more then. And I'll deserve it. Today has spiraled, and every moment I think I'm getting ahead of it all, I just fall deeper into the red."

Jac didn't like the sound of that. "Hard to imagine hating you any more, right now."

"Well, I'm asking for your help, and I know I don't deserve it."

"You don't," Jac said, but he was already climbing down the stairs. Because even if he did spend the night on a church pew, he'd just lay awake worrying about what Levi meant and wasting prayers—and then he'd be right back here in the morning.

Levi sat down on the edge of his bed, gingerly touching the places on his arms and chest where he'd been bruised. "This morning, I had a run-in with Harrison Augustine."

"A bad sign if I ever knew one," Jac responded darkly. He didn't know much about Harrison, but the man shared his mother's name, and thus her talent for omertas. That was enough of a reason to steer clear of him.

Levi recounted their conversation in his getaway car—how

Harrison was replacing Sedric Torren as the First Party's candidate for the New Reynes representative, how the monarchists actually held a strong chance of turning the election, how Harrison needed Levi's influence to help him sway the North Side.

"He knows the only thing to your name is your bounty, right?" Jac asked. "Even if Chez is gone, that doesn't mean the Irons will take you back."

"It won't be easy to convince the Irons to trust me again, but I have to try."

"*Why?*" Jac demanded. "You're wanted dead or alive, and playing Iron Lord will only make you more likely to get hanged."

"Because if he wins, he'll kill Vianca."

Jac stilled.

The omerta marked the exact moment in Levi's life when everything had gone wrong. Jac had spent years watching his friend scrape to hold his ambitions together while Vianca took everything from him. It was because of her scheme that the Irons had betrayed him. That Reymond was dead.

Which was precisely why Jac had been so furious that Levi would wager their friendship like that. Jac was one of the last good things Levi had left, and he'd basically offered that up to Vianca.

"That's why you made the wager," Jac realized out loud, "because Vianca was going to take away the Irons. And you—"

"Need them. Without the Irons, I can't help Harrison. And if Harrison loses—"

"You stay trapped with Vianca," Jac finished, his head spinning.

"That's why I'm asking you to forgive me," Levi said grimly. "And to help me."

Jac had lost his home today. He'd colored his hair and changed his clothes. He'd said goodbye to the job he'd grown comfortable with, the places he liked to frequent and called his own. In the two years since he'd hit bottom, Jac had struggled every day to rebuild his life. So it had infuriated him to think that Levi—who had played a part in causing all of this—could feel even remotely happy about their newfound reputations while Jac lost everything.

But it was Vianca who got Levi invited to the Shadow Game. It was Vianca who'd thrown their friendship on the line.

Like Levi, Jac had a precise moment when his life had gone wrong. And it had taken nearly a year of heartache and rock bottoms, but Levi had helped tear Jac out of it. So it didn't matter how many times Jac needed to start over—he would do the same for his best friend.

"Of course I'll help," Jac told him. "But what if Vianca finds out about Harrison?"

"She can't. If she did…" He shuddered. "I'm telling no one but you."

"It's no wonder she loves you so much, if her son hates her enough to kill her," Jac said, collapsing onto the other side of Levi's bed. The cot creaked with his added weight. "You're probably some sick replacement for him. The one who can never leave."

Levi looked like he wanted to snort, but his expression turned serious. "There's something else that Harrison needs, something I can't provide him. Without it, it doesn't matter how much I do for him—he'll lose the election. He's sure of it."

Jac squinted. He didn't know much about politics. "Like what?"

"The Torren Family's influence will ultimately be what makes or breaks his victory. And with Sedric dead, it's unclear who will end up the Family's next don. It's vital that Harrison is able to sponsor whoever wins. He asked me to watch the feud unfold from the inside, so he can make a clear bet on who that don will be."

It was Levi's expression, not his words, that gave him away.

Levi only wore his poker face when playing cards or keeping secrets.

"And how will do you do that for him, Levi?" he asked softly, even though he'd already guessed the answer.

"He told me to ask someone I trust," his friend answered, voice steady and practiced. "And you're the only person I trust."

Jac stood up abruptly and faced the wall farthest from Levi. Unlike him, Jac wasn't skilled at hiding his emotions, and he wasn't sure he could look at Levi right now with anything other than betrayal. Levi had saved him during the lowest points in his life, but now...he was asking Jac to return to them?

"No. *No.* I want to hear you say it. I want to hear you ask me," Jac growled. If Levi was willing to make such a bold request, then he could at least say the words. If words were too terrible to utter out loud, then they shouldn't be said at all.

Levi cleared his throat. "I'm asking you to be that person."

The words did sound terrible when spoken, but it wasn't the words themselves that left Jac so breathless. It was the strangled way that Levi said them.

"I'm sorry—" Levi started.

"You're *sorry*?" he spat. "What were you thinking, agreeing to that?"

Jac tried to summon the anger Levi more than deserved. He should throw over every last shelf in this cellar, just to hear something crash.

But all he felt instead was guilt.

"I..." Levi paused as his voice cracked. "I made a mistake. I never should have assumed you'd do this."

If Levi had any other friend in this city, Jac knew there would have been no question. Jac always said he would go down any road for Levi, but this was one road—the only road—that he'd sworn to himself he'd never cross again.

"Do you actually think I'm capable of this?" Jac asked. He liked to think he was stronger now. He'd survived Lullaby. He'd glued himself back together, piece by piece. He'd prayed hopeless prayers to never break again. But while their lives might have changed in two years, truthfully, the scars on his arms might as well have still been raw. Even once he'd sobered up, for months after, there'd been the drinking. The fighting. The smoking. And he'd still never kicked the last two.

Addiction had a way of changing courses like that. Jac was a far throw from lull trips in empty warehouse lots and taking his wages in stamps. But he wasn't exactly clean, either. This morning and its two whole packs of cigarettes had been one of his worst in a while.

"That's your decision," Levi answered him. "Do you think you are?"

"You don't get to ask me that now. You agreed to this with Harrison, so you must think I'm ready for it. Right?" Jac whipped around, expecting once again to see Levi's poker face. Instead, Levi was anxiously flipping a business card over in his hands, and Jac swore, from his bloodshot eyes, that his friend might actually cry. It brought back painful memories of the last time Jac had seen him like this, the morning after Jac had nearly died in New Reynes North General Hospital.

That had been his lowest point.

Jac could forgive Levi for betting their friendship as a wager for his freedom.

But betting Jac's health? His dignity? His life?

He didn't know if he could ever forgive him for this.

But if he didn't accept, he didn't know if he could ever forgive himself, either.

"I trust you," was all Levi said. It wasn't exactly the enthusiastic vote of confidence Jac needed, but it was something. "It was wrong for me to agree to this without asking you, but I can still decline. There are more important things."

"No, there aren't." Jac ripped the business card out of Levi's hands. "If this was another scheme for volts or admirers, then I'd tell you to go to hell. But this is the end of Vianca. You're the slickest, cleverest person I know. Watching the way she treats you... I thought she'd *kill* you today. And I felt like I couldn't even stop it, not without killing us both." The way Levi had simply stood there as he choked, standing his ground like he'd been in that position many times before, made Jac delirious with fury. "Of course I'll do it. Anything is worth seeing her rot."

Levi's smile was bright even as he blinked back tears. He gradually lowered himself onto his back, as though every inch brought its own pain, and stared up at the ceiling.

"You're worth more to me than all the other Irons put together," Levi told him, and it was the best thank-you Jac had ever received.

"Yeah, well, you better be able to handle them when I'm gone. If I'm spending all my time at Luckluster Casino, I won't be able to save you from Chez a second time."

"Don't worry. Next time you see the Irons, they'll be the richest gang in the North Side." The determined sound to Levi's voice took Jac back. If he closed his eyes, they could have been thirteen years old again, fantasizing about all the fortune their futures held. Now Jac couldn't envision their futures with anything other than dread.

"Did you tell Enne about Harrison?" Jac asked. After all, Vianca's death would free her, too.

"No," Levi said firmly. "That would only give Vianca another opportunity to find out. It's better that Enne doesn't know, for both our sakes."

Jac agreed with that, but he was still surprised. It didn't seem like Enne and Levi kept secrets from each other.

Jac let several moments pass before he worked up his nerve. Because yes, Jac would do absolutely anything for Levi, but that didn't change the fact that what Levi had asked of him was almost unthinkable. Had it been anything short of this prize, it would have been despicable. But this was the price it took to end Vianca Augustine.

And if Levi's suffering was worth all of this, then Jac refused to watch him walk down a path that would only lead to more heartache. Especially when that path was so obviously what the donna wanted.

"Can I ask you a favor, when I'm gone?" Jac asked.

"Anything," Levi replied quickly.

"Don't be with Enne." Even as he noticed Levi tense beside him, Jac didn't let himself falter. "Vianca used me to play with you, and she already suspects that you're both together. Don't give her any more ways to hurt you. To hurt *both* of you."

It took Levi several seconds to say anything, and when he did, his voice was strained. "Of course. I said anything. And you're...you're right."

"It's better for both of you."

"Until Vianca is gone."

Jac cringed at the hope in Levi's voice, but he didn't take his request back.

After a few minutes, Levi's breathing slowed into a rhythmic sleep. Jac shifted uncomfortably, his heart racing with an all too familiar dread. Although he desperately wanted to sleep, for the next several hours, the sensation of drifting off terrified him. Every time he felt his consciousness slip, he yanked it back, as though he might fall off the edge. His mind kept revisiting the same memories over and over, unraveling the threads he'd spent years knotting.

When he did eventually sleep, he did so fitfully. It wasn't deep sleep. It certainly wasn't a lull.

And for the second night in a row, Jac Mardlin dreamed of his own death.

ENNE

♥ ♠ ♦ ♣

Church bells tolled across Olde Town, making the wrought-iron gates and window bars tremble. Everything in Olde Town was sharp—the spindly towers, the spear-like points atop the fences, the crumbling spires. It was a neighborhood of thorns and barbed wire. And with every new haunting graveyard or condemned building that Enne passed, she wondered how Levi and Jac could possibly be so fond of this place.

The address Levi had given her over the phone this morning led her down the Street of the Holy Tombs, to an abandoned, overgrown park and an impressive marble building hidden among the trees. She tread up its stone steps and peered at the graffiti painted over its once beautiful oak doors. The building was grand enough to be a palace, with the columns and sweeping windows to match. But over a period of probably many years, after hurricanes and infestations and general waste, Olde Town had swallowed it whole.

The door creaked open, making Enne jolt, and Levi peered out with a smirk. "Did I spook you?"

Enne *hmph*ed and straightened her skirts. "What is this place?"

"The remnants of an art museum that was looted and closed during the Revolution," Levi explained. Then he grinned. "Pretty swanky, right?"

Enne slipped inside. The floor was coated in dust and broken glass, and the magnificent dome ceiling was home to several bats. "That wouldn't have been my first descriptor."

"Well, it's vacant, and no one comes here," he said, shrugging. "The Scarhands have Scrap Market. The Doves have… whatever hole they crawl out of. So the first thing on both our agendas should be finding our own places to claim. This is right in the middle of Olde Town, safe, large—"

"You intend for people to *live* here?" Enne asked in disbelief.

"Yes, myself included."

"It's *filthy*."

"There's history here."

"Not anymore."

Levi cracked his neck. "Then there will be." He made for the stairs and motioned for her to follow. "Come on."

They climbed to the third, top floor, where a large set of windows offered a magnificent view of the Brint, and, beyond it, the glittering skyscrapers of the Financial District. The stairwell forked, leading to two separate hallways, each one lined with rooms.

"This is it," Levi declared, rubbing his hands together. "I have a good feeling."

Enne grimaced at a dead rat on the floor. "Your good feelings are not to be trusted."

He rolled his eyes. "You'll be happy to know I *did* do some thinking last night on how I'm going to help you."

"That's interesting you say that," she said, trailing after him as he continued down the hall. For someone so injured, he walked very fast, and she suspected he was running on nothing but his delusions of grandeur. "Because I have an idea myself."

She rummaged around in her purse. It was filled with invitations Vianca had recently sent her for political salons and parties in the South Side, some of them dated as soon as two weeks from now. She dug around them and found the worn edges of *The City of Sin, a Guidebook: Where To Go and Where Not To*. She pulled it out and flipped to the map.

"The gangs have each claimed a neighborhood of the North Side. You have Olde Town and the Casino District. The Scarhands have the Factory District. The Doves have the Deadman District. But no one has this one." She held up the book and tapped the Ruins District, in the northwest corner of the map.

"That's because no one goes there," Levi said. "It's where the royal family and the nobles used to live. It's just rat nests and empty estates now. The Faithful think it's cursed."

Enne triumphantly snapped the guidebook closed. "Then it's simple. I could claim anything in the Ruins District that's still standing."

"It's not a bad idea," Levi admitted. "But you'll still need to recruit members—"

"I have an appointment with the Orphan Guild today at three o'clock."

"The Orphan Guild?" he echoed, his brown eyes wide. "But that's—"

"Lola's already spoken to Bryce." Lola had woken up early today to meet with him—partially on Enne's behalf, partially to hear for herself if the news was true. She'd returned to St. Morse several shades paler and with an appointment scheduled for this afternoon.

Levi shook his head. "I don't like the Orphan Guild. Reymond always relied on them, but I won't pretend that Reymond had a straight moral compass."

Enne didn't think she was in a position to limit herself to good morals. "Well," she responded, "Vianca told me to, so I don't really have a choice."

They turned down an archway and into the final room in the hallway. Inside was a bench covered in a thick film of dust, and walls decorated with a mélange of cobwebs.

Levi took one look at the bench and sat down with a sigh of relief, dust and all. He winced and held a hand to his abdomen. "Even the wicked need to rest sometimes," he breathed.

Enne sat down beside him and flushed, remembering how she'd kissed him last night. The memory had replayed in her mind a few times on the walk here.

But there was still business to attend to.

"I have another idea, too," she said quietly. "I have something to ask you. I'm pretty sure you'll say no…"

Levi shot her a coy smile. "For all your ideas, are you sure you need my help at all?"

She cleared her throat and tried not to look too pleased. "The Scarhands sell weapons, the Doves kill people, you…" She didn't particularly understand how the Irons made volts. "Steal from people?"

"I contract dealers and workers to casinos," he said flatly, as though offended she didn't care more about his business.

Enne nodded like she understood what that meant. "I need a way to pay for this gang, and it *occurred* to me… Of all the worries we have, why should volts be one of them? When both of us—"

Levi shook his head. "Enne, making volts is dangerous. What you *are* is dangerous."

His concerns weren't anything she hadn't considered herself only the day before. But she could feel the volts in her skin constantly, pulsing in tune with her heartbeat. It was an incessant reminder that real power was so easily within reach.

"We could be *rich*," she said.

He threw his head back and let out a sound somewhere between a sigh and a groan. "Careful. You're appealing to my vices."

"When Lourdes led me to you, we could think of no good reason why she'd give me your name. Now it seems obvious. An orb-maker and a Mizer, of *course* she—"

"Enne, do you know any other orb-makers?" Levi asked seriously.

"No." It wasn't a very common talent.

"That's because almost all the orb-makers are dead. The estates in the Ruins District belonged to them, too." Levi took a deep, steady breath. For all his broken bones and bruises, it was obvious the pain on his face right now was a different sort. It came from older wounds. "This is all very new for you. Not only did you not *know* your true talents until a few days ago—a shock I can't even imagine—but you also didn't grow up on the Republic's mainland. There aren't Revolution landmarks on every other block in Bellamy." His expression darkened. "I grew up in the shadows of that history."

Enne knew that Levi hadn't been born in New Reynes, as much as he liked to call himself a Sinner. But the details of his past were a mystery to her. "Do you want to talk about it, then?"

"I... There's nothing to talk about. I'm a different person now." He said it like he was trying to convince himself. "My father's father was the personal orb-maker to the king of Caroko." Enne knew Caroko was the capital of one of the seven Mizer nations that existed before the Revolution. "The monarchists believe the First Party went too far after the Revolution. Families like mine, who served the Mizers, were forcefully relocated closer to New Reynes, where we could more easily be watched. My parents lost their home and the lives they knew, but they were considered the lucky ones. Plenty of other orb-makers were executed."

Enne realized how insensitive she must've sounded. "I'm sorry. I shouldn't have suggested it."

"We'll think of something else," he offered.

"Before I meet Bryce?"

He closed his eyes. "We have to try."

Enne allowed a few moments of silence to pass between them. Part of her was still ashamed for her suggestion, and so she glanced at the empty space between their hands, looking for assurances.

Later, Levi had promised her. *I will be the most attentive listener.*

There was no one to interrupt them now.

And so she placed her hand on his.

Levi stiffened and looked down to where they touched with a pained expression.

"Enne." All of his wry smiles from last night were gone. He moved away from her with slow, reluctant restraint. "This is dangerous."

Enne's cheeks burned. "Everything in our lives is dangerous—"

"This is different," he said suddenly, almost forcefully. "I'll help you—of course I'll help you—in any way I can. We're a team. We're partners. But this…it's not a good idea, for either of us."

"But last night…" Enne swallowed. "You seemed—"

"It was a mistake," he answered, looking away from her.

Enne didn't pretend to understand everything going through Levi's mind these past few days, while his entire life had fallen part. But a memory stirred in her of Luckluster Casino, when Levi had been a moment away from kissing her, like it was the last chance he'd ever have.

So that was it, then. She was a danger he would only risk when he had nothing left to lose.

He was allowed to feel that way, but that didn't make it hurt less. They had faced the worst together and sacrificed for each other. She could tell he was holding back from the way he spoke, that he wanted this as much as she did.

But he'd decided he wouldn't. He couldn't.

Well, she wouldn't push him into something he would only regret.

"I should go meet with Lola," Enne said, as an excuse. It was silly to let her feelings get in the way of the help she needed, but she couldn't remember last night and feel anything less than humiliated.

"You don't need to leave," he told her weakly.

"Don't I?" she asked, her words somewhere between a question and a challenge.

"What will you tell Bryce? What sort of associates are you looking for?" Levi asked. "Or are you expecting to find others who follow your finishing school curriculum?"

She gritted her teeth. "No, but—"

"If you'd like, I'm sure you can make them call you a lady, rather than lord."

The comment shouldn't have struck her like it did. She'd heard those jokes before. But in that moment, seconds after his stinging rejection, she decided she didn't need this sort of help.

Muck Levi's jokes, she thought to herself, not even cringing at the curse. She'd already decided yesterday not to be ashamed of who she was. When Enne did hire her gangsters, she would do so in pointed toe heels. She would shake hands for business deals in lace gloves. She would claim *herself* a palace.

Enne stood up. "I should head back." Levi made to get to his feet, but Enne quickly stopped him. "Don't rush up and hurt yourself. You've been enough help today."

"Have I?" He bit his lip. "Don't answer that. I know I haven't. And I'm sorry. I... I've had a lot on my mind."

Enne shouldn't feel petty. Levi was her friend—and no matter how many times he claimed they were in this together, he was allowed to draw this line between them. But she was also allowed to be hurt.

"Goodbye, Levi," she said, and then she walked out, in the direction of an empire of her own.

LEVI

♥ ♠ ♦ ♣

The Catacombs nightclub wasn't much to look at on the outside, all decrepit and centuries-worn. It'd once been a church to the old Faith, and the flying buttresses and unlabeled crypts along its walls still gave off the air of someplace sacred.

Levi only knew its owner, Narinder Basra, by reputation—the Catacombs was the most famous nightclub in the city after all. And while Harrison trusted Narinder enough to recommend him to Levi as a contact, Levi wasn't sure he could trust anyone while he had a three-thousand-volt bounty on his head.

Not that I have much of a choice, he thought as he rapped on the back door.

The music inside paused. A moment later, one of the musicians—a violinist, which seemed a strange choice for a dance club—answered the door, and a cloud of pungent smoke escaped from inside. He ran his eyes over Levi with a bored expression and spoke with his cigar between his teeth. He didn't seem to recognize Levi's face. "We're not open."

"Is Narinder here?" Levi asked.

"Who's asking?"

"A neighbor."

The musician rolled his eyes and opened the door.

The Catacombs was an apt name for this place. The decor varied somewhere between macabre and distastefully irreverent. Surrounded by chandeliers of human bones, clacking and vibrating with each note of the music, the stage stood where the altar once had. The band was a half orchestra—complete with a grand piano, a saxophone, a variety of strings and woodwind instruments, even a harp. Skeletons unearthed from their crypts had been cemented to the walls, piece by piece, casting unnatural red and purple shadows in the light from the stained glass ceiling. The pipe organ in the back had been painted ivory, its gold crowning lined with teeth.

It was pretty over-the-top, even for Levi's taste. "Cozy," he commented sarcastically.

"I've always thought so, too." The voice came from the bar, where a lone young man sat on a stool drinking a mug of coffee. He had dark brown skin with a delicate face and straight black hair tied at the nape of his neck. Beneath his jawline, on the left side, was a tattoo of a pair of dice.

Levi's voice dropped somewhere deep in his stomach, and he gaped at him, speechless. No matter how drunk he'd been, he never forgot a face. The memory of him felt like the trace of lips against his neck.

"Neighbors, indeed," Dice murmured. "All this time you've claimed Olde Town, yet only now we officially get to meet." His eyes roamed over Levi's body, pausing on places he'd previously claimed himself. "Don't you look dashing with your designer suit and matching black eye."

Levi cleared his throat. "You never mentioned, um—"

"My name? No, I didn't." Dice smiled wickedly. "I'm Narinder Basra. I own this place."

Levi had met Dice—Narinder—at the Sauterelle, a burlesque cabaret in the Casino District where he and Enne had gone searching for information on Lourdes Alfero.

Narinder finished his drink and left it on the bar. "Come on. We can reacquaint ourselves in my office."

Just because Narinder had helped Levi once didn't mean he wouldn't sell him out now. There was no loyalty between them. When they'd met before, Levi hadn't even asked his name. He had no idea how to treat their relationship.

He followed Narinder to his office, which was plainly decorated and well-lit—far different from the rest of the nightclub. He kept a number of instruments behind his desk: a flute, a sitar, and a harp. The Basra family must've had a musical blood talent.

Levi's gaze fell on the couch, then, remembering his last encounter with Narinder, he flushed and loosened his shirt collar.

"You look terrible," Narinder commented.

"Eh, just a few broken ribs is all," Levi said, wincing as he lowered himself onto the couch. "A friend of mine suggested I pay you a visit. I'm recruiting. He seemed to think you were well connected."

Narinder lifted an eyebrow as he sat behind the desk. "I hear things about the Irons, us being neighbors and all. Like how Chez Phillips went missing two nights ago, and now here you are, looking for replacements. I guess dead chancellors make the news, and dead gangsters get nothing."

Levi stiffened. "I didn't kill Chez." He would never have gone so far.

"I wouldn't blame you, if you did." Narinder leaned back in his chair and aimlessly plucked a few strings on the harp. "That's how it works in the gangs, isn't it?"

"Not mine," he said.

Narinder rolled his eyes. "You can't have a heart of gold

and do the work you do. The greedy would only carve it out of you."

Levi thought a heart of gold might have been stretching it. "I'll take my chances. As I said, I was told that you have a lot of connections, and I came here to see if you knew anyone who might be interested in working for me."

"Joining a gang has just been made a capital offense, and either way, yours hasn't exactly been doing too well lately," Narinder said in an accusatory tone. "Why should I recommend anyone to you?"

He doesn't like gangsters, Levi realized. Considering their last encounter, Levi liked to think he was the exception.

"Because my luck has changed," Levi said smoothly, "and because this 'street war' is about more than crime. It's about the rich watching from their ivory towers in the South Side while the North Side becomes a battleground. This is our city, not theirs."

"You sound like a politician," Narinder said.

"But what I said is true," Levi told him.

Narinder gave him a look of approval and stood up. He sat beside Levi on the couch, and Levi noticed he still smelled like honey. He stared at the dice tattoo on Narinder's jawline, pushing away intrusive thoughts of the look on Enne's face when he'd lied to her about how he felt. Jac's request had been reasonable, but that didn't make it ache less.

"It's funny," Narinder said with a smirk. Levi could see why the musician was well-liked; he had an easy smile. "At the Sauterelle, you were so preoccupied with being recognized yourself, you had no idea everyone else there recognized *me*."

"I haven't spent enough time in Olde Town," Levi explained with a pinch of embarrassment. "But I'll be around more now."

"A dangerous idea," Narinder murmured coyly.

A heat swept through Levi, starting in his stomach and spreading across his neck. Levi did his fair share of flirting, but this wasn't how he typically did business. He preferred to have a level head, and nothing about the way Narinder smiled kept his head clear.

He thought of Enne, and her look of betrayal found its way back into his mind. He didn't think starting something between him and Narinder was wise. And if Enne ever found out...

Levi shifted, putting a little more distance between them. "So, do you know anyone you'd recommend? If not, I'll be leaving. I only came on a referral."

"You don't trust me," Narinder observed.

"It's nothing personal." Even though it was. They clearly had unresolved history.

Narinder leaned in. "It feels personal. I'm not interested in turning you in, you know, and it's not because we've...met before. Olde Town is my home, but Olde Town is all that stands between the rest of the North Side and the South. Like you said, last time there was a war, my home was the battleground, while Veil and Havoc watched from elsewhere."

Levi searched for a tell in his expression, but found none. The history was true: Veil and Havoc had sacrificed Olde Town for the good of everyone else. Even now, barely anyone lived here. "You're the only other person with any power in this neighborhood," Narinder said. "So I have a personal stake in helping you rise, if you'd see my home protected."

The word *rise* lingered in Levi's mind. He was a sucker for anyone who saw potential in him. He couldn't help it—his gaze darted to Narinder's lips.

"And..." Narinder added, noticing Levi's stare and grinning. "Maybe it's also because we met."

"I'm grateful, either way," Levi told him truthfully.

"I have someone for you. You could interview her now, if you'd like." Narinder's gaze flickered from Levi's eyes to his lips and back again. "Well, it doesn't have to be just now."

Levi swallowed. He'd come here with a purpose, but maybe he could also use a distraction.

You have three thousand volts on your head, he scolded himself. But, for better or for worse, he trusted Narinder. Twice now, he'd agreed to help Levi for little in return. Levi had spent so much time clearing his debts that he forgot not every good deed came with a price.

He could get used to that again.

Levi leaned closer to him, and it only took the brush of Narinder's mouth against his for his desire to win out.

Last time, they'd both been far from sober, but the feeling of Narinder's hands on his waist and the honey smell of his skin still brought flashbacks of a secluded booth in the Sauterelle. Of ragtime music drowning out the sounds of their breaths. Of Enne wearing a fur coat several sizes too large and looking every bit a Sinner.

He shoved that last thought away. He'd made a promise—a mucking awful promise, he was already realizing—but it couldn't be helped. Falling for her was no good for either of them, and kissing Narinder felt good enough to forget everything else.

Levi's back met the edge of the couch, forceful enough to make him wince, and Narinder paused and rested his forehead against his.

"When you say you'll be in Olde Town more, will it only be for business?" the musician asked.

"You tell me," he murmured.

"Pay me another visit, when you're not so bruised."

Levi smirked. "The shiner doesn't look *that* bad."

Narinder's breath was hot against his neck. "It's no fun hurting you if you're already hurt."

Levi felt so dazed he barely noticed Narinder open the door and ask for someone named "Tock."

While they waited, Levi cleared his throat, no longer as keen to return to business. "I have a free morning."

Narinder shook his head. "Remember when I said your ego was too big to notice mine?"

"Ah," Levi said, embarrassed. "*You're* busy. But you're the one who suggested we wait."

"I'm successful, not responsible."

Someone knocked on the door, and Narinder opened it. A girl strode in, a saxophone hanging from a cord around her neck. Her short black hair looked as if she'd cut it herself, and her laced leather boots appeared military grade. She had thick thighs and a knife strapped to each one.

She smirked when she saw Levi. "You're better looking in your wanted poster." Behind her, Narinder gaped in exasperation.

Levi shrugged and sent Narinder a sly glance. "At least I'm wanted."

"Levi, this is my cousin, Tock Ridley." Narinder said it like an apology. "Tock, this is Levi."

Levi had already noticed the resemblance. Though Tock's tan skin was a few shades fairer than Narinder's deep brown, they both had warm, dark eyes and brows with the same determined set to them.

"So this is why I should trust her? Because she's family?" Levi noted.

"Yes," Narinder said, wrapping an arm around her shoulders. Tock bristled and elbowed him in the side. He winced. "We're very close."

Levi had to admit her clothes and weapons gave her an intimidating air—a quality he certainly didn't possess. But she didn't look like she'd be thrilled about taking orders. "What are your talents?"

She tapped her sax. "A split music talent—"

"That's worth nothing on—"

"And a blood talent for explosives."

Levi stilled. He'd heard of those talents, of course, but they were extremely rare. Before the Revolution, those with Talents of Mysteries had largely populated the upper classes. When the First Party overthrew the Mizers, those with Talents of Aptitudes, like dancing, music, strength, and others, rose to power and removed or relocated those they viewed as a threat. Someone with the ability to conjure a potentially deadly explosion shouldn't have survived the Revolution.

"Her father—my uncle—created the blast that blew open the National Prison's gates during the Revolution and freed Chancellor Semper," Narinder said, as though he could hear Levi's thoughts. That explained the reason Tock had been spared.

"Impressive," Levi told her. "Do you have any leadership experience? Done any casino work?"

She inspected her fingernails with disinterest. "Nope."

With her talent, if Tock approached the Orphan Guild, the Doves or the Scarhands would fork over a fortune for her. But she hadn't gone to the Guild, and judging by her current bored expression, Levi had no reason to believe she actually wanted this sort of work.

"Narinder, can I talk to you for a moment?" he asked. Narinder followed him out into the hallway, and Levi hastily shut the door behind them. "Is she really the best you've got?"

Narinder looked away sheepishly. "I promise you—she's good at what she does."

"She doesn't seem to want gang work."

"She does. She's just…like that." He gestured toward the door helplessly. "She's wanted to do something like this for months. I'm finally giving in."

"Giving in?" Family members didn't normally encourage each other to join the gangs.

"Well, I'm tired of her blowing my things up. This cathedral has stood for four hundred years, through fires and disasters and revolution. But it's never had to face Tock when she's in a mood."

"You're not really selling her," Levi said warily. "And I'm having a hard time believing that you'd put your cousin at risk with this job."

"That's always been my fear, but I know Tock is capable of protecting herself." His eyes fell on the bruise around Levi's eye. "Far more than you are."

Levi ignored the gibe. "If she really wanted this, I'd think she'd act a little more interested."

"She knows you're broke," Narinder admitted. "She thinks she wants volts and thrill, but I know her better than that. She's not shallow. And the way you talk about Olde Town… I think this would be good for her. *That's* the only reason I'm okay with this. Because it's not the other gangs—it's you."

Maybe he did have a heart of gold, because Narinder's words struck Levi in all the right places. And whatever his thoughts about Enne and his promise to Jac, he liked Narinder. Narinder's help might've been freely given, but Levi wanted to do something for him in return.

"Fine," he breathed, praying he wouldn't regret it.

Narinder sighed in relief and kissed Levi in a way that said *thank you*. Levi decided he could, as it turned out, grow fonder of doing business this way.

They returned to the room, and Levi announced, "You're hired."

"I am?" she asked.

"Yep. You can start immediately. If you want the job, that is."

Tock straightened, her surprised expression turning smug. "Doing what?"

"You're going to round up all the Irons around Olde Town, armed with that natural intimidation you wear so well. And you're going to make it clear to the whole neighborhood that Chez Phillips is gone, war is coming, and I'm the only chance they've got." He hid a smile. His little speech sounded pretty impressive, if he said so himself.

"You sound as desperate as you look," she said. "And that job sounds pretty boring."

Levi's irritation rose. "Joining a gang is cause for execution these days. If you were scared, I'd understand, but exactly what about this is boring?"

"I don't get scared," she said.

"Well, you should," he snapped. He'd spent the past two days—before and after the Shadow Game—scared out of his mind. Every day working with Vianca was a day lived in fear. He might've been the youngest street lord by at least ten years, and he might've been so injured he could barely walk, but of all the things he could be belittled for, he wasn't a coward.

"The Orphan Guild was attacked last night without warning, with automatics that fire five bullets a second. The Guild might work primarily with the gangs, but you know where else the workers go? Casinos. Dens. Bars. Night clubs." He lifted his arms up, gesturing to all of the Catacombs. "I'm willing to bet someone who works here has a past. I'm willing to bet gangsters find their way here every weekend, just like any other patron. The wigheads are only going after the gangs now, but at some point, what they call a gangster just means a criminal. Then what they call a criminal means an accomplice. Then what they call an accomplice means a bystander. Sit it out, if you want. But the life I want for the people loyal to me isn't one of violence. Sorry if that's boring to you. Maybe one day, if they ever come for this place with automatics or matches, you'll get to see something exciting."

Levi clenched his fists and whipped around, if not to storm out the door, then to drag Narinder back into the hallway and ask for someone better. He didn't care if she could blow up the entire South Side—maybe the violinist or the pianist would have more moral fiber.

But before he could leave the office, he was grabbed by the shoulder. His knees nearly gave out with the sudden pain of it, like a bolt of lightning straight to his ribs. He shouted out a curse.

"Muck," Tock said, startled by his volume. "You're delicate."

"And you're—"

"*Sorry,*" she said, cutting off the insult before he spat it. "I'll take the job."

"What job?" he growled, turning around.

"Convincing people you're a smart-ass, or whatever you said," she said. Narinder's face, which had seconds ago brightened, slid back into a scowl. "Not being a bystander when the Great Street War happens all over again. I don't care that the Chancellor is dead, or that you and this Séance person killed him. I don't think anyone in the North Side cares about politics and the laws that doesn't affect them. But like you said, it's the whole North Side that will go to war."

Levi had heard far better apologies. "Is that the best you can do?" he asked.

"I'm sorry I called you delicate."

He cringed. That wasn't what he meant, but it did strike him as just absurd enough that he could laugh. "How do I know you mean it?" Levi asked.

"Because I'll say the oath."

If Tock grew up in this city, then she knew the legends of the North Side. When you swore a street oath to your lord, it wasn't simply for show. There was a power to the words. It wasn't like the omerta, which was power taken. An oath didn't force you to do someone's bidding. An oath was loyalty given, a solemn promise not to harm the lord or others who had sworn to them.

Levi nodded. "Go ahead then."

She crossed her heart and recited the words. "Blood by blood. Oath by oath. Life by life." When she finished the rest of the speech, there was an unmistakable tingling in the air. If Tock noticed it, though, she paid it no mind.

"There's a tattoo parlor across from St. Morse," he told her. "Tell her I sent you, that you need a diamond and a ten. She'll do it no charge." At least, with the papers saying what they did, he hoped that was still the case.

Tock's gaze flickered to the set of tattoos on Levi's forearms: the black A and spade. "What does the suit mean?"

"Diamonds mean you'll get to blow things up."

She grinned. Then she took the saxophone off her shoulder and heaved it ungraciously onto the couch. Narinder winced and picked it up.

"After you get your tattoos," Levi continued, "find Mansi Chandra, at the Sauterelle. She'll help you find the others."

Mansi was a card dealer in the Irons. Levi had always considered her his protégée, and she'd once looked up to him like a little sister. Then she'd betrayed him and sided with Chez. That blow had hurt more than any of the ones Chez had landed.

Levi should've been angry with her. But really, he just wanted her admiration back.

"Yeah, I know the Sauterelle," Tock said. "So I find your gangsters, I give them your message, and then what?"

"We'll all meet tomorrow at the abandoned art museum," he said. If Levi was going to lead differently this time, then he needed to appear more present in the Irons than before. He'd been too distant, and he wouldn't make that mistake again. "Seven o'clock. Make sure they know."

"And for the ones who say no?" she asked.

Unlike the Scar or Dove Lords, Levi swore he'd never run his gang on fear. But the Irons had betrayed him, and there had to be a better line between being weak and being a monster.

"They bear the tattoos, which means they each have bounties on their heads," he said. "Tell them, as long as they stay in Olde Town with me, they have my protection."

"And if they leave?" Tock asked.

Levi didn't know what he'd do if the Irons left. He couldn't help Harrison. He couldn't help Olde Town. He might not like it, but in New Reynes, power wasn't a commodity freely given. If he wanted it, he had to take it.

"Then they can face the gallows."

JAC

♥ ♠ ♦ ♣

By eleven o'clock the next day, Jac had smoked another half a pack of cigarettes—far more than he typically burned through in a morning. Every time he finished one, after twenty minutes or so passed, his fingers started to tremble and his heart palpitations sent him reaching into his pocket for another. All his new clothes already reeked of smoke.

He'd left Zula's nearly as soon as he'd woken up, and the walk to the eastern side of the Casino District had cleared his head. For a while, he stood outside Luckluster Casino, staring at its slick black stone and flashing scarlet lights, and thought about how choosing a don for Harrison to sponsor would only help the Family to survive.

Jac would prefer to see them burn.

But Jac was one man against the entire Torren Empire. That included Luckluster Casino, the only other casino in New Reynes as large as St. Morse. It included the profits of drug sales all across the North Side, particularly its two most popular substances: Rapture and Lullaby. It included thirty-four different pubs they'd bought and converted into smaller gambling enterprises or drug dens. It included hundreds of employees, thousands of addicts, and millions of volts.

And he was just one man.

At eleven thirty, Jac slid into a yellow phone booth and called St. Morse. He knew Levi had scheduled a meeting with Enne around now, but it wasn't Enne he wanted to talk to.

"'Lo?" Lola answered. Her voice sounded strangely on edge.

"It's me."

"Is that supposed to mean something? Who is this?"

Jac choked in surprise and coughed out a puff of smoke. "It's Jac. Why do you sound all wrung out? What's wrong with you?"

"I just spoke to my bosses, and now we have an appointment scheduled later today," she explained. Jac supposed her bosses meant Bryce Balfour and the two others who ran the Orphan Guild. Judging from what he'd heard about that trio, that seemed a reasonable excuse for anxiety. "Why do *you* sound all wrung out?" Lola asked snidely.

If Jac explained all that over the phone, he'd run out of volts to feed the call. "Can you meet me?"

"*Now?* Where?"

"At, um…" He gave the first cross-street he could think of in this neighborhood that wasn't near a Torren place. "18th and Rummy."

"Fine," Lola huffed. "But you better not be in trouble, because I really don't have time today to save you."

There was a bench on the corner, just as he remembered. He sat on it, his back to the building, trying to convince himself to wait an hour before his next smoke. He stared at the line of pubs across the street, a sight that had once been the view from his cramped bedroom window for nearly eight years. From here, it was a short walk to the factory where he'd worked. Jac imagined one of the wardens walking past him on the sidewalk, not recognizing him with his dyed hair or glasses.

It made him feel powerful.

It also made him feel like a ghost.

Lola appeared across the street. Even though no cars were coming, she waited for the light to turn before she crossed over. For nearly a whole minute, Jac watched her just stand there and thought…maybe she'd gotten herself lost. But when the light finally flashed green, he realized she was actually a rule-abiding, knife-collecting fraud.

Lola sat on the bench beside him. She wore her usual top hat, but it was strange seeing her hair down, now that she no longer needed to hide it in public.

"You're less scary with the red hair," he commented.

She frowned. "It's blood red."

"It's…cherry red."

"Why are we here?" she asked, ignoring him and turning around to look at where the address had brought her. "Is this some kind of school?"

"It's my old One-Way House," Jac explained.

Because many had fled the city during the Revolution, the wigheads had started shipping in children from orphanages across much of the western coast about two decades ago, in an effort to bring workers and "community" back into New Reynes. Most of those children ended up in One-Way Houses like the building behind them.

The worst part of the One-Way Houses wasn't the work—it was the debt. From the moment Jac arrived when he was six years old, he was given a tally. Everything he was provided had a price, and the earnings he made at the factory were supposed to pay for his necessities. But within months, the charges quickly surpassed his earnings. Once in the indenture, it was nearly impossible to work his way out. Jac finally managed it when he was thirteen, through the volts he'd earned helping Levi with his schemes.

Lola crinkled her nose and turned back around. "Well, that's depressing."

"I'm going to tell you a few things that you have to promise not to tell Enne," he said. He remembered how she'd ratted him out about the teacup, but he liked to think that'd been a joke. He liked to think that he could trust her.

She sighed. "Why not?"

"Because none of this can get back to Vianca." He rubbed his hands together. Even talking about the donna made him nervous.

"Fine," Lola said, though she didn't sound happy about it.

And so he told her everything that Levi had confided in him last night—and what he'd asked Jac to do.

"What happens when everything doesn't go to plan?" she demanded once he finished.

Jac pursed his lips. "It's a gamble."

"It's a disaster," she hissed. "You're right—Enne can't know about this. So why are you telling me?"

Because he didn't have anyone else to share the burden with—not that he would admit that.

Lola took off her top hat and ran her fingers nervously through her hair. The shade from the buildings behind them was creeping back, and now that they sat in the sun, both their faces were slick with sweat. "This will end badly."

"Your catchphrase," he muttered, because he couldn't help himself.

"And when Levi's deadline with Vianca expires? How is he going to help Harrison then?"

"I'm honestly not sure," Jac answered. "Which is why the most important piece is the Torrens. If anything happens with

Vianca, or if—muck—if Levi *loses* this wager, at least there's still the Torrens' vote. At least Harrison could maybe still win. And then the wager won't matter, because Vianca will be dead." It was an awful lot of pressure, far more than he felt he was capable of taking on. His fingers shook as he reached for another cigarette, hating himself for it.

Lola stared at her knotted fingers for several silent moments. Finally, she looked up, her expression dark.

"Was it Rapture or Lullaby?" she murmured.

Jac's fingers slipped as he flicked the lighter. He hated the idea that she could know such a thing by looking at him, but he also suspected she'd known for a while.

"Lullaby," he admitted. "I'm two years sober."

He lit the cigarette and inhaled deeply. It was almost too hot outside to take a full breath. He hated the stifling feeling of smoking in summer, but he didn't feel like he could breathe without the nicotine.

"I have it all figured out," he said quickly, coughing a bit. "There's this place that's Torren-owned. It's called Liver Shot. It's the only den that—" he counted off on his fingers "—one, has a boxing pit. An easy way for me to get an in. And two, that sells exclusively Rapture, not Lullaby."

"And you'll... What? Fight your way into getting a job? Is that how that works?" she asked.

"That's about as far as I've worked out, yeah."

"*Muck*, Jac, you can't do this. The fact that Levi even *asked* you is... It's repulsive. He knows, right? Of course he must know—"

"Levi literally pulled me out of a Lull den when I overdosed and saved my life," he told her seriously.

"That makes it even worse, and you shouldn't be defending him," Lola chided. "You might have this all planned out now, but you don't really know what sort of situation you could walk into. If this family feud gets messy, you'll be right in the middle of it. It'd be dangerous for anyone, but for *you*—"

"Well, it's not like Levi has anyone else he could ask, does he?" Jac snapped. Maybe Lola was right. Maybe he shouldn't defend Levi, but he still felt he had to. "Anyone else could handle this better, but instead, he has me. Unlucky for him, I'm the only friend he's got."

He threw the stub of his cigarette behind him, toward the One-Way House. "I grew up in that place, trapped by a debt I never thought I'd escape until I met him. And I think all the time about how easy it is to get trapped in this city. How my first real job after that really wasn't any type of improvement. How I kept feeling trapped, so I took the Lullaby when they offered it to me the first time, and then I trapped myself when I kept going back.

"I might be the absolute worst person for this job, but he's my best friend. If it means *he's* not trapped anymore, then maybe it's worth it."

Lola leaned back on the bench, still knotting her fingers together. "You realize what this means for the city—for the whole Republic, right? An election that the monarchists could actually win?" She shook her head. "It's just one seat, but that isn't what matters. What matters is that, ever since the Revolution, we've pretended this is peace. But there are talents that don't exist anymore because people were systematically *killed* by the First Party. And not just Mizers—anyone with true power, anyone who could be a threat. That's been the heart of the monarchist platform for years. That this is *not* peace. That we can*not* stop changing. And to think—the fate of an entire history-altering election could rest on your shoulders."

Jac didn't actually think he could have felt worse, but now he did. "Very eloquent. You have a real way with words, you know that?" he snapped. "But you missed the last bit you meant to say. The 'we're doomed' part."

She half smiled, the sort of expression that told Jac there was an element of truth to his joke. "You know how they say this city is a game? Well, I always felt like I was surrounded by players. My bosses at the Orphan Guild, my brothers, and now Enne... I'm the sort of person who watches from the outskirts of the story. Who hopefully lives to tell the story."

"I get that," Jac said, and he did. At least up until the point about living to tell the story. He'd honestly never been quite so optimistic.

"So when are you going to this place? Liver Shot?" Lola asked. "Tonight?"

"No, it's a Thursday. If I wait until tomorrow, it'll be busier, and my chances of talking to the right people will be better. I have a few volts. I'll stay at a hostel." He could save his volts and go back to Levi's, but he didn't think he had it in him to face his friend a second time.

Lola checked the expensive watch she'd stolen from him. "I have to meet Enne soon. I..." She bit her lip.

"You know, I only told you because I thought you of all people wouldn't worry about me," Jac said.

She punched him in the arm. "Of course I'll worry about you, muckhead."

Jac smirked. "That didn't hurt much. You won't jaywalk. You've got no strength. No wonder you collect all those knives—how else would you convince people to fear you?"

She scowled. "I have my methods."

Jac wondered why someone like Lola would stay in New Reynes. When they were in the National Library a few days ago, she'd claimed she had people she cared about in this city, but as far as he could tell, she was alone. But she was smart, and she could read, and even if it was sometimes easy to forget, the world was a lot bigger than the City of Sin. And a lot kinder, too.

"If volts weren't an issue," he started, "if you weren't some assistant to the Orphan Guild, if you weren't Enne's second… What would you be? What would you be if you could be anything?"

"A librarian," she answered matter-of-factly.

He couldn't help himself. He hollered. "I can't believe you just admitted that you're actually a softie."

She crossed her arms. "What's your answer, then? What would you be?"

"I don't know," he said. It was a depressing thought. "But thanks for coming out here. I don't… I don't actually have a lot of people to talk to, other than Levi. But you get things that he really doesn't. You're a good friend."

"Friend." She squinted. "That's pushing it, don't you think?"

"Acquaintance?" he offered.

"Better," she said, smirking.

The two of them stood up, and she eyed him with suspicion. "You look like you're about to hug me. I don't like hugs."

He held out his hand. "Fine. Acquaintances."

She snorted and shook it. "The ones who never wanted to be players." And with that, she gave him a final order to be careful and a wave goodbye. Jac watched her walk down the block and disappear around the corner.

He was glad he'd called her—he did feel better now, with far less of an urge to smoke, at least for a few hours.

But there was still something that bothered him. Something about the last words she'd said.

The ones who never wanted to be players.

Sure, maybe Jac had never *asked* to be a player.

But Lola's words about him weren't entirely true.

ENNE

Lola scanned Enne's ruffled sleeves, visible even beneath her black trench coat. *"That's* what you're wearing? To meet my bosses?" Her voice was barely more than a squeak.

"I like the blue." Enne pouted her lips and followed Lola into the Tropps Street Mole station. Though it hadn't rained in several days, the cement steps were mysteriously and disturbingly covered in puddles, which Enne carefully avoided.

"You have a reputation now," Lola groaned. "You have to look the part, otherwise we won't attract the best."

"And what attracts the best?"

Lola frowned at Enne's necklace. "Not pearls."

"This city thinks I killed the Chancellor. Everyone knows I killed Sedric Torren. And I did so while wearing pearls."

"You're in a mood," Lola grumbled as they slid their tickets through the turnstile and followed the signs for the gold line.

Enne thought of her meeting that morning with Levi and soured further. "Maybe I am."

They descended the steps and waited along the platform.

"If you could buy anything you wanted, what would it be?" Enne asked her.

Lola narrowed her eyes. "Why do you ask?"

"I've just been thinking about it lately."

"Well, you shouldn't. It's—"

"Only a question." Enne leaned her head back, smiling to herself wistfully. "I bet I can guess it. You strike me as a Houssen girl. In silver? In—"

"In black," Lola answered quickly. This was clearly a fantasy she'd already given some thought. "Are you trying to buy my contentment for some reason? Because we should really be discussing the plan for today. You said Levi would—"

"There is no plan," Enne responded. "I'd hoped Levi would have one, but he didn't." Her voice dripped with resentment. At least she'd learned her lesson: if she wanted something in New Reynes, then she needed to learn to depend on herself.

The train sped its way to the platform in a rush of wind, saving Enne from having to look at Lola's undoubtedly frustrated expression. They claimed seats in a shadowed corner of the train. Advertisements by the doors featured perfumes held by famous opera stars and prima ballerinas of the South Side, or the address of a real estate agent selling "Once in a Lifetime" properties on the up-and-coming New Reynes boardwalk.

"Then what were you and Levi doing all morning?" Lola hissed. "No, no, I don't actually want to know."

"It wasn't like that," Enne said, flushing. "But I'd rather not talk about it."

"So that explains the mood," Lola remarked. "Regardless, you can't be distracted. Not today. In fact, we need to be *very*, *very* careful. I don't like Bryce on a good day, and after what happened at the Guild, he's distraught." She looked around the train car nervously, as though Bryce might've been able to overhear. "And he's not typically a stable person."

The more she heard Lola speak of Bryce, the more the prospect of this meeting intimidated her. "Tell me more about the Guild?" Enne asked.

"It works like a temp agency," Lola explained. "If you're interested in work, Bryce will find it for you, whether it's with the gangs or otherwise, temporary or permanent. Bryce sets the price of each guildworker based on their talents and various skills. Two thirds goes to the worker, and one third goes to him."

"Why give a portion of your earnings to Bryce when you could find a job yourself?" Enne asked.

"Some people aren't looking for steady work. And some places only hire from the Guild, like the Doves. Expect a lot of assassin hopefuls there."

Enne nervously tucked her ruffles into her sleeve. Maybe everyone else's jokes were right. Maybe she *was* about to be eaten alive.

Lola drummed her fingers on the metal seat. "So we have no idea how to earn an income. No idea what sort of talents we're looking to hire. No place for them to live—"

"I want to find a place in the Ruins District," Enne told her.

"By tonight?" Lola asked with exasperation.

"Well, I don't want to bring them to St. Morse. Can't they stay with you?"

"I live in a studio. I'm not hosting some would-be killer for a slumber party in six hundred square feet."

"Who said they have to be a would-be killer?" Enne asked.

"Well, it's not like you're going to find a lady," she muttered, piquing Enne's irritation. "I've convinced Bryce you're some aspiring street lord, and so you'll need to act like it. For starters, we need a trademark. The Irons have tattoos—"

"I already have that covered," Enne said hotly, pulling two

pairs of lacy, cream-colored gloves from her purse. "Let me guess, you hate them."

"These are…ridiculous," Lola sputtered with exasperation. "They'll stain. A bit of dirt, a bit of blood—"

"Well, then," Enne replied, her voice weary with fatigue and nerves. "Don't get blood on them."

Fifteen minutes later, as they wove through the Deadman District's maze of alleys, Enne slipped on the black silk mask that she hadn't worn since the Shadow Game. She and Lola walked the path side by side, dressed all in black except for the whites of their gloves and the bits of blue ruffle peeking out from Enne's jacket. As they approached the end of the street, Enne suddenly wished she'd listened to Lola's advice and changed her shirt.

After the attack, the Orphan Guild had relocated into what had once been called the National Prison. It was the tallest building for a mile in either direction, with a watchtower that overlooked the entire North Side. The metal gate stood open, one door broken off its hinges and leaning against the adjacent wall, the other in pieces on the ground, rusting away to nothing. The pathway inside was littered with loose barbed wire, cigarette butts, and wrappers of Tiggy's Saltwater Taffy.

Unlike Scrap Market or Olde Town, which crawled with Scarhands and Irons, the National Prison looked vacant, a ruin from a ruined time. If they were to encounter anyone here, it would probably be the ghost of a prisoner executed within these walls, or a revolutionary who'd given their life to see the building blown apart.

Enne and Lola walked inside. There was no noise, no sign of life, except for the scurrying of a rat.

"Are you sure they're here?" Enne whispered.

"They were this morning," Lola answered. A crow cawed

from outside. Lola jolted so much her top hat fell off, and she had to pick it up and dust it off. Even though Enne knew much of Lola's tough exterior to be a farce, it was still strange to see her so openly on edge. "Let's turn through here."

A hallway spanned a hundred feet in either direction, lined with cells—most of them empty. The few occupants slept on cots or hung cheap artwork and torn pages of *The Kiss & Tell* in their new living quarters.

Enne had already decided she would pick a girl—she had enough male gangsters in her life. But the girls she passed were unbathed and ungroomed, slouching, stinking, with a ferocious look in their eyes. Enne had been naïve to think Lola had ever seemed frightening. She merely collected knives. These girls *were* knives.

Everyone looked up as they passed. Some whispered. Enne heard Séance's name murmured behind her.

She'd seen her own wanted posters across the city, but here, she *felt* the effects of her reputation. And, seeing the skepticism on their faces, she already knew she wasn't living up to it.

Lola held out her arm for Enne to stop walking. She nodded toward their right.

A young man sat in a cell, just like the rest of them.

But he was not like the rest of them.

His clothing—a white undershirt and black trousers—hung on him, an extra notch cut several inches into his belt to hold the ensemble together. His bones jutted out at unusual angles, all broad shoulders and crooked elbows and protruding hips. The way he stood, with one arm bracing him as he leaned against the wall, his head down, his other arm limp at his side, accentuated the harsh curve of his vertebrae and protrusion of his adam's apple.

He looked starved enough to slip through the cell's iron bars—ghostly enough to haunt the prison, not to own it.

He made no gesture to show he'd noticed them, and Lola called no greeting.

Beside him, a show played from a radio. "No," a female actor murmured. "No, I couldn't. What would my family think? It wouldn't be right."

"George knew this was the last time he'd ever see her again," the narrator voiced. "And he knew nothing he could say would change her mind. She was meant for that six o'clock train to somewhere, just as he was meant for his father's twelve acres of nowhere."

"'Dorothy,' George said, in spite of it all, 'Don't leave like that. Without even saying goodbye.'"

The narrator returned. "The look Dorothy gave him was not what he expected. It was full of reluctance. The sun was rising, the train was whistling, and Dorothy had one hand on her ticket and the other fiddling with her parents' ring on the chain around her neck. Just as the train's whistle sounded across the tracks, he pulled her in for a kiss to make her forget all those dreams of New Reynes, to make her forget about saying goodbye."

The Guildmaster reached over and turned the radio's volume down. "The world isn't like that anymore," he mourned.

Lola rolled her eyes. "It never was."

He looked up for the first time, giving Enne a view of his features. His eyes were black; his smile was taut. His lips were full and swollen red, matching the marks trailing across his neck and collarbone.

"No," he said. "Dorothy stays with him, in the story. And they marry and have a child and die—tragically—of the fever. And their only child takes that six o'clock train to New Reynes, where he either becomes a victim…or he crawls to me."

Enne flinched at the statement. The hall was silent, everyone clearly eavesdropping on their conversation, and the

Guildmaster had described the workers here as little more than strays. She supposed that must truly be how he felt, for how else could he suffer a brutal attack from the whiteboots, see several of his associates murdered, and still be open for business in a new location the next day?

Looking at the Guildmaster, panic rose like bile in her throat. She'd come in the wrong clothes. She'd come without a plan. She was silly and naïve for thinking she was anything other than silly and naïve.

"I was hoping you'd come," Bryce Balfour said to Enne. "I didn't realize until this morning that you knew our little Lola, here."

Anyone who described Lola as "little" or in the possessive, Enne suspected, was eager to lose several teeth. But Lola made no sign she'd heard. Although she was over eight inches taller than Enne, she seemed smaller than she ever had, her gaze fixed on the cement floor.

"She's my second," Enne explained. Even to herself, she sounded timid and quiet.

Bryce gave her a tight-lipped smile. "Abandoning me, blood gazer? We've been through so much together."

Lola took the smallest, almost imperceptible step back. "It was time for a change."

"You hate change."

Lola didn't reply.

Enne didn't like the way Lola had gone silent, or the implication that Bryce knew her second better than she did. She cleared her throat. "Is there somewhere private we could speak?" The air here was thick with tension and stares.

"Of course."

Bryce unplugged his radio and led them through the hallway, to the warden's office.

A girl sat in the desk chair. She was beautiful, someone

who belonged on the front page of the *Guillory Street Gossip*, sporting the latest designs of Regalliere or taking tea at the South Side's trendiest salons. Instead, she was in a ruined prison, wearing a dozen strands of fake gems the color of blood and drinking murky coffee out of a tin beggar's cup. Her hair was golden blond and hung down to her hips. Her eyes were wide-set and her face soft, like a model from an oil painting. At first, she looked like someone lost, but the keenness in her expression as she watched them enter told Enne otherwise. She was exactly where she belonged.

When Bryce arrived, she got up and kissed him so passionately that Enne flushed a shade as deep as the girl's necklaces. The display—groping hands and labored breaths—looked more unappealing than erotic, clearly meant to make Enne and Lola uncomfortable rather than show intimacy. Now Enne knew where the numerous marks across Bryce's neck and chest had come from.

In a corner of the room, Harvey Gabbiano scowled. Enne recognized his corkscrew curls from the night she'd met him at the Sauterelle, when he'd used his Chainer blood talent to try to coax Enne into joining the Guild. He referred to himself as a salesperson, but Reymond had called him a poacher.

When the couple finally broke apart, Bryce said, "This is Rebecca."

Rebecca looked Enne up and down. "I'm his partner."

Harvey scowled a second time.

Enne watched Harvey with unease. When they'd met, she hadn't been wearing this mask. But unlike the other members of the Guild, he showed no interest in her or any hint that he recognized her. His gaze only followed Bryce as the Guildmaster sat on the edge of the desk and crossed his arms.

"Can we call you something other than Séance?" Bryce asked.

"Séance is fine," she answered, not wanting to compromise her identity. "Um, please," she added.

Bryce gave her an odd look and scratched at the marks on his neck. "And what business have you come for?"

"I'm looking to hire a girl."

"What sort of girl?"

"I don't have anyone particular in mind," she answered blandly.

"How...unusual. For a permanent position?"

"Yes." Though, after paying Bryce his cut, she'd only have enough volts to compensate this person for two more weeks. Maybe whoever she hired could find a solution for their income predicament.

"Whatever you need, we can assist." Bryce snapped his fingers. "Lola, the files."

Lola immediately responded to the order. She hurried to the file cabinet, pulled out a handful of folders, and laid them neatly across the desk. Bryce licked his fingers and perused the papers. Occasionally, he'd show one to Rebecca or Harvey, who would shake their heads or shrug. Rebecca often leaned over to stroke Bryce's hand or play with the edges of his shirt.

Finally, he handed Lola several files. "Go fetch these girls."

Lola took them, shot Enne a warning glance, and left the room.

Enne took the seat beside Harvey—not because she particularly liked him, but because it was the farthest position from Bryce and Rebecca. Harvey hummed a ragtime under his breath and fiddled with a Creed necklace, one that matched Jac's, except for the set of gold keys that shared its chain.

"You called Lola your second," Bryce said. "Do you call yourself a lord?"

If you'd like, I'm sure you can make them call you a lady.

Enne's cheeks reddened. "Yes."

"Do you know how many lords there have been, since the Great Street War?" Bryce rolled up his sleeves, revealing a bandage and gauze peeking beneath one. Judging from the fresh scratches below it, Enne guessed he'd sustained some sort of injury from the attack last night. When he caught her looking at it, he quickly tucked it away again.

"No," Enne replied.

"Take a guess," he pushed. Enne had heard enough condescension in her life to recognize it in his voice.

Harvey cleared his throat, saving her from answering. "Don't mind us. We're only anxious, as I'm sure you can imagine—plus it's thanks to you that this war was called. And it's thanks to this war that eight of our associates are dead."

Harvey rested a hand on Enne's shoulder. Even when his words were harsh, his tone was still warm. She had no reason to trust him, yet suddenly, she wanted to.

"Not that you're the one to blame, of course," he said, flashing her a gap-toothed grin.

Enne was about to respond with apologies, or explanations, or whatever else Harvey wanted to hear, but even as transfixed as she was, she didn't miss the dark look exchanged between Harvey and the Guildmaster. Harvey immediately wrenched his hand off her and leaned away, and the spell was broken.

Enne's skin prickled, remembering just how dangerous Harvey's talent was. With only a touch, he could probably convince her to spill her deepest secrets. And if she ever accepted a favor from him, Enne would be forever trapped where he pleased.

Every time she thought she'd decided which of the three intimidated her the most, one of them introduced some new kind of threat.

"Courtesy," Rebecca snapped at Harvey, clicking her tongue.

"You know he can't help it," Bryce told her, as though Harvey weren't even there.

Rebecca narrowed her eyes at Harvey, then she slid her arm around Bryce possessively. Enne leaned back into her seat to avoid their mutual glares. She realized that their attempts to challenge her weren't what made her so uncomfortable— rather, she felt trapped in the intimate squabbles of someone else's dysfunctional home.

She sighed with relief when Lola returned. Four girls followed behind her, most old enough to be called women. Enne examined their yellowed teeth and knotted hair with uncertainty.

"All of them are looking for full-time work," Bryce said. "A variety of talents. A runner, a wordsmith, a truthseer, and a singer."

Lola rifled through the papers with confusion. "Why didn't you include Talia? I thought she wanted something full-time."

Bryce faltered, and a haunted expression crossed his face. "Talia was injured last night. She's here." He looked suddenly young as he spoke. There was something darker than grief in his eyes, something that Enne recognized as guilt. "But she won't be working."

"Well?" Rebecca asked Enne sharply. "What do you think?"

Enne snapped her gaze away from the Guildmaster. "Is this really all you have?" Enne might've been playing at being a real street lord, but she would've preferred someone a little... cleaner, at least.

"You haven't been very specific in your request," Harvey said flatly.

"I'll know her when I see her," Enne said, which she realized sounded absurd. What sort of decision-making was that? Lola scowled in the corner.

"Fine," Rebecca sniped. She grabbed a heap of files off the

desk and thrust them into Lola's arms. For the first time since coming here, Enne's annoyance piqued. Lola wasn't their servant. "Let's go find this mystery person, then."

As the others left the warden's office, Lola and Enne lingered behind.

"You've irritated them," Lola whispered.

"I'm not sure I could've helped that," Enne said. "I've never seen you so...submissive. Are you afraid of them?"

"Aren't you?" Lola responded pointedly.

Enne was, and it probably showed. But now she was also irritated.

In the courtyard were close to sixty people, soaking in the warm June sunshine, playing games of backgammon or Tropps. Many of them stopped what they were doing to stare at Enne. Shoulders straightened, chests puffed out, knives danced between fingers. They were showing off, she realized. The thought bolstered her confidence.

Enne's gaze wandered until it settled on a book. It was a romance novel by one of her favorite authors, Sadie Knightley.

The girl holding it, however, made Enne pause. Despite the summer heat, she wore black from head to toe. She had dark hair, dark eyeliner, and dark fishnet gloves. A collection of necklaces hung from her, chains and rusted nails and the largest Creed Enne had ever seen, the bottom of its knot sharpened into a blade. Her skirt was obscenely short, making her stockings more suggestive than functional—she was clearly trying to cover nothing. Unlike the other members of the Orphan Guild, she didn't bother to vie for Enne's attention, as her gaze was focused on the book.

"Who is *that*?" Enne asked.

"That's Grace Watson," Lola answered. "Her blood talent is counting."

Enne considered this. A counter was exactly the sort of person who could unravel their financial problem.

"You should know," Rebecca said, her voice smug, "Grace never does jobs as a counter, even if that's her talent. She's one of our most skilled blades. And her price is steep."

Enne withered. Slumber parties with would-be assassins, indeed.

"And I'm not sure she'd want..." Rebecca's eyes wandered to the ruffles slipping out of Enne's trench coat, and she pursed her lips.

Enne's caution and restraint snapped like brittle cords. The North Side had a host of unspoken rules: how criminals looked, how they talked, how they behaved. If Enne was about to become a street lord, then she could make her own rules. The City of Sin would learn that a pistol painted pink was just as lethal.

Without a word, she marched herself toward Grace. What did Enne care if Grace Watson dressed like a harlot at a funeral? If she was a killer? Enne had killed, too, and if Grace was reading a three-time award-winning romance author, she could hardly be that bad.

"That's one of my favorites," she told Grace, nodding at the book. "I've read it four times."

Grace ripped her gaze away from the page with an annoyed expression. She squinted at Enne's mask. "I'm not interested."

"You don't even know what I'm going to ask."

"I don't know who you are, but I'm not interested in killing your ex-boyfriend." She glanced around the courtyard. "Are you famous or something? Why is everyone looking over?"

"I killed the Chancellor and Sedric Torren two days ago." Unlike earlier, she now spoke clearly, confidently. *Speak up,* her instructors at finishing school had often snapped at her. *Ladies do not mumble.* Not even about murder.

Grace snorted and looked over Enne's clothes. "Right." She returned to her book.

Enne mustered up every bit of frustration she'd felt over the past few days and pressed the assassin further. "I'm going to sit here." She wedged herself between Grace's leather boots and the bench's railing.

Grace held the book up to her face and said nothing.

"The love interest dies at the end," Enne told her.

"Nice try," Grace said, sounding bored. "But I've read this book *five* times."

"Have you read the author's other work?"

"I'm not looking for a job right now, so you might as well stop trying."

"I want to hire a counter."

"How boring." Grace licked her finger and turned the page. "Hire one of the other counters. They come much cheaper than me."

That was undoubtedly true, but at this point, Enne was determined. Hiring Grace didn't need to make sense anymore. She'd pay top voltage if it meant wiping the sneers off Bryce's and Rebecca's faces. If it meant proving to herself that she could earn the respect of anyone in the North Side.

"Tell me what it would take."

"Hmm." Grace smirked and drummed black-painted nails on the glossy cover of the paperback. "You can find me a licentiously rich South Side man to dote over me and cater to my every expensive whim."

Of all the requests she could've made, that had been the one Enne had least expected.

Without thinking, Enne reached into her purse and removed one of Vianca's salon invitations. She tossed it to Grace.

"Deal," Enne said.

Grace looked over the invitation with interest. "You said the job would be boring."

"*You* said that. The job will be permanent, it will involve counting, but it won't be boring."

Grace handed her back the invitation and returned to her book.

Enne's stomach dropped with disappointment. She'd thought she'd managed it.

"Yeah, I'll do it," Grace muttered.

Enne jumped to her feet and shot the others a victorious, smug smile. While Grace slowly got up and squinted into the light, as though intimidating the sun into disappearing, Enne was already at Bryce's side. She held out her hand to shake. "It's a deal," she told him.

Harvey bit his lip to suppress a grin, even as Rebecca and Bryce frowned. But Enne was no longer intimidated by them. She'd passed their tests. And she'd done it wearing pearls.

"It's done, then," Bryce said, and he grabbed her hand.

When their skin touched, the air around her instantly turned cold. The ghost of a thread appeared in the corner of her vision, and with it, a thousand more, much like she'd seen during the Shadow Game. Every movement and sound plucked them like eerie violin strings—all tied to Bryce's hand.

Enne gasped and jolted away. The world, once again, grew still. She briefly wondered if she'd imagined it. Or maybe there were still reasons to fear the Guildmaster.

Bryce's eyes widened, then the corners of his lips twitched into a smile. He raised her hand and kissed it. "It's been a pleasure… Séance."

LEVI

♥   ♠   ♦   ♣

Levi straightened his tie as he waited. It was the day after his meetings with Narinder and Enne, and he'd spent all of last night in the museum, cleaning. His body ached, both from his broken ribs and from the work he'd put himself through in preparing for this moment. It was almost a good sort of hurt. His back felt stiff from sweeping; his arm muscles ached from repetitive motions. But the result of his efforts surrounded him: a clean lobby and at least two habitable rooms.

It wasn't much—not yet. But standing there, wearing his new suit, he felt like it counted for something. For every hour spent cleaning this place, he was also paying penance for his mistakes. And he'd certainly made a lot of them.

Outside, Tock knocked on the front door, and for a brief moment, his courage faltered. He'd spent the past seven months stealing from the Irons, and even if they didn't know that, he hadn't faced them—all of them—in a long time.

He took a deep, shaky breath and opened the door.

Tock stood on the stoop, her arms crossed. Behind her, Levi

counted about thirty heads. He didn't recognize most of their faces, a realization that made him increasingly uncomfortable, but his eyes fell on someone familiar in the back: a thirteen-year-old girl with bobbed black hair and ruby earrings.

Mansi.

She wasn't looking at him or the museum, just at the ground. The last time they'd faced each other, Mansi had watched as Chez Phillips nearly killed him.

Levi plastered on a smile, trying not to let his feelings of inadequacy faze him. All his confidence from the past few days shriveled away, as he watched his gang inspect the remnants of his wounds with uncertainty. He needed their loyalty—not just because the streets had turned more dangerous, or because of his ambitions, or because of his promise to Harrison Augustine...but because he had failed so many times, and he needed to believe he could really change.

And for their loyalty, he needed to put on a show.

"I know times have been hard lately. We've been putting in the work, but we've had nothing to show for it." Levi slapped the marble of the doorframe. "Today your fortune has come."

Some of them frowned, staring up at the museum. Admittedly, it still looked a mess from the outside, and it was probably best they keep it that way—let the place continue to appear abandoned. But most of the Irons kept their gazes fixed on Levi.

He stepped aside, letting them pass. They gathered at the foot of the grand staircase, staring in awe at the gleaming white steps and some empty, broken frames Levi had found and glued back together. Levi circled around them, careful to conceal his subtle limp.

"You might notice the frames are empty," he said, his voice practiced, like a tour guide. "But this place will be a museum no longer. We aren't here to memorialize history—we're here to make it."

They stared at him blankly. He was getting ahead of himself. Tock stood behind the group, smirking, and Levi wished Jac was here to support him. Tock might've come through on her responsibilities to round up his gang, but she definitely took pleasure in wounding his ego.

"You haven't seen me in a while," Levi continued. "And I'm sorry about that. But as you can tell, the Irons will be beginning a new chapter. And I brought you here not to enlist you, but to ask you to be a part of that."

Levi took a deep breath as he looked them over. Even if he didn't recognize all their faces, if he walked into any gambling den in the city, he would always be able to point out the Irons. They all had a certain look to them—glitzy jewelry meant to distract, secondhand yet expensive clothes not quite tailored to fit. They were charmers and smooth talkers, whether they were dealers or otherwise. But while they all had a look like they were up to no good, there was something alluring about each of them, in their easy smiles or slender fingers or confident ways they carried themselves. Even after they kissed you and tricked you, you'd still be walking away with red lipstick on your cheek and a foolish grin on your face.

Levi looked at them with pride. They were his, and he *would* win back their loyalty.

He had to.

Levi led them around the stairwell to the first hallway. He'd moved a rickety desk he'd uncovered in a vacant room to this spot, to become a makeshift poker table. With his injuries, it was easier for him to sit down, and he always looked more impressive with cards in his hands.

He slid into the dealer's seat and motioned for a few others to join him. He recognized the faces of those who sat down—

his dealers. Each member of the Irons had a different tattoo depending on their work, and dealers—like Levi—wore spades. Of all his gangsters, he knew these kids the best. Many he'd taught himself.

Mansi sat directly across from him, her expression still downcast.

"What will it be, everyone?" Levi asked, loud enough that the others huddled around could hear.

The boy beside him—Tommy, his name was—tossed in a single chip. The others followed.

"Let's play, then," Levi said. He dealt everyone a classic game of Tropps, starting with three cards. "I bet you all have a few questions. Tommy, you play first. What's on your mind?"

Tommy reddened at being singled out. He was Levi's age, clumsy and awkward, but with a face so pretty that everything he did seemed charming. He could even make cheating look endearing.

Tommy took his cards. "I'm wondering what happened to Chez Phillips."

Levi had been prepared for this question, of course. He'd practiced his forced smile in the mirror this morning. "Chez got in over his head." Levi handed the next player a card. "Stella, do you know how many clients we work with full-time?" When Stella shook her head, he moved on to the next player. "Hwan, any idea what we charge as fees? Do you know what you get paid per hour? How much of your earnings go to the gang?"

"I keep seventy percent," Hwan said uncertainly.

Levi licked his fingers and dealt Mansi the next card. "Nice try. You keep eighty percent. So, Mansi, our client lists, our fees, our contracts, our profits. Do you know who *does* know the answers to all those questions?"

She narrowed her eyes. "You do."

"That's right." He tapped his temple. "I do." The others gave small, approving nods.

Linton didn't wait for the next question prompt. "We heard you helped kill the Chancellor. That's what they're saying, isn't it?"

Levi fiddled with a chip on the table, trying to stay casual. As good as his poker face was, it was hard to fake that smile, to pretend he didn't still hear the time ticking down when he closed his eyes, didn't still feel the weakness of draining his life into those orbs. Three days later, those memories still felt fresh.

But the Irons didn't want to hear about that. They wanted a tale of bravery and glory—a real-life legend. So Levi leaned forward conspiratorially, shaping his mouth into a grin. "Have you ever heard of the Shadow Game?"

Each of their eyes widened. Of course they had. It was one of the many legends whispered on the streets of the North Side; a legend shrouded in equal parts awe and fear.

Levi continued to deal the cards as he talked. "The Phoenix Club claims that the players always lose." He nodded for the other players to keep going, keep betting. They did so, but they weren't really paying attention to their cards. They kept their gazes fixed on him. "The stories were right about everything except that, otherwise I wouldn't be sitting here now."

"You beat the Shadow Game?" Mansi asked incredulously.

Levi reached into his breast pocket and pulled out a gleaming silver Shadow Card: the Fool. He threw it in the center of the table, but none of the others dared to touch it. Everyone held their breaths.

"Why are we called the Irons, Tommy?" he asked.

Tommy blinked—he'd still been gaping at the card. "Because we fix games. We're mechanics. Cheats."

Levi nodded. "That night, I didn't just cheat the odds— I cheated death. And now Semper is rotting in a grave, and

I'm here." He raised his arms, indicating the entire building. His palace.

"And Séance?" Stella asked. "The papers said she was there, too."

"Are you rivals now?" someone behind her asked.

"I heard she's as deadly as Ivory."

"I heard she *is* Ivory."

Levi pursed his lips. Maybe this entire time, he'd just needed to don a mask in order to fashion himself a legend.

"Séance is a new ally," Levi said. "And this is the part where you listen closely." They leaned in further, some standing up off their seats. They might've all been charmers and smooth talkers, but Levi was the one who'd taught them, and he was the best of them all. "You heard about what happened at the Orphan Guild, right?" They nodded. "Eight gangsters dead. Before we focus on volts or glory or anything, we need to focus on staying alive."

Levi stood up, and they trailed after him as he walked back to the stairwell. He pointed upstairs. "I'm sleeping in the back room of the second floor."

They blinked at him. "You're staying here?" Linton asked.

"I'm done at St. Morse. I want to be here, watching over Olde Town, watching over you."

They shared appreciative glances. Even Mansi gave him a smile.

"There's some work to be done," he continued. "Rooms to clean. Things to buy. Dens to talk to. When we're not on our shifts, I want everyone here. Not only do we want this place to be habitable, we want it to be safe. This location stays secret. Watches around the clock. Olde Town has always been our claim, but now we have a home." After a pause, he added, "Well? What are you waiting for? Go check it out."

While the others scattered to explore the rest of the museum, Tock hung back. "Impressive show," she said, yawning. "It was the most ridiculous thing I've ever seen."

Levi pursed his lips. "Yes, well, I'm not sure if I have their trust yet, but their admiration counts for something. Plus, I don't know how the dens are reacting to the news. What casino will want Irons dealing if there are bounties on all their heads?" If the Irons didn't have work, they'd run out of volts fast. "That's our first priority—making the den owners feel secure."

"That won't be enough," Tock said. "Right now, if we call this a real war, then the South Side has already won one battle, and the North Side has won zero. The dens will need to think you can protect them. And you've done nothing so far to prove that."

Levi grimaced. Tock might have been lazy, but she wasn't thick. He was just one person, though—one very *broke* person. So he had no idea how to do that. Not alone.

A desperate thought occurred to him. "Then this is what we'll do—we'll send a message to each of the other lords named in *The Crimes & The Times*: Ivory, Scavenger, and Bryce Balfour." He could tell Enne himself. "You know where to find them, right?"

Tock nodded hesitantly. "Sure, I guess."

"Tell them, after what happened with the Orphan Guild, we need to meet. All of the lords together. Ten o'clock at the Catacombs, tomorrow night."

Tock raised her eyebrows. "You think you can convince Narinder to agree to that?"

"Well, what do you think? You know him better than I do."

"He doesn't like risk. Doesn't even like gangsters. He just likes you because you have a pretty face."

Levi wasn't positive how he felt about that, but he settled on flattered for now.

"It's the only place I can think of." With the whiteboots bribed to stay away from Olde Town, it was the safest. It was also public and crowded, so it would be difficult for the other lords to try something. "Let's hope my face is pretty enough."

"When should I send the messages?" she asked.

"Right away. I don't want to wait too long."

"Do you think they'll agree to this?"

Levi straightened. His messages to the other named lords might not even be acknowledged. Sure, he'd helped kill the Chancellor, but to them, he'd always been Pup, the boy playing at being lord, the punchline of the North Side.

Still, he let himself imagine his call being answered. He would meet Ivory, a street legend. He would gather all the lords in a single room, a feat never before accomplished in criminal history. He'd be able to provide Harrison the intel on the others, like he'd asked for. Everything he'd ever wanted would be right in his grasp.

"Let's hope so," he said. "I'd also like Jac there." Last night, Jac had called from some pay phone in the Factory District. He'd chosen a den to approach, and it seemed like the right move to Levi. Even though the specifics had made the job feel suddenly all too real, their conversation had actually put him at ease. Jac had given his plans a lot of thought. "He'll be at a den called Liver Shot tonight."

"I'll leave now, but you better hope Narinder says yes to all this," she said drily.

Levi flushed and straightened his tie. He could use another distraction. "I'll do my best."

She rolled her eyes. "You just convinced a whole room of people you're some genius, but you're just a hustler and a harlot."

He furrowed his eyebrows. "You're a dagger to my ego, you know that?"

"Somebody needs to be."

As she marched to the door, Levi added a quick, "Be careful." Walking into the lairs of the other lords was a dangerous assignment, and even if Tock gave him a hard time, he admitted she was growing on him.

Tock paused at the door and turned around to smirk at him. "I'm not someone who needs to be careful." She rolled up her sleeves, as though ready to get her hands dirty, exposing the fresh tattoos on each of her arms. As she left and let the door close behind her, Levi decided she wore the Irons well.

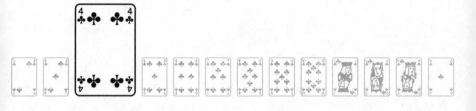

"I know it's just a Faith story, thickhead. But I swear it.
A fellow I knew—Sullivan, his name was—he saw one
once. A malison, they're called. He said it looked like a
human, and that it had eyes the color of blood."

—*A legend of the North Side*

JAC

♥ ♠ ♦ ♣

Jac Mardlin knew a bad idea when he saw one.

Liver Shot didn't look like much from the outside—no signs, no music, no welcome of any sort. But customers found it all the same. Its acidic aroma wafted all the way down the block, guiding you toward it as firmly as a hand on your shoulder. It smelled of harmless curiosity and a chemical rush, and even if it wasn't the soothing smell of Lullaby, it made his heart pound all the same.

A man knocked shoulders with him, and Jac staggered on the front steps.

The man cursed. "You shouldn't be here, kid." It wasn't clear if he meant "in the way" or "at this drug den."

Either way, Jac didn't need a stranger to tell him that. He mumbled something and darted aside, fiddling with the tape around his knuckles. The man opened the door, letting out the faint sounds of cheers.

The door closed. Once more, Jac waited in the darkness.

He took a deep breath.

Jac Mardlin knew a bad idea when he saw one. But rarely—hardly ever—had that stopped him from greeting it.

He followed the man inside, over the red paint along the threshold that marked the den as Torren-owned. It was dimly lit, and everything smelled of Rapture. The cheering he'd heard had come from the back room—the boxing pit.

He shuddered as he made his way down the hallway. He'd never tried Rapture. Unlike Lullaby, which quickly lulled you into a haze after injection, Rapture did the opposite—it was euphoria, designed for bright lights and loud rooms and lots of space. Jac's eyes flickered to the den's shadowed corners, expecting to find someone lost in slumber. He fiddled with the chain of his Creed necklace, which was tucked beneath his shirt.

This place is different, he reminded himself. *I'm different.*

As soon as he stepped into the back room, Jac's shoulders relaxed, if only slightly. The odors of sweat, the sloshed beer on the floor, the shouts of the men in the ring—this he recognized, this he knew. Levi always hated it when he fought, but truthfully, Jac didn't know what he would do without the fighting. No matter how broken and bloody he left the ring, he would always jump back in. It was his favorite bad idea.

Jac found the bookie hunched over a table in the corner. He was scrawny with wide-rimmed glasses, chewing on the ice in an otherwise empty glass. "Do you have any spots?" Jac asked.

The man's eyes roamed over Jac's frame, but showed no sign of recognizing him. Despite his wanted posters being in every city newspaper, Jac really did look different with his dark hair. "Do you have a name?"

"Todd Walsh." It was the name of someone he used to know, someone who wouldn't need that name now. He'd met him in a place sort of like this.

"There's a slot in a half hour. Nine forty."

Jac scanned the room, searching for the usual uniforms of Torren grunts: pin-striped suits, red ties, breast pockets bulging with switchblades and orbs. He spotted several at a table in the back, smoking cigars, watching the fight.

"You hear me?" the bookie grunted. "Nine forty? You want in or not?"

"Yeah," Jac answered, distracted. As he turned his attention away from the suppliers, he noticed someone else—a girl. She wore an oversize black smoking jacket with a red rose tucked into its breast pocket. Jac might've thought she worked for the Torrens by that getup, if she wasn't standing across the room from them.

If her gaze wasn't trained on *him*.

He adjusted his glasses—as if they offered much coverage to his identity—and nervously turned away.

"Stand by the entrance when it's about time," the bookie told him. "They'll let you in." He nodded at the group of Torren suppliers. Jac was about to ask for one of their names—anything to get him a means of introducing himself—but the competitor waiting behind him pushed him aside.

Jac turned around and coughed as he accidentally inhaled a cloud of Mistress, an Augustine drug that must've been snuck inside. He swatted it away, even if it wasn't enough to give him a contact buzz. The woman who'd blown it laughed, high-pitched and too loud. "You're going to fight?" She batted her eyelashes and reached toward him. "A shame to do any more damage to that handsome face."

Jac was used to this. More than once, girls had scrutinized his features in the light of tired mornings after, and told him he was better looking each time they looked.

"But you don't give people the chance to look twice, do you?" one girl had murmured, while Jac was already muttering an apology, collecting his clothes, and making his way out the door.

But he wasn't used to it in a place like this. As the woman's nails traced down his cheek, Jac ducked away, the touch overwhelming. His palms were sweating. He itched to have something in his hands, something to distract him.

He lit himself a cigarette. When he turned around to watch the fight, the girl from earlier stood in his way. Up close, he noticed her brown curls reached her waist, and she had a diamond piercing just below her lips, which were lined in cherry lipstick. She was tall—an inch taller than him, and at least several more in those boots. She was prettier than a Guillory Street heiress, she dressed like a casino crook, and she had a look in her deep green eyes like she was daydreaming—of glamour or murder, he couldn't tell.

She smiled at him, and Jac's stomach clenched. This night was full of bad ideas.

"You've never been here before," she purred. "I'd remember that face."

Jac ran a sheepish hand through his black hair. "You don't look like a regular, either."

"What do I look like?" She tossed her head to the side.

"Trouble." He took a drag from his cigarette and tried to squeeze around her. He was here for a reason.

"If you get a job, you'll be working in places like this, you know," she said, and he paused. How could she tell he was looking for work? "They won't want someone who doesn't look comfortable here. And you *are* uncomfortable, aren't you?" It was worded like a question, but it sounded like a statement.

He didn't respond. There were a thousand and one things in this den making him uncomfortable, and she now topped the list.

She handed him something—a piece of Tiggy's Saltwater Taffy, the signature absinthe-flavored treat of New Reynes. "The bookie will have you as the underdog. See that I win back my bet."

She was challenging him, but he wasn't sure what for. She strode away and, to his surprise, collapsed into a chair at the table with the Torren suppliers, chewing on her taffy and twirling a dark curl around her finger. She paid him no more attention.

Of course, Jac saw the red flags. She had no reason to take an interest in him. This was some sort of trap, and even if it wasn't, his heart was racing so fast that his mind was already thirsting for old, familiar ways to calm it. He scratched at the old abscess scar on his inner arm and took a long drag of his cigarette. Feeling trapped and anxious always set him off, and he'd been here barely fifteen minutes.

He considered leaving—was even making his way to the door—when he bumped into someone. The girl looked about his age, with unevenly cut short hair, light brown skin, and—to his surprise—Iron tattoos.

"Jac Mardlin?" she asked, crinkling her nose at the smell of his cigarette. "Pup said I'd find you here." She looked around the place disapprovingly. "Not sure why."

"Who are you?" Jac asked. His heart pounded with guilt. Had she noticed he was about to leave? Would she tell Levi?

"Tock Ridley. I'm the new Chez." She leaned in closer and whispered in his ear. "Tomorrow. Ten o'clock. The Catacombs. The other lords and seconds will be there."

Jac's eyes widened. He didn't know Levi had been planning such a gathering, but of course the others had agreed to come. When Levi asked, the city answered.

"But what about the Torrens? What about the job?" Jac asked.

"I don't know about the job, but this is just for tomorrow night. And you know how Levi is. He'll want his second there. A proper show." Jac couldn't argue with that statement. "This is a sorry lot, isn't it?" she commented, looking around the establishment.

"I've seen worse," he muttered, and he had.

Tock gave him a look like she already knew that. No matter how many tattoos he inked, what color he dyed his hair, how he changed his clothes—it still lingered on him, a scar everyone could see, and that he always felt.

"Will you be there?" she asked him.

Jac's breath hitched. *Muck.* He was already anxious from being in this den, confused about the girl, nervous about letting Levi down, and now he had to worry about tomorrow night on top of everything else.

"Yeah, I'll be there," he muttered. Because when Levi asked, Jac answered, too.

She slapped him on the shoulder. "Don't do anything I wouldn't do," she said. Jac wasn't sure how to take that. Tock looked like the sort of girl who came with a warning label. Before he could respond, she nodded and headed back the way she'd come.

The Torrens tonight, the lords tomorrow. Jac tried to douse the nerves burning inside him. He couldn't leave now, not when he knew he'd see Levi tomorrow. Levi was depending on him. Jac needed to bring good news.

Jac put his cigarette out in an ashtray and made toward the ring. He held his breath as he walked, trying to focus on the sweat, the whistles, the cheers. He had a routine before his fights.

It started with a song.

I sold it all but my pride when I came to this town.

The song wasn't about him. It was about legends and glory

and ambition, but sometimes, when Jac's stomach churned with anticipation and the room around him thundered with shouts, he could convince himself otherwise.

Bought my ticket at a crossroads for the long way down.

Someone slapped him hard on the back. Jac turned and stared into the yellow-toothed smile of a Torren supplier. The man removed his jacket and placed it on the referee's table. He would be Jac's opponent.

Jac hesitated—he hadn't been expecting to fight someone he'd hoped would hire him. But maybe this wasn't bad luck. Maybe it was an opportunity.

Jac stripped down to his undershirt, laying his orbs, his pistol, and his belongings with the man's. He examined the tape around his knuckles. "You fight much?" he asked.

"I'm in the mood." The man turned over his shoulder and waved at the girl from earlier, who shot him back a winning smile. Jac's eyebrows furrowed. What sort of game was she playing? Hadn't she bet on him? "You look like a fighter, though."

"I'm out of work," Jac responded smoothly. "Need some voltage."

"There's always work here if you're willing to look." The man offered him a grin.

The referee whistled and motioned for them to enter the ring, and Jac held his breath. Should he let the man win, or try to win himself? He examined the man's broad shoulders and impressive height. Without a doubt, the bookie would've marked Jac as the underdog. The girl said she'd bet on him, but she worked here, and Liver Shot would pocket more volts if Jac lost. If he wanted a job here, he should think about the den first.

Wanted the name on my tombstone to match my crown.

He swallowed down his disappointment. He wouldn't be a legend tonight.

Jac and his opponent readied their stances, fists raised, shoulders squared. For a brief moment, the den was silent. Then the referee blew his whistle, and the room erupted.

His opponent threw the first punch. Jac dodged it easily and went for the man's stomach. Another miss, another jab. Soon the man's shoulder dug into Jac's abdomen, shoving him against the wall. The crowds around them cheered as Jac grunted and kicked his opponent off him.

They circled each other. Jac was hyperaware of the smell of Rapture, of the gaze of the girl from the suppliers' table. It all made his head spin. It made the scar on his arms itch.

The rest of the match passed in a blur. He ended it on his stomach, the man's knee in his back, the taste of blood in his mouth from his split lip. The man didn't look much better—a cut on his jaw, a hobble to his step from a kick in his groin—but he'd won, and that was what mattered.

The man held out his hand to Jac, and Jac grabbed it gratefully and got to his feet.

"You've got more to you than you look," he said. "You should come sit with my friends. Let them buy you a drink."

Jac flashed a smile, even though he usually tried not to drink. "I can't turn that down," he lied.

After collecting their possessions from the referee, they made their way to the table. There were six suppliers sitting there—four men and two women, one of them being the girl from earlier. Jac tried to keep his expression neutral even as she winked at him.

His opponent gestured at the open seat next to the girl. "We all work here most nights. We bring in the supplies and oversee the orders and the stock…and make sure there isn't trouble. We can always use extra help."

"Who pays you? The tavern?" Jac asked.

"We get our volts directly from the Torrens. Sophia's the manager. She keeps charge of all that, and transporting the stock here." He nodded at the girl, who smiled. "Plus, a name like Torren will get you places. The Family really watches out for us. Pays for doctor bills or emergencies if they come up. It's more than you could ever ask for."

Jac cleared his throat nervously. "And none of... I mean, I heard about what happened to Sedric—it was all over the papers—"

They exchanged wary glances. "We've been assured our volts are still coming."

He hesitated. Jac wanted to press further—*who* were the volts coming from?—but he also didn't want to arouse suspicion. Todd Walsh was jobless and needed volts, and the Torren Family name carried weight in New Reynes. This was his ticket to the inside and, soon, he *would* find out all Levi needed him to know.

"Well," Jac said, smiling. "I can't say no to that, either."

His opponent slapped him on the back. "Great. Why don't you grab drinks for the table? There's no charge for us here."

Jac nodded and stood up. As he made to move to the bar, the girl—Sophia—stood up, as well. "I'll go with you," she offered, and didn't bother to wait for Jac to accept or decline. She popped another piece of taffy in her mouth as she walked beside him. "So, did it feel good throwing that fight?"

His mouth went dry. How could she tell? "I don't know what you're talking about."

They reached the edge of the bar, and she leaned one elbow on it, crinkling a green taffy wrapper between her fingers. "I won two hundred volts."

"I thought you bet on the underdog."

"I did," she said, nodding at Jac's opponent from earlier. "Just not the one the bookie picked."

Jac wasn't sure if she was trying to flatter him or not. Something about the girl gave him a bad feeling, but he'd need to ignore that if he was going to work with her. And from what the man had told him, Sophia wouldn't just be his colleague—she'd be his boss.

"Well, I'm happy to earn anyone a few volts," he answered carefully.

"What's your name again?" she asked.

"Todd Walsh."

She pursed her lips. "Well, *Todd*, I'm Sophia Caro." She said both of their names like they tasted of phoniness. "Welcome to the Torren empire."

ENNE

♥ ♠ ♦ ♣

The doors lining the hallway alternated black and white, extending endlessly in both directions. The architecture resembled a palace, with checkered marble tiles to match the doors and numerous scalloped columns that made Enne feel as though she wandered in a forest of grandeur and stone.

As she treaded past door after door, Enne's thoughts were muddled, as they usually were when she was dreaming. She'd visited this place before. She'd dreamed this dream before. And like always, only one clear thought took hold in her mind: she was searching for a particular door.

She paused in front of a black one and ran her fingertips over its smooth, glossy paint. She remembered this place well enough to expect one of three things behind it: a memory, a fantasy, or a nightmare.

She pushed open the door.

It was a nightmare.

A chandelier of murky glass offered meager light to the room, obscuring the features of most of its occupants. They sat, ghostly silhouettes surrounding a long table covered in black felt. Silver gleamed as each new Shadow Card was turned over and tossed into the table's center. It was deathly quiet except for a familiar *tick, tick, tick.*

Enne's breath hitched as she entered. She was back. She couldn't be back. She whipped around to flee, but the door behind her slammed closed, like the lid of a coffin. She shakily turned around, working up her courage to once more take a seat at this dreadful table. But then she realized she wasn't the invited player.

Lourdes was.

Lourdes identified fluidly between female and as neither male nor female. Currently, she was dressed in gender-neutral clothes, her long blond hair braided behind her, a linen blazer draped over her shoulders. She smoked a cigarette with trembling fingers as she played.

Enne looked at her mother's measly stack of Shadow Cards, then at the timer, panic lodging in her chest. Lourdes was losing. Lourdes *would* lose.

This was the night she'd died.

"You're not trying," Malcolm Semper told her.

"There were other ways you could've chosen to kill me," Lourdes answered. They spoke as though they knew each other well. She even laughed. "I know you think the North Side corrupted me, but I've always been terrible at cards."

"This was the only way." He turned over another Card. It was Death. To Enne's surprise, the Chancellor cringed when he saw it. When he dealt out a new hand, he did so quickly— quite the opposite from what he had done for Enne, and Enne could think of no good explanation for it. "I had to—"

Lourdes cleared her throat, and her gaze shot in Enne's direction. Enne froze in the room's corner. Her mother couldn't *see* her. That wasn't possible. But she narrowed her eyes as though she sensed Enne standing there, eavesdropping on a memory where she didn't belong.

"Go," she murmured under her breath. Enne couldn't tell if this was real or the dream playing tricks. But of course, none of this was real, her practical mind told her. Her mother hadn't actually *known* the Chancellor. The hallway was a recurring figment of Enne's imagination.

Then the door opened, and a force wrenched Enne out of the room. And Enne woke up feeling like, even in death, Lourdes Alfero still kept her secrets.

The Ruins District was as vacant and silent as a graveyard. It sprawled across the northeastern region of the city. Grass and beachy sand from the nearby shore coated its cobblestones, left untamed in the twenty-five years since the Revolution. The estates of noble families still stood, their belongings looted, their doorframes painted with crude, bloody words. Bits of glass cracked beneath Enne's heels as she walked—pieces of the windows that had been shattered when the city of Reynes fell.

"I did some researching in old newspapers," Lola said, indicating for them to stop at the street corner. "I thought this would be a good laugh."

Enne read the sign with irritation.

MADAME FAUSTING'S FINISHING SCHOOL FOR GIRLS

"I get it!" Enne seethed. "I went to finishing school! I'm not from the North Side!"

"I think it's funny." Grace smirked.

"It *is* funny," Lola said smugly. "But it's also perfect."

Enne's gaze swept over the abandoned campus, with its overgrown gardens and ivy-covered white brick. It looked nothing like her own school, which was all stone and woods and baskets of flowers underneath every window. But Lola was right—it was spacious, secluded, and exactly what they were looking for.

The front doors hung on their hinges, the wood splintered and broken as though hacked with a dull axe, and cobwebs filled the missing slivers. Much like Levi's museum, the Revolution had carved out the school like a carcass and left it to rot. The girls crept inside. Sunlight shone through the dust-coated window glass in fractured rays. The display cases in the lobby had been smashed, their contents stolen or discarded, and Enne gingerly stepped over the fallen photographs that age had yellowed and curled like dying flowers.

"This is not the glamor I was expecting," Grace said. Enne imagined sleeping in Lola's six hundred square feet apartment last night had left quite a lot to be desired.

"Not yet," Enne admitted. "But with a little cleaning—"

"I don't get it," Grace snapped as they turned into the first classroom. The remnants of a lesson still lingered on the chalkboard, and she wrinkled her nose as she inspected the dirt coating each of the desks. "You've written yourself some kind of checklist for what a gang looks like. You call yourself a lord, but as far as I can tell, you're just some tourist with almost no experience, no voltage, and no common sense. You haven't even asked me to swear, yet you're touring me around your future hideout."

Enne could've easily risen to her provocation. By the way Lola grinded her teeth beside her, she clearly wanted Enne to.

But then Enne pictured the gray, lifeless faces of the Phoenix Club fading out one by one. The practice soothed her, grounded her.

She'd never thought this would be simple. But checklist or not, she refused to still be taken as a joke.

"You're right—we're not a gang. Not yet. That's why you can swear when you choose to." Even if an oath was different from an omerta, Enne had no desire to push Grace into anything. She'd rather earn her respect.

Grace gave her a pointed look. "That isn't the way things work in the North Side."

"As you can tell, I'm not like the rest of the North Side," Enne said. She marched over to the blackboard and grabbed a piece of chalk, which she thrust into Grace's hands. "Lola and I will clean this place. You have a different job."

Grace stared at the faded arithmetic on the board with displeasure. "I can already tell I'm not going to like this."

"You're a counter, and we need volts," Enne said.

Grace tossed the chalk over her shoulder. "I have quite literally killed men to avoid doing math. Besides, I'm a counter, not a Mizer. I can't make volts appear out of nothing."

Behind them, there was a crash as Lola tripped and dropped all the cleaning supplies. She sheepishly muttered an apology and bent down to pick everything up.

"We don't need a miracle," Enne told her. "Just a business model."

"Set up a flower shop, then."

"You know that's not what I'm trying to do. I'm a wanted criminal. Design me a crime."

Grace's face twisted with anger. "You don't get it. There used to be dozens of gangs in New Reynes, and not that long ago, either. The Doves weren't the only killers. The Scarhands weren't the only forgers and arms dealers. But over time, as lords died and turf wars were fought, the gangs condensed. Whatever crime you decide to claim, one of the other lords has already claimed it. And it would be a bad idea to make an enemy out of Ivory or Scavenger."

Enne agreed with her there. "Then all we need is something that no one has thought of before."

Grace scoffed. "If that were simple, you wouldn't need me to come up with it."

Enne ran her gaze over Grace's chain-link belt and sharpened Creed jewelry and wondered how they both cherished the same romance novels. But they did, and Enne had to believe that somehow—very, very deep down—that made them kindred spirits. No matter if she wore a lacy blouse while Grace wore studded boots.

"The first South Side party is in two weeks. You haven't sworn to me, and until then, I don't need to explain myself to you. But if you still want *this*." Enne held up one of the invitations. "Then you better figure out that business model, because it's going to take time to prepare you to pass as a South Sider."

Grace stalked to the blackboard. "I hate puzzles," she growled.

"I hate cleaning," Enne said flatly.

"And I hate both of you," Lola muttered.

The cleaning was backbreaking, disgusting work, and no matter how many times Enne scrubbed the windows, they never seemed to shine. Lola had been attacking cobwebs and dust mites all morning, and she looked it. Her trousers were covered in dirt, and both girls smelled of sweat and disinfectant. After three hours, they'd removed the disturbing film from the walls, leaving only faint stains behind, and scrubbed the wooden floor clean.

But while Enne and Lola might've been miserable, Grace had lied about hating puzzles.

For the first hour, Grace had merely stared at the blackboard while muttering curses under her breath. When the second hour struck, she scribbled furiously over every inch of it. By the third hour, she'd screamed profanities, thrown her chalk against the wall, and stormed out of the room. Then she'd skulked back in a few minutes later and started over.

When she at last shouted out, "I am a *mucking* genius," a mess of numbers covered the board that made Enne's head throb.

"What is this?" she asked warily.

"*This* is your answer. Something to help the North Side, not to hurt it. Something to make allies of the other lords, not enemies. Something to make you *rich*." Grace swung herself around on the teacher's desk and faced them, like Enne and Lola were both her students. She had a terrifying gleam in her eyes that Enne suspected was also there when she talked about murder. "*This* is a stock market."

Lola frowned. "Like in the Financial District?"

"If it were like the stock market on Hedge Street, what would you invest in?" Grace asked, though she didn't wait for either of them to answer. "You'd invest in corporations, like motorcar companies and product manufacturers. But we're not on the South Side, are we? So what will the North Side invest in?" She pointed to the board's corner, where she'd written DVES, SCRH, IRNS, and OPHG. "The gangs."

Enne squinted at the garbled tickers long enough to see the names of each of the gangs hidden within them. "I don't have any idea how a stock market works."

Grace then launched into a frightening explanation of finance, including words like *equity* and *options* and other terms that were meaningless to Enne. Whereas she'd merely struggled to keep up in her dancing classes, Enne had always been properly hopeless at math. She'd comforted herself with the notion that there were no real-world applications for algebra, no matter what her teachers claimed.

Now Enne was finding those real-world applications right

in front of her, and despite having faced far worse, that dejected, self-loathing feeling from school set in all over again.

"Let me simplify it," Grace said. "I'm an entrepreneur. I tell you and Lola that I have these great business plans, and I need one hundred volts to start them."

"That's…nothing," Lola pointed out. "You can't start a business with one hundred volts."

"It's pretend," Grace snapped. "Now, I convince you the plan is genius—which it is, of course—and so you each give me fifty volts. That makes you both investors. I use those volts to hire people, to purchase supplies, to run my business. Then when I start making profits, I pay some to each of you, since you each own half the company. That's sort of how the stock market works, but instead of one hundred volts, it's millions. And instead of two investors, there are hundreds."

Enne needed at least several more minutes to process that, but Lola was already pushing forward. "So who would be investing in the gangs?"

"Regular North Siders. You want the North Side to feel united?" Grace asked. "Then unite them where it matters—their wallets. If the North Side citizens have their volts invested in the gangs, then they'll want the gangs to succeed. And the gangs, in return, will want their investors protected."

"But you're assuming the lords will *take* investors," Lola said.

"They'll receive a ton of volts," Grace told her.

"That is still a *very* big if," Lola countered. "How are we even supposed to approach them about it? Knock on Ivory's front door like some kind of carpetbagger?"

"This isn't a bad idea," Enne said, still letting it seep in.

"A bad idea? It's a *genius* idea," Grace said. "If we keep a ten percent cut of investments as an advance against dividends, then a fifteen percent—"

"*Please* stop," Enne begged. "No more numbers. Just…break it down for me again. Then I'll ask Levi about it."

"Levi Glaisyer?" Grace asked. "Do you know each other?"

"Don't you read the papers?" Enne asked at the same time Lola answered, "They do, and they're awful."

"Well," Grace said, shrugging, "I hardly think we need Pup's permission."

"I'm not asking for his *permission*," Enne hissed. "I'm going to ask him if he knows a way we could speak to the other lords. Just…" She gestured at the board. "Let's go through all this one more time."

Grace sighed. "Those South Side men you promised me better be worth it."

Thirty minutes later, into a pay phone in the Casino District, Enne dialed the direct number Levi had given her.

He answered immediately. "Enne?" he asked. "Where have you been? I've been trying to call you since yesterday."

"Why? Is something wrong?"

"The lords of each of the gangs are meeting tonight in the Catacombs—it's a nightclub in Olde Town. And you're invited."

Normally, Enne's first reaction to such news would be fear. If she was going to have a place at a table with the other lords, then certainly she would be the dinner.

Instead, she let out a triumphant laugh. "Levi, this is *brilliant*."

"I know. I didn't expect them to say yes, at least, not to me. This could really change things for the Irons. It could—"

"What? No. Levi, this isn't about you. Be quiet for a moment and listen."

And so Enne Salta, a finishing school dropout who knew far more about pirouettes than profits, explained to Levi how she could save the whole North Side.

LEVI

♥　♠　♦　♣

At eleven in the morning, the floor of the Catacombs was sticky with spilled drinks from the night before. The stools sat upside down over the bar, the instruments rested in their cases, and the lights burned unusually bright.

Levi slipped down the hallway to Narinder's office and knocked on the door.

"Come in," his voice called from within.

Inside, Narinder sat behind his desk, his fingers dancing over a harp's strings. He wore an oversize shirt that looked like he'd slept in it. His shoulder-length black hair hung down, unbrushed. He glanced up as Levi approached and grinned slightly, but continued to play. "You look better," he commented.

Pay me a visit, when you're not so bruised, Narinder had said to him a few days ago. Levi's face heated at the memory. This wasn't the time to lose his wits.

"The Catacombs has a reputation for being a place where gang affiliations don't matter," Levi started.

Narinder nodded and took a long sip of his coffee. His

other hand continued to dance across the strings, dexterous and confident even when he didn't look where his fingers fell. "That's true. We don't play favorites here."

"In light of what happened to the Orphan Guild, the lords want to have a meeting. This location has been volunteered."

Narinder's fingers struck a clashing chord. "By you?"

Levi fiddled with his tie awkwardly. Narinder's tone was sharper than he'd expected. "It's the best place for it, and the lords have to meet. If there's another attack—"

"I don't see why you get to decide any of that is my responsibility," Narinder snapped. Levi withered—the location had already been agreed upon. Tock had warned him to ask sooner, but he'd wanted to wait for assurances from the other lords—and he'd assumed from their last meeting that Narinder would want to help him. "The lords of every gang of the North Side, in my club? What could go wrong?"

"Tock said—"

"Tock doesn't own this place. I do." He crossed his arms. "Tock doesn't make decisions. You do."

Levi didn't need someone he barely knew reminding him how he ran his own gang. "I'm sorry. I think I must've misunderstood. When you said you wanted to keep Olde Town safe, you actually meant to send the problem to someone else."

Levi stormed out, cursing under his breath. He'd have to find somewhere else on short notice. Get a message out to the other lords that the plans had changed. He prayed that would be enough, with both the Irons and now Enne depending on this meeting.

As Levi hurried through the club, he heard Narinder running after him. "Levi, wait!"

With one hand on the back door, he shot Narinder an annoyed look. "I don't have time to wait. I only have a few hours to let everyone know the plans have changed."

Narinder swallowed. "It's tonight?"

"Eight people died a few days ago. I didn't want to wait longer."

"So are you trying to be a saint, or are you just taking advantage of the situation?"

Levi clenched his fist. "If I don't, somebody else will. And my interest is in alliances. Give Scavenger or Ivory the reins, and they might have other ideas."

"You understand why I'd be wary to welcome you all here tonight, don't you?" Narinder asked. "It's a dangerous risk."

"I know that. I shouldn't have asked you."

"But you didn't ask me."

Levi's blood boiled, and he shoved open the door. "Forget it."

Narinder grabbed his arm. "So ask me."

"I said forget it."

He let go. "If you'd asked beforehand, I would've said yes."

Levi took a deep breath, trying to suppress the urge to shout. Narinder was right—he shouldn't have assumed. It'd been a lot to ask, but he'd also thought Narinder would pay him this favor; that he would *want* to help him out.

His pride told him to keep walking. But his head told him that Narinder's words were still an invitation, one he desperately needed. If Levi was going to learn from his mistakes, then he needed to swallow his ego.

He let the door close. "Then I'm asking. And apologizing."

"Alright, then. Now tell me—what exactly are you asking for?"

"Everyone agreed to meet here at ten o'clock. Do you have private rooms?"

"I do."

"There'll be five of us. You can collect weapons at the door. Whatever it takes to keep the club safe."

"And these five would include…?"

"The lords of the Irons, the Scarhands, the Doves, the Orphan Guild—and Séance."

"So the worst criminals and crooks of the North Side," Narinder said flatly.

Levi shrugged and gave a sly smile. "If that's what you think of me."

Narinder's shoulders relaxed, but he still took several moments to speak. "Fine. But if anything goes wrong, or you spring something like this on me again, there will be no more gangsters in the Catacombs."

Levi understood that he was included in that statement. He tipped his hat and reopened the door.

"It's a long time until ten o'clock," Narinder murmured.

Levi had admittedly come prepared for flirting, and he liked Narinder, but he didn't like ultimatums. He was tired of all his relationships feeling like a gamble.

"Yes," he agreed, checking his watch and giving the musician a wave goodbye. "Volts to make. Hearts to break. Empires to build."

But as he closed the door behind him, both he and Narinder were smiling.

When the Iron Lord returned to the Catacombs that night, he did so with an entourage. Dressed in the swankiest suits each of them could steal, their polished leather shoes gleaming in the spotlights, reeking of whatever cologne they'd swiped from off-brand department stores, the Irons slipped through the back door behind the stage. Levi walked among them, his hat tipped down to conceal his face.

His silver jewelry—necklace, rings, cuff links—shined, expensive, and new. Something silver gleamed out of his breast pocket, as well—too small for a handkerchief, too large for a ballpoint pen.

It was a symbol.

It was a rumor.

It was a legend.

A hush fell as the Irons entered. The crowds parted. Many stopped their dancing or conversations to get a better look, to lean toward a friend next to them and whisper. They couldn't tell who the newcomers were, but they understood they were important, players in a game everyone else was spectating from the front row.

Tock led the Irons through the club to a hallway, and from there, up a narrow stairwell to the choir floor. Narinder waited at the top of the landing, his arms crossed. He, too, wore his best—a gray suit, cut tight along his slender frame, a violin case slung over his shoulder. Bouncers flanked him on either side.

"Lords only," Narinder said sternly. "Everyone else can enjoy complimentary drinks downstairs tonight."

The other Irons grinned at each other and headed for the dance floor.

"You look smart," Narinder said to Tock.

She wore a skintight gold dress that accentuated all of her curves, her favorite knife displayed prominently on her bare thigh. "I haven't gotten to blow anything up yet."

He smirked. "The night is young."

Levi turned to her. "Jac should be here. Wait with him. See if he looks…" He swallowed. He'd only sent Jac away two days ago, and he was already worried.

Tock squeezed his shoulder, as though reassuring him. It would've been considerate if she hadn't pressed a bruise, making him wince. "When I saw him yesterday, he was fine."

She turned to leave, but three girls blocked the stairwell, each wearing white gloves. Lola Sanguick stood at the front, dressed in a full pin-striped suit and her top hat. Levi blinked at her, still unused to the vibrant red of her new hair.

"The Irons boys are here," Lola said, seeing him.

Tock cleared her throat. "Not just the boys."

Levi didn't recognize the girl beside Lola, whose eyes were rimmed in thick black liner and whose studded dress revealed more than it left concealed. Levi had assumed Enne hired a counter from the Orphan Guild, because he knew her well enough that there was no way she'd conceived that stock market plan on her own. But this girl looked far more vicious than someone just meant to keep the books.

In the center, Enne wore Séance's signature satin mask, black lipstick, and a pink drop-waist dress that made Levi's heart stutter. Her aura, a vibrant storm of purple and espresso, circled around him as she climbed the stairs. When they locked eyes, the way she looked at him was twice as dangerous as the gun bulging in her pocket.

"So you're Séance," Narinder said. "I thought you'd be taller."

She cleared her throat. "Who are you?"

"I own this place." He turned to Levi. "No weapons. We're going to check you." Levi lifted his arms up for the bouncer, but Narinder shook his head and pulled Levi up the last few steps onto the landing. While the bouncers moved behind them to check Enne, Narinder motioned for Levi to stand against the wall. Levi obeyed, lifting his arms for inspection.

"I see you're wearing silver now," Narinder said. He knelt, starting at the bottom of Levi's trousers. His hands felt their way up both his legs. "Not very subtle."

Levi bit back an amused smile. Nothing about Narinder's touches were subtle, either. But no one was looking, so he didn't mind. His thoughts were too focused on the meeting to dwell on their argument this morning, and Narinder's charm was always an appealing distraction.

"Shoes," Narinder ordered, and Levi lifted his soles up, ensuring him there were no dangers tucked within. Narinder stood and moved his hands to Levi's stomach. "Just because I've forgiven you doesn't mean I won't warn you—you're letting your newfound reputation go to your head."

"This is an important night," Levi reminded him. "I need to look confident."

"For your big show, yes," Narinder said. He stepped needlessly closer to feel Levi's arms, his touches slow and lingering. "Most people would leave the Shadow Game with a bit more humility."

"Most people don't leave at all." Levi lifted an eyebrow. "*I* left it with urgency. I've no intention of dying before I get what I want."

Narinder grabbed Levi's shoulders and turned him around. Levi kept his fingers interlaced behind his head. "And what is it you want?" Narinder said lowly in his ear. Levi's skin prickled.

"Everything. But tonight I'd settle for an alliance."

"That's it?" Narinder's chest pressed against Levi's back, and his hands moved lower down his waist. Since Narinder was taller—which Levi liked—Levi could feel his breath against his ear. Narinder slid his arm around Levi's stomach, slipped a hand into his pocket and pulled out Levi's pistol. The act left Levi's head dizzy.

"There's always an opportunity for more," Levi managed.

"Ahem," said a voice, and he realized it was Enne. She flushed and stepped around them, pushing Narinder closer to Levi. Levi watched her disappear into the corner room, and he fought the urge to go after her.

And do what? Levi berated himself. If he confessed how he

felt about her, how his stomach knotted just seeing her in that dress, then what would he achieve? He'd made a promise to Jac, and that choice was the right one. He wished he could have the chance to explain—and maybe he would, once Harrison won the election and this game of secrets was over.

Narinder traced a finger along the chain of Levi's necklace, grazing his skin from back to collarbone. Levi focused on the gleam in Narinder's dark eyes, and all the other things he liked about the musician. Even if he couldn't be with Enne, he didn't need to be alone.

"Remember—don't do anything sinful here. This is a holy place after all," Narinder warned him. "Even the lords of the North Side can behave themselves in a church."

"Can *you*?" Levi asked, turning around, his eyebrow raised.

Narinder answered with his gaze fixed on Levi's lips. "I haven't decided if I want to." Then he swung the violin off his shoulder, nodded at the two bouncers, and disappeared down the stairwell.

Levi took a deep breath to cool himself off, then made his way into the back room. Inside was a long table, empty except for him and Enne.

"I see you've been here before," she said. Her voice didn't betray any jealousy, but she had one of the better poker faces Levi knew. Not that he wanted her to feel jealous. Not that he was in any way torn and frustrated.

Without answering, Levi claimed the head of the table.

Someone else entered the room: Jonas Maccabees, otherwise known as Scavenger, the Scar Lord. Levi's stomach clenched as he took in Jonas's foul odor—the stench of rotting bodies, a token of his blood talent for stealing volts off the dead. He had a mane of greasy dark hair and lips blue as winter frost.

Reymond, his predecessor, always had a soft spot for kids

like Levi—clever and eager. Levi didn't think Jonas had a soft spot for anyone.

"This is very official, Pup," Jonas said, beginning the meeting with Levi's hated nickname. His gaze fell on Enne. "We haven't met properly. I'm Scavenger. But you can call me Jonas."

"I'm Séance," Enne said, and offered him no other name.

His lips spread into a smile, an unnerving expression on the Scar Lord. He took a seat, rested his elbows on the table, and leaned toward the two of them. "You know, you look awfully familiar." He peeked over his shoulder at the door, but they remained alone. "Seems a great coincidence that two weeks ago, Pup shows up with some missy to see Eight Fingers, and only a little while later, Pup and some missy are together on the front page." His gaze roamed over Enne's features, and both she and Levi tensed at his inspection. "Dark hair. Same height. Same voice."

Muck, Levi thought. He'd thought they'd covered every loose end, but of course there was still Jonas. He could think of no worse enemy for Enne than one of the people who had always despised him. And now that person was the new Scar Lord.

Enne, to her credit, managed to respond, "I don't know what you mean."

"Don't you realize who you're talking to?" he asked. "I'm the man you see when you need to bury a secret, when you need a new identity. I know how to find records. I know how to make them disappear. I'm curious…if I research hard enough into the name Lourdes Alfero, will I find yours, as well?"

"What would it take?" Levi asked, because he could think of no other option than to beg.

Jonas smiled and leaned back. "I'm not sure—what do I want? Other than to make you squirm?" He squinted, considering. "How much are each of your bounties, again?"

"I wouldn't share this information with anyone, if I were you," Enne said darkly. Levi could hardly believe her words—was she *threatening* Jonas? He kicked her under the table, but she didn't even blink. "You're right—I was the one with Levi that day. And if you searched deep enough, you could find my name."

"Are you trying to scare me, missy?" Jonas asked, sounding more amused than he did angry. "You seem a long way lost from the South Side."

"I might be," Enne said, and Levi kicked her a second time. She kicked him back. "Only a handful of people know my actual identity, all of whom I trust wholeheartedly. Which is why, if something were to happen, she would know it was you."

"She?" Jonas echoed, eyebrows furrowed.

"Vianca Augustine."

Levi let out a mangled breath; he would've never played such a dangerous card. Even though Vianca was one of the few people in this city more powerful than the Scar Lord, no one in New Reynes was drawing a connection between Séance and the donna. Not like they did with Vianca and him.

Jonas's eyes flashed with something close to fear. "I don't believe you. Why would you tell me something like that?" Because Enne might not have come out and said it—the omerta would never have let her—but it was still obvious what she meant.

"Well, I suppose it's just another secret I'll have to ask you to keep."

There were only so many times Levi could kick her under the table without leaving a bruise, but there were also only so many ways to discreetly tell her that she was acting completely shatz.

But then Jonas did something that the Scar Lord *never* did. He backed down. "Very clever. This meeting has already been more interesting than I expected, and no one's even spilled blood yet."

A figure appeared at the door, leaning against the frame. "Oh, there will be time for that," Bryce Balfour said.

Levi and the Guildmaster had only crossed paths once, outside St. Morse several years prior. Bryce had recognized Levi, with his orb-maker hair and Iron tattoos, but he hadn't seemed pleased to see him. Even the brief introduction had felt strained, as though there was bad blood between them, even though they'd never met and they were both associates of Reymond.

Two others appeared behind him. The first was a girl, who nestled her head into the curve of Bryce's shoulder. She had golden hair that hung wavy and frizzy down to her hips, and she was attractive in an overtly sexual way—swollen lips, cleavage spilling out of her dress, pale skin flushed as though breathless.

The second figure was a man, one Levi didn't recognize. He was tall, his black hair dusted with gray, and his light brown skin wrinkled around his forehead and eyes. Since Levi knew the Dove Lord was female, he could only guess that he was the second of the Doves: Scythe. The latest rumors claimed he'd killed over forty-six people, and, like the other members of the gang, he was named after his weapon of choice.

Scythe peered around the room, looking displeased to be in the company of those so much younger than himself. But he said nothing.

Bryce sauntered toward the table and took the seat opposite Levi, while Rebecca sat beside him. He leaned back into his chair, crossing one leg lazily over the other. "Séance, it's a pleasure seeing you again. And Pup, it's nice to more formally meet."

"You, as well," Levi forced out. He wondered why Rebecca had joined them, when none of the others had brought a companion, but after Enne's words to Jonas, he wasn't looking to anger anyone else.

"I admit, I'm flattered to have received an invitation. And to be in the presence of such…" Bryce looked at Levi disinterestedly "…celebrities."

"We needed to meet," Levi began, ignoring his dig. "We've all heard rumors about what happened at the Guild, but it doesn't seem like anyone has anything specific to say. There was open fire without instigation."

Bryce paled but maintained an easy smile. "A dreadful business."

When he didn't elaborate, Rebecca leaned forward, frizzy hair hanging around her, as though telling a scary story over a fire. "There's not much we know for certain. It happened two nights ago, and it was a planned attack. A team of whiteboots—it's impossible to guess how many—opened fire with assault rifles. It was clearly meant to be a bloodbath. Eight of our workers died. Six more were taken to the hospital and apprehended there."

Jonas lit a cigar and leaned back in his seat. "Where did the whiteboots acquire those automatics? That's what I want to know. Those permits don't extend to standard law enforcement. Only the Families have—"

"We're at war, didn't you hear?" Rebecca snapped.

"I forge those permits," Jonas told her. "I know how the process works. One day after the papers cry blood, and the whiteboots are already equipped for such an attack?" Jonas shook his head. "Hard to believe the force organized that fast, even for this."

"They managed operations like that during the Great Street War," Levi pointed out.

Jonas snorted. "Captain Hector is so old he was probably

captain then, too." He shot an apologetic glance at Scythe, who remained impassive at the comment, despite obviously being the oldest one at the table. "It's all hard to believe."

"I don't understand why the whiteboots didn't apprehend anyone at the scene," Levi said. "What was the point of such an organized operation if the objective wasn't to capture Bryce?"

"I don't think the objective was to capture me. It was to kill me." Bryce rolled up his sleeve, exposing a gash on his forearm, covered in stitches. "The bullets all came from the back side of the property, where my office was. I got nicked with some glass—Rebecca and Harvey thankfully were in a different part of the building, which was how we were able to evacuate in time."

"Evacuate where?" Scavenger asked.

Bryce's eyes shifted between them and rested on Enne. "We're not accepting any business for the next few days. Not until we can be certain we're safe."

It was Enne's turn to kick Levi under the table. Enne had paid the Orphan Guild a visit only yesterday, so clearly Bryce *was* open for business. Maybe just not for Jonas. Someone had ratted out their last location, and so now Bryce had no reason to trust the Scar Lord...or Scythe.

But Levi needed the lords united against the South Side. A united front would mean fewer whiteboots north of the Brint. It would mean business as usual and volts flowing in the Irons' accounts. To make that happen, they needed to work together. And if that cooperation wasn't going to be built on trust, it needed to be built on something else.

"So what are you going to do?" Levi asked.

"What do you mean?" Bryce asked.

"Eight of your associates are dead. Considering the sort you employ, I would've thought you'd have returned the favor by now at Humphrey Yard."

"We're an agency, not a gang. I find them contracts. Not trouble."

"You're right. This is the responsibility of the lords," Levi said seriously. "This attack wasn't just on you—it was on the North Side. If we do nothing, then we let it happen."

Jonas laughed and flicked his soot in the ashtray. "I don't care what you and this missy—" he pointed his cigar at Enne "—did at the House of Shadows. The Scarhands overwhelm the size of your operations, of your connections, of your manpower. And you," he added, gesturing to Scythe. "Your lord doesn't even bother to show. Should we all be offended? We not good enough for her?"

"Ivory doesn't need to show," Scythe answered coolly. "Her presence is felt all the same."

Levi shivered, proving Scythe's point.

"You're all shatz if you think I'm going to send my own on such a stunt," Jonas said. "We have no interest in what happens to any of you."

"Half of your men came from me," Bryce growled.

"You provide a convenience, not a necessity," Jonas countered.

"And *you* know what's best? How long has Eight Fingers been dead? A week?" Rebecca cocked her head to the side. "You sit rather comfortably in his seat."

"You insult rather comfortably in a room full of killers."

She grinned. "Bryce is the businessman. No one claimed the same of me."

Levi felt the goal of this meeting slipping away from him. He needed to act, otherwise the lords would leave here not just as rivals, but as enemies. And everything would end up worse than it started.

"I would never suggest an idea I wasn't willing to execute

myself," Levi began. Enne gave him another kick under the table, hard enough that Levi cringed.

"Oh, you have a scheme?" Jonas said with a sneer. "We all know how good you are at those. Forgive me—I didn't think you meant outplaying Captain Hector in a game of cards. I can't guess what other service you'd provide."

"I don't want to play the captain," Levi said. "I want to play you—all of you."

The room fell silent, and Levi knew he was at that moment—like in the twelfth round in Tropps, when you were asked to turn over your cards, to back up your bluff with something to show for it. Right now, Levi might've found his palace, and he might've earned back his gang's respect, but he still needed to rewrite his reputation.

It was lucky for him he had more than a bluff: he had an alliance with Harrison Augustine, and he had Tock's blood talent.

Already, a plan began forming in his mind.

"Séance," he murmured. "Why don't you tell the others exactly what *you've* been planning?"

Enne cleared her throat. Levi expected her to kick him again for putting her on the spot like this, but she'd obviously come prepared. "During the Great Street War, the gangs lost because the North Side betrayed their lords." She gave each of them a significant look. "I have a way of ensuring history doesn't repeat itself."

She explained the same plan she'd already shared with him.

"My gang is mine," Jonas barked. "I work for no one but myself and the other Scarhands. I'm not putting my volts into the hands of some girl gang run by a South Sider."

Enne squeezed her hands into fists. "I killed the Chancellor. And Sedric Torren."

"And both of them preferred the South Side, didn't they?"

Scythe inspected her coolly. It was the first words he'd spoken unaddressed. "Until you've killed a worthier opponent, you've proven nothing."

Clearly, Enne wasn't going to win tonight. But she'd already hired her counter, and Levi wanted to hold true to his promise to help her. He needed to make this work.

"How about this?" he offered. "Each of you can make a wager. Let *me* take our vengeance on Captain Hector. Let *me* claim the North Side as ours. If I manage it, then you'll each open twenty percent of your gangs for investment. If I fail, then we return to how it was—every gang for themselves, every lord opposed to one another."

"What are you planning on doing?" Jonas asked, his voice low enough to be a growl.

"That would ruin the fun of it," he said, because even he couldn't finish crafting such a plan on the spot. "But you'll know it when it happens."

The room remained quiet. Jonas took another puff of his cigar. Scythe stared at Levi like he was assessing him for a second time. Bryce still looked as though he'd swallowed a bug.

"No skin off my bones," Jonas said finally. The others nodded, as well.

Levi stood, his heart hammering. That feeling of destiny stirred inside him. "Then excuse me—I have ruin to plan."

LEVI

♥ ♠ ♦ ♣

When Levi and Enne returned to the main level of the Catacombs, they found Jac, Tock, Lola, and Enne's new counter sitting in a circular booth in the VIP section, bouncers blocking any view between them and the other patrons. Levi recognized some of the faces at the other tables—a Guillory Street heiress always gracing the tabloids, a few famous musicians, and, of course, Narinder. He greeted every guest by name, all charming smiles and small talk. Levi was beginning to realize exactly how humiliating it was that he hadn't recognized Narinder at their first encounter. He really was as connected as Harrison had claimed.

Levi and Enne slid into the booth.

"How did it go?" Jac asked, and Levi immediately searched for signs of the symptoms he knew too well. Thankfully, he found none.

"Levi decided to stake all of *my* plans on a reckless wager," Enne growled. "Apparently he's planning some stunt on the whiteboot captain."

The others' eyes widened.

"Not enough wagers in your life already?" Jac asked darkly, as if Levi hadn't thought to merely ask for the things he needed. As if Levi wasn't constantly resorting to desperation. "What are you planning?"

"I'd tell you," Levi assured him, "but I haven't decided yet."

"So all that was just talk?" Enne asked, her tone accusatory.

"I said I haven't decided yet. Not that I didn't have a plan at all." No blood had been spilled, despite Jonas's expectations, so Levi considered the meeting a success. And he didn't appreciate everyone else dampening his mood.

Levi sent a pointed glance at Enne. "I don't think you should be calling *me* reckless when you argued with Jonas like that."

The new girl with the eyeliner shrugged. "Did you leave an impression?" she asked Enne.

"Oh, she left an impression, all right," Levi grumbled. He met Enne's eyes, and saw she had her nose crinkled in annoyance. Levi was all too used to that look, and he hated the way he'd grown to like it. He hated that the way Enne had talked back to Jonas only made her more attractive.

"Jonas has some information I'd rather he didn't," Enne said, unflinching as she held Levi's gaze. "And I wasn't about to let him use it."

The new girl threw back her head and laughed. "You're right. None of this is boring."

"And who exactly are you?" Levi asked her.

"My name is Grace." She wrapped an arm around Enne on her one side, Lola on her other. She offered no other introduction. Enne couldn't have hired anyone more different from herself—her black dress held together by shredded fabric and little else, her jewelry doubling as a weapon or a prayer piece. "Who are you?" she asked.

Levi gaped. "Don't you read the papers?"

"You're *absurd*," Tock groaned from across the table.

"So was Ivory there?" Lola asked, craning her neck to see into the crowds. "I don't see any Doves around."

"Scythe came. She didn't," Levi answered.

"I still can't believe what you promised them," Jac said, shaking his head. "You just can't help yourself, can you?"

Levi frowned. "You used to have more faith in me. What happened to, 'You'll think of something. You always do'?"

Jac's face darkened. "That was before the Shadow Game. Before you started keeping secrets and making bargains with half the city."

"They're all a means to an end," Levi said.

"*Your* end," Jac snapped.

Enne watched them both with a furious intensity. "What are you talking about? What other bargains have you been making?" When Levi didn't answer—didn't know *how* to answer—she stood up. "You know, I believed you when you said you'd help me. But if you're keeping secrets, I'm not sure why I'm still giving you chances. We've figured out everything we needed without you."

Levi felt like he was trapped in an endless loop of games, and every time he came close to beating one, another began. It was wager after wager. If the other lords demanded Levi take revenge for the Guild, then he would do it. If Vianca asked him to bet Jac's friendship on his success, he would do it. If Jac asked him to keep Enne at arm's length, he would do it. Promises and secrets, promises and secrets. There seemed no way to help himself other than to hurt someone else.

And the last person he wanted to hurt was her.

Lying to Enne about Harrison was the right choice, he knew, but the longer she stood there—her expression changing from frustration to hurt with each passing heartbeat—he couldn't help but feel like a coward.

"I hope whatever you want is worth it," she growled at him. Then she stalked off in the direction of the bar.

If only she knew that of all the things he wanted, he didn't want any of them as much as he wanted her.

Grace stood. "If a girl like that saved *me* from certain death, I'd at least kiss her." She grabbed Lola's wrist and pulled her up.

Levi winced. "Tell her—"

"Tell her yourself," Lola snapped, and the girls stormed off into the crowd.

Levi took a deep breath. He'd deserved that. He slumped deeper into the booth and buried his head in his arms.

"Yeah... That got awkward." Tock grabbed the drinks the girls had left behind and cupped them in her arms. "I'm gonna go, too."

Once they were alone, Jac started, "When I asked... I didn't mean to—"

"Don't," Levi said, in the most even-toned voice he could manage.

But Jac did anyway. "I'm sorry about how it's turned out, but I'm not sorry for asking."

Levi's skin heated with anger, but he didn't respond. He understood why Jac had asked this of him, but he wondered if his friend knew how much it hurt.

Finally, he murmured, "How was last night?"

"I was offered a job." Jac gave him a weak smile. "Didn't take me long, huh?"

It was good news, but Levi still felt like he needed to muster up enthusiasm. "That's great."

A bartender stopped by, and behind him, Narinder. Before Levi could order, Narinder rested his hand on the bartender's shoulder. "They'll both have Gambler's Ruins," he said smoothly. Then he slid into the seat across from Levi where Enne had sat moments before. "Enjoying your night?"

Five minutes ago, Levi told himself, *you were in a better mood.* Five minutes ago he had called the night a success. He had plenty of cause to celebrate.

"Thank you," Levi told Narinder. "And I'm sorry about this morning. It was selfish of me." It was one apology, but he felt like he had dozens more to make.

Narinder cast a look around the club. "Scavenger, Scythe, and the Guildmaster have already left. As far as I'm concerned, this night has played out without incident."

Jac laughed darkly. "I wouldn't be so sure." Then, when Levi shot him an annoyed look, Jac scratched his head sheepishly and slid out from the booth. "I'm going to find the others. Well, actually, that might be a bad idea." He looked up and scanned the crowd, meeting the gaze of a girl who had been giving him eyes for the past five minutes. "And that looks like a worse idea." With that, Jac slipped off.

Within moments of being alone with Narinder, the bartender returned with their drinks. Levi took Jac's as well, and quickly downed them both. The guilt quieted in a rush of bourbon.

"Do you know what people are saying about you?" Narinder's lips tilted into a smile as he slid to Levi's side. "Nearly everyone I spoke to tonight had a different take on the famous Levi Glaisyer."

Levi suppressed a grin—he couldn't help it, even as morose as he was. "What sort of things?"

"Well, I'm not sure if all of them are true," Narinder said. "There's one about you winning so many volts in a night that you bled out a whole casino."

"That *is* true," Levi said. "The owner was a muckhead. It was revenge."

"I heard you still carry the Shadow Card around in your pocket." Narinder reached into the pocket of Levi's suit jacket and retrieved the Fool card. Even several days after the Game, even after Levi had turned it into a story, the look on the character's face still made his heart hammer. "I see that's true."

Levi quickly grabbed Narinder's hand in a mute plea for him to return the card—he didn't want to look at it. But Narinder stilled as they touched. The alcohol had sent Levi's mind into a pleasant sort of tilt; his gaze fixed itself on Narinder's lips.

"You gangsters are very direct," Narinder said, obviously noticing Levi's stare. Even so, he inched closer and pressed a hand against Levi's thigh.

Levi swallowed. Did he want to take this further? Flirting with Narinder was an easy distraction, but even so, he wasn't sure. He tried to think of a reason to stop, but instead his mind kept playing the same reel of what Narinder had said, of all those he had spoken with. Narinder possessed an influence that Levi could use. And even if it was a means to an end, Levi had certainly rationalized doing worse for causes half as noble, and as far as he could tell, the only thing wrong with Narinder was that he wasn't a particular someone else.

Levi pressed his forehead against Narinder's. "Tell me what else they say about me."

Narinder smirked. "That you're full of yourself." Levi felt his breath on his lips, sending shivers through him. He could want this. So easily.

"That's true."

"That you're reckless."

Levi traced his fingers over Narinder's tattoo. "Yes. That's also true."

"That you're a terrible lover."

Levi faltered for a moment and pulled back, until he realized Narinder was joking. He smirked and grabbed a handful of Narinder's collar. "Not sure about that one."

Narinder laughed, and even that sounded like music. It wasn't hard to see why the whole city was in love with him—

Levi was equally mesmerized when watching him play his harp as he was when they were talking about business. He decided he liked just about everything about Narinder.

"That did admittedly sound phony to me," Narinder murmured.

"Only one way to be certain."

Levi closed the space between them and pressed his lips to Narinder's. There was something angry about the way they kissed each other, yanking at shirts, squeezing shoulders, biting lips. Maybe Narinder was still annoyed about this morning, even if he wouldn't admit it. But even when it hurt, none of it bothered Levi. No matter what he had to celebrate, he'd still be angry—a little bit at Jac, and a hell of a lot at Vianca, but mostly at himself.

He'd made his decision. He was kissing probably the most attractive boy he'd ever kissed. He was close to achieving the reputation he'd always wanted. So why couldn't he be satisfied?

At some point, when Narinder's thighs were wrapped around his and his lips were teasing at Levi's ear, he whispered, "I'm still not convinced." Levi understood this was more of a question than a statement.

"Where do you live?" he answered.

He felt Narinder pause to smile. "Upstairs."

They wove through the crowds, their fingers hooked around each other's. Levi tried to focus on Narinder in front of him, but he couldn't resist the urge to look at the faces around him.

He didn't find her.

They climbed up a narrow winding staircase that led to the bell tower, then stopped breathlessly at the top. The stained glass window offered a view of the entire Street of the Holy Tombs, and a good portion of Olde Town beyond it.

Views like this always took Levi's breath away. This was his territory. His home. And there was something satisfying about looking at place you owned—that also owned you.

A door to their right led to Narinder's bedroom.

Before he opened it, Narinder playfully tugged at the buttons of Levi's shirt. Then he whispered something in Levi's ear that made his face heat.

"I remember you saying something earlier about this being a church," Levi murmured.

"No one comes here to confess their sins," Narinder said. "They come to commit them." With one hand clutching the belt loops of Levi's trousers, he fumbled with his other to open the door.

Levi laughed as they nearly toppled inside. But lust hardly seemed the deadliest of sins he would commit tonight. Every time he kissed Narinder—even though he liked his honey scent, the slopes of him, the way his voice sounded when he was breathless—Levi started picturing something else. How Narinder had so easily spoken to the most famous patrons of his club. How he'd growled at Levi this morning that *he* owned this establishment, and no one else. How people talked about Levi, about Narinder—and maybe about Narinder *and* Levi.

Because no matter how much Levi liked him, he was doing this for a reason…and not one so frivolous as a distraction. Maybe this was his worst quality; one that had led Enne straight into Vianca's hands, had handed him a one-way invitation to the House of Shadows.

But maybe it was also his best. The start of Levi's life had been a sad story, and ever since he'd come to New Reynes, he'd set his sights on rewriting it into one worth telling. Every decision he made factored into that desire. Even letting Enne walk away. Even letting Narinder take her place.

Levi let himself be guided onto the bed.

Ambition was the deadliest sin of all.

ENNE

♥ ♠ ♦ ♣

Enne, Lola, and Grace huddled together in the lone habitable room of Madame Fausting's Finishing School for Girls, staring at the four orbs on the desk in front of them. It was beastly hot—each of them had stripped down to the barest clothing they possessed, save for their undergarments: Enne in a lacy camisole, Lola in an oversize men's undershirt, Grace in a black slip. In the room's corner, a radio played popular songs from the South Side's music halls that sounded overly cheerful for their strained moods.

"There's only seventy volts left," Enne said, examining the orbs, as if willing them to multiply. "How long will that last us?"

"How long until Pup pulls whatever stunt he promised?" Grace asked.

"*If* he manages it," Lola muttered.

Enne would rather avoid thinking about Levi. Thoughts of him brought up unpleasant memories from last night; of how he'd shut her out without so much as an apology. Of spotting him twenty minutes later with his lips pressed against someone else's. She had far more important problems in her life than romance, but—as she'd learned these past few days—she could apparently carry multitudes of pains and worries all at once, even if they contradicted each other.

But it didn't matter how she felt about him. Levi had wagered everything she'd worked for on a gamble, just to feed his own ego.

How *dare* he?

"We could find something temporary," Enne suggested.

"You're right," Lola said sarcastically. "We could set up a lemonade stand on the beach."

Enne rubbed her temples, trying not to feel hopeless.

"You know, I once read somewhere of a girl making friends with wealthy South Siders and convincing them she was some sort of heiress," Grace said. "And she attended all sorts of parties, ate at all the most expensive restaurants, with everyone around her paying the tab."

"Very funny," Enne muttered.

"It's a viable option. When exactly are these parties? We're all sitting around here sweating and counting milivolts when we could be preparing to become wealthy widows."

Lola pursed her lips. "If that's what you want, why have you been working as an assassin?"

Grace winked at her. "Practice."

The song on the radio changed, this one even peppier than the last. It was a duet about how love was easy, and it infuriated Enne so much that she huffed over to the radio and quickly changed the station.

"For someone who's been gone from New Reynes for so long," an interviewer spoke, "what thoughts crossed your mind when you were asked to return?"

"Well, I was very flattered, and interested. New Reynes is my home, and I've been wanting to return for some time," the man answered. "Over the past several days, I've been traveling around the city—through both the North and South Sides. Since the terrible night of the Chancellor's assassination, violence has already broken out in the lower income, higher crime neighborhoods. And that's what is ugly about this business—"

"Turn that off," Grace complained. "Just because you're feeling all sour doesn't mean we can't listen to music."

"I want to listen," Lola argued, and so Enne turned the volume up higher. She wanted to listen, too.

"To claim no tolerance against the gangs makes the North Side a battleground," the man continued, "but the North Side is also a home. It's *my* home. And my plans are to see the North Side flourish—not destroyed."

"Speaking of your background in the North Side, many have expressed concerned about your candidacy with the First Party when your mother, Vianca Augustine—"

"What?" Lola shrieked, loud enough that both Enne and Grace jolted. *"Harrison Augustine* is running for Senate? Against his mother?"

"Is Vianca running?" Grace asked, eyebrows furrowed.

"She might as well be," Lola answered. "I've heard Worner Prescott is a buffoon."

Enne switched the radio off. She wondered if, a few miles across the city, Vianca was listening to this same interview. Enne knew so little about the donna's personal life, but this election meant everything to her, so what would she think about her son running against her party? It would be an ongoing public humiliation, and though Enne hardly had it in her to feel sympathy for Vianca Augustine, she *did* feel anxious. The donna would likely take her displeasure out on *her.*

"Why do you have that look on your face?" Lola asked her uneasily.

"Because she's been in such a great mood all day," Grace said sarcastically. "I'm not sure Pup is worth this."

"This is *not* about Levi," Enne snapped. "This is about how two weeks from now, I have to show up at these South Side parties and pretend like I know anything about politics, when I don't. How we're down to two meals a day until Levi comes through on his promises, which might never actually happen. How even if he *does*, it just means I'm in another meeting with the other lords, surrounded by people who are better criminals than me, talking a whole other sort of politics and history that I don't understand. And no matter how everything turns out, I am helpless, and ignorant, and...and..."

"Pathetic," Grace offered.

Lola shoved her. "Don't be—"

"*Yes,*" Enne agreed, nostrils flaring. "Pathetic." It wounded her pride just to say it, but that only meant it was true. "And I hate feeling this way."

Enne remembered how it felt to sit beside the other lords and understand only fragments of their conversation. She hadn't said anything until Levi introduced her, and without having a memorized spiel about Grace's stock market, she wouldn't have contributed at all. She might've warded off Scavenger—for now—but at some point, if the others didn't see her as a peer, they would surely see her as prey.

She'd known this wouldn't be easy—nothing in her life ever had been. But when the day came that she returned to the House of Shadows, when she sat in the place where her mother had died and where she almost had, too, she needed to be ready.

"Well, you don't know much about New Reynes, but *I* do," Grace told her. "I know all the history, every legend. I can't fix your prissy accent, but I can make sure that the next time you sit at a table with the other lords, you'll be able to throw words around like a North Sider."

"You'd do that?" Enne asked.

"Of course, and in return, you have two weeks to teach me how to blend in at *these* sort of tables." Grace waved the invitations in the air. "Lola, too. She knows all about the politics stuff. I can tell."

Lola flushed. "I know a little about politics. But I'm not interested in lace and cream puffs."

"Just be a good sport," Grace snapped. "We're in this together."

We're in this together, you and I, Levi had said to her once. She shouldn't have been foolish enough to believe him.

"Fine," Enne agreed. "I'll turn both of you into ladies, and in return, the two of you will turn me into a Sinner."

Several hours later, the classroom's blackboard was covered in list after list of details—the names of the most respected artists and musicians of the modern age and the works they'd contributed to society; the most influential politicians in the Senate, which districts each of them represented, and what scandal they were known for; and every major street lord in New Reynes history, along with how and when they'd died.

Grace, it seemed, had an uncanny ability to rattle off facts down to exact dates and quotes. She quickly memorized all the information the others wrote, and then had the gall to act bored afterward. "You need to learn this quicker. With everyone calling this a street war, all anyone will talk about is the last one."

Enne didn't enjoy Grace's teaching methods, which mainly involved insulting her students into submission. "Of the two warring lords, Veil and Havoc, Havoc died second, in December of Year 9," Enne recited. Grace didn't call her any names, which Enne took as a sign of approval. "Did her blood really run black?"

Grace shrugged. "I doubt it. But we like our street legends."

"That's not the full history, though," Lola told her. Her lessons always sounded drier than a textbook. "After all the Mizer kingdoms fell and the Revolution ended twenty-five years ago, New Reynes was named the capital of the new Republic. Eventually, times began to improve. The manufactured volts made the economy more stable, and people believed there was a real future in New Reynes. The population swelled with opportunists and the disillusioned, and two street lords rose to power. But they became so powerful that the wigheads had to declare a war and finally execute them. It basically destroyed the North Side."

"I like my version better," Grace said. "You literally made blood and guts sound boring."

"Sorry for caring more about facts than legends," Lola grumbled.

Grace hopped off the desk and pouted her lips. "I want to learn something *interesting*. Teach me how to curtsy."

"To curtsy?" Enne echoed, eyebrows furrowed. Curtsying was rather old-fashioned, even for Bellamy and the South Side.

"That's what they do in all the Sadie Knightley novels."

"But those aren't *real*, Grace. Not anymore." While Enne loved those books, she found it difficult to understand Grace's fascination with them. But Grace seemed full of unexpected contradictions.

It made Enne like her even more, though. After all, she was full of contradictions, too.

Grace pouted her lips. "Neither of you are very romantic."

"I can teach you both some dances," Enne suggested.

"Please don't," Lola said.

AMANDA FOODY

Enne rolled her eyes. "You can play us music for now, but you'll have to learn all of this later."

Enne directed Grace to stand in front of her, then she positioned Grace's hands on her shoulders. Enne was quite short to lead the dance, a role usually assigned to the man, but Grace hardly seemed to mind. While Lola played her harmonica, Enne showed Grace the steps to a few dances common in both Bellamy and the South Side. Grace laughed at the conservative twirls and kicks.

"This isn't how I'll be dancing next time we go to the Catacombs," Grace said.

"This isn't relevant. You should be teaching Enne something more important than just street legends," Lola told her. "After all, *I'm* no criminal, but I know all of the history."

Grace took a step closer to Enne, looming over her with a frightening gleam in her eye.

"What did you have in mind?" Grace asked her. "I could teach you all the ways to kill a man. My favorite technique, unfortunately, takes hours." She purred the words, which made it difficult to decide if Grace was truly talking about killing a man...or lying with one.

Enne took a careful step back. "I'm just looking to impress."

"You're five feet tall and look like you're thirteen years old. You're not exactly going to instill fear in the hearts of many."

Enne stood on her tiptoes, smirking. "I mean, you don't *know* that."

"You're a good dancer—which means you're good on your feet," Grace admitted. "That's helpful. What are your talents?"

Enne still hadn't shared that information with Grace. After all, Grace had yet to swear to her, and until then, there were some secrets that simply couldn't be told. But there were other truths that, alone, wouldn't be a cause for alarm.

"I'm an acrobat," she told her. Lola shot Enne a warning look.

"That's useful," Grace said. "If you spent some time train-ing, you could be a strong fighter. Hand-to-hand combat is my specialty. Do you have a preferred weapon?"

Weeks ago, that question would've scandalized Enne. Now she considered it without hesitation.

She'd once fought Lola with a broken wine bottle. She'd used a poisoned dart to kill Sedric Torren. And she'd shot the whiteboot at the House of Shadows with a revolver. Of all of them, she preferred the last—it was quick, and the least personal.

"A gun," she answered.

"As an acrobat, you'd be able to reach otherwise inaccessible places. You could be a proficient sharpshooter. But..." Grace frowned. "You obviously don't see well enough for that."

"What?" Enne asked. She had perfect eyesight.

"Your eyes are always so red and irritated. I just assumed. You always look like you're about to cry."

"Oh." Enne rubbed her eyes, as if that would make the red-ness from her contacts disappear. She would have to resign herself to feeling uncomfortable and looking emotionally dis-traught for the rest of her life. "I can see fine."

Grace's lips slid into a smile. She reached into Enne's purse and pulled out a tube of black lipstick. "This color suits you," she told her, before drawing a circle on one of the invitations lying across the desk. She walked to the back of the classroom and pinned the card stock to the wall with a hair clip.

A target.

Once she moved away, Enne pulled her revolver out of her pocket. The feel of it in her hand made her breath hitch. Last time she'd held it, aimed it...

Tick. Tick. Tick.

"Two hands," Grace instructed. "Keep your legs and shoul-ders square."

Enne did as instructed, but memories and nightmares were already rushing into her mind. Her heart sped up. For a moment, she was standing on the steps of the House of Shadows again. Shark was answering the door, his eyes widening with recognition. If he yelled out, she'd be exposed. She'd be dead.

Head swimming with old fear, Enne cringed as she pulled the trigger.

The noise of it rang in her ears—drowning out the ticking of the timer, drowning out everything she'd been feeling all morning—and her bullet landed several inches below the paper. She frowned.

"You're distracted," Grace said. "You need to aim. You're not focused on the target."

When Enne raised the gun again, a different image came to mind. She was lying on the grass in front of the House of Shadows, and Sedric Torren was pointing the gun at *her*. Fear and anger bubbled up inside her at the thought of him. She'd been so certain, so determined when she killed him, and she would always make the same choice when it came to him. So when Enne fired the second time, she tried to hold on to that conviction, to picture his sickening smile at the target's center.

This one landed even farther than the one before.

Grace walked over to Enne and adjusted her posture. In the corner of the room, Lola had her arms crossed protectively around herself. Enne sent her a look of concern, remembering how much Lola hated guns, but her second motioned for Enne to continue practicing.

"Take a deep breath and relax," Grace instructed. "You don't need to perfect this overnight."

Except Enne did, and always had. When Vianca had asked her to poison Sedric, Enne hadn't been given time to prepare. When Lola had threatened to kill her, Enne had no choice but to act. When she realized Levi was in danger and the Shadow Game was already beginning, she'd run inside after him.

A whole ocean away, in a finishing school much like this one, Enne had been mediocre, invisible. But for the first time, Enne had new ambitions. And maybe it was her own worst qualities talking—her pettiness, her competitiveness—but if Levi believed he could make an impression on this city, then so could she. If she was thrown into an array of parties and asked to be a lady, then she would charm. If she was seated at a table with notorious street legends, then she would impress. If she was invited to play a game with the City of Sin, then she would win.

And when she crossed paths with the Phoenix Club again...?

Enne pulled the trigger.

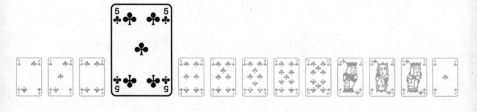

"Before Ivory was the Dove Lord, she was part of a different gang. More like a cult, I've heard. The lord, Abbess,
kept a journal, and in the weeks leading up to her murder, she wrote that she was being stalked by a figure in
white. Some credit that person as Ivory. Me? I think it was
Death."

—*A legend of the North Side*

JAC

♥ ♠ ♦ ♣

Two weeks had passed since Jac saw Levi at the Catacombs. Whatever thickheaded plan he'd been concocting since then, Jac couldn't worry about it—not when he really needed to worry about himself.

He stood in a back office at Liver Shot. One of his associates—Ken, the opponent he'd fought his first night—was bent over the desk, a cigar dangling out of his mouth. Since he'd started work, Jac had learned all their names, what other dens they liked, how they got paid, how much Rapture they sold...but he'd only learned two things that truly mattered.

One, the Torren Family was assuredly without a don. The volts for this den came from Delia Torren, but other dens worked under Charles. The empire was split in two, and it was only a matter of time before all of them were recruited into a war between the siblings—a fact none of his co-workers seemed to consider or worry about.

And two, Jac's boss knew exactly who he was.

Sophia Caro hadn't come right out and said it, of course,

otherwise Jac would've left by now. But the air between them always felt charged with secrets. At every opportunity, her eyes flickered to his arms, as if she could see his Iron tattoos through the sleeves. Once, she'd laughed and flicked his glasses, claiming he had the best vision in the world for someone with bad eyesight, after he'd read her the scoreboard numbers from across the room. And just last night, she'd run her hands through his hair—an act that left him both nervous and weak-kneed—and told him that black really *was* his color after all.

Each time, Jac wasn't sure if it was flirting or blackmail. It didn't matter if they were alone or not; she always acted this way. The others all thought she was in love with him, and half of *them* were in love with *her*.

"Delia sent us a message," Ken said, reading over a note on the desk, one stapled to an obituary photo of Sedric Torren. "She wants us to pick up at a new location. It's not far from Chain Street."

"She's taking us out of the way of Insomnia." That was a Charles-claimed tavern.

Ken shook his head. "You're so paranoid about all this. It's probably just routine."

Jac attempted to look sheepish and shoved his hands in his pockets. "You'd know better than me."

"I don't know about that, but I'm not going to worry. That's Sophia's job." Sophia was the only one of them who communicated directly with Delia.

"Did I hear my name?" Sophia popped her head in through the doorway. Jac yelped and instantly grabbed his Creed necklace. Sophia smirked. "That was cute."

"Todd's being a downer again," Ken said.

Sophia sauntered into the room and slapped a volt jar. "We talked about this, *Todd*. Pay up."

Jac frowned. "You guys already have half my paycheck in there."

"It's our tab tonight at Kaleidoscope," Sophia said. Their group often liked to finish a shift at this den and immediately patron another. "We keep toasting to more misfortune. You keep our glasses full." Then, without warning, Sophia ran her thumb over Jac's brow and forehead, as though wiping away a stain. "They didn't get that right, did they?"

Jac flinched, assuming she was referring to the scar he'd earned a few weeks back—a scar that wasn't on his wanted poster.

"I'm going to check on the others," Ken said. He shot Jac a wink as he left—he had a bad habit of constantly leaving them alone. Sophia might have been stunningly beautiful— the type anyone would want flirting with them—but at this point, every kiss she blew at him seemed more like a threat.

Ken closed the door, leaving them alone.

Jac shoved the volt jar away. "I'm not paying. You're all running me broke."

"Fine, don't pay." Sophia shrugged. "You're lucky I won't tell anyone." Jac knew that statement wasn't about the volts.

"Stop doing that," he growled.

"Doing what?"

"Oh, you know exactly what you're doing." Confrontation was a dangerous move—Sophia had all the leverage, and Jac had nothing. He didn't know anything about her. Not where she lived, not how she'd gotten this job, not what her talents were. She was a complete mystery.

She pulled a taffy from her pocket and unwrapped it, leaning against the desk. "I keep waiting for you to ask me. After all this flirting the past two weeks, I figured you eventually would."

Jac's mouth went dry. Did she... Did she think he was going

to ask her out? He was far more concerned about the thousand volts on his head, dead or alive. She looked like the sort of girl who might take her men either way.

"Ask you what?" he managed.

She grinned and popped the candy in her mouth before saying, "Walk with me, Todd."

And so he did, because he felt like he didn't have a choice. Jac followed her into the hallway and out the den's back door. It was dusk, and the rain from earlier had lightened into a drizzle. Sophia marched forward, paying no mind to getting wet.

"Where are we going?" Jac asked.

"We're going to meet with Delia. She wants to reorganize our pickup locations again," Sophia answered. "Normally I go to those meetings alone, but it's been sort of touchy around here lately. Plus…" She winked at him. "I thought we could use a little *alone* time."

Jac wasn't sure he liked the sound of that. He wouldn't have thought it possible to be as frightened of someone as he was attracted to them, but so it was between him and Sophia.

But this could be a great opportunity to gather information for Harrison. Too great of an opportunity to pass up.

"Touchy?" he pressed, ignoring her other statement.

"The state of the Torren business is…precarious," Sophia told him. "Neither Delia nor Charles want a messy war. But the Apothecaries, the ones with the talent for brewing their drugs, are loyal to different siblings. If it gets too messy, some of them might turn toward the Augustines instead."

"So what's going to happen?" Jac asked.

"Either Delia and Charles fight petty territory battles until the other goes broke…or real blood gets spilled, and all of this goes to hell." She unwrapped another taffy and popped it into her mouth. It was a wonder her teeth weren't rotten through with all the sugar she ate. "One can only hope."

One can only hope what? Jac wanted to ask, then thought better of it.

They turned down Tropps Street in the direction of Luckluster Casino, and even from a distance, its lights shone scarlet into the overcast evening sky.

"So whoever has the favor of the Apothecaries wins the empire?" he asked.

"Yes, and no. The Apothecaries are vital, but the hierarchy is far larger than that. At the top of the Family is the don, which was previously Sedric Torren, and not long before him, his father, Garth Torren." Jac nodded—this was all information everyone in New Reynes already knew. "Then there are the other family members, mainly Charles and Delia, Sedric's cousins. They're followed by consiglieres, advisors, underbosses, bookkeepers, den owners...it all filters down to people like you and me at Liver Shot."

Jac furrowed his eyebrows, trying to follow. *This* information was new. "Are the Augustines the same?"

"Yes, except Vianca has no family left. She has no heir. She's destined to fall."

"One can only hope," Jac echoed. "So do you know all this just from working at Liver Shot?"

"Not exactly."

Before Jac could ask her to elaborate, Sophia stopped them in front of an alley, dark enough that Jac couldn't see the end of it. She pulled a coin out of her pocket, flipped it, and caught it again. It landed on heads. "Fifty-three," she muttered.

"What's that about?" he asked.

"It means we won't encounter any danger," she said, pushing him forward into the darkness.

Jac knew a lot of superstitions, but he'd never encountered one like that before. And even if Sophia strolled with confidence—her thigh-high boots clicking with every step—he couldn't be certain some Charles-paid Dove wasn't waiting for them at the alley's end. So he kept his eyes trained ahead and one hand on the gun in his pocket.

Eventually, they approached a set of double doors. Sophia opened them, and they entered a cheap hotel—the counters nicked, the floor stained, the floral wallpaper faded. A few men and women, all Jac's size or larger, played a game of Tropps at a table in the corner. Several others stood in front of an elevator, dressed in dark suits and red ties—Luckluster colors. They nodded at Sophia as she approached and stepped aside for her and Jac to pass.

It wasn't until the elevator's gate closed that Jac realized what was about to happen. He was going to come face-to-face with Delia Torren, an actual member of the Family that had nearly destroyed his life. Jac had never met Sedric or Garth, never had a living face to attach to the evils of the Torren empire.

Until now.

"Don't make a face. Don't say anything," Sophia warned him. "Especially about the smell."

"The smell?" Jac asked, then quickly went silent as the elevator lurched to a halt. The doors opened to reveal a room cloudy with cigarette smoke and filled with steel tables, lining the walls side by side, gleaming under bright fluorescent lights.

Each of them held a body.

Jac couldn't help it. He grimaced and swallowed down a wave of nausea. The room looked like a morgue, and it reeked—not just of cigarettes, but of whatever slew of concoctions boiled in the glass beakers on the shelves, of the phlegmy coughs of those lying on the tables. It smelled chemical and rotten, and even when he snapped his mouth shut, he could still taste the stench on his tongue.

He would've almost preferred the bodies to be dead. Instead, he stared, horrified, at the labored rising and falling of their chests, at the empty looks in their eyes, at the IV drips in their arms.

A woman—Delia Torren, he assumed—stood over one of them, attaching a new packet of saline to the IV. Her brown hair was tied back in a slick, low ponytail, and she wore a pair of glasses and a pristinely white lab coat, its pockets overflowing with paper receipts, pens, and vials. Jac had seen Sedric's picture a few times in the papers, and Delia looked at least ten years older than him—almost forty, with a seriousness so unlike Sedric's pursuits of bright lights and constant entertainment.

She looked up as Jac and Sophia entered, then abandoned the man trembling beneath her on the table and walked toward them. "Sophia," she cooed. Her voice was comically high-pitched, and she herself was quite petite. "You're early."

"I'm always early," Sophia pointed out.

Delia raised an overgrown eyebrow. "Yes, always hoping you'll cross paths with whoever pays a visit before you. I know how you think. So ambitious for a den manager. My consigliere thinks you're a spy."

Jac caught his breath—even if Delia didn't sound angry, it was clearly a threat. But Sophia didn't even stiffen. Instead, her gaze roamed around the room until it settled on one of the tables. "*That* consigliere?" she asked, nodding at a balding man whose skin was a strange green color, matching the liquid that flowed in through his IV.

"Yes," Delia answered, her lips pursed with disappointment. "As you can see, I didn't take his advice."

Jac had heard appalling rumors about the Torrens—so many it was impossible to believe them all. But here, he could see that the truth surpassed even the most monstrous tales. To Delia, these bodies weren't people—they were experiments.

This was the woman he worked for at Liver Shot. Whenever he played bouncer at the door or referee to the boxing pit, *she* benefited from the profits. The thought made him sick.

"I'm accepting your request for increased shipments," Delia told Sophia. "I managed to sway the Arzt family to my side. They find my brother...distasteful."

If they preferred Delia to Charles, Jac wondered, what must Charles be like?

"That means you'll run him out by August," Sophia said. "He won't get by without being able to sell Rapture."

Jac perked up. That was all the information he needed to call Harrison and give him Delia's name. Then Jac could return to being the second of the Irons and leave the Torren Empire behind him.

"That's true," Delia mused. "But I don't expect Charlie to be so easily defeated. He lashes out when he feels threatened." She handed Sophia a folder of documents. "These are the new pickup locations. I'm glad you brought muscle with you, by the way." She nodded at Jac, making him stiffen. "I'd play it safe until this finally ends. Double up the men on each pickup and the bouncers at the den. Start denying firearms at the door. I don't want mess or headlines."

Sophia nodded and tucked the folder into her bag, then pulled out several green saltwater taffies. She offered one to Delia. "Candy?"

"Trying to poison a split Apothecary?"

Sophia rolled her eyes. "They're just Tiggy's."

Delia smirked and drew something out of her own pocket—a coin. Jac frowned as she flipped it, repeating the same ritual Sophia had only minutes earlier. For the life of him, he couldn't understand it. The coin landed heads, and Delia reached forward to snatch the taffy.

"One day," Sophia said, "you'll explain that trick of yours to me."

Jac frowned deeper. Was Sophia playing thick?

"You act too confident around me. Are you so eager to take his place?" Delia nodded at her green-skinned consigliere on the other side of the room.

Sophia shrugged. "You're right. I'd rather wait until you're in Luckluster."

Delia smiled. Then she wrapped an affectionate arm around Sophia, and this time, Sophia *did* stiffen. Jolted, even.

The coin Jac had seen her flip earlier slipped from Sophia's pocket and clinked to the tiled floor. Sophia hitched her breath as Delia bent down to pick it up.

"How curious," Delia murmured. She held up the coin to the light to inspect it. It was cheap nickel, like something from a carnival. Delia retrieved her own gold coin from her pocket. "We match."

Sophia laughed. "It's just a memento. Something from an old boyfriend."

Delia narrowed her eyes, and Jac's heart began to race. He had no idea what was going on, but he didn't like it.

Then Jac noticed something strange: a flicker of Sophia's reflection in Delia's glasses. It didn't match the face Jac saw before him. Her deep green eyes, her fair skin, her everything...

She was a different person. A different girl.

Then Delia turned, and Jac lost sight of the reflection. She dropped the coin back in Sophia's palm. "Better not lose it, then."

She waved her hand, dismissing them both. As they returned to the elevator, Jac sighed with relief, more than ready to escape the unnerving presence of Delia Torren and the putrid smell of her lair.

"So," he said darkly, once the doors closed and they began

to descend. "Is this when you tell me what sort of game you're playing?"

Sophia laughed hollowly. "You don't get to ask me that."

"Then how about this?" Jac retorted. "How could you want to be an assistant to that…monster?"

"I don't. Not exactly." Again, she didn't elaborate, and Jac decided that was for the best. He didn't care, anyway. He had the information he needed to leave Liver Shot tonight.

The doors opened, and they left the motel from down the same darkened alley they'd come. Night had fallen, and Tropps Street was loud with drunken activity. It was always especially rowdy in summer, when tourists traveled to sample the casinos and nightlife, when the entire city craved something cold and strong to drink.

Jac kept several feet of distance between him and Sophia. He replayed the scene from earlier in his mind—of the empty-gazed people on Delia's medical tables, of Sophia offering her a piece of candy, of the horrifying smell of the place.

That was how evil smelled, he decided. That was how it looked, how it spoke. With total and utter indifference.

He'd been working for Liver Shot for two weeks, and so far, none of his worst fears about the job had been realized. But every sickening notion about the Torren Family had… and then some.

He would give Delia's name to Harrison tonight, and then with Harrison's sponsorship, Delia's likely victory would become a certainty. And then she would relocate that awful laboratory to Luckluster. And that evil would keep on going, and it wouldn't matter if Jac was long gone—he would still feel he played a part in that.

Helping Harrison meant destroying Vianca, who ruled an empire no different than the Torrens', full of drugs and crime and misery. But while Jac hated Vianca for what she'd done to Levi, when it came to the Torrens, it was personal. It was his own demon, not someone else's.

As they passed a yellow phone booth, Jac held back, fingering Harrison's business card that Levi had given him in his pocket. "I'll meet you back at Liver Shot," he lied.

Sophia turned around, her expression downcast. "Don't make me do it."

"Do what?" he asked nervously.

"Blackmail you."

Jac took a deep breath. For two weeks, he'd waited for this. But it didn't matter now. Nothing would stop him from making this call.

"Isn't that what you've always been doing?" he challenged her. "I'd rather you just say it and stop pretending like you have power over me."

"Fine," she snapped, stepping closer. "I know exactly who you are, *Jac Mardlin*. I know you have a thousand volts on your head. And even if I don't know what game you're playing, I know you're a spy. And whatever phone call you think you're about to make right now, you won't."

He'd suspected she'd known his name, but it still made his heart stutter to hear her say it. Sophia had always been a bad idea waiting to happen. Jac had once liked bad ideas—when their consequences used to entail hungover mornings or awkward, half-clothed stumbles out the door. But lately, bad ideas meant execution.

"Why is that? Will you pull a gun on me?" he asked, drawing his own out of his pocket. It was a crowded street, so he kept it close, tucked beneath the flap of his jacket. He had no intention of shooting her, but he had every intention of making it out of here.

"You won't kill me," she answered matter-of-factly.

Then Sophia reached into her pocket, and Jac clicked off the safety. "Put your hands where I can see them."

She did so, but she'd already removed what she wanted— the coin. She flipped it again and murmured, "Heads."

"Why do you keep doing that? What does it mean?" His voice came out harsh and biting, and he realized how fearful he sounded. He didn't mess with superstitions.

"It means I won't get hurt tonight," she said. "Listen, I didn't bring you along with me to threaten you. I wanted you to see what we're up against."

"Who's 'we?'" he asked.

"You came here for a job—I know that. I don't know if it was for Pup or someone else, but it's clear you're not here by choice. If it *were* your choice, you wouldn't be anywhere near the Torren empire. You hate it. Every time I've watched you light your cigarette outside Liver Shot, I've wondered if it would be the time you lit something else instead."

She took a step closer to him, close enough that Jac felt nervous about hurting her accidentally. Putting his gun away meant relinquishing the last bit of control he had in this conversation, but he'd never really had any power to begin with. She'd seen right through him. About everything.

Still, he held it. Better safe than sorry.

"That's why I wanted to bring you. Because I have a proposition." Sophia took another step closer. "After I tell you what it is, I want you to take the night off and think about it. If you still want to make that phone call in the morning, then fine. But at least consider what I'm offering."

"I'm not interested," Jac told her flatly.

"You don't even know what I'm going to say," Sophia insisted.

"I know I won't like it."

She was close enough to reach out and touch him now. Jac swallowed hard.

"I know your secret," she whispered. "So it's only fair that you know mine. I'll give you a hint, *Todd*."

Jac waited for her to finish her statement, then it slowly dawned on him that she already had. And all at once, he knew what she was going to say. Her brown hair, her wicked smile, her matching coin. He should've realized it the moment he saw her and Delia Torren in the same room. He should've realized it the moment he looked at Sedric Torren's obituary photograph on the desk in Liver Shot's office.

"Your name," he said hoarsely.

Sophia leaned forward and rested her hand on his—the same that held his gun. Then she moved her lips dangerously close to his ear. "My real name is Sophia Torren, and I want you to help me bring this empire down."

LEVI

♥ ♠ ♦ ♣

Levi lay on the hard marble floor of a hallway, the tiles and the doors alternating black and white. A familiar chill crawled up his spine, and he remembered that there was something unnatural about this place.

But he also remembered it was only a dream. And so Levi stood up and crept to the closest white door, filled with an instinct to explore.

When he pushed it open, he was home. At least, at the time, he'd still thought of this place as home. Their house was modestly small, not unlike the many others that trailed up the winding roads overlooking the beach. Inside, however, his family kept their many treasures. Old portraits of dead kings were tucked, secretly, into the pages of books. Amid typical trinkets—bouquets bought from the local market, wooden coasters, a cheap cigar box—hid more expensive collectibles, concealed within the clutter of plain sight. There was an heirloom family brooch swathed within the bundle of roses on a side table. The key to their grandfather's home was glued beneath the third coaster. A map of a distant city was rolled up beneath a cigar.

In this memory, Levi was ten years old and resting a broken leg after colliding his bike into a motorcar—one of the first he'd ever seen. He'd chased after it to get a closer look…and he'd gotten one. As punishment, he had to spend the whole summer indoors, waiting for himself to heal. And his favorite place to do so was here, in his mother's studio, watching her paint.

A long time ago, his maternal grandfather had worked for a railroad company as an engineer, and he'd traveled the world with his family, designing new lines of public transport in all the major cities and kingdoms. His mother had collected stories from all the places where she grew up and the people she'd met, and it was her sentimentals that Levi knew to look for, knew to ask about.

She bent over her easel, a brush perched in her fingers. She painted stories as well as she told them—flourishes of color and texture that Levi knew to be auras, even though he'd only ever seen one. Because he took after his father, his split talent for glimpsing auras was weaker. What his mother could sense about the world—the essences of every person she encountered, every emotion they felt—was so far beyond his own abilities, he could only look on her art in awe. Levi had spent most of his childhood trapped within that house, but it seemed to him that his mother had experienced everything, and he thirsted to see more of the world through her eyes.

"Which story do you want to hear again?" she asked, tucking a coarse curl behind her ear. Her brown skin was freckled from always sitting by the window, occasionally staring out of it for hours on end. Levi sometimes suspected she felt as trapped as he did.

"This one." Levi pointed to a city on the map hanging

above her desk, one not so far from where they lived. It still felt a world away.

"Why that place?" She gave him a sly smile. "Should I be worried?"

"You said it was your favorite."

His mother laughed. "Did I admit that? Don't ever tell your father." Then she leaned back in her stool and her gaze drifted toward the window—toward elsewhere.

"When I was fifteen, your grandfather was offered a contract to help construct an addition to the subway across the city's South Side..."

Levi woke tangled in familiar sheets. The morning sunlight shone red and gold through the stained glass windows, casting Narinder in holy light as he sat up and stretched his back. "It's been over twenty-four hours," Narinder muttered. His voice was still heavy with sleep.

"Since what?" Levi asked groggily.

"Since I've had coffee." He cast him an annoyed look. "It doesn't help that you steal the covers."

Levi frowned at the pile of blankets on his side of the bed. In the past two weeks, he'd spent so much time at the Catacombs that he'd apparently begun to claim things as his own. "Here." He shoved them at the musician. "We don't need to get up yet."

Levi intended to put off the day as long as possible, even if he had plenty of reasons to be in a good mood. He hadn't heard from Vianca in ages. Most of his injuries had healed, except for his ribs. And his relationship with Narinder was in a better place than he'd ever hoped it could be.

But all of those facts were overshadowed by the promise Levi made to the most powerful criminals of the North Side. One he'd staked his entire reputation on.

And in two weeks, he'd come through with nothing.

Narinder sighed and lay back down. "You're making that face like you want to be pitied."

Levi frowned deeper. "I don't have a pity face."

"You know, you could always come up with another idea." But Levi already had the perfect idea—it was grand, brilliant, and would spell catastrophe for Captain Hector and the South Side.

But it was also dangerous, and Levi didn't want to spill blood, even if the whiteboots had already spilled theirs. And for that, he needed Harrison's help. Unfortunately, Harrison had gone silent since he announced his Senate candidacy, leaving Levi to wait while his reputation withered to nothing.

"There is no other plan," he answered grimly.

Narinder turned on his side, head propped on his hand. "Should I be nervous?"

"That depends on what you're nervous about."

"That you'll get yourself killed."

Levi laughed bitterly. The world wasn't giving him the opportunity to try. "Save your worries." Narinder's face darkened, and Levi realized his tone had been too bleak. He quickly threw on a card dealer smile. "I grew up listening to stories about New Reynes, and so I came here to make a story of my own. I think about it constantly—*what sort of story am I writing? Where does all this lead?*"

"I never thought criminals could be so self-reflective," Narinder teased.

Levi scowled. He was being serious. "Maybe I'm different— I *want* to be different. I'm only holding off because I don't want anyone to get hurt."

"You can't ensure that."

"No, but at least, if something goes wrong, I'll know I tried."

"You're a terrible gangster," Narinder told him, with a playful shove. Levi would've pushed him, if turning himself over wasn't still so dreadfully painful. "But you're a good person."

No one had told Levi those words in a long time, and he hadn't realized how much he needed to hear them. Lately, all he could think about was the Irons losing their faith in him all over again, Enne's expression at the Catacombs dissolving from hope into hurt, Jac finding his way into a Torren drug den he wouldn't be able to fight out of.

Maybe he didn't deserve Narinder's words. But at least he still cared.

"Can't I be both?" Levi murmured.

Narinder pursed his lips, like he wanted to say no. But instead he told him, "I guess we'll find out."

Over the past two weeks of refurbishment, the Irons had decorated their museum as lavishly as the dumpsters of Olde Town could provide. Discarded Faith charms and trinkets hung along the staircase, clacking and chiming as people brushed past. Every piece of wooden furniture wore a new silver coat of paint.

As Levi entered, the Irons straightened in their rocking chairs and splintered barstools, pausing their card games and whispered conversations to stare at him. The air felt uneasy and still.

Confused, Levi sauntered over to Tommy. "Don't stop your games on my account." When Tommy looked away instead of responding, Levi grabbed the magazine out of his hands. "*The Kiss & Tell*? Bit of a trash tabloid, isn't it?" He glanced at the title on the opened page: "Most Eligible Persons of the North Side."

"Oh," Tommy said, clearing his throat. "It's, um..."

Levi furrowed his eyebrows. "Why are you all acting like

someone died? Did Scavenger make it in here or something?" He scanned the sketched faces and recognized Narinder as number one. "Bet he's pleased," Levi muttered, though secretly, he was, as well.

Then, past a few famous cabaret vedettes and businessmen, down at number nine, Levi found his own face, straight from his wanted poster. He tried very hard to suppress his grin. Tabloids were ridiculous, of course, but—Levi straightened out his shirt—he did look pretty good.

Levi slapped Tommy on the back, making him wince. "Muck, Tommy, I'm the one with the broken ribs here." He scanned the other faces around the foyer. It seemed the tabloid wasn't why they looked anxious. "Anyone going to fill me in on what I've missed?"

Mansi stood abruptly, making her stool skid across the stone floor. "Chez is dead."

Whatever Levi had been expecting her to say, it wasn't that. "Dead?" Levi rasped. "From what?"

"From burns." The look in her eyes made it clear her words were an accusation—no, a conviction. Chez had tried to challenge Levi, and so Levi had murdered his third.

Mansi stalked past him, bumping painfully into his side, and stormed out of the building. Levi watched the door close behind her with nausea churning in his stomach. He squeezed Tommy's shoulder and bent over, certain he was about to be sick.

No, he wasn't like the other lords.

"You're hurting me," Tommy told him, and Levi wrenched his hand away.

"Sorry," he said. "I'm sorry."

"So it's true?" Tommy asked nervously.

Levi remembered it all with disturbing clarity. The starved look in Chez's eyes when he'd found Levi in that alley. The feeling of Chez's gun pressed against his temple. The burning mouthful of Gambler's Ruin that Levi had spit on him. The bloody flesh and exposed bone circling Chez's wrists where Levi had grabbed him.

They'd been friends, once.

Now Levi actually did taste vomit. "I…"

"Levi!" Tock called from the top of the stairwell. All the charms and chimes clattered as she descended a few steps. "You have a phone call."

Levi barely even registered her words before he rushed up the stairs, fleeing from the other Irons. Tock grabbed him by the wrist and yanked him up the last step. "I didn't hear you come in," she hissed. "They've been sitting there all day like this." She grabbed the copy of *The Kiss & Tell* he was still holding and threw it on the ground.

"Is it true?" Levi whispered.

"It's true." She led him to his room, and he numbly followed. "But you need to pull yourself together. Harrison Augustine is on the phone."

Levi's stomach lurched again. *Finally.* He ran to the telephone resting on a repurposed absinthe crate in the room's corner. "'Lo?" he breathed into the receiver.

"You called?" The purr in the voice was unmistakable.

"Yes," Levi growled. "Two weeks ago. Where have you been?"

"It's been busy since the announcement. Interviews, visits, speeches—"

"I need your help." Levi didn't have time to listen to Harrison's rehearsed excuses. He'd already been waiting too long.

"Yes, I got that from your message. It's an incredible request to make, yet you've provided me with almost nothing I originally asked for. There's still no word from your associate at the Torren den, and I'm not even sure all the information you gave me from your meeting with the other lords is reliable."

"What do you mean?" Levi asked sharply.

"I'm not accusing you. I just have a few questions about what happened at the Orphan Guild. I don't believe the white-boots were responsible."

Levi frowned and swatted at Tock, who kept trying to press her ear against the other side of the receiver. Levi's entire promise to the other lords was built on vengeance for what the whiteboots did to the Orphan Guild. Was someone else responsible? And if so, did he care enough to change his plan?

"Why do you say that?" Levi asked.

"Because I was with Jameson Hector that night. He was of the same mind as me—he didn't want to see the conflict be-tween the North and South Sides escalate."

"If Hector didn't do it, why would he claim credit?" Levi asked.

"I haven't spoken to him since the attack, but I believe he feels it's best that the people believe the authorities have the situation under control."

"So someone else is pulling the strings." Levi furrowed his eyebrows. "It might be Scavenger." Tock rolled her eyes be-side him. "He has access to those sort of weapons. He admit-ted as much during our meeting."

"It's not him. He has no motive. He does business with the Guild."

"Well, we won't learn anything by doing nothing," Levi said. "I agree with you—this will only escalate the conflict further—but if I don't do this, I can't get you the informa-tion you want, and I won't be able to figure out who's actu-ally behind this."

"Are you that confident in your associate? We've heard nothing about the Torrens in weeks."

"I am," Levi said, even though he wasn't—not entirely. "Let me do this tonight, and I'll have the name of the new don for you by tomorrow." When Harrison didn't respond right away, Levi pressed further. "I only need your help ensuring it's shut down."

Harrison sighed. "You want to do this *tonight*?"

"Yes," Levi answered. He was tired of waiting.

After another moment of silence, Harrison said, "Fine. I'll arrange for an anonymous tip to go to Hector, but tomorrow, we'll meet at the Kipling's Hotel at four in the afternoon. Bring your associate along. The waiting on both our parts ends tonight."

The line went dead.

It wasn't until Levi hung up and looked back at Tock that the weight of everything crashed down on him. The pressure to pull this off. The news about Chez.

His plan was finally coming to fruition; his empire would rise tonight. But for the first time, he thought, *Maybe I don't deserve it.*

"Did he agree?" Tock asked.

Levi looked up and nodded.

She pumped her fist in victory. "So it's happening. It's *happening.*"

Levi looked out the window, where the magnificent, historic structure of Revolution Bridge crossed the Brint. The city's most symbolic landmark.

This evening, Tock was going to blow it up.

But even the thought of that did nothing to change Levi's mood. He couldn't shake the image of the way the Irons had looked at him. Like they were afraid of him.

"I murdered Chez," Levi breathed. "That's what everyone is saying, and they're right."

The words finally pushed his nausea over the edge, and he vomited behind the absinthe crate.

Tock made a disgusted noise as Levi heaved and awkwardly patted him on the back. "You don't need to explain yourself to me. If anything, this is good news. Everyone is shocked. They didn't think you had it in you."

"How is that a good thing?" he gasped, trying not to throw up again.

"Your silver jewelry, your ridiculous palace... You're trying to write yourself a legend, but you forget—all stories from the North Side are penned in blood."

"Not mine," Levi ground out.

She tilted her head to the side and gave him a pitiful look. "Maybe you're just too good for all of this."

Levi grew up in a family whose power had been forcibly removed from them. He'd listened, enraptured, to the stories of the North Side gangsters, people who'd come from nothing but seized power all the same. When he thought of those legends, of the Phoenix Club, of the sort of people who held power in this world, it sickened him to realize that the only path to it was a wicked conscience. He didn't pretend to be a saint, but he'd foolishly hoped that he could change the repeated theme of all the stories. He'd thought his story could be different.

Maybe it wasn't that the wicked always gained power— maybe power itself corrupted. Maybe Levi had spent so long calling himself a victim that he hadn't noticed that he'd become a villain.

Maybe you're too good for all this, Tock had said. So had Narinder, and Reymond before him.

Levi spat out what remained of the vomit in his mouth. "Not anymore."

ENNE

♥   ♠   ♦   ♣

Three girls walked down Guillory Street wearing pearls, frocked jackets, and impeccable plumberry lipstick. Their hair was tucked into dainty feathered hats, showing off slender necks and feminine collarbones. They clutched pastries and ruffled purses in delicate, white-gloved hands. Nearly everyone tipped their hats or smiled at them as they passed. They looked like a photo shoot from *The Guillory Street Gossip* waiting to happen, an exclusive clique the South Side didn't know, but felt they ought to.

Never might they have expected the ladies to be gangsters.

According to Enne's guidebook, Guillory Street was the social center of the South Side. Like the buildings, the cobblestoned streets were white, barely besmirched by the wheels of motorcars or the soles of brogued oxfords and kitten heels. Twinkling string lights crisscrossed overhead, illuminating shopfronts selling such luxuries as imported chocolate, fine jewelry, and overpriced real estate. The gardens were blooming and well-manicured. The street performers on clarinets and violins were Von Ballard–trained. The passersby carried colorful shopping parcels and smelled of high-end cologne.

"What a muckhole," Lola muttered under her breath. An elderly woman who passed shot Lola a horrified look.

"Don't be ridiculous," Enne told her. This was easily the nicest place in New Reynes she'd ever visited, one that came with glowing recommendations from her guidebook. She itched to tour some of the sights—the famous Kipling's department store, the boutique cupcake shop, the opera hall. But they had come for one reason today: an afternoon salon that Worner Prescott was attending.

It had been two weeks since she'd last seen Levi. Their plans for the stock market were entirely stalled until Levi fulfilled his reckless promise to the other lords. She was depending on him, had no idea what was going on, and he hadn't even bothered to contact her.

That stung worse than she cared to admit.

With their volts nearly gone, all three of the girls were irritated and hungry. And their clothes, though beautiful, were stolen from expensive Tropps Street boutiques and the laundry at St. Morse Casino.

Enne took a deep breath of the sweet-smelling South Side air, as though it could cleanse her bitterness from the inside out. She might've felt betrayed, petty, and mildly faint from a lack of sugar, but that was nothing a box of rose macarons and the scream of a whizzing bullet couldn't fix.

"This is it," Lola said, looking up from the guidebook.

The condominium complex was painted peony pink, and a flower box of lilies perched on every windowsill. The girls stepped through the revolving doors and into a pristine lobby, and Enne slid her invitation to a nearby attendant.

"My friends and I are here for the salon," she told him. He looked at her lace and pearls and smiled pleasantly.

"Right this way."

After a short elevator ride, the three girls stepped into a cheerful common room, crowded with people in seersucker and satin. Pastries were stacked into towers, teacups rested on end tables, and crowds gathered to discuss the recent editorials and columns in *The Gossip*.

"Oh, sweet muck," Lola muttered, her expression growing ever more horrified.

Across the room, Enne locked eyes with Vianca Augustine. Vianca beckoned with her bony finger, and Enne felt the terrible, familiar squeeze of the omerta around her throat.

"I'll be right back," Enne told the other girls hoarsely. "Introduce yourselves." The two of them shot her alarmed looks as she pushed through the party to Vianca's side.

"Get up," Vianca snapped at the scrawny man beside her. He paled and jumped to his feet, gesturing for Enne to sit.

Once Enne did, Vianca clamped a hand around her arm and leaned toward her. Enne cringed. "I see you've brought your associates with you," she whispered. "You dressed them up well. They both look like little dolls."

Vianca was probably the only person in New Reynes who would ever feel comfortable describing Lola and Grace like that. "I can't be everywhere at once," Enne answered. "And I trust them." That was the truth. Even if Enne hadn't yet won Grace's oath, she'd earned her respect. And while Enne might've softened the edges of her friends, she'd also sharpened her own.

"Is Worner Prescott here?" Enne asked.

Vianca nodded to a man across the room. He was short and fair, with shoulders made broader by thick pads and balding hair half-concealed beneath a top hat. He had the sort of face you could pass in the street unnoticed, even if you knew him.

Enne fought to contain her surprise. She associated monarchists with arson and vandalism, not cherry cheeks and tea parties.

As they watched, Worner made his way over to Grace and Lola. "He likes to introduce himself to everyone," Vianca muttered. "He's a buffoon, but he remembers names and faces. Some people find that charming."

Enne wasn't sure she'd ever heard Vianca share such a comment with her, as though Enne were a confidante. It was deeply uncomfortable, especially with Vianca's hand still latched on her arm.

"You feel so thin," the donna said, shaking Enne's skinny wrist. "Don't tell me the pressure is getting to you."

Enne considered telling Vianca about how Levi's ambitions were getting in the way of her own. She couldn't imagine any real consequence to Levi—after all, *he* was Vianca's favorite. But even if they hadn't been speaking, it still felt like a line she couldn't cross.

"Of course not," Enne answered.

"Then why don't you talk to Worner?" Vianca suggested. "Feel him out. He's been terribly awkward around me lately. As if I care about what my son does or doesn't do."

Lola had advised her to avoid this subject, but Enne couldn't contain her curiosity. "So it doesn't bother you that Harrison is running for the First Party?"

Vianca's nails dug deeper into Enne's skin at the mention of her son's name. "Of course not," she said, echoing Enne's own words and tone. Then she released Enne's arm and carefully tucked a loose strand of white hair behind her ear, gazing into the distance. Enne realized that every few moments, the others in the room stole curious glances at the donna, followed by whispers.

Maybe the pressure was actually getting to *Vianca*.

"I'm very glad you're here," Vianca said, surprising Enne

once again. She patted the back of Enne's hand, as though her presence was a comfort.

Enne had never seen the donna betray vulnerability before, but still, she remained wary. After all, it wasn't as though Enne had a choice about being here.

"What will you get if Worner wins?" Enne asked. "More power?"

"There are a thousand ways to power. You think I'd go to all this trouble if it were that simple?" Vianca's voice grew colder and colder, and Enne leaned back into the comforting support of the cushions. "Do you know how it feels to have no value? For every person to see through you, no matter what you've accomplished?"

Enne didn't look at the donna when she spoke, in case she saw something common in their expressions. She didn't want to share anything with Vianca. Not ever. "I might," she answered carefully.

"I was never supposed to be the donna of this Family," Vianca said. Her bitterness was so palpable, Enne could nearly taste the vinegar in her words. "A long time ago, when there were still kings, my Family lived like royalty, too. And though Reynes was always a City of Sin, it felt different then, and my grandfather was adept at concealing his secret lifestyle. He spent his nights throwing dice and his mornings clutching prayer beads. He was a self-made man, but he was obsessed with his legacy. From nothing, he had built something. My father, my uncles, my brother—those were his something. I was not."

Vianca's voice remained cool, steady. Enne wasn't sure she herself could speak about the things that had hurt her without them hurting her all over again. Maybe that was weak, but she also felt it was human.

"I was always overlooked," the donna continued. "Even

when my entire Family was executed for supporting the Mizers, I was spared."

"But you've continued to support them. Because that's what the monarchists want, isn't it?" Enne asked quietly. "New kings?"

"It was, once. My family died because they wavered in their convictions, not because they upheld them. I am stalwart. The only one who *ever* continued the family legacy. After all, family is everything. *Conviction* is everything." Then Vianca laughed under her breath, far too light and cheerful to match their conversation. "I know you believe me to be the enemy, but I do wish you'd told me about the stock market earlier. It's very clever. And very unfair for Levi to throw *your* work into jeopardy."

Enne froze. "How did you know about that?"

"It's not exactly a secret that the lords met in the Catacombs, is it? Everyone in there saw you. Of course I find out these things." Vianca reached over Enne's shoulder to a drink tray and grabbed herself a glass. "I think it's a marvelous idea—both of yours, really. I'd love nothing better than to see the North Side united against the South. I told Levi I wouldn't interfere—not for six weeks. But the clock is ticking, and…it really isn't fair to *you*, is it?" She leaned down to whisper into Enne's ear. "Should I punish him for you?"

Enne coughed, startled. "No. You don't need… I mean…"

Vianca raised her eyebrows and sipped her drink. "I'm surprised by how all this is turning out. I would've thought you two would be more than happy to work together. You're such a pretty set on the front page."

Vianca still wanted to play matchmaker, for whatever reason beyond her own cruel entertainment, Enne couldn't fathom. Well, lucky for everyone, those plans had failed.

Vianca removed a pouch from her purse and pressed it into

Enne's hand. Enne felt the shape of glass orbs inside. "Your last gift. No point in wasting it on the boys this time."

"Thank you." Enne was horrified to realize she actually meant it.

Vianca smiled. "I always wanted a girl."

Enne muttered a shaky goodbye and stood up. As she tried to shake off Vianca's last words, she approached the spot where Worner Prescott was giving Lola and Grace the most exaggerated bow Enne had ever seen, his nose nearly scraping his knees. While Grace stifled laughter, Lola nervously attempted a curtsy of her own. She looked like a crow bar straining to bend.

"Oh!" Worner said, spotting Enne. Lola and Grace turned to her with relief. "Are you all here together?" He extended a hand, pastry crumbs stuck between his fingers.

"We are," Enne said, and she introduced herself.

Worner squinted at her. "You look familiar. Have we met before?"

Enne smiled wider, making her face look even more different from her wanted poster. "I don't believe so. I've only recently arrived from Bellamy."

"Bellamy!" he trilled. Worner spoke at a volume not quite appropriate for the indoors. "Why, I vacation there often in the summer. My house is right on Hawthorne Street. It's by this bakery, the Gooseberry." He beamed, as though quite pleased he'd remembered.

"I've been there a few times," Enne told him politely.

"Well, what a delightful coincidence!" He looked around the room cheerily. "I'd be happy to introduce you to anyone here. I know them all."

Before he could make any suggestions, a young woman appeared behind him. She had the sort of willowy figure that made Enne immediately identify her as a dancer.

"Oh, this is my daughter, Poppy," Worner said. "Poppy, this young lady lived in Bellamy. Perhaps you went to school together?"

Enne tried not to gape at the girl. She looked far too elegant to be Worner's daughter.

"The Bellamy Finishing School of Fine Arts," Poppy said, twirling a blond ringlet around her finger. "I was only there a few months, though."

"That's where I attended, as well," Enne answered. "I'm currently taking a gap year. For travel." That was one of the prettiest lies she'd ever told.

"I still write to a few friends from there," Poppy said, her voice suddenly filled with excitement. "Maybe you know Madeline Tanzer? Or Georgiana Glisset?"

Both girls had been far more popular than Enne ever was. She would've been shocked if they'd even known her name.

But Vianca had instructed Enne to insert herself into Worner's inner circle, so she smiled tightly and lied. "Yes. I knew them well."

Worner beamed brighter.

Within five minutes, Enne and Poppy were seated on a loveseat, Lola awkwardly hovering beside them while Grace scoped out the men in the room with an almost predatory stare. Poppy held a copy of *The Guillory Street Gossip* on her lap as she told them all a scandalous story surrounding the city's favorite prima ballerina, who seemed to be Poppy's rival and—in their not so distant past—former lover.

Poppy turned the page and pointed to a column called "Most Eligible Persons of the South Side". Poppy had dated nearly all of them.

"Except *her*," she said, pointing to an heiress who was listed at number six. "She set fire to my Regalliere purse in our ninth year." Poppy turned the page. "Or him." She pointed at a face Enne nearly didn't recognize, since she'd only seen him through the hazy violet lights of the Catacombs. Narinder Basra. "I don't think he likes women. Very disappointing."

Enne suddenly had a bad taste in her mouth, which Narinder probably didn't deserve—she didn't even know him. Lola shot Enne a warning look, then asked, "Wouldn't he be in *The Kiss & Tell*'s version? He's from the North Side."

"Oh, I'm sure he'll be in both," Poppy said. "He knows everyone in New Reynes, and the Catacombs is full of South Siders, as well." She lowered her voice. "Though I heard a few weeks ago there was some sort of gangster turnout there. Kind of frightening, isn't it?" But she sounded more excited than scared.

"I positively have goose bumps," Grace said flatly.

"I'm still trying to get my hands on the other version," Poppy admitted. "My father forbids me from reading it, but of course I do anyway." She shot him an annoyed look from across the room, but he was too immersed in a discussion with a group of campaigners to notice. "He's one to talk—getting a quarter of his donations from Vianca Augustine. Everyone knows what they say about *her*."

"She's here," Enne rasped. "Best to lower your voice."

"Oh, I know," Poppy replied airily. "The whole room reeks of her off-brand perfume."

"Do you mind if I see that?" Grace asked, indicating *The Gossip*. Poppy nodded, so Grace took it and flipped through the pages. While the others discussed the model who'd been interviewed for the cover, Grace announced that she'd spotted one of the most eligible persons at the party. She pointed at a photograph of a young man with red hair wearing a glittering family brooch against a suit jacket.

"Wealthy, working for his father's company on Hedge Street," Grace read. "He's number eight, but do you think he really measures in at eight?" Grace winked at the three of them, and Poppy let out a shocked howl of laughter.

"I wouldn't know," Poppy mused, "but I'd be curious should you happen to find out."

Grace tossed Enne the magazine. "Oh, I'm sure I will." Then she left to stalk her victim.

Poppy looked between Enne and Lola, a mischievous smile brightening up her features. She reached behind her and grabbed three cocktails off a rose-gold serving tray and handed them out. "This afternoon might be a lot more fun than I expected."

Enne sipped the drink. It was sweet and bubbly—far more palatable than a Gambler's Ruin or a Snake Eyes. "What is this called?" she asked Poppy.

"It's a Hotsy-Totsy—you drink it for luck, or good times, or any occasion, if you want. It's the real reason I couldn't stay in Bellamy. The whole island is dry!" Poppy wrapped her arm around Enne's shoulders. "You're about to be *thrilled* that you took a gap year. And that you met me."

Poppy clinked glasses with Enne and Lola and downed nearly all of her Hotsy-Totsy at once. "So are you from Bellamy, as well?" she asked Lola, and Lola nearly spit out her drink.

"No. I'm not. I'm, um, starting my first term at the university in September. I'll be studying history."

Poppy laughed. "Don't tell that to my father. History is a passion of his. He'd talk your ears off."

"I don't know—I'd be rather interested in what he has to say. He studied history, too, didn't he?" Lola eyed Poppy seriously. "And journalism?"

Poppy shifted and took another sip of her drink. "I'm surprised you know that. He did, before he switched to law. It's not really something he likes to talk about."

"Why not?" Lola pressed.

"Oh, he failed at it miserably, I think." Poppy quickly reached for the magazine again and launched into a discussion about one of its writers. The whole time, Lola bit her lip and sipped little from her glass.

By the time Grace returned, Enne and Poppy had grown gradually more buzzed and giggly. Enne realized she very much liked Poppy. She was brazenly frank and easy to talk to, and no matter how out of place Lola seemed, Poppy went out of her way to try to include her in the conversation. Enne's logic told her Poppy was an advantageous link to Worner—and her homesickness told her Poppy was a perfect distraction from the affairs of the North Side.

"Well?" Poppy asked, examining Grace's sly smile. "How did it go?"

Grace wiped away her smudged lipstick with the back of her hand. "I've been very entertained. He was about as charming as old tuna salad, but I've had three of…whatever those are." She pointed at Enne's Hotsy-Totsy. "And I've complimented almost every single girl here, like, twice. That's three drinks. Twenty girls. Sixty compliments."

Lola furrowed her eyebrows as Grace crashed onto the chaise between them. "Not sure that's right."

"I am a *counter*," Grace said sternly. "I'm always right." She looked at the magazine spread across their laps. "What did I miss?"

"Poppy's trying to set Enne up." Lola crossed her arms. "I'm sure we can all imagine how well that will turn out."

"With who? Him?" Grace snorted, pointing at the photograph of a young man wearing a clover-green suit. "She'd eat him alive."

Enne flushed. "What does that mean?" She, for one, liked the boy's genuine smile. It was refreshing. If Vianca was going to be dragging her to several of these parties, she didn't see why she couldn't turn them into more distractions.

Poppy's eyes lit up. "Do I get to hear secrets?"

"They just like to tell stories," Enne said hurriedly.

"Well, I'm glad to hear those, too. The scarier the better."

Grace grinned. "They're *very* scary. I should warn you."

"I'm a big girl. Scare me."

"Well, I once heard a street legend. It's from the North Side." Grace paused dramatically, waiting for Poppy to widen her eyes and think better of her request. When Poppy only leaned in further, she continued. "About eighteen years ago, there was a street lord named Veil. Of all the legends, he is *the* legend. He built the North Side into what it is today."

"Ooh, I haven't heard this one," Poppy purred. Enne recognized the story as one Grace had already told her—and one Levi and Jac often bickered about.

"During the Great Street War, Veil made the city a promise. He said that if you wrote the name of your enemy on any wall of the North Side, then he would personally see to your enemy's death. So, as you can imagine, the walls were soon covered in names, and he drew them like a lottery. With Veil as lord, anyone could be a killer. Cross someone, and you could end up dead tomorrow."

Enne shivered. What a horrifying idea. Poppy was grinning beside her, as though Grace's story was a fairy tale.

"They say copycats still exist, even now," Grace murmured. "That if you find yourself in the Deadman District, and you cross paths with your own name...you won't live to see morning."

"What did this Veil character look like?" Poppy asked. "I bet he was good-looking."

Grace laughed. "They say he kept his whole face covered. To this day, no one knows what he looked like. He asked to be hanged and buried like that, and they have to honor last requests…even from criminals." Grace grinned and nudged Lola's side. "Tell her the one about the Bargainer."

Lola scoffed. "But that isn't history. The Bargainer isn't *real*—"

"Depends on who you ask."

"But that's ridiculous—"

"Everyone! Everyone!" Worner Prescott's high-pitched voice echoed shrilly through the room. He clinked a spoon against his glass, and the party fell silent. "We've just received some disturbing news on the radio. There's been an anonymous tip about a threat on Revolution Bridge, and it's been cordoned off for the foreseeable future. If you need to make new arrangements to return home, the attendants will be more than happy to assist you."

"Ooh," Poppy whispered to them. "This is exciting."

Enne met Lola's eyes warily, and she knew her second was thinking the same thing. This had to be connected to Levi somehow.

"I'm sorry," Enne said, quickly getting up. "But we need to leave. That's where we've been staying…" She cleared her throat and added, "Terrible hotel mix-up."

"You won't stay longer?" Poppy pleaded. "There are other ways to cross the Brint."

"We'll be here next time," she assured her, and kissed both of Poppy's cheeks in farewell. As they made their way toward the door, Enne stealthily stuffed a dozen crumpets in her purse, beside the pocket where she kept her gun.

Grace tried to wink at her, but she was so drunk that she actually just blinked both eyes. "I guess it's showtime."

JAC

♥ ♠ ♦ ♣

Jac crept down the stairs of his apartment building, a carpet bag stuffed with his meager belongings slung over his shoulder.

He opened the door onto Tropps Street and came face-to-face with Sophia Torren.

She eyed the bag. "You're in a hurry."

He was, because he'd been hoping to avoid her. It didn't matter who she was or what she wanted—as soon as Jac found a pay phone, he would call Harrison Augustine, and he would leave the Torren Empire behind.

Sophia flipped a coin into the air and closed it in her fist. She peeked at it between cupped fingers and smiled.

"You know where I live now?" Jac grunted.

"Now?" She gave him a pitying look. "I've known where you live for weeks." She reached into her pocket and tossed him something black—a ski mask.

He scoffed. "I don't have time for this." He shoved the mask back into her hands and stormed off.

Sophia grabbed his shoulder and yanked him back. "So that's your decision? To leave?"

"What decision?" Jac demanded hotly. "You act as though I have any information. As though anything you told me or showed me last night makes sense. All I know is that you're a Torren, and you want my help. And I say no." He brushed past her, and she scrambled to block his path.

"Don't make me—"

"What? Blackmail me?" he asked darkly.

"If that's what it takes."

"Why are you doing this?" Any of the others at Liver Shot would be happy to help her. Where she went, they followed. "Why me?"

"Because...you're *Jac Mardlin*. Your smile is plastered on wanted posters all over the North Side. You're *someone*."

Jac possessed his fair share of vices, but rarely did anyone try to appeal to his pride. He was only famous as an extension of someone else. Everything he'd done for this job, he'd done for Levi.

The ones who never wanted to be players. That was how Lola described the two of them. That was who he was; the periphery of someone else's story. And never, not once in his life, had anyone ever thought of him otherwise.

He'd never realized until this moment how much he wanted someone to.

"Just let me explain," Sophia pleaded. She was clearly not used to begging—her face could barely hold the expression.

Jac was intrigued, but not enough to change his mind. "You lied to me about who you were."

She crossed her arms. "And you didn't?" She took an intimidating step closer to him, and Jac pressed his back against the brick wall. "Playing it safe isn't really playing at all. And that's what you want to do, isn't it? To play?"

It was, and it always had been—even before Jac had met

Levi. But he'd never said those words out loud. It was far easier to bet on cards or fights, when losing only cost a few volts or a black eye. The game Sophia played was far deadlier than those.

That, too, was a reason Jac wanted it.

But he didn't tell her that truth. Instead, he gave her a different one. "I nearly died thanks to your family, and what you do."

Her expression sobered. "I'm sorry—I am. But even if Charles and Delia are my half siblings," she admitted, "they're *not* my family."

"But the drugs are still your family's business," Jac snarled. "And I don't want to get caught up in it. I can't afford to."

"Yes, you *do*. You do. You just won't admit it. And I won't leave until you say it. So say it."

"Say what?" he countered.

"That you want to see the Torrens burn."

Jac froze. A desire simmered inside him like a hunger. "You're shatz," he whispered.

"What will it take, then?" Sophia asked. "Should I say please? Because I will. I'm saying please." She glared at him, as if he'd forced her to suffer being polite. As if she'd much rather be threatening him.

Maybe it was her looking like that. Maybe it was because the words were true.

He did want it more than anything.

To be a player.

"Fine," he growled, chest heaving. "I want to see the Torrens burn."

Sophia grinned, as though she knew she'd already won, and thrust the mask at him again. "Good. Now throw that bag back inside and let's go. I planned out the whole date."

Jac knew by now that whenever Sophia alluded to romance, she was actually thinking about something destructive. Anyone who went on a date with Sophia Torren probably needed to sign a waiver first.

Sophia winked at him before she walked away. "You know you want to."

Of course he wanted to. It was dangerous—terribly dangerous—but he still wanted to.

I already regret this, Jac thought as he opened the door to his apartment building and tossed his bag inside.

He caught up to her and asked, "What's the mask for?"

"What I just said. For our date."

He raised his eyebrows and held it up higher between two pinched fingers. "Kinky."

"I took you as a moonlit stroll, picnic-in-the-park sort of fellow, so I thought I'd meet you halfway." Sophia fluttered her eyelashes. "How do you feel about arson?"

Jac hesitated on the corner of Chain Street and Tropps Street. A yellow sign for a drug den flickered above them, dull and dirty in the daylight. Rusted chains dangled from it like party streamers. Even this early in the morning, glassy-eyed patrons—trapped in their cruel indentures to local Chainers—wandered up and down the street. Others sat in clusters on the pavement, hunched over and clutching bottles of absinthe. Some of them didn't move at all.

Even during the worst of his addiction to Lullaby, Chain Street was one place Jac had refused to go. He'd always known that the moment he walked in there, he'd never walk out.

Sophia pointed at a den at the other end of the street, called Insomnia, painted black with white dots to resemble the night sky. It looked like a place plucked out of dreams.

Or for him, out of nightmares.

Jac reached for his Creed to steady himself. He was a different person now. He was stronger for what he'd overcome. He was no prisoner here.

But the sight of it still left him gasping for air. He struggled to maintain a straight face in front of Sophia, who was grinning and crossing her arms to conceal the two bottles of gasoline hidden beneath her shirt.

"You probably have questions," she said.

"One or two," he managed.

"Insomnia is currently being operated by Charles," she explained. "Delia said Charles will run out of volts by the end of the month, and knowing Charles, he's itching to act out. So whatever we do to the den, he'll assume it was Delia, and he'll retaliate."

Letting them destroy each other was a clever plan, but it came with a heaping amount of risk. Like the possibility of Jac and Sophia getting caught and killed before they finished their "date."

Still, Jac didn't object when Sophia took his hand in hers and led him down the street. His heart constricted when he smelled that familiar waft of chamomile, and a phantom noose tightened around his neck.

In every legend, the hero was forced to face the worst of their adversaries. As Jac passed the foggy windows of each of the shopfronts, he saw the ghost of his old reflection—twenty pounds skinnier, skin ruddy, eyes sunken.

His worst adversary was himself.

At this hour, the shops were still closed, and the prisoners of the street paid them no mind as they passed. Still, Jac didn't let go of Sophia's hand until they'd made it to Insomnia. She retrieved two lock picks from her pocket and made surprisingly quick work of the door.

"Do all girls know how to pick locks?" he asked, thinking of Enne.

"I can rewire a radio, too." She winked at him. "I know, I'm quite the catch."

"Yeah, like the flu."

Sophia ignored him and eased open the door. When Jac reached for the light switch, she swatted his hand away. "If it looks like the den's open, they'll come."

Jac's stomach clenched. She meant those sitting outside, waiting for their next Lull.

"Taffy?" she offered gently.

"Oh, yeah, sure." It would distract him from the haunting smell of this place, which had already settled into his lungs, making him anxious and dizzy. Sophia handed him the taffy, and he unwrapped it with shaking hands and popped it into his mouth. The anise and fennel flavors made his head clear, and he sent her a grateful smile.

Sophia flipped her coin. "Seventy-eight," she said. "I think we'll be okay, but let's make this quick."

"Are you going to finally tell me why you do that? Or do you just like annoying me?"

She shot him an irritated look, as though Jac's questions were spoiling the romantic mystery of their date. "Haven't you ever wondered why the Torrens' casino is called Luckluster?"

"Can't say that I have."

"The Torren blood talent is luck. We can measure it, manipulate it. Every time I flip heads, I know my luck is on the up. The more I've flipped in a row, the luckier I am."

"And when the luck runs out?"

"Good deeds make your luck rise. Bad deeds make it fall." She made a slashing motion across her throat. "Fall too low, and you might even die."

"How has your family lasted as long as they have, then?" Jac asked. "They're as rotten as they come. Um, no offense."

She grinned, showing off the taffy between her teeth. "None taken. And in answer to your question, there are tricks to raise your numbers. I carry charms on me. My cousins have their own methods." She didn't elaborate, but her tone was dark enough that Jac didn't want her to. "It all depends on your conscience, and it's unlucky for me I've got one. Noble cause or not..." She uncapped the bottle of gasoline and started pouring it over the front of the shop. "This is still destruction. We'll need to be fast—my rabbit's foot won't last much longer."

Jac took a deep breath and looked around. The Lull den resembled so many of those he'd seen before, sparsely decorated, with cushions crowding the floor that made it difficult to walk—especially when using. The first thing he did was pick one up, pull at it with two hands, and tear it clean in half. The down feathers drifted onto his boots.

It was very satisfying.

Another cushion—ten, twenty. Then he went for the lights, pulling wires out of the walls, chucking bulbs onto the ground. Every shatter soothed his nerves. He would destroy this place, brick by brick. And, if given the chance, he would destroy the next den, and the next.

He kicked the bar so hard the wood broke through. He let out a shaky, freeing laugh.

When Jac turned around, panting and exhilarated, Sophia was standing by the door with a match in one hand and her coin in the other.

"Wish me luck, Todd." She struck the match and held the flame to her lips, as if giving it a kiss. With her free hand, she flipped the coin, and Jac waited for her to say "seventy-nine."

Instead, she frowned.

"Tails," she whispered, her eyes widening.

Bullets shattered through the window glass.

Sophia screamed and dropped to the ground. The match caught the gasoline, and the den quickly engulfed in flames. Jac swore and ducked behind the remnants of the bar. Sophia rushed toward him, scrambling for cover.

The sound of gunfire rang in his ears. Jac had been beaten, trampled, and stabbed before—never had he been shot. He reached for the pistol in his pocket, but he knew it would be useless against the automatic rifles.

"There's a back exit," she breathed.

"They'll already be there by now, waiting for us," Jac said.

Sophia paled. They couldn't crouch here forever. Even if the bullets didn't kill them, eventually, the fire would. Already the smoke filled the den.

Jac coughed into his sleeve. "What's next door?" he asked.

"A Mistress parlor."

Jac didn't hesitate. He jumped to his feet, took a running start, and kicked at the wall as hard he could. Drywall and cement caved in a haze of dust. He ducked through the hole to the parlor on the other side.

"Come on," he called to Sophia. "Mistress is Augustine-owned. And if I'm right about Vianca, she has secret ways out of all her dens."

He led Sophia to a rear hallway, where he busted through several locked doors. First, a closet. Then a bathroom. Then, at last, a stairwell, leading down into blackness.

Sophia let out an uncharacteristic whimper. "It's so dark."

They didn't have time to stall, so he ignored her comment and pulled her down the stairs. They felt their way lower and lower, until they reached a series of tunnels. Sophia lit a match, her hand shaking, but it offered little light beyond her fingertips.

"Where does this lead?" she asked.

"St. Morse Casino, I'd guess. The Augustines had the tunnels built decades ago."

They walked in silence for several minutes. Behind him, Sophia took deep, steady breaths, in that rhythm of someone forcing themselves to stay calm. Meanwhile, Jac was finally at ease, the scent of Lullaby replaced by the stench of gasoline.

"So how does a girl like you become afraid of the dark?" he wondered aloud.

"We're all afraid of something."

That was probably true, but he wouldn't have guessed it about her. She trembled beside him, the same way he'd trembled when they'd entered Insomnia.

As he studied her in the matchlight, he caught a glimpse of something red on her arm. Sophia wore a lot of red—but this red didn't belong.

"You were grazed," Jac said. He brushed his fingers against the cut, and Sophia winced. "Does it hurt?"

"A little."

"Here." He reached out and pressed his thumb against the wound, staining his skin with blood. The pain seeped into him and settled into his stomach.

She jolted away from him. "How did you do that?"

"It's my split talent. The Dorner side."

"The Dorner..." She shook her head, letting go of whatever she was going to say. "Thank you."

They came upon an exit, a narrow set of stairs leading to the street above. Jac led the way as they climbed and threw open the hatch at the top. They emerged in an alley. A few blocks behind them, smoke billowed into the blue sky.

Jac let out a whooping laugh. He'd committed a lot of crimes, but never one as dangerous as this one. He wondered if they'd freed a few of the prisoners on Chain Street who'd been bound to that den. He hoped so.

"What's next?" he asked, grinning.

Sophia examined the street they'd ended up on. "Don't you live near here?" She laughed at the expression on his face. "Don't look at me like that. It was a question, not an invitation."

"But you've known where I live for 'weeks.'" He mimicked the pitying way she'd spoken earlier.

"You're right. I know you live three blocks down. Sometimes I like to play coy."

Nevertheless, when they began walking, they *did* walk in

the direction of his apartment. Jac came close to asking if she was following him—and why—when he realized she'd only been heading in the direction of a dumpster.

"You don't want what's under these clothes, anyway," she said casually. Then she pulled a half-rotted rabbit's foot from beneath her shirt and threw it in the trash. "Unless you're into that kind of thing."

But Jac was no longer listening, distracted by a sudden idea. This entire time, he'd been balancing his wager between Charles and Delia.

But there was a third Torren.

If Sophia entered the feud and won, she could control the empire long enough to give Harrison his votes, then destroy it after the election.

Jac muttered a goodbye so he could mull over the possibility, and continued toward his apartment.

To his surprised, he found one of the Irons sitting on his front stoop—a runner named Stella. She stood up with a groan. "Finally," she complained. "I've been waiting for over an hour."

Jac's eyes widened as Stella relayed the message from Levi. "All the Irons are invited, of course," she added. "Pup says he'll really do it. And there's a great view of Revolution Bridge from—"

Jac didn't wait for her to finish. Normally, he'd be furious at Levi for devising something so reckless. But, now, a impulsive plan began to form in his mind, pushing all other thoughts aside.

Jac sprinted and caught up to Sophia along the sidewalk of Tropps Street.

"Todd," she said, tilting her head to the side. "Miss me already?"

"You got me—I'm smitten," Jac huffed, resting his hands on his knees to catch his breath. "So do you want to go to a party?"

LEVI

♥ ♠ ♦ ♣

Levi stood on a rooftop porch above the museum, gazing at Revolution Bridge ahead. It hadn't always been the magnificent structure it was now. The statues of famous rebels had been added after the Revolution, their polished bases glinting in the sunlight. It was one of only three bridges in the city wide enough to accommodate motorcar traffic, and sidewalks and benches lined the sides for tourists to sit and take pictures.

Soon it would be gone.

Tock stood behind him, clad in a skintight black party dress. "Is everything arranged?" Levi asked.

"Yes, I bought plenty of hooch."

"That's not what I meant." He should've been excited, he knew. He should've been hearing explosions in his mind like music. After all, he'd envisioned this plan a thousand times over the past two weeks—but in none of those visions had he painted himself a murderer.

"There's nothing *to* arrange," Tock said impatiently. "You just tell me what to blow up, and I'll do it."

"I'd still rather go with you." At least if he was present, he'd feel more in control.

"We talked about this. The whole area will be crawling with whiteboots after the bridge goes down, and you're still too recognizable."

Levi hated that she was right. He hated even more that sitting out meant he'd need to wait here with the Irons, who stared at him as though Chez's blood still stained his clothes.

"And you're sure your explosion will be enough?" Levi had never witnessed Tock's blood talent in action.

"I'm positive," she assured him. "I just need to run fast."

According to Tock, her power worked with touch and time. With a touch, she could lay down a "line," as she called them, and then she fled the initial drop point. The farther she traveled, the more taut the line grew. When she let go... Well, the bigger the snap, the bigger the explosion.

Except, as Tock had told him, there was a time limit. After thirty seconds, the line would snap on its own.

"Don't joke about it," Levi snapped. "Your safety is what matters most tonight." He wouldn't be responsible for another death.

"I don't need anyone to worry about me." She said it like she meant it, but Levi couldn't help but think that everyone needed someone to worry about them once in a while.

Levi rested his hands behind his head and breathed deeply, trying to trust her, trying to relax. "When we met, you told me you don't get scared. Is that really true?"

"Of course," she said matter-of-factly.

"Never mind, then," Levi muttered. He should've known better than to seek comfort from Tock. The party tonight had been her idea, to boost morale. Levi had agreed to it, even if he found it distasteful.

Chez tried to kill you, he reminded himself. His third hadn't been an innocent bystander. This had always been how their story would end: one or the other.

"You care about things too much," Tock told him. "You *want* things too much. What happens once you get everything you want, Levi? Will you be happy then?"

Levi winced. He didn't have an answer to that. Every time he achieved something he'd sought after, he set his sights on something else. He would never get everything he wanted because he would never stop wanting.

"Am I supposed to not care?" he snapped. "Is that your secret?"

"You're supposed to pull yourself together. There's no such thing as destiny. Street legends aren't real. I know you wouldn't mind dying tragically, so drunk poets could sing songs about you in two-volt cabarets, but I don't give a muck about your dreams—you're not allowed to fall apart when thirty kids have *your* tattoos on their arms and *your* bounty on their heads. You think the city revolves around you, but this isn't just your story. It never has been."

Tock's words stung, but only because she was right.

Levi lowered his hands and forced his shoulders to relax. "Fine, but I'm still going to worry."

"That's what all the hooch is for." She slapped him on the back, and he groaned. He wasn't all the way healed yet. "I keep forgetting you're delicate."

"Yep," he choked out.

"Make sure to find yourself a good view. It's time to tell the whiteboots that the North Side is ours."

Several hours later, Levi nursed a Snake Eyes on the top floor of the museum. His drink was supposed to bring luck, and so he planned to drink copiously. They needed good fortune tonight.

Amid the Irons playing cards and eating street cart dinners, Levi heard the door open and the sound of heels clicking on hardwood.

He turned. She always arrived too early.

Enne wore a dark violet dress covered in intricate black beading that shimmered as she walked. Over it, she'd tied a robe made from a fabric so translucent that Levi could still make out the low cut of the back and the shape of her shoulder blades.

Levi supposed the dress was what South Siders might sport to get drunk on champagne and lounge in music parlors. He wouldn't normally consider it his type, but he had also never seen Enne in it. As he watched her approach, Levi tried to remind himself that he'd also invited Jac and Narinder to the celebration.

After all, tonight was for fulfilling promises—not breaking them.

Enne's gaze flickered to his, and he swallowed hard. Levi could nearly see the two weeks of distance between them in her eyes, and each day of his absence sliced into him like a cut.

Then she looked away, and Levi promptly downed the rest of his drink.

Tommy appeared beside him with another Snake Eyes, and Levi relaxed, grateful for the company so he wouldn't stare at Enne from across the room like a fool. "It's getting late," Tommy said.

Levi checked his watch. He was right—Tock should've finished by now. In the view from the window, Revolution Bridge looked unchanged.

He glanced back at Enne. Lola had joined her now, dressed in the same pin-striped suit she'd worn to the Catacombs. She spun a shiny pair of motorcar keys around her fingers. Grace had taken Levi's empty seat at the bar and motioned for the other girls to join her.

Levi's last interaction with them had been far from warm, but even so, he needed something now, from Lola in particular. So he swallowed his nerves and marched toward their group. He laid a friendly hand on Lola's shoulder, hyperaware of Enne standing beside them, though he didn't dare look at her.

Lola peeled his hand off her. "Touch me again, and you'll wind up with a third broken rib."

Levi cleared his throat and shoved his hands in his pockets. "I see you've acquired a car."

"A *car*," Lola repeated, grinning from ear to ear. "Not just any car. A *Houssen*. In black, of course." She dangled the keys in front of his face.

"Good. I need a ride."

"Away from your own party?" she asked.

"I'm not looking for a joyride." Levi lowered his voice. "Tock should've finished by now. I'm worried."

Her expression softened. "Oh, fine," she muttered.

A few minutes later, Lola and Enne climbed into the front seat, with Levi and Grace in the back. The car radio played a jazz tune with a heavy bass as they roared through the narrow alleys of Olde Town in the direction of the river.

"How did you afford this?" Levi rubbed his hands over polished leather.

"Vianca gave me some more volts," Enne said.

"And you *took* them?"

"I wouldn't have needed to if you hadn't wagered all of our plans."

He scoffed. "If you were that desperate for volts, you wouldn't have bought a swanky motorcar."

"Exactly what I said when I saw how Lola spent her third of it," Enne grumbled.

"You said we should be practical!" Lola answered. "A motorcar *is* practical!"

A crowd gathered about a quarter of the mile from the bridge, where whiteboots had quartered people off to prevent them from crossing. Levi spotted Tock wedged among the pedestrians. Neither of them had expected such a large group of spectators—she couldn't lay her fuse if she couldn't get on the bridge.

"Muck," Levi groaned.

"Levi," Enne said nervously, "what's happening here?"

He threw open the door, and the three girls followed him out of the motorcar. "Tock needs to get on that bridge."

Levi spun around, searching for anything he could use. The apartment buildings were bleak and bare, overlooking a large traffic circle and the riverfront beyond it.

His eyes fell on Lola's Houssen.

"What are you doing?" Lola screeched as Levi pushed around her to the front seat.

"I'll buy you a new one." He closed the door, and Lola reached through the window to grab at him.

"Pup, I will *kill* you if—"

"Distract the whiteboots so Tock can get onto the bridge," he said. "And so I don't get shot."

Then, before anyone—even his own logic—could stop him, he slammed his foot down on the pedal. The engine roared, and he lurched forward. As he drove, Levi turned up the radio twice as loud, so loud he felt the bass in his stomach, drowning out all of his fears and thoughts of self-preservation. He aimed the motorcar in the direction of the crowds.

And so he drove, in the direction of his destiny.

The people began to scream and disperse as he roared around

the traffic circle, careful not to hit anyone. He screeched to a halt where the crowd had once been and peeked out the window just long enough to glimpse Tock sprinting across the center of the bridge.

And to spot the whiteboots raising their pistols.

He floored the engine a second time and sped around the circle once again. Bullets pelted the back of the car, shattering the rearview glass. Levi ducked his head down and spun the wheel so he didn't collide with the adjacent building.

As the whiteboots swarmed closer to him, Levi only had a few moments of panic in which to formulate a new plan. Several of the whiteboots had already noticed Tock and begun a pursuit, guns firing. Though the pedestrians were clearing away, many gathered around the edges of the square to watch, and Levi searched their faces for Enne and the others.

In a few moments, Tock could be shot.

In a few moments, he could be, too.

He could surrender, but no—he was wanted dead or alive. That would only doom them both. He needed a bigger distraction. A bigger play. And he needed it now.

The whiteboots raised their guns, and Levi drove again. He'd circle the roundabout over and over if he had to. A bullet punctured his front tire, sending the car into a tilt and spin. Levi cursed as the world funneled around him—buildings and river, buildings and river. He slammed the brakes and slid to a stop mere feet from the Brint's edge.

I should make my escape, he thought. *I should run and trust Tock to do the same.*

But Tock had told him she would blow up the bridge, and he trusted her word more than any other part of his plan. And so he wouldn't abandon her.

Just as the whiteboots raised their guns again, and as Levi braced himself for another stomach-lurching turn around the circle, he spotted Enne behind the building beside him. She motioned to the left, but there was nothing to his left but the river. Then she screamed something at him, and it took him a moment to make out her words.

"Get out!" In her right hand, she waved a gun.

But the whiteboots were already firing, and so Levi could do nothing but duck. The glass windshield shattered.

Then he spotted something on the floor. A history book, thicker than a North Side brick.

Levi lurched open the driver's side door, slammed the book down on the gas pedal, and flung himself out of the motorcar. He hollered in pain when he landed on his side, then swallowed it down as he shakily got to his feet. The car sped forward, and the whiteboots leaped to get out of its path. Levi sprinted to the right, in the direction of Enne, but just before he reached out to grab her and pull her away with him, she fired her gun.

Her bullet hit the motorcar just as it slammed into the roundabout's obelisk, and Lola's shiny black Houssen exploded into flames.

"Nice shot," he said in awe.

"Terrible driving," she answered.

BOOM!

It was the loudest, sweetest sound Levi had ever heard. The streets around them shook violently as Revolution Bridge collapsed inward on itself, wires snapping and columns crumbling into the murky waters of the Brint. Levi would've waited to watch every single stone fall, but Enne's hand was already pulling him into a run. They turned a corner and met up with the other girls.

We did it, he thought, victoriously punching the air in front of him.

Then Enne slapped him across the face.

He stared at her for a moment, shocked. "What was that for?" he asked, rubbing his bruised cheek.

"That was for Lola's motorcar."

She slapped him a second time.

"And that was for almost getting killed."

"I told her I'd buy her a new one," he said sheepishly. To her other point, he had no defense.

"We should get back to the museum," Grace said. "The whiteboots will be looking for you."

"I need to wait for Tock," Levi told her.

"Tock ended up on the South Side. They'll close all the bridges and ferries," Lola countered. "What's she gonna do? Swim?"

Levi plucked a shard of glass off his suit jacket. "I can't see Tock missing a party."

"Then we should wait for her there. That's where she'd go."

Levi hated that they were right. Right now, the Irons were probably popping champagne bottles and cheering at the black-stained sky. Somewhere across the city, Jonas was scowling, and Harrison was impressed. Levi had won his wager with the other lords and earned himself the respect he'd always wanted from the North Side, but none of that would matter if Tock had paid the ultimate price for it.

But she'd asked him to trust her. And so Levi swallowed down his nerves and followed the girls home.

LEVI

The party erupted into cheers as Levi entered, and the loudest among them was Tock.

Levi rubbed his eyes, certain she was some kind of trick. Her party dress was damp, her short hair frizzy and air-dried, and she wore a blanket draped over her shoulders. Apart from a bandage on her right elbow, she otherwise looked fine. The Irons crowded around her, screaming and slapping her on the back.

"How are you here?" Levi sputtered.

Tock wrapped her arm around his shoulder and raised her Gambler's Ruin. "To Pup!" she shouted.

"To Pup!" the room chorused. Levi was too excited and relieved to cringe at the sound of his nickname. Glasses clinked, and every Iron rushed to congratulate him or shake his hand.

The next fifteen minutes were a whirlwind. Before Levi knew it, he had a glass of something cold in his hand. Music started playing as Tock explained her spectacular rescue—how she'd fallen into the Brint and was dragged to shore in the arms of a handsome whiteboot who'd mistaken her for a victim in her sequined party dress. And so while Levi had walked the mile home in zigzagged, backtracked patterns in case they were followed, Tock had received a personal escort.

"Pup! Pup!" the Irons called, pounding their fists onto card tables like a drumroll. He turned around, a thrill shooting through him. It seemed unbelievable that only two and a half weeks ago, these same gangsters had cursed his name. As he turned and climbed onto a poker table, whiskey glass in hand, he could barely remember why.

Levi had always been the Iron Lord, but now, it finally meant something.

Before he could begin his speech, the door across the room opened, and Jac walked inside. He was dressed in the swanky plaid suit Enne had bought for him, a cigarette hanging out of his mouth and his arm wrapped around a girl Levi didn't recognize.

Levi's chest swelled with pride. The Irons were all here.

He lifted his glass in a toast.

"Twenty-five years ago," he started, "revolutionaries tore the Mizer palace down and marched across Revolution Bridge. And all this time, they've left the North Side to burn."

Hollers chorused throughout the room. Levi swigged the rest of his drink before continuing, then wiped the whiskey off his lips.

"The South and the North," he mused. "No matter how many parks and universities they build, none of it matters. The North reigns. The capital of the Republic isn't New Reynes— it's the City of Sin." Boots thumped on the floor, and glasses clinked in cheers. "But who owns the North Side?"

No one responded, and Levi hadn't expected them to. The answer was no one—the North Side was divided. But he'd convinced every lord to bet on his wager, and so soon the gangs would be united. And the Irons would be rich.

"The whiteboots killed eight people, people the papers have labeled as gangsters," Levi said. "And now the Irons have claimed vengeance." He raised his glass again to Tock across the room, and the others cheered for her. "Scavenger and Ivory didn't think this was possible. They bet against us, but we all know what happens when you play against an Iron."

"You get played!" a few dealers shouted.

He raised his now empty glass. "Why beat your enemies when you can own them?"

As everyone toasted for the last time, Levi's eyes fell on the only group that hadn't joined in—specifically, on the girl in the middle, laughing over a martini glass of something pink and bubbly. As he stumbled off the table, Levi got it into his head that he should thank her. She'd helped him pull off his stunt tonight—maybe even saved his life. He remembered how cleanly her bullet had torn through the Houssen's combustion engine, even while it was in motion. When had she learned to shoot like that?

As he passed through the crowd, receiving slaps on the back and applause all around, the door opened once more. Narinder walked inside, dressed plainly in an oversize black shirt. It wasn't exactly a party outfit, but Levi figured he had enough swagger for the both of them. He delayed his plans of gratitude and walked toward the musician. Narinder was always good-looking, but tonight, he seemed almost painfully so. Burning with victory and whiskey, Levi pulled him in for a kiss.

But as Narinder drew away, Levi realized that he wasn't really looking at him. He was looking at Tock, relief relaxing the tightness of his expression.

"You're late," Levi said, grinning and twisting his fingers through Narinder's belt loops.

"Do you think we could talk in private?" Narinder asked.

Levi frowned. This was his party, and Narinder knew how much this meant to him.

"We could have a drink first," Levi suggested.

"You've already had too much to drink."

Levi was buzzed, not drunk. He was just in a good mood. "Fine, but I don't know why you're in such a rush. The Catacombs can live without you for a night." He followed Narinder out into the hallway and toward one of the empty spare rooms. The parts of Levi that were tipsy realized what exactly they could get up to in such a place, and he was suddenly in less of a hurry to return to the party.

"Do you have a death wish?" Narinder asked him. His face was unreadable as Levi slid his arms around his waist.

"It's the opposite. I wish to *live*." He could hear an edge in Narinder's voice, but if he were really angry, he wouldn't let Levi press himself against him. He wouldn't let Levi trail his lips from his tattoo down his neck. "I can tell you don't like it," Levi said teasingly. He felt the tension in Narinder's shoulders disappearing. "But I can also tell you *do*."

Narinder laughed, but it was hollow. "I see what you're doing."

"I'm seducing you until you relent and agree to stay. A trick out of your own book, to be fair." Levi pressed his lips to Narinder's, easing them open with his tongue. "We should celebrate. It's finally…it's finally all happening." His voice cracked a bit, and he swallowed his wave of emotions in embarrassment.

Narinder sighed, a sound of both of exasperation and surrender. Normally, he took the lead, but for once, Levi wanted to do to Narinder what Narinder always did to him. As he unbuttoned his collar, slid his hand behind his neck, and pulled him closer, Levi aimed to make Narinder's head foggy, to make his heart race with thrill and recklessness, to make him feel the same sense of destiny Levi felt each time he walked into Olde Town. He wanted to impart all of this with a kiss, and lose themselves until the morning.

But then Narinder broke away. "You could've died. *Tock* could've died."

"I know that," Levi said quietly. "But we didn't."

"You can't just risk yourselves like that. You told me not to worry about your plan. But when I heard…" He fiddled with Levi's belt angrily, and Levi put out a hand to stop him.

"What did you come here for?" Levi demanded. "To yell at me? Or something else?"

"I… I don't know." When Narinder tried to reach for him again, Levi backed away.

"I don't get it. All this talk about protecting Olde Town—you never really mean any of it."

"I *do* mean it. But that's not what you're doing, is it? You're setting the city on fire to claim what's left behind."

The words pierced Levi deeper than Narinder probably intended. Levi wasn't like the other lords, so Narinder had told him this morning—and Narinder didn't even know about Chez.

"I would go to *your* party, if you asked," Levi told him.

"I believe that," Narinder said. "But would you also *not* do something, if I asked?"

It seemed a comparable request, but really, it wasn't. Levi would take the world on his shoulders if it meant helping someone he cared about, but as Tock had told him, he couldn't slow down, couldn't afford to fall apart. He had a destiny to reach, and Narinder could either keep up or watch him walk away.

"It's good I'm not asking you to, then," Narinder murmured. He placed his hand on Levi's shoulder, but Levi swatted him away.

"What are you asking of me, then?" Levi said. "What even are we to each other?"

"What do you want us to be?" Narinder asked, and Levi grimaced.

"More than this."

Something in Narinder's restraint seemed to snap. "You always want more. You can't have everything, Levi. You can't invite all the city's gangsters into my club and expect me to welcome it. You can't throw yourself and my cousin in danger and expect me to applaud you for it." Narinder rubbed his temples. "You're honest, and you're clever, and you're ambitious, but you're also selfish. You didn't even know my name after we first met. And after weeks into this, it's still you doing all the talking, and me doing all the listening."

This wasn't how today was supposed to go, Levi thought desperately. First the news about Chez, and now Narinder chose tonight to lay into him?

"I didn't realize I was such a burden," Levi growled. "No wonder you kiss me all the time. That must shut me up, right?"

Narinder's face darkened. "I didn't meant it like that, and you know it."

"Did you ever mean *any* of it?" Levi was talking about more than just Narinder's words, and he was already making his way to the door. He could find a new club. A new connection. A new distraction. "All that stuff you said to me about Olde Town? Tock *cares* about something now. The Irons—well, we're all still broke, but soon we won't be. And they're *happy*—"

"I thought I cared about those things," Narinder said. "But I guess...maybe I don't. Not enough for the worry."

Levi clenched his fist as he reached for the doorknob. Then he whipped around. "Tock won't leave."

"I know that," he said darkly. "And I regret that, now."

What Levi had liked about Narinder—more than the connections and the opportunity—was that he'd actually seen good in him. But all he saw in Narinder's eyes now was wariness, and the worst part was that Levi was starting to believe he deserved it.

He kept pulling himself together only to fall apart.

"I can't do this anymore," Levi said suddenly, his voice hitched. "I'm done."

Narinder let out a long sigh, and it almost sounded like relief. That only infuriated Levi more. Narinder might complain that Levi did all the talking, but clearly he'd wanted Levi to say the words for him.

"My mother always told me to stay away from gangsters," Narinder said, as though Levi really was just like the other lords. "Because first they break the rules, then they break your bones...and then they break your heart."

"Your mother was right," Levi snapped, slamming the door behind him.

He stormed back into the party with a bitter taste in his mouth. A few more cheers went around at his reappearance, and he tried to manage a smile in return. But Narinder's words kept coursing through his mind. It didn't matter what he'd accomplished—there was blood on his hands, and there always would be. Levi knew exactly who and what he wanted to be, but in the end, his story was being written for him.

Levi circled around the bar and grabbed the bottle of bourbon. As he poured himself a new drink, a girl in a red dress leaned over, dark curls nearly spilling into his glass.

"I bet you've looked better," she said.

Levi recognized her as the girl Jac had brought and gave her a tight-lipped smile. "I can't always be as dashing as the stories."

He remembered that he'd promised Harrison to have a decision about the Torrens by tomorrow, so he searched the room for Jac. Instead, his gaze fell on another face: Mansi. When she locked eyes with Levi, any remnants of his triumphant mood sank until they hit bottom.

Then he noticed something even worse—she wore bandages around both her forearms, where her Iron tattoos were. The gauze peeked out from beneath her sleeves, stained red.

He swallowed as she crossed the room to his side. "'Lo, Mansi."

"Is it true?" she hissed. "Were you stealing from the Irons for your scam?"

The alcohol no longer sat still in his stomach. "What? Why would you ask that?"

"I don't want to challenge you," she warned.

Levi leaned in so no one could hear them over the music. Gangsters didn't casually throw around the word *challenge*. It was a duel to the death for lordship. Chez had nearly killed Levi during their duel, until Levi later ended the challenge on his own terms. He'd always thought of Mansi as his protégée, but she stood by and watched as Chez kicked him over and over. When it came down to it, she'd chosen Chez. And maybe she was making that choice again now.

"I don't want to fight you, either," Levi rasped.

"Even if I tell everyone what you did?"

She pulled a knife out of her pocket and flipped it expertly between her fingers, just like Chez once had. Levi had taught Mansi how to deal cards, but it seemed he hadn't been her only mentor.

"Even then," he said, and he meant it.

"If you're wondering how I know, it's because you missed the same loose end again. He sends his congratulations about the bridge." Then she turned and walked away, and when the door closed behind her, Levi knew it would not open again.

The same loose end. Levi and Enne had already forgotten about Jonas once, and now he'd made the same mistake again—of course Jonas had known the details of Levi's investment scheme. Reymond had been Levi's business partner.

"Congratulations," Levi muttered to himself. He grabbed his bottle off the bar and skulked off to an armchair in the room's corner, to watch the rest of the party from his broken throne.

JAC

♥   ♠   ♦   ♣

Even with all the Irons' past glory, Jac had never seen his gang celebrate like this. Drunk and obnoxious, the party was exactly the sort he and Levi would've fantasized about years ago, when all their dreams revolved around cheap liquor and dropping volts on outrageous, one-night sprees. Jac's eighteenth birthday had recently passed, but that didn't seem a good enough explanation for why he looked around the room and suddenly felt old.

Sophia perched on the edge of the bar, shaking a mixer, flanked by Enne and her girls. She was the only one here who knew how to make a Hotsy-Totsy, some South Side drink Enne liked that was basically a Snake Eyes with so much syrup it tasted like cotton candy. The five of them stood in the room's corner, away from the rest of the crowd.

"I don't get this," Grace mumbled. "He'd be dead if it weren't for you. Where's your applause?"

"He'll thank me later," Enne answered. But Levi had been absent for some time. Jac suspected he was lost among his admirers, showing off card tricks and counting how many hands he could shake.

"I owned a motorcar for a grand total of four hours," Lola said bitterly. She polished her harmonica with a bar napkin.

"You shouldn't have bought it in the first place," Enne chided. "What a waste."

"You're the one who planted the idea in my head."

"I heard it was a Houssen," Jac told her, smirking. "I knew you didn't have taste, but if you ask me, it's for the best that Levi—"

"Shut up, Polka Dots," Lola snapped.

Sophia slid Enne her drink. "I'm in the mood to dance. Everyone else is dancing."

Jac had brought Sophia to introduce her to Levi and convince them both of his plan, but so far he'd spent the entire night gaping at her in that red dress.

"I'll dance," he said, trying to sound casual.

Lola rolled her eyes. "You can't dance."

"How do you know?" Jac challenged.

"I know things."

"Lola, you have no room to talk," Enne told her in between sips of her Hotsy-Totsy. "You're as lithe as a lead pipe."

Lola stood up, several shades of pink. Jac realized he'd never seen her drink before. Apparently she was a lightweight. "I'll prove you both wrong." Then she tripped and slammed awkwardly into the person beside her.

Grace snorted. "I think you both broke her."

The person caught Lola by the shoulder. Jac recognized her as Tock, though she dressed far more nicely than when they'd last run into her at Liver Shot. She smelled like the Brint mixed with cheap perfume.

Tock hoisted Lola back up and looked her over. "I don't really know you," she told her. "But I could."

Lola flushed a shade so bright it matched her hair. Both Grace and Enne choked on their drinks.

"Um," Lola sputtered.

Tock nodded at Lola's harmonica. "Do you play? I brought my sax."

Lola nodded, looking dazed, and let Tock lead her away into the party.

Jac had no intention of being upstaged by Lola, aspiring librarian, so he pulled Sophia away from her set-up of mixed drinks and loose candy wrappers. "We need to talk," he told her.

When they reached the dance floor, Sophia slid her arms around his shoulders. "Then let's talk," she said.

Having her so close to him made his heart squeeze nervously. He wasn't Levi—he wasn't the one who came up with the plans. He suddenly had sick feeling he was about to make a fool of himself.

"I don't think your plan for Delia and Charles to destroy each other is going to work," he told her.

She pursed her lips. "Way to kill the romance, Todd."

Jac coughed out an awkward laugh. "Even if one of them kills the other, one of them *will* win, and then what will you do?"

"I'll do what I've been doing—I'll weasel my way into their inner circle. I know them better than anyone—"

"But they don't know who *you* are, so how can you really know them?" Sophia had told Jac they were half siblings, so Jac assumed Sophia must've grown up estranged. But clearly there was something she hadn't told him.

A dark look crossed her face, and she dropped her arms from his shoulders. "Why are you asking me these questions? You haven't told anyone who I am, right?"

"No. No, of course not," he said quickly. He wasn't good at

this. He was losing her. "But I have a better idea for how de-stroy your family." Jac peeked over his shoulder, but the Irons were too lost in their dancing and card games to pay them any attention. Still, he leaned closer and explained Levi's agree-ment with Harrison Augustine.

Sophia's green eyes widened in shock. "That's who you were going to call last night. You were going to give him Delia's name."

"I *was*, but I've decided to wait. I'm working for Harrison as a favor to Levi, but I keep feeling like all I'm doing is helping another monster rise to power. I don't want to be complicit."

"So what *do* you want?" Sophia asked.

"I want it to be *you*. You should become the next don."

Sophia backed away, out of his reach. "I can't do that."

"But you *could*. You're their sister! You have as much claim as they do. And after the election is over, we can burn it. All of it."

Jac flushed. Maybe he shouldn't have said "we." This was why Jac was never the smooth talker—he didn't open up; he unraveled.

"But this is suicide." Her voice was high-pitched, and she trembled the same way she had in the tunnels beneath the Mistress parlor. Maybe her fear of the dark and the fear of her siblings were one and the same. "They can't know who I am. If they find out…"

"You've been getting close to Delia for months," Jac pointed out. "There's always been that risk."

"Close enough to interfere, yes, but to *rival* them?" She let out a strained, hopeless laugh. "You either underestimate them, or you overestimate me."

Jac had witnessed enough of Delia's twisted laboratory to know to fear her and her brother, but that was *him*. Where was Sophia's easy confidence? He'd never seen her this vulnerable.

"Everyone at Liver Shot eats out of the palm of your hand. You bet on and win every fighting match." One of the other dancers bumped into them, causing them to stumble even closer together. Jac caught Sophia by the side and steadied her, and her chest pressed against his. He swallowed and tried to focus. "You're the most confident person I've ever—"

"That's because I'm *lucky*," she snapped at him. "I told you how my talent works. Of course I win all my bets. I was lucky I got my promotion. Lucky we made it out of that den today alive."

Jac's hands started to sweat. He wasn't convincing her—he was only making her angry.

"And I might be lucky," Sophia continued, "but Delia and Charles are *invincible*. It doesn't matter how many charms I have—their methods are much more effective than mine. I'll never outplay them. I'll only expose myself and undermine everything I've worked for."

Jac recognized the fear in her voice. It was the overwhelming nausea he'd felt when he walked onto Chain Street this afternoon. It was the nightmares that woke him up in cold sweats. It was when he took the long way home simply to avoid certain places.

Jac had felt that terror when he agreed to enter the Torren empire, and clearly, Sophia had, too. And they'd both braved that fear in order to do something they believed in.

That made them the same.

If Sophia could confront him and show him that he could want more, that he could *be* more, then he could do the same for her.

"It meant something to me today, to burn down that den," Jac said quietly.

Sophia averted her eyes. "I know that."

"Why did *you* want to do it?"

"Because they're both monsters, and they're my family. It's my responsibility to bring them down." She hugged her arms to herself. Jac got the feeling he was watching her unravel, too. "I've already sacrificed so much to do this—more than you could ever guess. I owe it to myself to make those sacrifices worth it."

After a moment of hesitation, he grabbed her hands and squeezed them reassuringly. All it had taken was the smell of gasoline, and Jac's decision had been sealed. He would do whatever it took to see Luckluster Casino and all the Torren dens reduced to rubble.

Maybe he didn't know Sophia well; maybe she didn't know him. But if they were both bound to this path, then they might as well walk it together.

"I won't tell you what to do," he said, "but if you choose this, then I'll help you every step of the way."

She looked down to where their hands touched, and her expression softened. "But it's not the same for you. All you need to do is give Harrison a name and leave. You're not in it like I am. You could go back to..." She crinkled her nose and looked around the room. "Overly greased hair and suits with the tags still on."

He grinned wryly. "Well, I won't pretend like the Irons are a class act—"

"That girl is literally vomiting in the corner." Sophia nodded at Stella, who was indeed bent over a waste bin.

"I..." Jac couldn't argue about the Irons, but she was wrong about him. He was at a party surrounded by friends but feeling like an outsider, because what he wanted wasn't here anymore.

"I could get a new job," he murmured, "but I could never *leave*. There will never be a time when I walk past Chain Street and don't get chills. When I won't have nightmares that send me into a spiral for days. When I won't wake up telling myself I have to fight, that I never get to stop fighting."

Sophia bit her lip. "You're right. Of course you're right." She squeezed his hand, and it made his stomach tie in knots. "I'll do it," she murmured. "But if I regret this several hours from now, I'll blame you and that face of yours."

"What's wrong with my face?"

"Nothing, and it's very upsetting."

Jac grinned as he led her to the corner of the room, where Levi sat, staring into the bottom of his glass.

"'Lo," Jac said to him.

"'Lo," Levi echoed, not looking up.

Jac had no idea why Levi would be sulking at his own party, but what he had to say couldn't wait for Levi's mood to improve. He cleared his throat. "I want you to meet someone. This is my boss."

Levi took a look at their hands and raised an eyebrow. Then he wearily set his glass down and stood up. "I'm glad you came—I've been meaning to talk to you. Harrison needs a name by tomorrow. He wants to meet and everything. I know it hasn't been long—"

Jac cleared his throat a second time. "That's actually why I came over. This is—"

"Sophia Torren," she finished for him, holding out a taffy as an offering. All her nervousness from earlier had vanished, as though confidence was a switch Sophia could simply turn on and off. When Levi just stared at her instead of reaching for the candy, she dropped it into his empty glass. "I'm going to be the next Torren Family donna."

ENNE

♥ ♠ ◆ ♣

Enne's stomach was still recovering from her drunken gossip with Poppy that morning, but she sipped her Hotsy-Totsy, anyway. It was an excuse to sit even as the party grew wilder around her. She wasn't in the mood to dance. She wanted to think.

Her bullet had provided the diversion needed for Levi to escape and for Tock to destroy the bridge. It wasn't that Enne was bitter about their lack of gratitude—well, she definitely *was* bitter—but she couldn't stop replaying the moment in her mind when she'd fired. When she squeezed a gun in her hand, she felt capable. She felt *powerful*.

Her thoughts drifted back to her familiar fantasy: the figures of the Phoenix Club disappearing around her like smoke. This time, they vanished in a puff of gunpowder.

"Are you just going to sit there and mope all night?" Grace demanded.

"I haven't been moping," she answered. It'd be nice to share her thoughts with Grace, but Grace had yet to swear to her, which meant there was still so much about Enne that she didn't know.

"That was a good shot earlier." Grace peered around the room, and her gaze settled on one of the tables. She winked at Enne. "I'm sure there are more ways to upstage the Irons. Do you know any card games?"

"Just one," Enne answered darkly.

"Well, you should play a game of Tropps with me. I already know what I'll bet."

"And what is that?"

"My oath."

Enne stiffened in surprise. "You shouldn't bet that on a card game."

Enne expected Grace to laugh, but instead she asked, "Why not?"

"Because swearing to me is about more than loyalty. There are…secrets. Things you don't know." Grace had worked as an assassin. She wore weapons as though they were accessories. But when she learned the truth, would she also look at Enne differently? As a danger to them all?

Enne's secrets always seemed to push everyone away.

Rather than argue, Grace grabbed Enne's hand and dragged her through the crowd. The air smelled of spilled bourbon, sweat, and cigarettes, and it was hot from the many bodies pressed together.

They approached a table and slid into the two available seats, Enne in between Grace and a pretty-faced card dealer.

Grace slid an orb into the pot, and it glowed dimly with a couple volts. "We'll be boring for now. Loser has to buy the other dinner."

Enne nodded shakily and took the hand the dealer slid her.

You may take your cards.

She heard Malcolm Semper's voice as though he stood behind her, and her hands trembled as she stared at her hand. But they were only normal playing cards. This was only a game.

The dealer shot her a charming, lopsided smile. He had dimples and a dusting of freckles beneath his eyes. "You look nervous. Have you ever played before?"

Enne shook her head.

His face lit up, and he began to explain the rules. "All players, as you can see, start with three cards. Every round, you'll be given a new card if you continue to bet." As Enne leaned in to show him her cards and ask a question, he pushed them away with a laugh. "This isn't like blackjack or poker. In Tropps, the dealer is another player in the game. You can't go showing me your hand."

But even as Enne lowered her cards, he continued to lean closer. Enne might not have minded if she wasn't so on edge. He was attractive, and he had a smile full of innocent intentions, but Enne knew better than to believe that about an Iron.

They played for a few rounds. Each time Enne reached for a new card, she held her breath, preparing for a Shadow Card's vision to take over. Every so often, she looked across the table, expecting to see Levi, sickly and draining of life.

"This party is mostly Irons," the dealer told her. "How do you know Pup?"

"We're friends," she mumbled. Friends who'd barely spoken in weeks.

"They're not close," Grace said, then nudged Enne sharply in the ribs, scooting her another inch closer to the dealer. Enne shot her a stormy look.

"Didn't you come back with him?" The dealer furrowed his eyebrows. "I remember, when he came back from the bridge, you were behind him."

Enne was surprised anyone had noticed them at all, amid the hollers and cheers for Levi.

"I was there," she told him drily, turning away from him and attempting to focus, once more, on the game. This was supposed to be a party, but all Enne felt was irritated. "I was there for all of it."

"At the bridge?"

Enne should've been more careful, but she couldn't help herself. "For the bridge. For the meeting at the Catacombs. For the death of Semper." As she spoke, the image of Semper behind her vanished, like a bullet tearing through smoke.

Enne didn't know much about the game, but she had a pair of queens, and she was certain that counted for something. "Fifth round is the first reveal, right?" She threw the pair down on the table, then scooted the extra inch closer to the dealer, close enough that their legs touched.

But the dealer was no longer paying attention. He stared at the cards, or maybe at the table—anywhere but at her.

He swallowed uncomfortably. "I…" His eyes flickered to something over her shoulder, and he quickly stood up, stumbling over a chair leg. Enne supposed others might find his clumsiness charming, but his lopsided smile seemed rehearsed, the more she saw it.

"I'll take over this game, Tommy."

A drink was thrust into the dealer's hands, which he nervously accepted before hurrying off.

Levi slid into his place and collected the cards. "Why don't we start over?" he asked, but the players, too, were leaving the table.

"Look who finally graced us with his presence," Grace said flatly.

Levi ignored her and shuffled the cards, cascading them nimbly between his fingers. Enne stared at the bit of silver peeking out of his breast pocket. She'd been given a similar card by Sedric Torren, but she'd left hers behind in the House of Shadows. It only brought bad memories, and she didn't want to wear her pain like a trophy. She wondered if that's how Levi looked back on the night that haunted her—just another victory, just another story.

Levi dealt out hands for only him and her. Grace cleared her throat. "What about me?" she asked.

"I'd like to talk to Enne," he said. He had a seriousness to his voice that told her he'd come to talk about business. That was what they were after all—business partners. Nothing more.

Enne nodded for Grace to leave, and then she and Levi were alone.

"I'm going to send messengers to the other lords," he told her. "We need to meet again. Tomorrow night. And if they're true to their word, they'll open up twenty percent to your market."

"You shouldn't have put my plan on the line like that," Enne snapped at him. "You had no right."

"They were going to decline it. It's thanks to me they now have to give it a chance."

"And what would you have done today if I hadn't been there? I have nothing to thank you for."

Levi pursed his lips. This would've been the perfect opportunity to actually thank her, but he seemed intent on ignoring it. "Are you prepared? Because I already made a list of businesses to ask to invest."

"That's great. You can give the list to Grace. She'll help me take care of it."

Maybe she was even more bitter than she'd thought. Enne sifted through her cards so she could look at something other than him wincing.

"I want to help you, Enne." He whispered her name—it wasn't an apology, but there was fear in his voice.

"Do you?" she asked. "Because I never hear from you. You've been keeping secrets. How did you get the whiteboots to evacuate Revolution Bridge? Why aren't there any whiteboots in Olde Town?"

He stiffened. "I can't tell you that. It's too—"

"Dangerous?" she guessed, letting out a quiet laugh. She squeezed her cards so hard they bent. "If we were really in this together, we actually would be—risk *and* reward." She didn't want to be the forgotten face in Levi's legends. Being partners was a pretty thought, but if it wasn't meant to be, then she would rather become a legend on her own.

"You're right." He put his hand on hers and pried her fingers away from the cards. She hadn't realized she'd been trembling. "Why don't we leave? I don't want anyone to overhear."

That proposition seemed dangerous in its own way, but even so, Enne nodded and let him lead her out of the party. They crept down the corridor into an empty room, one that was still uncleaned and coated in broken window glass. Levi closed the door behind them, silencing the music. A breeze from outside swept through the room, sticky and smelling of the sea.

"I didn't want to tell you this. Because Vianca *can't* know." Levi paused. "This is the part where you agree with me. That you're too easily compromised. That I shouldn't tell you."

"No, I think you should," Enne said indignantly. She blew a sweaty strand of hair out of her face.

Levi sighed and walked toward what remained of the windows. Enne measured the distance between them and took a step back to make it wider.

"The morning after the Shadow Game," Levi started, "I met Harrison Augustine, and I made a deal with him."

Enne's thoughts returned to Worner Prescott's party that afternoon, how Vianca had trembled under the scrutinizing, judgmental gazes of everyone in the room. Levi was playing with fire.

"So that's why there aren't any whiteboots in Olde Town?" she asked. "That's why the bridge was already cleared?"

Levi nodded. "I didn't want to tell you because—"

"Because it's another secret to keep from Vianca," she finished. Admittedly, that was a worthwhile reason. If the tables were reversed, she wasn't sure she'd have behaved any differently. "But...if she *does* find out..." A shiver of fear ran down her spine. Maybe—as irritating as it was to admit—he shouldn't have told her after all. "She'll kill you, Levi."

He snorted. "Vianca would never kill me."

"You didn't see her today, since Harrison's candidacy was announced. She was humiliated...and furious." All that belief in legacy, and her legacy had betrayed her.

"Even so, we won't need to worry about Vianca forever. Harrison intends to kill her."

Enne's eyes widened. It felt wrong to wish for murder, but Vianca Augustine was an exception. "When?"

"After the election, should he win," Levi said. He leaned against the wall, his gaze fixed out the window. "I can't be the one to pull the trigger, but I'll help him...in whatever way I can. It's not just about my freedom—it's also about yours. I want to make that right."

"I don't blame you for introducing me to Vianca," she murmured. "You know that."

His expression told her he felt otherwise. Despite everyone in the museum toasting his triumph, Levi looked ill. His eyes were sunken, and his voice weak.

"You were sent to the Shadow Game for no fault of your own, but I wasn't," he said. "I'd cheated half the city. And I can't take back the things I did to you, or to Chez, or to Reymond, but I *can* make penance."

She'd had no idea Levi felt that way. Maybe she'd been too harsh with him. It'd been hard not to look at this party and the silver card in his pocket and assume his fame had gone to his head.

"I don't think you made that many mistakes, Levi," she told him, joining him beside the window. The cool air made chills creep across her skin. "You're just punishing yourself. I was at the Shadow Game for hurting Sedric Torren—and not just because Vianca made me. Because I *wanted* to hurt him."

Levi shook his head. "I found out this morning that Chez died from the wounds I gave him. Sedric deserved to die—Chez didn't."

Enne stilled. "Do the Irons know?"

"Everyone knows."

"But...the party... I thought Chez used to look after them."

"He did." Levi's voice was distant, somewhere else. "For months at the end of the scheme, I was paying my way out by stealing from the Irons. And I'm scared there's nothing I can do to make up for that."

Enne could never imagine stealing from her friends, but Levi had been desperate. Before she'd come to New Reynes, he'd suffered Vianca alone.

"Did Chez know?" Enne asked.

Levi shook his head. "He would've tried to kill me much earlier, if he had. Mansi found out, and now she's gone. I don't blame her."

Enne was about to tell him that she didn't think any less of him, that she *knew* him. He was loyal and clever and good, and no matter what mistakes he'd made in his past, he deserved his successes now. She was even about to reach for him, her own embarrassment and bitterness be damned.

But then he continued. "There's something else. Harrison wants information on the Torren Family. He asked me to send someone inside their empire, to find out who the next don would be. Someone I could trust."

"Jac," she said. The person Levi trusted most in the world.

"He wouldn't want me telling you this." He sighed and rested his head against the doorframe. "But I think it's important you understand why I've done what I have."

"You don't need to keep making me understand. I don't think you're half as terrible as you seem to. Selfish and infuriating, maybe, but not terrible."

He smiled weakly. "A few years ago, Jac was working a job that got him mixed up with Lullaby, a Torren-owned drug— one sold all up and down Chain Street."

Enne's breath hitched. She hadn't known that.

"He was addicted for almost a year. It happened around the same time I started working for Vianca, so I hardly ever saw him. Sometimes he'd disappear for weeks on end. He ran himself broke. Every time we met, I didn't know which Jac I would face—the one lulled and empty, or the one who was withdrawing...and *angry*. For a while, I hated him. He'd say awful things. He'd go through these cycles over and over, until it nearly killed him." Levi drew in a shuddering breath, a haunted look crossing his face. "After I dragged him out of that place and he realized he'd overdosed, he promised he'd get clean. And he did."

Enne stared at the sparkling city skyline because it was easier than looking at him. "And after all of that, you sent him to the Torrens?" In some ways, that seemed a worse crime than killing Chez. Jac was Levi's *best friend*.

"I never should've asked him to do this. But he agreed. He *wanted* to do it." Levi squeezed his hands into a fist. "So if one more person smiles at me or cheers for me, I think I'll be sick again."

Enne noted the word *again* and softened her voice. He

didn't need someone else to hate him when he clearly already hated himself. "Lucky for you I wasn't going to do either of those things."

"What will you do then? Leave?"

"Do you want me to leave?"

He laughed hollowly. "No. I want everyone else to leave, but not you."

Enne tried not to dwell on what his words could mean. He was the one who'd taught her to second-guess herself.

"I thought the deal with Harrison would make me feel more in control. And then the wager with the other lords. What happened today at the bridge." He closed his eyes. "I don't feel in control."

"For what it's worth," she told him, "I forgive you. I forgive the terrible choices you made, even if you don't forgive yourself. Because I understand why you made them, more than Mansi or Jac or anyone. I know what it's like to feel helpless around Vianca. I know how it feels to have no control."

For the first time since they entered the room, he turned to look at her, and the city lights shining through the window cast splintered shadows across his face.

"You understand better than anyone," he murmured. "But you have no idea how hard it is to control *myself*, when…"

He stepped closer, close enough to touch her, and Enne didn't trust herself to move. She shouldn't still want him, not after the rejection, the secrets, but it was hard not to reach for him. And so she focused her gaze on the floor and the shards of glass beneath their shoes, reminding her how easily another move could cut.

"I don't…" Levi swallowed and slid his hand around her waist, pulling her into him. His hand cupped her cheek, and he tilted her chin up to look at him and the distress in his eyes. "I don't accept your forgiveness."

He squeezed the fabric of her dress, making its sleeve slip from her shoulder. Gently, he slid her hair to the side and brushed his lips against her bare skin. She shivered. All of his touches were slow and deliberate, as if he'd given each of them some thought. And that realization enraged her.

He wanted her. He'd wanted her even when he'd told her he didn't. He'd wanted her even while he'd spent his nights with someone else.

She wanted to slap him. She wanted to kiss him and draw an apology from between his lips.

Instead, she whispered. "You're still keeping secrets." Because Levi was right—she understood better than anyone, and so she was the only one with the power to forgive him. And that meant there was another secret he still hadn't told her.

He froze, his forehead pressed against hers. "You're right," he breathed, but he didn't move. "Before Jac agreed to the job, he made me promise something in return. And so... I told him I wouldn't... That I wouldn't be with..."

Enne didn't need to ask him what he meant. It was obvious from the way his hand tightened around her waist, tugging her closer when there was no space left between them. The truth wasn't that he wanted her. The truth was that he wanted her, and it ate at him.

She *should* kiss him, just to break his promise and see if it broke him, too.

Instead, Enne hissed, "Why would he ask that?"

"Because Vianca would use us against each other," Levi answered. "That's what he said, and he's right. She loves the idea of us together. We'd be giving her what she wants."

But even as he spoke those warnings, his gaze still fixed on her lips. Still, this wasn't desire, she realized. It was defeat.

Enne pushed herself away from him, and he staggered back. "You're unbelievable. Did you *like* knowing that I wanted this?

That you could go home with whoever you wanted, and that I would still be here waiting?"

He cringed. "No. Muck, no. Of course not—"

"Then you must be terribly thick." Enne swallowed. She was working herself into tears, but she didn't care. "If Vianca asked me to save you again, right now, I would. If she hurt you to get to me, then it would work. Wouldn't it be the same for you?"

"Of course it would." He started to reach for her, but Enne swatted his hand away.

"You do *not* get to touch me." Tears finally spilled down her cheeks. She didn't care how broken he felt tonight—he couldn't use her as a weapon for his own self-destruction. "Your promise was useless from the start. Only now it's worse, because if Vianca used you to manipulate me, it would still work, but I would hate myself for it."

Levi flinched as though she'd slapped him for a third time that night.

"I'm glad you have your gang back," she said, reaching up to wipe the tears away. "I'm glad Jac came here with a girl and looks so happy."

"You *know* I'm not happy," he rasped. "I don't deserve any of their praise up there, but I'm trying so hard to be better. I just don't know how to be better if I don't keep this promise to Jac."

"Fine," she snapped. "Then I'm glad we're both miserable."

She stormed out of the room and slammed the door behind her so he wouldn't follow. When she returned to the party, she immediately made for Grace, who was dancing with an Iron boy. Grace took one look at Enne and pushed him aside.

"That bastard," she muttered. "What happened?"

"We're leaving," Enne answered. "Tell Lola." While Grace hurried to find their friend, who'd abandoned her music with

Tock so they could dance to someone else's, Enne retreated to the edge of the room. The last thing she wanted was to run into Jac right now.

Lola stormed over, Grace behind her. "Are you alright?" she asked.

Enne wiped away her smudged makeup with the back of her hand. "All this time, I've felt like a thickhead, but then he told me that he made a promise to Jac not to..." It felt pathetic even to say it.

"That's a muck promise," Grace snapped, "and we'll kill them both."

Grace grabbed her dagger necklace, and Enne thought, for a moment, she would actually have to tell her *not* to murder the Iron boys. But then Grace drew the blade across her palm. Blood spilled on the floor.

"Tell me your real name," she said.

Enne knew what this was. And she also knew from the fierceness in Grace's dark eyes that she had earned it. It was the only thing Grace could've given her to make her feel better, to make her feel powerful once more. So Enne whispered her true name into Grace's ear, and Grace spoke the words. "Blood by blood. Oath by oath. Life by life."

"Thank you," Enne said when Grace finished.

Grace wiped the blood off on her dress, which was too black to show the stain. "Let's build our own empire."

"Sometimes they call them the Bargainer. Sometimes the Devil.
I guess it depends on who tells the story.

"Legend goes that either the Bargainer approaches you,
or you have to summon them. Some people claim you need to
stand at a crossroads. Others say to make a sacrifice.
But all of them are wrong.

"The only thing that summons the Bargainer is chaos."

—*A legend of the North Side*

JAC

♥ ♠ ♦ ♣

Jac stared out the black-tinted window of the motorcar as they passed over the Brint. He'd only visited the South Side a few times, and he always felt dreadfully out of place. Jac wore the suit Enne had bought him—with a checkered shirt and leather shoes worth more than a week's salary at Liver Shot—and even though it fit perfectly, it still felt like a costume.

Levi sat across from him, reading today's copy of *The Crimes & The Times*. Dark circles hung beneath his eyes, like he hadn't slept all night. Jac wanted to ask about it, but then he remembered how Enne had returned to the party yesterday in tears. How Levi hadn't returned at all.

Sophia was the first to speak. "You don't like this," she said to Levi.

"I don't," he agreed. He set the newspaper down in his lap, revealing a front-page photo of the destroyed Revolution Bridge.

"Why not?" Jac demanded. Last night, after listening to their plans, Levi had merely muttered to Jac, "I trust you," be-

fore abandoning them to interrupt Enne at a card table. Now
Jac realized Levi hadn't listened at all.

"Harrison wants to quietly back the winner of this feud,"
he answered. "Nothing about you is quiet. How are you even
connected to the Family?"

"I'm Charles's and Delia's sister," she answered. "We're all
half siblings."

"Do they know about you?"

"No," she answered, but Jac knew that wasn't the full
answer—he just didn't know what the truth was.

"How do you plan on winning this?" Levi asked. "At best,
you control one den."

"I know all the supply routes." Sophia's words were smooth
from her rehearsal that morning with Jac. "I've met nearly all
the Apothecaries, who are more interested in stability than loyalty. With Harrison's resources, we could convince them of my
leadership and block Delia's and Charles's shipments. We—"

"'We'?" Levi repeated. His gaze flickered to Jac, and he
narrowed his eyes. "All Harrison needed was a name. That's
the whole assignment. The whole p-promise." He stuttered
a bit on the last word.

Jac straightened. "I'm helping her."

"You don't need to."

"I *want* to." He kept his voice firm, but he still withered at
the dark expression on Levi's face. Even though he'd braved
some of his worst fears these past few weeks—and set them
aflame—part of him still looked to Levi to anchor him.

Silence fell a second time, and it didn't let up until the motorcar stopped.

At least Levi trusted him enough not to turn the car around,
Jac told himself. The thought didn't make him feel any better as
he climbed out and stared at the Kipling's Hotel in front of him.

Even more than its adjacent high-end department store, the
hotel was famous for murder. On the first day of the Revolu-

tion, the best friend of the prince of Reynes was shot in the head in the bathtub of the grand suite. Now the hotel had been transformed into a sort of museum, with tours open during business hours. The decorations inside had a disturbing sort of glamour, with vases full of glass eyes, and scarlet carpets dripping down marble stairs.

Jac shook his head and rubbed his Creed. He was a sorry excuse for a member of the Faithful, but even he could tell this place was unholy.

A man stood up from a chaise in the lobby, wearing an eyepatch and a slim-fitting suit. Jac guessed him to be in his thirties, and like his mother, his eye was so green it looked like a jewel you could pluck out.

Despite his haggardness, Levi plastered on a million-volt smile and smoothly shook Harrison's hand. Unlike Jac, Levi wore his suit like it was made for him.

"Have you seen the papers?" Harrison asked Levi. "If I'd known your stunt would have *this* level of repercussions, I never would've agreed. They're adding travel and licensing restrictions to those with Talents of Mysteries, like we've gone back in time twenty-five years. It's barbaric. Even if it barely affects the South Side, I still—"

"They're *considering* restrictions—"

"It'll happen, mark my words," he said darkly. Then Harrison shifted his gaze to Jac.

"Harrison, this is Jac Mardlin, my second," Levi introduced. Jac took Harrison's hand to shake, even though it felt wrong. An ex-Family prince and an ex-addict weren't the sort of men who usually crossed paths.

"And this is Sophia Torren," Levi told him.

Harrison cleared his throat with surprise. "You look like a Torren," he managed, and Jac couldn't tell if that was a compliment or an insult. Sophia's brown curls did resemble those of her siblings, but the differences between them still seemed obvious to Jac. Her green eyes, for instance. And her lack of bloodlust.

Harrison shot Levi a wary look, one that twisted Jac's stomach like a corkscrew. They might fail before they'd even had a chance to plead their case.

Sophia seemed to share his thoughts, because she told Harrison, "I've heard a lot about you."

"I'm afraid I can't say the same."

"Yes. Purposefully so." She flashed a winning smile, and Jac had to admire the confidence of her bluff. It was hard not to be charmed by her.

Sophia's response relaxed Harrison's shoulders. "We can talk in my room." He led them to an elevator, and from there, to an upper floor suite. The morbid decor in Harrison's rooms matched the rest of the hotel. From the coffee table, a radio replayed Sergeant Roy Pritchard's same statement about the explosion at Revolution Bridge, assuring the citizens of New Reynes that they were still safe and that the efforts to clean out the North Side would be tripled.

"Ever hear of this station?" Harrison asked.

"Can't say I have," Levi answered.

"The host—Bobby Vance—is a friend of mine. By the end of this show, I told him he'd receive a phone call with information about the next don of the Torren Family." Harrison tapped his watch. "We have twenty-eight minutes. I hope he's not left disappointed."

Jac grimaced as he sat on the sofa. Augustines, Torrens, they were all the same. Even if Harrison had exchanged casinos for opera houses and Tropps Street for Guillory, he was still running an elaborate power scheme.

Regardless, they still needed him. So Jac sat on the couch and said, "We better hurry up, then."

Sophia took the spot beside him, and though neither Harrison nor Levi could see it, she hooked her fingers around Jac's behind their backs. He didn't know if she'd done it to comfort him or for her own support, but, either way, he liked it.

"I'm Charles's and Delia's half sister," she explained. "I grew up in an orphanage in the Factory District and didn't know my talents until I met a blood gazer." It was a sadly common story in the North Side, but Jac didn't believe a word of it. "Over a year ago, I began working at a Rapture den to get a better sense of my siblings. I was...curious. But by the time I was promoted to manager, I realized how despicable each of them was. So I've spent my time interacting with the underbosses, collecting knowledge on the inner workings of the empire, and growing familiar with their Apothecary network."

"All to become donna?" Harrison asked. "Ruling a casino and narcotics empire hardly seems a likely dream for a young woman."

A comment like that might've made Jac stumble, but Sophia betrayed no such weakness. "At my age, what was yours?" she asked.

A ghost of something unpleasant crossed his expression. "I know better now."

"Then you'll sympathize when I tell you I don't wish to run my Family's empire. I want to destroy it."

There was an unmistakable glitter in Harrison's eye. "Well, that's...interesting."

Interesting is good, Jac reassured himself, but his anxiety was much louder. *Interesting is bad, very bad. Interesting is a disaster.*

"I can get you your votes, but after the election, I'll watch Luckluster burn," Sophia said. "That's the deal I'm offering."

"I thought I was the one making the offers," Harrison said with amusement. Then he sat down in the armchair across from her, and the two of them leaned forward, matching each other's serious expressions. "It's been a long while, but I know Delia and Charles. They take pleasure in torment. And as much as I hate to support either of them, how can my conscience allow me to support *you*, someone so young and in-experienced, when *they* are your opponents? They won't care that you're family. They won't want to kill you, they'll want to *crush* you. And they'll enjoy doing it."

Jac remembered the terror on Sophia's face last night when she'd agreed to this. Harrison was telling her nothing she didn't already know.

Jac squeezed her fingers tighter. She squeezed back.

"I understand perfectly," Sophia answered coolly. "I've always understood this, but even if you choose not to sponsor me, I won't back down. Delia already sees me as a member of her inner circle. I'll bide my time until I have the chance, and I'll still try to destroy her, no matter the price."

"You don't know what you're saying," Harrison said.

"Actually, I do," she snapped. She let go of Jac's hand and stood up, her voice rising. "I have already gone to extremes to see this through, and I *will* win. Every time I look in the mirror, I see them and the evil they do. I'm tired of that guilt. I'm tired of doing nothing."

Harrison said nothing for a long while, only examined Sophia with growing unease. Jac wanted to add something, even just useless words about Sophia's management of Liver Shot, but it was Levi who spoke next.

"Jac?" he asked. "Can I talk to you in private?"

Jac nodded and followed Levi to the room's corner.

"I think I know why you feel you need to do this," Levi started.

"You *think*?" Jac countered.

"But even if Harrison agrees to this, you don't need to stay with her. You could come back."

Jac hesitated. He liked the Irons—missed the Irons. And he missed his friend. But working with Sophia meant something more to him than the Irons ever had, and he didn't want Levi to make him say that.

"It would be amazing if you stopped the Torrens from selling Lullaby," Levi said. "But even if the Torrens fell, one of the gangs or some other Family would pick it up. It'll never end. And you heard what Harrison said. This isn't just a game. It's dangerous."

Jac rolled his eyes. "Wouldn't you know a thing or two about that?"

"I would." Levi's voice was slipping back into the same weariness from earlier. He'd gotten nearly everything he'd ever wanted when Revolution Bridge fell, but Jac had never seen his friend act so defeated. "So I won't ask you not to do this. I'm just worried."

If Levi didn't want to worry, then he shouldn't have given this assignment to him in the first place. But he didn't say that. It frustrated Jac that Levi only seemed to understand pieces of why this mattered to him, but that didn't mean Jac needed to be cruel.

"If Harrison agrees," Jac continued, "then Sophia *needs* to win. She needs to provide votes so that Harrison can join the Senate and kill Vianca. I told you I'm going to help free you, and I am. I'm going to see this through."

Levi gave him a cheap excuse for a smile. "The Irons aren't the same without you."

Somehow, Jac doubted that. But he told Levi what he wanted to hear. "Only a few months until everything is normal again."

Then he turned, eager to end their conversation. In the sitting area, Harrison was on the phone.

We did it, Sophia mouthed, then shot Jac a wink.

A thrill stirred in Jac's stomach as he sat back down beside her. She threw an arm around his shoulder. It was a thoughtless touch—the sort she might've done during a shift at Liver Shot. He didn't know if he should read more into it, but he wanted to.

"I knew we'd manage this." Sophia grinned and twirled a dark curl around her finger. "You were amazing, Todd."

"I didn't do anything," he mumbled. "And you can stop calling me Todd, you know."

"I *could*," she said, with a smirk that told Jac she probably wouldn't.

"So if we're going to be partners," he said, keeping his voice low. "You need to tell me—all this talk about knowing your siblings or not knowing them. Which is it?" He thought of the strange reflection of someone else in Delia's glasses. "What really happened between you and them? Why don't they recognize you now?"

Sophia's smile fell. "I can't tell you that."

"Of course you—"

"I can't," she said flatly. She slid her arm away. "You wouldn't believe me, anyway."

Before Jac could argue, Harrison hung up the phone and adjusted the volume on the radio. "Vance was thrilled," Harrison said. "This will be the biggest story of the week."

"There has been a fascinating update in a story currently playing out on the North Side." Jac assumed it was Vance speaking on the radio now—he had one of those fast-talking radio voices, exactly the sort to be narrating their victory.

Jac should've felt excited—he was finally part of a story, a legend in the making—but he didn't understand why Sophia had shut him out. Whatever happened, he thought they were partners.

"After the death of Sedric Torren, it's been uncertain who would inherit the Family's casino business. Although it seems likely to pass down to one of Sedric's two older cousins, Charles or Delia Torren, we've just been informed of another candidate in this race—Sophia Torren, a family relative."

Sophia gave a whooping cheer and jumped to her feet.

As Vance continued, Harrison dialed down the volume and

turned to the window. "Across the river right now, your siblings and my mother are deeply unhappy."

"Good," Sophia said seriously.

"Wait," Levi said, his voice sharp. "Can you turn the radio up again?"

Harrison obliged.

"What an incredible back-to-back story. Captain Hector has just called to say that Delia Torren has been found dead in her Tropps Street hotel, the cause of death being eight gunshot wounds. Though it remains undetermined who killed her—"

"Charles," Sophia whispered hoarsely.

Harrison rubbed his temples. "I'm sure Charles hasn't heard the news about you yet."

"Yeah, he's probably driving back to Luckluster with his sister's blood on his hands, thinking he's won," Levi said darkly. He glared at Jac, but Jac avoided meeting his eyes. "You think you made him deeply unhappy? How about furious?"

Jac fingered his Creed necklace. There was no going back now. Not for Sophia. Not for either of them.

Sophia's confidence from earlier was gone. When she reached for Jac's hand, he felt a taffy wrapper crushed between their fingers.

Jac leaned closer to her. "I told you I would help you, no matter what."

He meant his words to be reassuring—they were both scared, but they were in this together. She could trust him.

"I know," she whispered, and pulled her hand away.

Jac's face burned. She still wouldn't tell him her secret, and he now had a terrible feeling he didn't know what he was getting into. And even worse, that his story was slipping away from him.

"Well, that's one less opponent standing," Harrison declared. When he spoke, his gaze was fixed on Sophia—he didn't look at Jac at all. "I guess it's time to play."

LEVI

♥ ♠ ♦ ♣

To a casual observer, when the Irons strutted into the Catacombs that night, it was a repeat performance—even if the circles under Levi's eyes told a different story. His associates flanked him on either side, dressed in smart suits with flashes of silver—the shimmer of jewelry or the glint of a concealed blade.

Several guards stood at the top of the stairwell, and Levi noted that Narinder wasn't among them. Then he turned and saw Narinder playing onstage, his violin propped against his shoulder, his eyes closed. Levi knew he needed to thank Narinder for letting them continue to use his club—and Tock for convincing him—but he didn't feel brave enough to face him again. Enne would be at this meeting, and that—more than the musician, more than business—pressed anxiously on his mind.

Then I'm glad we're both miserable, she'd snapped at him. Those words had kept him awake all last night.

After the guards confiscated his weapons, Levi made his

way into the meeting room. This time, he was the last one to arrive. He'd planned it like that.

Enne looked away the moment he entered, her gaze fixed firmly on the table. Levi should've been strutting into this room with pride, but he stopped dead at the threshold when he saw her. All he could feel was shame, and want, and shame for wanting.

"We've been kept waiting," said a woman's voice, turning his attention away.

Levi had never seen her face before, but he instantly knew who she was. She looked maybe forty-five years old, with hair so white it appeared translucent. She wore white clothes as well, but there was something unnerving about her dress. It hung on her like a hospital gown, and its hemline was filthy, its sleeves dotted with what Levi assumed were specks of blood. She wore white bandages around her hands and bare feet that fluttered like ribbons.

For someone who had a reputation for never being seen, her eyes had a look in them that told Levi she saw everything—and a certain madness, like she'd seen too much.

"My apologies," Levi told Ivory, trying to keep his voice steady, even though he was speaking with the most notorious murderer of the North Side. He took his seat at the head of the table and surveyed the others around him. Rebecca was missing, and Bryce, seemingly incapable of coming alone, had brought Harvey Gabbiano in her stead. Levi didn't know Harvey much beyond his reputation: he'd briefly dated Reymond Kitamura, he was a Chainer estranged from his family, and he called himself the salesman of the Orphan Guild.

"So Revolution Bridge now lies at the bottom of the river." Jonas smiled wide, a cigar dangling between his teeth. "Consider me impressed, Pup."

Never before had Jonas paid him a compliment. Levi trusted it about as much as he trusted drinking water out of the Brint.

"Consider me flattered," he answered coolly. "But now that we've struck back against the South Side, we need to be prepared for what's next. Captain Hector will rally."

Ivory let out a laugh. "Scythe told me you were entertaining fantasies of cooperation. We may all live on the North Side, but we're not on the same team." She waved her hands around the table, the unraveling gauze dancing between her fingers. "What do I care if each of you burn?" She said it as if considering that very possibility.

While Levi nervously loosened his necktie, Jonas snapped, "You'd go against us?"

"You'd go against *me*?" she echoed. She looked around the room, and everyone stayed silent. Levi knew he should argue with her—*he* had called this meeting, *he* had won this wager—but this was *Ivory*. She was one of the bloodiest legends of the city, and Levi hadn't spent years enraptured by those stories to disregard them and interrupt her now.

She pulled something out of her pocket and placed it on the table in front of her. It was a knife, serrated all the way around, in the shape of a white tusk. Levi sucked in his breath as he examined it. Every member of the Doves was named after their weapon of choice, and he'd never thought he'd see hers.

"Seventeen years I've carried this, since before some of you were even born. I've lived longer, fought longer, killed more. I built everything from this blade. How did you all get to be in this room?" Ivory peered around the table.

"Eight Fingers died, and you couldn't save him," she told Jonas.

To Bryce: "An idea that wasn't even yours."

To Levi: "Because of *her*." She nodded at Enne, and Levi clenched his fist under the table. That wasn't true.

And to Enne: "I don't even know about you." Ivory cocked her head to the side. "Why are you here?"

"Because I was promised something," she answered with impressive yet frightening coldness. Levi fought the urge to kick her under the table, but he no longer felt he had a right to.

"Your little stock market scheme?" Ivory raised her eyebrows. "No one will go along with it. Not if I don't. Not if I *forbid* it."

Enne crossed her arms. "Why would you do that?"

"Because the Doves aren't a public offering. My followers aren't assets."

"Your second gave his word."

"And now I'm giving you mine, and the answer is no."

Levi tried to come up with words to fight her, but he knew he'd lose. She was right. The legend of Ivory was more fearsome and older than any of them, and the threat of her wrath was enough to ensure no one invested in Enne's market or opened their casinos to the Irons again.

"That's disappointing," Enne said drily. "I don't like people who go back on their promises."

Levi sucked in his breath. Enne knew better than to anger Ivory—didn't she?

And muck, *he* knew better. But that didn't stop him from saying, "I'll do it. I'm with Séance."

He swallowed and stared at the ivory knife, wondering if he'd made a deadly error.

Ivory narrowed her eyes. "A mistake," she hissed. In that moment, Levi was grateful that a table stretched out between her and him. Not that distance would serve as any real protection from a woman credited with sixty-three kills.

Enne needed their support for her stock market, but Levi needed this, too. If the North Side came together, then the casinos would open their doors to the Irons again. Their pressure of the gangs could drive the whiteboots out.

If they united, the city would be their kingdom.

And if not, the city would be their ruin.

"I couldn't save Reymond, either," Levi murmured, meeting Jonas's eyes. He thought Jonas was slimier than a rotting eel, but at least they'd both cared about Reymond. Maybe that would be enough.

Jonas turned over Levi's words carefully. "So it's the three of us, then." For perhaps the first time in their acquaintance, Levi looked at Jonas and smiled.

Just as Ivory reached for her knife, Bryce cleared his throat. "The four of us."

Ivory's hand froze in midair. *"What?"*

"Eight of my friends are dead," Bryce said darkly. "I'll protect the ones I have left. Whatever it takes."

Levi wasn't sure in that moment where to look—at the fury that crossed over Ivory's face, or the thrill that filled Harvey's.

"I see," Ivory seethed. Without another word, she picked up her knife and stormed out.

Enne stood, chair screeching against the wooden floor. "I'll be in contact with all of you soon." And then, to Levi's shock, she walked out, as well.

Abandoning Jonas, Bryce, and Harvey in the meeting room, he ran after Enne and caught her at the bottom of the stairwell. The music from the club pulsed around them.

"Wait," he rasped.

Enne spun around and looked up at him. "Why? I got what I came for."

"You threatened *Ivory.* Maybe you don't know—"

"I know," she snapped. "I've learned a lot in the past two weeks, and, you see, I was the one that had everything on the line tonight. Thanks to you, I don't get to play it safe."

He stormed down the steps, even if it still ached in his ribs to do so. "Like I said last night, had I not stepped in and made the wager, your plan would have sunk. They—"

"Do you want me to thank you, then? If this all fell through, we would've thought of something else. I don't need—"

"I know that," Levi said. He white-knuckled the railing across from her, trying not to shout, trying not to reach for her. She had clawed her way inside him and buried herself there, and that meant every one of her words could wound or cut. He didn't know how to force her out—and he didn't want to.

Her aura filled the stairwell, but it didn't storm like it usually did; like he would've expected. It was trembling, and that was how he knew not to bite back.

Instead, Levi pulled a piece of paper out of his pocket and handed it to her.

"What is this?" she asked, unfolding it. Then her eyes narrowed. "This is for the market."

Last night, Levi had written the list of every possible investor they should approach. Enne had asked him yesterday to give it to Grace, but Levi hadn't made a promise to Grace. He'd made it to her, and he was determined to keep it.

"I'm sorry," he told her. "I'm sorry about every deal I've made." He swallowed, thinking of the events that had transpired at Harrison's this morning. Levi understood why Jac felt the need to destroy the thing that had nearly destroyed him, but he couldn't fathom why Jac was putting himself in such danger to do so.

It went far above and beyond Levi's original request, and it was of Jac's own volition…so Levi couldn't help but wonder if all their initial promises still applied.

One promise, in particular.

I told you I'm going to help free you, and I am. I'm going to see that through.

The memory of Jac's words instantly triggered another rise of shame inside him. Levi should've felt only gratitude for Jac's sacrifice, but all he could think about were his own desires. He'd already come close to breaking his promise.

Levi raised his eyes to Enne's. "Please let me try to fix this."

Enne slid the paper into her pocket, and for a brief moment, Levi thought she would walk away again. He didn't know how many more cuts he could take.

"Fine," she huffed. "Tomorrow night. The first place on the list."

And then she disappeared into the club.

Levi sighed and let go of the railing. He could still keep both his promises.

Bryce Balfour descended the stairs, so silent Levi barely heard him until Bryce stood right beside him. He looked as terrible as Levi did, his eyes red and bloodshot. But then again, Bryce always looked like that. "Destiny has a mucking awful sense of humor, don't you think?" he asked with a tinny laugh.

Lately, Levi's feeling of destiny had been replaced by a sense of hopelessness. "What makes you say that?"

"Because the hero of one story is the villain of someone else's. It's all just a matter of who wins." Bryce sighed and sat at the bottom of the stairs, clutching the railing like he needed the support. Levi didn't know Bryce and was in no mood for a heart-to-heart, but he also didn't want to leave him there alone. Bryce looked lost without a companion.

"Where did Harvey go?" Levi asked.

"Gloating. I hate him when he gets like that." Bryce put his head in his hands. "What do you think of this Harrison Augustine business?"

"Why do you ask?" Levi snapped, harsher and more obvious than he intended.

"Everyone knows about you and Vianca."

Levi relaxed. Of course. Everyone knew about him and Vianca. "She's a witch. Even her son hates her."

"But you can't actually want him to win the election," Bryce said matter-of-factly.

Levi furrowed his eyebrows at Bryce's assumption of familiarity. "Why wouldn't I?"

"Because you're a Glaisyer. Wasn't your grandfather's head put on a spike outside the palace with the Mizers?"

Levi didn't talk about these sort of things—not with anyone. He knew the crimes the revolutionaries had committed against his family. He knew that, for most of the orb-makers, their final act of service to their kings had been dying with them. But Levi didn't know how to hate his father and also sympathize with him at the same time, so it was easier to pretend that politics didn't affect him. That Levi's Caroko skin and family history were like anyone else's in New Reynes. Even if that was a lie.

"That was a long time ago," Levi answered.

"The papers mentioned restrictions. Dividing talents by Aptitudes and Mysteries. History is repeating itself."

Just dwelling on this subject brought back painful memories. Grief could reveal the ugly parts of anyone, but his father had let his fester for so long that it took everything that was left. These weren't Levi's first broken ribs.

"Times are different now," Levi said.

"Yes. This time, we're the new kings."

Bryce held out his hand for Levi to help him up. Levi certainly didn't need to, nor had he enjoyed his conversation with Bryce, but he obliged the Guildmaster anyway.

A chill swept through him the moment they touched, making the hairs on his neck stand on end. Levi jerked his hand away as soon as Bryce staggered to his feet.

And then he saw it.

Bryce's aura. A curling mixture of black and scarlet, thicker than smoke. The metallic taste of it overwhelmed Levi, and all of his senses ignited in warning. His split talent was weak—he could only sense the auras of those he knew well, or, in Vianca's case, someone who had power over him. The fact that he could now see Bryce's...

Levi took a step back in alarm.

"What's wrong?" Bryce asked, frowning.

Levi opened his mouth, but he could think of nothing to say that didn't sound shatz. His mother had once told him to run if he ever encountered a black aura. That a black aura belonged to nothing human. A dozen different street legends crossed his mind, each more outrageous and horrifying than the next.

Levi didn't believe in superstitions, but he did trust his instincts.

So he took off. He pushed his way through the crowded dance floor until he was out the door in the humid July night air, and by the time he returned home, Levi had convinced himself he'd only seen a trick of the light. Yet as he lay in bed, he could picture nothing but that noxious darkness, with its red veins and coppery taste.

Like his own blood.

ENNE

♥ ♠ ♦ ♣

Enne vowed that the first purchase with their stock market earnings would be a bed. She tugged the sheet over herself, trying desperately to avoid thinking about what the previous owner had done on this mattress to leave such disturbing stains. Grace and Lola had retrieved it from a Casino District dumpster, crowing as though they'd stumbled upon lost treasure, but Enne would treasure nothing more than to toss it back into the filth it came from.

"So we starved for two weeks for no reason," Grace grumbled on Enne's right. "If you would just make volts, then I wouldn't need a rich South Side man to cater to me. I've got *you*."

Enne had told Grace the truth about her lineage that morning, the day after she'd given Enne her oath. Grace had taken it surprisingly well. In fact, she'd been most upset about how Enne refused to use her blood talent, as though she'd taken pleasure in their recent bout of poverty. Lola had made Grace swear on every man she'd ever killed that she'd tell no one, but Enne already trusted Grace. And she was relieved that she'd no longer need to sneak around to apply her contacts.

"Enne's talent isn't a joke," Lola snapped at Grace on Enne's other side. She held her pillow over her head.

Grace ignored Lola and rested her head on Enne's shoulder. "I've just been thinking…" she mused. "Gabrielle Dondelair must've had it pretty good before, you know…"

"She died?" Lola said drily.

"Yeah, sure."

"You know that even if Enne *did* make volts, we couldn't just go flaunting them, right? We can't just be broke one day and wildly wealthy the next. People would start asking questions."

Grace shrugged. "So we reinvent ourselves as South Side heiresses. We basically already have."

"Both of you, quiet," Enne hissed. "The lords agreed to the market. I'm going to meet potential investors with Levi tomorrow night. We've gotten what we wanted."

"Maybe *you* have. But I'm going to have to do more math, and that has never been what I wanted."

"Boo hoo," Lola muttered underneath her pillow.

"I've *actually* killed people, unlike you, you fake, sneaky…" Grace reached over Enne to smack Lola, painfully leaning on Enne's hair in the process. "You act like a killer, but you're just a killjoy."

Lola swatted at her, refusing to remove the pillow from her face. "Well, you look like a twelve-year-old without your eyeliner."

Enne pushed Grace off her and sat up, running her fingers through the knots in her hair. "I would like to sleep if you two could shut up." She hadn't slept well in weeks. Every night meant a visit to the same hallway, and for someone who prided herself on her practicality, Enne could come up with no explanation for why this happened—only that it wasn't good.

"You mentioned that you can't make orbs without an orbmaker," Grace said, apparently not finished with their conversation.

"Yep," Enne answered tersely.

"And Levi refused you."

"Yep," she said at the same time Lola responded, "The only rational decision he's ever made."

"Have you ever tried just depositing them yourself?" Grace asked. "You know, the way anyone would deposit volts into orbs from their skin?"

Enne had never considered making volts without Levi. "Would that work?" she asked quietly.

"Of course not," Lola snapped. "What Mizers make *isn't* volts. It's energy. The orb-makers turn it into volts...*why are you getting up?*"

Enne crept across the classroom to her purse. She retrieved an empty orb and clutched the sphere of glass in her hand, her stomach in knots. Of course it couldn't be that simple. And even if it worked, like Lola said, creating volts would call attention to herself. But it was her talent. It was a part of her, and she wanted to understand it.

This was the power of kings. And now it was hers.

Enne held the orb to her inner elbow, where people usually deposited volts. She felt the energy pulsing in her blood, felt it leap in the direction of the glass—like a magnetic pull, like a snap. She wondered how many volts flowed inside her. There could be hundreds. There could be *thousands*.

The orb shattered, slicing open some of Enne's skin. She yelped in surprise and pain, and blood trickled down her arm. Being barefoot, she froze where she stood and peered through the darkness at the dozens of glass fragments littering the floor around her.

"It was worth a shot," Grace managed.

Lola stood up angrily, slipped into her boots, and helped Enne back toward the mattress. She tore off a piece of the aged bedsheet and wrapped it over Enne's cuts, not bothering to be gentle. "Are you all right?"

"It was a bad idea, anyway," Enne muttered.

The phone rang, making all three of them jump. It was a private line, and only two people possessed the number. Enne carefully tiptoed around the glass to answer it.

"Did you see the papers?" came the voice through the receiver. There was something rasping about the donna's tone, which was as unexpected as the call. It was well past midnight. "His poll numbers are higher than Worner's." Vianca laughed hollowly. "He's always been good at these sort of things—playing the part. Even when he was a child."

"It's...it's the middle of the night," Enne stammered.

"These restrictions they're proposing on Talents of Mysteries. How could he support these? *He* has a Talent of Mystery! The hypocrisy!" There was a strange slur to her voice, like Vianca was drinking. "He's a fool if he thinks he can beat me. I killed the last candidate—could I not do the same to him?"

Enne didn't answer. Honestly, she didn't think so. Not because Harrison was too powerful, but because she didn't think even Vianca had it in her to kill her own son.

"Why are you calling me?" she asked tiredly.

"Because this is important. It's what you're doing for me, isn't it?" Vianca snapped. Enne didn't remember Vianca ever asking Enne to become her late night confidante. "My son will lose. I know he will."

Enne slid down to the floor and hugged her knees to herself. She waved Grace and Lola away—there was no point in them losing sleep, as well. And then she assured the donna of everything she wanted to hear.

The next evening, Enne stood at the edge of Sweetie Street, wearing her black silk mask and swallowing down her ladylike sensibilities. She didn't consider herself a prude—at least, not by Bellamy standards—but seeing the man in front of her parading down the alley shirtless, red lips swollen, lipstick stains across his chest and shoulders, Enne couldn't help but feel out of place. She reached into her purse and rooted around for her black lipstick. As she applied it, she reminded herself that she wasn't the same girl who'd left Bellamy. Then she returned the tube to her bag, tucked right beside her revolver.

She was so distracted that she didn't notice the black Houssen motorcar brake in the alley behind her, splashing puddles onto the curb.

Levi slipped out of the driver door, his collar popped to conceal his face, his homburg hat casting a shadow over his eyes.

"Sorry to keep you waiting," he said.

"Is that your motorcar?" she asked. "Is that how this works now? I get one, so you need to get a fancier one? How did you even buy that?"

"I signed a bunch of contracts for the Irons today. I thought after this, I'd drive you home, and you could give it to Lola." He had the decency to look apologetic, but she'd already agreed to let him help her tonight. That seemed forgiveness enough.

A memory crept across her skin where Levi's lips had touched. She crossed her arms. "Or I could drive it home."

"Can you drive?"

She could not. "Yes."

He watched her warily, as though waiting for her to snap at him. Part of her liked that she knew exactly how to break

Levi Glaisyer. The other part of her found it depressing. He'd apologized, and he'd supported her in front of Ivory when no one else would. She was still hurt, still indignant, but she was also tired, and despite it all, she would rather see him smile.

Levi strolled to the edge of the street and took a step down it. Enne reluctantly followed. "So what does your guidebook say about Sweetie Street?"

"Shockingly, it didn't recommend touring the red light district with one of the North Side's top ten most eligible people."

She expected him to laugh, but instead he tripped awkwardly over a cobblestone. "You saw that?" he asked.

Enne smirked. "Nine seemed too high. Don't they know you're better looking in your wanted poster?"

Levi smiled at her, his expression hopeful. Just because they weren't hurting each other.

Of all the devastating secrets he'd told her, it was this moment that broke her heart the most.

She shook away her thoughts—she couldn't get distracted. Tonight, Enne would finally claim power for her own.

"Let's get on with it, then," Levi said, significantly more lightness to his step. Enne plastered on a business face and recited the words she'd perfected with Grace from earlier. *The gangs are opening up for investments and you—yes, you—now have the once-in-a-lifetime chance to buy in. After all, no industry in New Reynes is always on the up like crime.*

They headed into the first building on their right, its foundation of wooden beams resembling stilts and painted in rainbow stripes. The third and fourth stories leaned to the right, as if trying to spill into Tropps Street, and blue lights blinked from inside, making Enne's head spin.

"We'll start with a tame one," Levi said, pushing open the door. "It's called the Beck and Call. Pretty clever. So you can have me—"

"At my beck and call," Enne finished. "Not *that* clever."

They stepped into a lounge area. Because it was still early, Enne only spotted a few workers—dancing to the sultry music, wiping down the bar.

Enne felt her shoulders relax. This was no worse than any New Reynes tavern.

"Can I help you?" one of the workers asked. He was dressed in a suit jacket and matching trousers, but with no shirt underneath. His eyes widened as he took the two of them in, recognition dawning on his face.

"We've come to speak to the madame," Levi explained.

The man nodded and hurried off. He returned a minute later with a surprisingly young woman dressed in gold from head to toe. Although very little of her was exposed, her clothes were tight enough to be a second skin.

"I don't know why the pair of you are here," the woman said, "but I don't want any trouble."

"No trouble," Levi told her, "only opportunity."

The madame narrowed her eyes, but nodded and motioned for them to follow. She led them down a narrow hallway and opened a door to a small office, where Enne and Levi took seats on fur-lined chairs in front of her desk.

The woman pushed away this morning's copy of *The Crimes & The Times* to clear off the surface. "Dreadful things in the papers, all thanks to you two. Dark times repeating themselves." She looked between them accusingly.

"We're not looking to revive the old war," Levi said. "In fact, that's exactly why we're here. We all share the North Side, and we're doing our part to keep our home safe. We wondered if you might be interested in helping us achieve that."

She raised her eyebrows expectantly, but said nothing.

Enne cleared her throat. "Membership in the gangs is exclusive, but now, each of the gangs have committed themselves to supporting the North Side. However, as the attack on the Orphan Guild proved, the whiteboots have weapons, numbers, and resources we don't. So every business in the North Side is being given the once-in-a-lifetime opportunity to invest—"

"What you're saying," the madame snapped, "is that you want us to pay for our protection."

"Not at all," Enne said, all practiced smiles. "Every volt you invest gives you a share of ownership. When the gangs profit, so will you. When the North Side is protected, we are all made safe."

The woman was silent for several moments, and Enne wondered if they had sold it. According to Grace, everyone in the City of Sin spoke the language of volts, but this was no simple transaction—this was risk. This was history.

This was power.

The woman leaned forward, lowering her voice to a hiss. "And when you and every gangster hang in Liberty Square? Where do my volts go, then? Who protects us, then?"

Levi stood abruptly, the charm never leaving his smile. "If you change your mind, you can find the Spirits in the Ruins District."

Enne shot him an irritated look, but he pulled her outside before she could confront him.

It was drizzling now. Levi opened an umbrella and offered it to her, but Enne took a step back.

"The 'Spirits'?" she demanded. "Did you just name my gang, Levi?"

"I think it sounds good. It suits your street name—"

"It sounds ridiculous."

"Well, sorry. I just blurted it out." Seeing as Enne wouldn't stand close to him, he handed her his umbrella and let himself get wet. "Her words were making me nervous."

They'd unnerved Enne, too. Now, whenever she closed

her eyes, she pictured the two of them hanging side by side at the gallows.

"Don't be put down about her yet," Levi said. "We're hitting up lots of others."

Enne sighed. "Where to next?"

"Everywhere. Anywhere."

Two hours later, Enne and Levi had collected a mere fifty volts for the Scarhands, one hundred for the Doves, and eighty for the Irons. Most of the brothels on Sweetie Street had turned them down or accused them of coercion. Enne had seen more nakedness that evening than she had in her entire life, and she was desperate to leave the red light district behind.

The pair wandered into a quieter establishment called the Dirty Deed, and after being turned down yet another time, took a break to brood at the bar.

"The market is a good idea," Enne grumbled.

"This is still a novel concept to people," Levi said. "If you give them time, they'll—"

Someone tapped Levi on the shoulder, and both of them turned around. A woman wrapped her feathered boa around his neck and planted a large kiss on his cheek, leaving a mark of green lipstick behind. Enne startled so much she nearly toppled over. Her gaze dropped to the woman's cleavage.

"You should smile," the woman purred. "You look like you could have some fun."

Levi stiffened and spit a feather out of his mouth. "I *was* having fun."

The woman's smile faltered, and she shifted her gaze to Enne. Upon seeing Enne's mask, her smile fell altogether. She released Levi's shoulders and backed away. "I'm sorry. Enjoy your night."

As soon as the woman was out of earshot, Enne let out a fit of laughter. "I think I scared her."

AMANDA FOODY

"It's hard to tell how short you are, sitting on a barstool."

"And it's clearly hard to tell who you are from behind." Enne sipped her drink. "In fact, I wonder if she recognized *you* at all."

Levi shot her a look that was both amused and annoyed, and Enne could almost feel a sense of normalcy returning to them. Maybe she could pretend his smirks didn't make her heart beat faster, and he could pretend he wasn't looking at her like the way he was now.

Except they weren't pretending very well at all.

Levi bit his lip. "I want you to know that—"

But Enne didn't want to know, not when things finally felt bearable again. So she held up her hand. "Don't do that."

"Do what?"

"Ruin it."

He grimaced and stuffed his hands in his pockets. "Will you let me drive you home?"

His sorry face really was a work of art. She wondered if he'd practiced it just so she'd forgive him. If so...well, it had worked.

"Fine," she answered. "On one condition."

"Anything," he said seriously.

"You show me how to drive."

PART II

REWARD

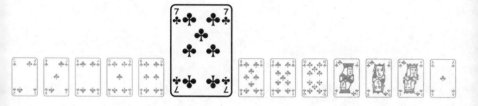

"There was a street lord whose name was a number,
and he changed it every time he made a new kill.
Whatever it was, he owned that number. If you said it,
no matter what you were talkin' about, he'd find you
and kill you. His name remains One-One-Six,
the name he claimed the day he died. That's why
none of the house numbers in New Reynes have
that number. All these years later, we're still afraid."

—*A legend of the North Side*

LEVI

Levi surveyed the casino floor from a balcony. At ten o'clock, the room was at its loudest: the clicks of a spinning roulette wheel, the cheers of winners, the chatter of patrons clustered around the bar.

A month had passed since Levi and Tock had destroyed Revolution Bridge, a month since Enne had launched her stock market. In that time, with the gangs united and the whiteboots forbidden from crossing the Brint, everything about the North Side had become *more*. Pubs that typically closed in mornings now kept their bars open twenty-four hours. Cabarets advertised their newer, more scandalous shows with vedettes in feathered corsets parading down Tropps Street. Gangsters strutted about the streets like kings, even as their bounties climbed three or four times as high. Levi had earned more, recruited more, and cheated more than any other time in his criminal career, and now he beheld his domain below with the pride of a prize rightfully earned.

The Martingale Casino, though smaller than St. Morse and

Luckluster, boasted a patronage of over a thousand gamblers every week—and it was now the Irons' largest contract. Spotting the Irons was simple: each of them, like Levi, wore silver jewelry. The spades dealt at the card tables, the diamonds kept careful eyes on the patrons from each of the exits, the hearts performed onstage or poured drinks at the bar.

The owner of the casino, a burly man with a beard that curled at the end like a corkscrew, slung his arm around Levi's shoulder. Now that Levi's ribs had finally healed, the touch no longer hurt like it used to. With his other hand, the owner handed Levi a leather pouch filled with orbs.

"This isn't due until tomorrow," Levi reminded him.

"I wanted to give it to you myself. From my hand to yours." He squeezed Levi's arm. "My only regret is that I didn't hire from you sooner. I gotta ask, how do you do it? What's your secret?"

"There is no secret. Just cleverness." Technically, his secret was cheating, but that was roughly the same thing.

The owner laughed. "You'll tell me one of these days. I'll wear you down." He checked his watch and slapped Levi's shoulder again. "Break time is over. I better send the other dealers back on the floor."

He disappeared down the stairs, leaving Levi to admire his work. After years buckled down by Vianca's demands, he'd finally built the empire he'd always wanted. He was wealthy in both volts and reputation. Tomorrow, when his six-week deadline with Vianca expired, it would be time for the donna to finally accept that Levi was more than just hopeless ambitions.

He was a legend.

A figure appeared at the edge of the balcony, a man Levi didn't recognize. He wore dark-rimmed glasses and an ill-fitting suit. "My apologies for barging in, but I was hoping to run into you." He pulled a business card out of his pocket and handed it to Levi. It had pink swirls, like some sort of carnival ride. "My name's Fitz Oliver. I'm a—"

"I know who you are," Levi said quickly.

Fitz Oliver was a real estate mogul who owned half the residential complexes on the North Side, and he was far wealthier than his cheap clothes would lead Levi to believe.

Levi shook his hand. "I'm here for business tonight, making rounds. I can't really—"

"I'll only take a moment of your time." He smiled until Levi reluctantly shoved the business card into his jacket pocket. "As I'm sure you've heard, the North Side is due for a change next summer."

"You mean the boardwalk," Levi answered. He'd heard some talk about that. He didn't realize it would open in less than a year.

"We're hoping to open several new casinos on the boardwalk—large enough to compete with St. Morse, Luckluster, all the greats. I've spoken to several other reputable dealers. But, well..."

"But I'm the best," Levi said, grinning.

"I can't walk down the street without seeing your face, whether it's on a wanted poster or a tabloid. This city can't seem to make up its mind about who it loves and who it despises."

Levi couldn't tell if that was meant to flatter him or not. "All that matters is people are talking."

"Nothing is decided," Fitz said hastily. "But we'd welcome you to contact us."

"Just to be clear," Levi said, clearing his throat. "This would be about—"

"Purchasing a casino, yes."

Levi's heart stuttered. He'd always thought about owning

his own gambling joint someday, a sort of wistful dream that any card dealer might have.

Two months ago, he'd been broke, scrambling to pay back the final investors of Vianca's scam and hold the Irons together.

Now, he had the whole city within his grasp.

"Well, thank you for considering me," Levi said smoothly, despite his stomach twisting into excited knots. "I'll give you a ring at some point. I have some ideas that might interest you."

"And we'd be happy to hear them," he answered. "But I warn you—the real estate doesn't come cheap. It'll be nearly sixty thousand volts—with a fifteen-thousand-volt down payment."

Levi nearly choked. Sixty thousand volts was six times higher than the payment he'd once owed Sedric Torren. Six times higher than the bounty the City of Sin currently had placed on his life.

"I'm sure that can also be arranged," Levi managed. He held out his hand for Fitz to shake. "I'd be careful talking about new dens around the Casino District, though. People might think you're trying to steal their dealers."

The man stood up and tipped his hat. "Why steal theirs when I could have yours?"

"What's this?" the owner of the casino asked at the top of the stairs, Tock lingering behind him. "Am I interrupting anything?"

"Not at all," Fitz answered. "I was just leaving." He grasped the owner's hand in a polite shake and left before he needed to introduce himself.

Levi avoided the owner's curious gaze, focusing on his third. "Tock?" he said. "Why are you here? I thought you took the night off." Lately, Tock had been taking a lot of nights off, and the Irons gossiped that she'd met someone she didn't want them to know about. "Stood up, were you?"

Tock rolled her eyes. "Just because you openly brood about your romantic woes doesn't mean I have to."

The owner let out a holler. "Romantic woes? Levi must be the richest person in the North Side. I can't imagine him having any trouble."

Levi was about to respond coolly that Tock was joking, but Tock cut in. "The richest *man*, you mean." She shot Levi a pointed look.

He scowled. Even though they'd repaired their friendship over the past few weeks, that didn't mean he wanted to think about Enne when he was otherwise having a great night. Not when he couldn't be with her in the way he wanted to.

"I came to tell you that Tommy didn't show up after his break," Tock said. "It's been ten minutes."

The owner shrugged and slapped Levi on the shoulder for the third time, making Levi scowl with irritation. They weren't *that* chummy. "That's not long enough to worry. Besides, we have a replacement! Levi can step in for him. Just until he gets back."

"I'm flattered, but I'm not sure that's a good idea," Levi responded. He hadn't dealt cards since St. Morse.

"Nonsense, it would give everyone something to talk about. You still got it, don't you?"

"Of course," Levi said, straightening his jacket. "If it's only one round..." Before he left, he leaned in and whispered to Tock, "But look around for Tommy, will you? It isn't like him to be late." Then he gave the owner a polite nod goodbye and slipped downstairs.

The casino itself was a repurposed theater, and the Tropps tables occupied the former orchestra pit. The players at Tommy's table, who'd been sipping at empty drink glasses and checking their watches, widened their eyes as Levi slid into the dealer's chair. Other gamblers at nearby tables turned their

attention away from their games to stare. Only in New Reynes would a wanted criminal be treated like a celebrity.

"I hope you don't mind the switch," Levi told the players,
and even those with the most experienced poker faces stuttered
out awkward pleasantries. He shuffled the cards and handed
them to the nearest player to split.

Levi had dealt many games in the past: poker, blackjack,
pilfer. But Tropps was his favorite. In Tropps, the dealer was
an equal player in the game. He dealt everyone three cards
and examined the king of clubs in his hand. It was lucky to
start out the game with a high card.

As the rounds went by, the guests continued to fill up the
pot. No one, it seemed, wanted to fold, and Levi realized with
unease how much pressure was riding on this single game. It
had seemed meaningless at first—he was only filling Tommy's
spot on a standard Friday night shift.

But he wasn't Tommy.

Many considered him the best Tropps player in the city. He
led a gang of gamblers, and he was currently New Reynes's
most notorious and favorite criminal. Every public appearance
defined his reputation now. It didn't matter if he was rusty;
he couldn't afford to lose.

It was lucky he continued to draw good cards.

The other players pushed and pushed him, and by the end
of all nine rounds, only two of them had folded. The three
remaining gamblers revealed their cards, and Levi was relieved to see that his hand was the strongest; a straight flush.

Levi flashed a victorious smile. "That's one for the house,"
he said, sliding the pot toward him. Tommy owed him a favor
for this—it was quite the haul.

Tock tapped him on the shoulder and leaned down to whisper in his ear. "Tommy isn't back yet, but look—" She hiked
up the bottom of her dress and pulled out a gun strapped be-

neath it. "We found this on the floor near the coat room. Stella said it's Tommy's."

Levi stood up from his seat, heart pounding. "You'll have to excuse us," he told the guests, then he quickly pulled Tock aside. "Were there any signs of a struggle?"

"I couldn't tell."

"What's the closest exit to the coat room?"

"The front door."

Levi nodded, and the two of them walked briskly out of the room. Once they made it to the lobby, they broke into a run. He pushed open one of the sets of dramatic gold doors onto Tropps Street, bright with neon signs and beckoning window displays.

Tommy was nowhere in sight.

"Don't panic," Tock said, her voice hitched. "Maybe Tommy just...lost track of time?"

"Doubtful," Levi answered. "He's one of our most reliable dealers. He wouldn't just wander off." He scanned the area, his mind racing. If Tommy had been abducted by a bounty hunter and turned in to the whiteboots, then he would hang. That meant Levi's best hope was that the bounty hunter would try to ransom him back to the Irons—if Levi was even given that chance. People didn't exactly associate gang lords with that kind of compassion.

Despite Tock's warning not to panic, her wide eyes as she scanned the passersby told Levi she was thinking the same thing. He kicked at the curb in frustration.

"Where's the nearest parking garage?" Levi asked. Even in the City of Sin, you couldn't get away with openly dragging someone down Tropps Street.

"Under the casino."

They tore through the crowds around the side street, making their way to the garage's entrance. They sprinted, pistols in hand, down the slope to the first level. The lights above them flickered, and despite the commotion of the city outside, in here, it was eerily silent.

Levi nodded at Tock, and the two of them split up—him taking the right side, her beyond a barrier to the left. He treaded carefully down the center of the lot, clutching his gun down by his hip with both hands. His gaze shifted through car windows, searching for movement.

He's already gone. Levi cursed.

Tires screeched loudly behind him. He whipped around to spot a black car speeding in his direction. Levi lifted his gun and fired at the driver's seat. The dashboard cracked but didn't shatter. He leaped out of the car's path just before it collided with him, and landed painfully on the hood of another car.

"What was that?" he heard Tock call from far away.

Levi stood up and turned in time to see a second car driving toward him from a different direction, a gun brandished out the window. Levi ducked behind another car and held his arms over his head as bullets fired and glass shattered all around.

Muck. Muck. Muck.

His back hit the garage's cement wall as both cars skidded to a halt in front of him, blocking his only escape route. The driver who'd shot at him climbed out of his car. He wore a black suit appropriate for an upscale casino.

Or a funeral.

Both he and Levi raised their guns. Levi slowly rose to his feet, his heart pounding so hard he thought he'd burst. "Who'll shoot first, then?" he demanded, praying it would be him.

"Me," someone else said. Levi's stomach did a turn as the second person appeared from behind the other car. She clutched Tommy by a fistful of his blond hair. Tommy's nose was broken, and blood ran down his face and shirt. The woman held a pistol to his temple.

Dread crept up Levi's spine as he came to a sudden realization.

They had never come for Tommy.

They had come for him.

"Put your gun down, or I'll kill him," the woman sneered.

Levi didn't even consider ignoring her. He crouched down and carefully placed his gun on the pavement, then lightly kicked it away and raised his arms.

"Let Tommy go," he ordered, though he was in no place to make demands.

"Get in the back seat." She nodded at her companion's car.

Levi knew where this future headed. A cell for the night, and the gallows in the morning.

Dead?

Or alive?

He'd found the answer to his question.

A gun fired, and Levi instinctively squeezed his eyes shut. Then the man let out a shout, and Levi saw that he'd been shot in the same arm that had pointed his gun. His pistol went skidding across the pavement.

"Run, you thickhead!" Tock shouted at him from across the lot.

The woman wrapped her arm around Tommy's neck and turned her back to Levi to shoot at Tock. The lot echoed with gunfire, and Levi seized his chance. He lunged for the man's fallen gun.

No sooner had he grabbed it that the man tackled him. The man was nearly twice Levi's size, and the weight of him sent Levi slamming chest-first onto the pavement. With his good arm, the man pinned down Levi's right shoulder, but

Levi managed to grab the gun with his left hand. He pointed it directly behind him, and fired.

The noise was deafening. Blood splattered on the back of Levi's neck and across the ground. His ears rang, so loud and overpowering he felt his entire world shift sideways. He groaned as the weight above him went limp, choking the breath from his lungs. He gradually rolled over and stared up into the bullet-mangled face of his assailant. At nearly point-blank range, his nose had been blown clean off, leaving a riddled mess of flesh and bone in its place. The blood dripped from him onto Levi's own face, and his stomach lurched as he pushed the man off.

Levi staggered to his feet, so dizzy and sickened that he could barely make out what Tock was yelling at him. She held Tommy by his jacket, one hand pressed to the back of the closest motorcar.

"Run! What are you doing? Run!"

She took off in the opposite direction, Tommy stumbling to keep up. The woman held her side as though she, too, had been shot. She leaned against a car hood for support and fired, her aim wild and haphazard.

"Run! Muck, Levi, *run!*"

Only then did Levi realize what Tock had done. She'd laid a line when she touched that car.

The car was going to explode.

Levi sprinted, his head pounding, his balance veering from side to side. Tock had told him her limit was thirty seconds. How long had it been? A bullet whizzed past him and shattered the mirror of a nearby car. He wasn't lucid enough. Wasn't fast enough.

Boom!

The explosion swept him off his feet. He felt the heat pass over him, but, of course, orb-makers couldn't burn. The crash hurt, though. He fell painfully on his shoulder, hard enough to bruise. When he turned behind him, the first car was engulfed in flames, the woman screaming and lost among them.

Levi half crawled, half staggered his way to a nearby stairwell. He found Tock and Tommy pressed against the wall, their arms still covering their heads. Tock jumped to her feet and threw her arms around him.

"Muck," she cursed in his ear. "If I'd killed you, I never would've forgiven you."

Levi stumbled down to Tommy's level and lightly slapped his face. The dealer's eyes had a glassy look, and Levi wondered if he'd been drugged. "Are you all right?"

"Never better," Tommy mumbled.

"You won't be pretty anymore with that nose," Tock told him.

"Don't be ridiculous. He's never looked sweller." Levi smeared some blood off Tommy's chin. Tommy was so delirious he barely noticed.

Levi stood and shook his head to clear it. The ringing in his ears had died down, leaving only a dull headache. The lot had gone silent, and Levi hoped that meant both of the assailants were dead.

Footsteps pounded down the stairs above them.

"None of that was quiet," Tock breathed. "People are coming."

Levi grabbed Tommy by the arm and hoisted him up. The Martingale Casino was his most lucrative client, and the Irons murdering people downstairs hardly spoke well of their business practices. "Get in the other car."

They ran across the lot. Tommy somehow managed to climb into the back seat without support, leaving Levi and Tock to deal with the bodies. Tock dragged the man Levi had shot across the ground, smearing the pavement with a trail of blood. Levi approached the flames, nearly vomiting from the smell, and pulled out what remained of the woman. His fingers sank into charred, crusted flesh.

By the time they dumped both bodies in the trunk, swarms of casino employees and other bystanders had begun flooding into the garage. Levi did his best to keep his face covered. He didn't want another headline in *The Crimes & The Times*. He just wanted to get out of here, crawl into the silence of his bedroom, and pretend this entire night had never happened.

Levi took the driver's seat, and soon the engine roared, their car speeding forward and onto Tropps Street. As soon as they screeched through the first turn, Tock rolled down the window and vomited.

"Delicate," he told her, even though he was a hairbreadth from being sick himself.

Tommy snickered from the back seat, then let out a low groan.

"Shut up, Tommy," Tock snapped at him as she wiped her mouth. "Your nose is broken. You're not dead."

Those were the last words they spoke for a half hour. At first, Levi wasn't sure where he was driving. They barreled down Tropps Street, passing St. Morse Casino, and eventually veered north, to the distant edges of the Ruins District. The lights and bustle faded behind them, and when he rolled down the windows, the air smelled of the sea.

Tock turned around to peer into the back seat. "He's asleep." She sighed and leaned her head against the window. "Was that the only person you've killed besides Chez?"

"No," he answered quietly. "I was the one who killed the Chancellor, not Enne."

Levi wasn't sure why he told her that. Even if Semper had been despicable, now Levi's actions had begun to feel like a pattern. Each time, he'd killed those who'd tried to kill him.

But with his reputation growing and the bounty on his head up to ten thousand volts... This probably wasn't the last time an incident like this would happen.

Tock let out a hollow laugh. "My father saved Malcolm Semper's life. When he blew up the National Prison, Semper had been next on death row for treason to the Mizer kings."

Narinder told Levi part of that story the first time he'd met Tock, but Levi had forgotten it until this moment. Tock's father ignited the Revolution that destroyed his own father's life. Levi felt that ought to symbolize something, but everything about the world suddenly felt meaningless.

"How did it feel to blow up Revolution Bridge, then?" he asked her. "Wasn't that part of your family's legacy?"

"My father was a mercenary. He wasn't some hero." Tock crossed her arms. "Heroes are overrated. That's why I never wanted to be one."

Maybe their family histories did have more in common than he'd thought.

Levi parked the car where the road gave way to sand. The ocean lay in front of them, its water black in the night. The city line was ten minutes behind them, and Levi suddenly realized, in his six years living in New Reynes, he'd never once left it.

"You don't have to help if you don't want to," Levi told her.

"But I will," she answered, and he breathed a sigh of gratitude, even if he probably depended on her too much.

They made two trips, the woman first and the man second. Levi did his best not to look at them, not to think about them, and so his mind wandered. He'd grown up on the beach, along this same ocean. He tried to focus on those memories rather than the one he was making right now. The bottom of his pants soaked as they rested the bodies face-down in the water. They sank slightly into the sand and broken shells, and waves lapped at their clothes.

Tock and Levi didn't linger. By the time they returned to the museum, Levi thought Tock had actually drifted off, as well. But as they passed through the darkened streets of Olde Town, she murmured, "The first person I killed was by accident."

Levi was about to ask how it had happened, but then realized he didn't need to. He'd watched a car burst into flames tonight. He'd seen the entire structure of Revolution Bridge collapse into the Brint as though it had snapped in two. If Tock wasn't careful, everyone around her could become collateral damage.

"I just wish it hadn't been," she added quietly.

Levi tried his best to give her a comforting smile while still navigating the narrow streets. "Don't let your fallen heroes stop you from wanting to become one."

"You always talk so highly of the old lords, like Veil and Havoc. Do you feel like a hero now?"

Levi remembered the weight of the man's body going slack on top of him. He hoped the prize of the Iron Lord's bounty had been worth it, to that man.

Then he thought of his view tonight from the top of Martingale Casino, and he hoped it was all still worth it to him.

ENNE

Lola pulled a stack of files from the metal cabinets and fanned herself with the manila folders. "I thought you said you had someone for us."

Harvey pursed his lips. "Yes, we suggested Vito. But you said no."

"Well, we're still only taking girls."

Harvey shot Enne an exasperated look. "You've hired all the female counters we had. How many more could you need?"

Enne perched by the windowsill of the warden's office, hoping to catch a breeze. It was the hottest week in New Reynes on record.

"More organizations have expressed interest in investing," she told Harvey, all businesslike. She was even dressed like a financier, with a pink button-up and a sleek skirt to match the ladies who worked on Hedge Street. Complete with her mask, her gang's white satin gloves, and her favorite black lipstick, this had become her uniform. "We need more girls."

"If you give us time, we'll recruit more," Bryce told her. He bent over his desk, his dark hair plastered across his forehead with sweat. For as many times as Enne came to visit, Bryce never looked pleasant. His clothes always hung on him, his eyes were always bloodshot, and despite all this sun, he actually seemed to be growing paler.

"How much longer?" Enne asked. With their stock market expanding by thousands of volts every day, Enne finally had the resources to begin digging up information on the Phoenix Club. But without new workers, she didn't have the time to spare.

"Soon," Harvey answered. "I'll make the rounds at all the pubs and cabarets, where workers tired of their jobs go to unwind. That's when they're most receptive."

Enne clicked her tongue in disgust. "You don't need to poach them, Harvey."

"I don't *poach* anyone."

"You talk like you do."

"Then come with me. It'll be an easier sell with you there. We can all go." He looked at Bryce and wiggled his eyebrows. "A few cold drinks could do us some good."

"How many times will you make her say no?" Bryce asked, and Harvey scowled.

"He has a point," Lola muttered.

Though Enne believed Harvey's intentions were good, it didn't matter how much time she spent at the Guild lately—they were associates, not friends. Enne wore her mask to every appointment. She'd still never given them a name other than Séance. And when Rebecca attended their meetings—though infrequently, as of late—she made it clear she still viewed Enne as a fraud.

Enne also suspected she wasn't the one Harvey was trying to convince to join him for a night out.

"But if you just—" Harvey started.

"I said no," Bryce snapped, making Harvey stiffen. Bryce stood up and sighed. "I'm not your villain," he murmured, and then he walked out of the room, and Harvey buried his face in his hands.

Enne and Lola exchanged an uncomfortable look.

Lola cleared her throat. "Well, I think we should be going."

"Yes, let us know about those recruits…" Enne gathered her belongings and followed Lola out the door.

The pair made their way through the prison's hallways, keeping their voices low.

"Why do they have to be so strange?" Lola hissed.

"They've always been like—"

Lola elbowed her sharply in the side. "It just got stranger."

Rebecca leaned against the wall by the exit with a gun in her hand.

"This isn't typically my weapon of choice," she told them, examining her revolver.

Both Lola and Enne froze.

"Is there something you'd like to say?" Enne demanded. When it came to Enne, Rebeca always had something to say—but not usually while brandishing a firearm.

Rebecca let out a hacking cough, splattering flecks of blood on her sleeve. "We don't need your business. It would be better for everyone if you stayed away."

Lola stiffened beside her, but Enne wasn't so easily threatened. "How do Bryce and Harvey feel about that?" Enne asked, reaching for her own gun inside her purse.

Rebecca let out a laugh. "As if Harvey's opinion matters."

Enne didn't want to get into an argument with someone who was clearly ill. Rebecca didn't look well enough to stand, let alone challenge them to a shoot-out. And either way, Enne felt she would win.

"You can either step aside, or we can go through you," Enne told her darkly. "It's your choice."

Rebecca narrowed her eyes and backed away. "Just don't come back."

Enne and Lola passed through the broken gates outside. Lola walked stiffly, like at any moment, she might be shot between the shoulder blades. Enne kept her hand on her own gun, trying to figure out when Rebecca had stopped treating her like dirt and started treating her like an enemy.

"I knew Rebecca was ill, but I've never seen her like that," Lola told Enne as they turned onto the block where they'd parked her motorcar. "No wonder Bryce has been a mess."

Bryce had unnerved Enne from the first time they'd met, but now Enne felt a pang of sympathy.

"What is the Balfour family talent?" Enne asked.

Lola eyed her uneasily. "Why do you ask?"

"I just realized how little I know him, is all."

Lola lowered her voice to a whisper. "The Balfour family doesn't have a talent."

Enne frowned. "Is that possible?"

"I don't think so, but that's how they're listed in all the archives."

"Then he's clearly hiding something."

"They're all hiding something," Lola muttered as she unlocked her car and they each climbed inside. She turned around to back the motorcar out of the narrow alley, then startled. "Did you see that?"

"See what?" Enne asked, whipping around. She only saw quiet rowhomes with their curtains drawn.

"I thought I spotted something," Lola murmured, frowning. "Probably nothing."

Enne shrugged and opened her Sadie Knightley novel. She'd

developed a habit of rereading the same books over and over, because she craved the certainty of knowing how the stories ended.

She'd listened to enough of Grace's lessons to know how legends ended, too.

And so each morning, before Vianca's direct phone line could ring, before Lola could fill her schedule with appointments, Enne completed a ritual. She pictured the faces of the Phoenix Club, she practiced her shooting, and she told herself the same thing.

Not mine.

Every day, over six hundred thousand illegal volts flowed through an old finishing school classroom in the Ruins District. It was decorated in pastels, and a gaggle of girls sat on the floor, papers spread around them, pencils tapping against plush fur carpet. They each wore curlers in their hair or green, sludgy masks over their skin. Every now and then, one would shout out a new number and phrase, and several others would adjust the statistics on the chalkboard.

As Enne and Lola entered, Grace jumped to her feet, cucumbers falling off her eyes. Enne wasn't sure the cucumbers could do her much good if she still wore thick circles of eyeliner beneath them.

Grace shoved Enne a clipboard. "We're getting calls. Lots of investors backing out."

"Define *lots*," Enne said. She squinted at the numbers on the paper.

"Two hundred thousand volts."

"*What*? Who's pulling out? From where?" Enne scanned the list. It seemed most of the investors were from gambling dens. Was Levi up to something?

"It's not the Irons," Grace answered. "They're all Torren-owned dens, which makes sense. Charles doesn't trust you. You *did* kill his cousin."

If too many investors pulled out, the gangs would each lose a fortune. And with tensions rising between the whiteboots in the South Side and the gangs patrolling the North, none of the lords could afford budget cuts right now. Wealth was their most effective weapon.

"If every single Torren den sold out, how much more would we lose?" Enne asked.

"Maybe sixty thousand more volts?" Grace told her. "I have the names of every person who backed out. Give me the word, and I'll kill them all."

"Terror," Enne said drily. "Because that worked out so well for past lords."

"Suit yourself, but I want you to know—I'm doing math, and I'm very bored."

"You're a counter. Isn't this what you do?"

Grace raised her eyebrows. "When's the last time you did a cartwheel?" She poked Enne in the side with her pencil. "I could think of other uses for your bendy talent that Poppy's list of South Side boys might find pretty appealing." She smiled wickedly.

The girl closest to them rolled her eyes. "You spent all morning telling me how satisfying it was to make the Irons' statements balance."

Grace clutched her knife necklace indignantly. "Yeah, well, Pup's books were a mess, so I fixed them."

"These aren't businesses—they're gangs. Who cares if the numbers don't add up?"

Grace bent down and snatched a glossy piece of paper hidden under the girl's notebook, pulling away the whole magazine with it. "Really, Charlotte?" She threw the copy of *The*

Kiss & Tell across the room. "So when you find an error, what do you do?"

Charlotte shrugged and grabbed herself a piece of candy from the bowl beside her. "I give it to Marcy. She lives for it."

Enne looked around at the girls and realized Marcy, the youngest girl among them, who wore glasses so large they made her face look bug-like, was the only one actually working. The others were reading from Enne's stash of romance novels or braiding their hair.

"This place is a mess," Lola said flatly. "It's a good thing we're not hiring a boy, otherwise none of you would get anything done." She tipped Charlotte's bottle of pink nail polish over on her magazine.

A number of voices chorused around the room.

"That was from *Kipling's*," Charlotte snapped first.

"We're getting a boy?" Marcy asked, flushing and dropping her piece of chalk.

"As if *you* ever do anything here other than chauffeur Enne around and sneak out every night," Grace muttered to Lola.

Lola whipped around, as though trying to decide who to strike first. Enne whacked her over the head with Grace's notebook.

"Enough," she hissed. "Charlotte, I want you to call the potential investors on the next sales list and see if you can make up these losses. Grace, if you're going to spend time fixing Levi's math, I expect you to charge him for it. And Lola— um, play nice."

Lola rolled her eyes. "I hate all of you. And I especially hate *this*." She kicked a pink fur pillow across the floor.

"I'm going to my office," Enne groaned, and then she swept off down the hallway. It'd been several hours since she last manned her phone, and knowing Vianca, she'd probably tried to call a dozen times in Enne's absence. Lately, the donna's list of requests grew ever longer and more absurd, including demanding the Spirits run election polls and forcing Enne to recite all the reasons why Harrison was a failure as a son.

Lola followed Enne to the headmistress's office, which the two of them shared. She slung her top hat on the desk and instinctively reached for the radio.

"The North Side isn't a no-go zone," Harrison Augustine told the reporter in a muffled voice, like he was pushing the microphone away. "The Mole lines are operating normally. In fact, violent crimes in the North Side have decreased by—"

"The Senate vote regarding the registration of the Talents of Mysteries is tomorrow," the reporter interrupted. "You've expressed reluctance regarding this in the past. How do you feel now that the vote is this close?"

Enne sighed and reached for the half-full mug of tea on her desk, sweetened with six teaspoons of sugar. The election wasn't for three months yet, and she already needed a vacation.

"Public fear is on the rise, and I think what everyone— North *and* South Side—wants is extra peace of mind. That's my only comment."

"What a mucking useless answer," Lola spat. "It's no won-der Prescott is beating him."

Enne's heart clenched. Even if she hated the First Party for its connections to the Phoenix Club, Enne had a vested in-terest in seeing Harrison win the election. If Harrison won, then she and Levi would be free of Vianca forever.

"Just because our polls say one thing, doesn't mean—" Enne started.

"Our polls are right." Lola fiddled with the radio dial, switching between talk shows, music, and static. "You know, Vianca would probably approve of a publication that shows the North Side's support for Prescott, since no one else will print the truth."

"Is that how you're pitching things to me now? How they would please Vianca?"

"You use the name Séance, which was Lourdes's pen name. It's her legacy."

Enne knew Lola felt more strongly about politics than she did, but she'd never imagined Lola would play such a card.

"It wasn't her legacy," Enne snapped. "It was her death sentence."

The words might've been harsh, but they worked. Lola quietly returned to changing the radio stations, and Enne slipped out of the room to clear her head.

Enne climbed the stairs to the dormitories and spotted a cat perched on the bannister. In an effort to make the finishing school feel more like home, Marcy had adopted thirteen strays, which she'd named after famous legends from the North Side.

"You're not supposed to wander," Enne told him, picking him up. Marcy had named this one Veil for the black fur on his head, matching the tales of how Veil had kept his face hidden. As Enne carried him back to the dormitories, she noticed the calico, Inamorata, curled up asleep in the hallway, and that one of the doors had been left ajar.

Suddenly a hand clasped over Enne's mouth. Another hand circled around her waist and held her firmly.

"Don't move," a male voice whispered in her ear. She ignored him and thrashed in his arms, dropping Veil. The cat paid no mind to her distress and ran down the hallway.

Then she felt a knife press into her back.

"I said, don't move."

Enne froze and swallowed down her scream. The man pushed her forward, walking her into the bedroom where the cats had escaped. The window was shattered, and a rope stretched down from it.

Keeping the knife pressed against her and his hand covering her mouth, he turned her around to face him. A mask concealed his features, except for a pair of dark eyes and a few tufts of dirty blond hair. Enne didn't recognize him, but she felt she knew his voice from somewhere she couldn't place.

"We're going to climb down," he told her, slapping a handcuff around her wrist and the other around his belt. "You aren't going to make a sound. You aren't going to fight."

Enne tried her best not to panic, but her bounty was worth the same if she was dead or alive. He might let her live for now, but if she fought back, there was nothing stopping him from slicing that knife across her throat.

The Spirits were all downstairs. How long would it take them to realize Enne had gone missing?

The man reached into his pocket and pulled out a gag. He stuffed it in Enne's mouth, even with one hand still clutching his knife. Enne guessed he favored his left hand, and judging from his size, she wouldn't overpower him in a battle of strength.

But she was not weak.

While he secured the knot around her gag, she grabbed the hand that held the knife and twisted it away. His balance veered, and she kicked his feet out from under him. It sent them both falling, but she landed on top.

She punched him as hard as she could in the face.

"*Muck,*" she cursed. It *hurt.* As she shook out the pain in her fist, he grabbed her by the shoulder and flipped them over.

He pressed his knife against her throat. "You're more of a pain than I expected."

"Yes," Grace said at the door, making him jolt. She dropped Veil onto the floor. "I'm very proud."

Then she lifted her boot and kicked him in the chest. He sprawled backward, his knife skidding across the floor, sending several cats dashing after it. Enne, too, was yanked by the handcuff, getting brush burn across her arms. Grace pinned him down with her knees and ripped off his mask.

He had a young, handsome face, with cheekbones so strong it was no wonder Enne had nearly broken her hand on them.

Grace reached over and pulled the gag from Enne's mouth. Enne sputtered out a thank-you.

"I'm not alone," the handsome man said sharply. "The captain knows my position."

"I was there when the whiteboots shot up the Orphan Guild," Grace said. "So either you've all lost your rifles, or you're alone. I'm guessing the latter." She dug through his pockets and removed a pouch of orbs, his badge, and the keys to Enne's handcuffs. She handed the last item to Enne, who quickly freed herself. "How did you find this place?"

He said nothing, only turned his head to the side and glared at the wall.

Grace punched him on his other cheek, and she didn't curse like Enne had. "You *will* tell us who you are and who else knows about this place, or I will kill you very, very slowly."

He seethed, but remained silent.

"Enne, get the rope," Grace ordered, and Enne pulled the whiteboot's escape rope up from the window. She and Grace forced him into a chair in the room's corner, then bound his arms and legs to it. "I say we kill him. I hate whiteboots."

"Kill him? Here?" Enne echoed. The Spirits were accountants—not assailants. "In Marcy's bedroom?"

"He knows our location now, and he's seen you without your mask. We can't let him live."

Grace had a point, but Enne still stopped her as she reached for his gun. *"No,"* she commanded. Even if she'd needed Grace to save her, she was still the lord. She would decide if and when they killed him. "I'm going to get the others."

"But… You can't—"

Two minutes later, all nine of the Spirits huddled in Marcy's bedroom. Several of them still carried the tabloids they'd been reading. Others clutched knives, as though a bruised man tied to a chair still posed a threat.

"Holy muck," Marcy murmured, which was the first time Enne had ever heard her curse. She squeezed one of her cats for support, even as it squirmed in her grip. "Look at his face."

"Let's keep him," Charlotte declared, and several of the Spirits nodded in agreement.

"Let's *kill* him," Grace growled, waving around his badge. "He's a whiteboot."

Enne didn't like the idea of murdering someone in cold blood, but Charlotte's alternative sounded no better. He would be a liability if he escaped, which meant someone would need to watch him around the clock. That was one less girl working, and they were already growing short-staffed.

"We can't keep him here," Lola said matter-of-factly, "or Marcy will have a stroke."

"He could be a hostage," Charlotte suggested.

"I am *not* a hostage," the whiteboot spat. He turned his face away from them, exposing the blossoming purple mark on his cheek. "You might as well kill me. Captain Hector won't negotiate with…" His eyes roamed over the girls, each dressed in little more than pajamas, with rollers in their hair or green charcoal masks still on their faces. "Gangsters."

"I know who you are," Lola said, stepping forward. "I know your voice. You're Sergeant Roy Pritchard. You're the whiteboot who led the Orphan Guild operation. You gave an interview on the radio afterward."

The other girls quieted. Nearly all of them had been present for the attack on the Guild.

They definitely weren't giggling anymore.

"If that's true," Enne said, "then why are you here alone?"

Lola picked up the mask that Grace had thrown away. "I knew I saw something strange earlier. I spotted someone wearing this when we were leaving the Orphan Guild. He followed us here."

Enne didn't like this. Why would the sergeant have acted alone? Once he'd spotted the finishing school, he could've left at any time and called for backup. And if he'd done that, he wouldn't have snuck inside by himself—he would've planned an ambush.

"If you don't want to kill him," Marcy suggested, "the Scarhands know people who can muddle memories. I've done jobs for them before."

Enne didn't fancy the idea of visiting Jonas, but that was the best idea they'd come up with. "Someone call the Scarhands and schedule me an appointment for tomorrow morning with Scavenger. Lola, see if you can find any information about whether the sergeant was recently let go from the force, or a reason why he'd be acting alone." Roy stiffened at her words, but still said nothing. "Grace, get everyone back to work. We'll need to spare someone every few hours to watch him, and we can't afford to fall further behind on work. I'll take the first shift."

As the girls scattered, Enne flopped down on Marcy's bed. She grabbed Marcy's pistol from her bureau and set it on the nightstand, then reached for the most recent edition of *The Kiss & Tell*.

"If you try anything, I'll kill you," Enne told him, and she meant it. She would protect her girls, no matter what.

Sergeant Roy Pritchard turned his pretty face away and glared at the floor. Enne ignored him as she stroked Veil and read the front page exposé, which speculated about the woman behind the criminal enterprise that had revolutionized the North Side.

After finishing it, Enne flipped back to the glossy portrait on the tabloid's cover and gave her own wanted poster a kiss.

JAC

♥ ♠ ♦ ♣

In the month since their meeting with Harrison Augustine, Jac and Sophia had mastered the art of persuasion. Defeating Charles Torren wasn't like a simple game of cards. It was night after night of sweet-talking dens and clientele and Apothecaries into abandoning the man currently paying them, all to support a teenage girl they'd never heard of.

It began with intimidation.

"How do I know you're really who you say you are?" a den manager might ask.

"Charles has never once denied who I am," Sophia would respond. "You should ask him, after you tell him how you agreed to meet with me."

Then they needed to charm.

"There's been trouble all across the North Side," Jac would say, taking a protective step closer to an Apothecary. The woman was nearly twice his age, but the team had learned her sort was the type he could most easily sway. "We all know Charles's reputation. If you were in trouble, would you rather be going to Charles, or to us?" He stood taller, arms crossed, trying to emphasize the build of his strength talent. "To me?"

"W-well..." the woman would stammer, a flush creeping across her face.

The last, most important step was to remind them that even though Sophia and Jac were inexperienced and risky, they were also rich—thanks to the under-the-table support from Harrison Augustine.

"We'll give you twenty percent more than whatever he pays you," Sophia would say, batting her eyelashes at the burly supplier. "Maybe even twenty-five, just for that smile of yours."

Now they controlled almost half of the Torren dens in the Casino District. They were *earning* volts in addition to spending them. And they could finally celebrate.

Jac was all grins as he swirled a straw around his glass of iced water, his head lazily propped on his hand.

"I don't know why you're so proud," Sophia teased from beside him. "I wouldn't be, if the only people I could make swoon were lonely, forty-year-old women."

"I believe what you keep meaning to say is 'thank you,'" Jac said.

"So you keep trying to remind me." She leaned into his shoulder.

Jac bristled. He didn't want to dredge up their same, familiar fight, but he couldn't help himself as he swept aside the taffy wrappers on the bar and pulled their ledger closer. On it was a list of dens, some circled, some crossed off.

"I don't understand why Charles hasn't made a move yet," he murmured. "That doesn't seem like him."

"Stop doing that," Sophia said sharply. She turned her head so her chin rested on his shoulder, and Jac could feel her warm breath on his neck. He'd seen Sophia flirt with enough den managers to know how she used charm like a weapon, but Jac wouldn't fall for it—not even if he wanted to.

"Then tell me the truth," he told her, forcing himself not to stare at her lips. "Tell me why Delia never recognized you. Tell me what happened between you and your family."

Sophia pulled away from him with pursed lips. Jac scolded himself—he *was* staring. "You're right—this isn't like him. Charles hits when you don't expect it. He hits where you are weakest, and he hits until you break." She shook her head. "Now I'm anxious. Does that make you happy?"

He sighed and stood up. "I'm going to find the washroom."

Before he moved away, Sophia reached into his pants pocket and pulled out his pack of cigarettes. She threw them across the bar.

"What was that for?" he snapped, even though he knew his smoking habit had worsened recently. "I'm just going to piss."

"Then it shouldn't matter to you." She waved him away, her face buried in the ledger, her fingers fiddling with her coin.

Jac groaned under his breath as he made his way around back. They made good partners, but she still kept a wall between them, between her and the world. And she only reached over that wall to steal his cigarettes.

So what if she cares? he thought angrily. If she cared more, she'd treat him like a real partner, and she'd tell him the truth.

After he finished in the washroom, Jac opened the door back into the hallway and was startled to find a man standing behind it.

"Oh, um, sorry," Jac muttered, moving aside to let him walk past.

The man shoved something in Jac's hands. A red envelope. Jac stared at the words on the front for several moments until he worked out what they said. *Todd Walsh.*

As the man who'd delivered it hurried out the back door,

KING OF FOOLS

Jac frowned and tore the envelope open. He spilled the contents into his hand, and a syringe gleamed on his palm. It was filled with a clear, murky liquid—a high enough dose of Lullaby to lull out for twelve hours, maybe even more.

Jac froze. He knew where the delivery had come from, and suddenly, it was like the past two years of sobriety meant nothing. No matter how many times he'd resisted, and prayed, and made himself stronger, he hadn't changed.

He hits where you are weakest.

Jac's palms began to sweat, and all of his worries from the past few weeks surged inside him. That Charles would come for them. That the North Side would crumble. That Levi's stunts would finally get him killed. All the scenarios he'd dwelled on returned to him in such vivid detail that he could almost convince himself they'd already happened. His heart beat furiously, his pulse anxious and all over the place. His lungs felt tight. His life might be different now, but he was still trapped, still overwhelmed.

And part of him still wanted the fix.

He tried to pull himself out of it. He thought about the smell of gasoline at the den he'd burned, and how good it had felt to destroy a place so like the others that haunted him. But still, he didn't let go of the syringe. He didn't move at all.

He thought about how he'd almost died. About the man whose name Jac now used as his own, and how cold he'd been when Jac had found him...only a few hours too late. Jac shivered, but it still wasn't enough to let go.

And so he thought about Levi. Who had dragged him unconscious to New Reynes North General. Who had trusted him. Who would blame himself.

Jac dropped the syringe on the floor and shattered it beneath his boot.

"Muck," he choked out, running his hands through his

353

hair. He took several deep, steady breaths, but he couldn't stop himself from shaking.

I didn't do it, he thought. *I crushed it.*

But another thought was louder. *He hits where you are weakest, and he hits until you break.*

Vomit bubbled up his throat. His fears were all he could see. The North Side falling. Levi dying. Himself fading.

And the worst part of it was that he knew the lull would take those fears away.

Before he knew what he was doing, Jac stormed across the den and wrapped tape around his fists. He dropped an orb with forty volts into the bookie's jar. "I'll take next. Whoever you got."

I sold it all but my pride when I came to this town.

Jac's opponent was no bigger than he was. In fact, he looked like he'd already been in a number of fights that night, his lip swollen and his knuckles chafed. Jac didn't mind. This just meant that he was faster. Each of his blows landed, one after the other. He would keep fighting with everything he had, and that was how he would win.

He continued for several rounds. Until he stopped winning.

His opponent's fist knocked him square in the jaw, sending Jac reeling back. His thoughts funneled, and he braced himself on the chain-link fence surrounding the pit as he spit out a mouthful of blood. He wiped what remained of it on his sleeve and straightened, his fist raised.

The next time he got hit, he landed on the floor. The air rushed out of him, and he groaned and rolled onto his back. His opponent stood over him, waiting for Jac to forfeit.

But Jac didn't want to give up. He wanted to win. He wanted to burn down a hundred more dens and smash a thousand more syringes. To hear the referee's whistle rather than sirens. To become so strong he wouldn't spiral the moment he caught a glimpse of Lullaby.

He lost, of course. No sooner did he climb to his feet than he was knocked back to the ground again. He clutched his stomach at the pit's edge, trying hard not to throw up.

The referee whistled, calling the fight for Jac's loss. Once his nausea passed, Jac limped to the exit and crashed in the nearest empty booth. He grabbed an abandoned glass on the table and fished out the ice to press to his lip.

He sighed as he leaned his head back. Logic reminded him that he never would've won all night, and he'd taken four fights to lose. Was that how long it would take Charles to wear him down? Or would it be next time? Would it be never?

Sophia appeared over him, her expression livid. "What was that about?" she demanded.

"I was in the mood," he grumbled.

"To get your ass kicked? Exactly what sort of mood is that?" She brushed her thumb over the cut under his lip, making him wince—and shudder. "You might need stitches."

He shrugged. "I've had worse."

She let go of him, shoving him away as she did so. "What aren't you telling me?" Jac didn't know how she saw through him so easily, but she always did.

"You were right about Charles. He did go for where we're weakest." He told her what the man had given him outside the bathroom, not quite meeting her eyes. "I shattered it."

Sophia reached into the pocket of her dress and removed a red envelope, identical to the one Jac had received. "You're not the weakest part of this. I got one, too."

A surge of relief went through him, followed by curiosity. "What was in yours?"

"An invitation…and a picture." Sophia's hand trembled slightly as she handed them to Jac. He traced his finger over the photograph first. It was clearly Sophia as a child, standing between two teenagers he realized were Charles and Delia. A family portrait.

Jac opened his mouth to ask about it, but she snatched the picture back and slid him the invitation. It was printed on luxurious black card stock with embossed red font. Luckluster colors. "Charles wants to meet."

"I bet he does. I bet he's thinking about bleeding us out on his carpet." Charles wanted to run the Torren empire, and Sophia wanted to destroy it. There was no room for negotiation.

"I think I should go," she said quietly. "I think I need to face him."

"I don't think we—"

"You're not going."

He frowned. "If you're going, so am I."

"You told Levi you'd get out if it became dangerous, and it has. If Charles keeps sending you Lullaby—"

"Don't you trust me?" he snapped. "I told you I destroyed it."

She pushed his hair off his forehead, pressing tenderly on what he felt was a bruise beginning to form. "You ran from one destruction to the next. Don't make me watch that."

His heart fell. That was the same as telling him no. She didn't trust him. Nobody did.

"Don't make me leave," he pleaded, even though he hated to beg. They were supposed to be partners. Equals. "You're the only one who knows why I want this. It was my idea. And if you send me away, then I'll keep hanging around here until you show up again. If you can hunt me down to where I live, then I can find you, too."

Her voice rose. "Just to prove something?"

"Isn't that what you're doing by going to see Charles?" he countered. "You're terrified of him. Even when you worked alone, you chose Delia over him—and she was every bit a monster. You know them, but they somehow no longer know you. How can I be your partner if I don't know the whole truth?"

She even looked pretty when she cringed. "You know me better than anyone else does. Isn't that enough?"

"No," he rasped. "It's not."

He pulled her down so she sat beside him. With the den loud with howls and whistles from the next fight, there was no one to overhear. She could either trust him, or she could at least be honest with him and tell him, flat out, that she didn't.

"I don't know what you want from me," she told him.

"Do you even want me here? Do you want me to stay?"

"Of course I do." She dug her nails into both her knee and his.

"Then tell me the truth. *All* of it." He didn't mean to growl, but he was angry—angry and frightened. Charles had *murdered* Delia. If they were going to face him together, then Jac needed to know what they were up against. Not the rumors—the truth.

Her gaze fell to the cut across his lip. "I don't want to." She leaned toward him, close enough for him to smell the taffy on her breath. He realized she wasn't actually looking at the cut. "I'm sorry, but—"

"No," he said, catching her hand midair as it drifted toward his waist. "You don't get to play this game." Because he was terrified that if they did, she would win. "The only game we'll play tonight is all or nothing."

Sophia pulled her hand back. "I can't make you leave. This is your war as much as mine. So we'll accept Charles's invitation together." She slid back and stood up. "But no games."

Then she left Jac to ice his wounds alone.

ENNE

♥   ♠   ♦   ♣

With the whiteboots trapped in the South Side, Scrap Market had taken up its first permanent residence in history. Gone were the days of varying hours, of packing up stalls and moving them at a moment's warning. The Scarhands had used their stock market wealth to purchase an apartment building in the Factory District, and vendors had taken up shop in each room. Every floor offered a different category of wares. The higher you ascended, the less innocent they became.

Enne climbed the stairwell to the topmost floor and entered a hallway filled with Scarhands. The doors to each apartment were open, revealing weapons displayed on lounge furniture and photographs of for-sale identities covering everything like wallpaper.

Though dressed primly for a South Side Party later that morning, the only attire Enne wore that mattered were her white gloves and silk mask. She paid no mind to the whispers and glances thrown her way as she walked past. Not until she came face-to-face with someone she recognized. Someone who, she immediately realized, was another loose end.

The girl straightened and lifted her head as Enne approached the door. She had brown skin and bobbed hair. Like all the others, scars crisscrossed her palms.

"Does Pup know you're here?" Enne asked. She hoped, for Levi's sake, that he didn't. Even if the Irons had prospered under the North Side's new regime, he wouldn't take it well if he learned his old protégée now worked for Jonas.

"No," Mansi answered coolly.

"What have you told Scavenger?" Enne asked, because of course Mansi would remember who she really was. Enne doubted the Irons received many visitors who burst into tears in their living room, as she had on her first day in New Reynes.

"Everything."

Enne's heart sank. That meant Jonas knew her name—and maybe more. She'd previously threatened him with Vianca, but how long would that threat retain its bite?

"I have an appointment," Enne told Mansi stiffly. The girl nodded and opened the door.

Jonas sat cross-legged in his desk chair, his greasy hair pulled back from his face. Enne braced herself for his usual corpselike stench, but the room actually smelled pleasant, due to whatever candle was burning on the end table.

"Enne Salta," Jonas said, grinning wickedly. Enne scowled at hearing her name and hastily shut the door behind her. "I've been looking forward to this appointment all night." As she took a seat in front of him, he opened a folder and slid her a photograph across the desk. It was Enne's last school portrait. "The Bellamy Finishing School of Fine Arts. Bottom of your class."

"I don't want trouble, Jonas," she said, since they were apparently on a first-name basis now.

"Trouble?" He lifted his eyebrows. "Do you have other secrets I should know about?"

"My associate called you yesterday about hiring someone who can alter memories. Do you have someone who could help us?" The sooner they disposed of Roy Pritchard, the better. She didn't want a second handsome whiteboot to come looking for him. Or worse, for the Spirits to grow any more distracted. When he wouldn't stop sneezing and they realized he was allergic to Marcy's cats, every one of the girls had offered their rooms as a replacement.

"Of course I do," Jonas answered. "Maybe you're unaware of what we offer here, but there's nothing we can't provide. Skin-stitchers, trackers, protectors. There's no information in New Reynes that I don't already know, or that I can't find out."

Enne's skin prickled at his last words. "Are you trying to sell me something, or are you trying to threaten me?"

"What would I gain by threatening you? The Scarhands have never been richer, thanks to you." He flashed her a too-wide smile. "My only ulterior motive is curiosity. I mean, why would a hopeless finishing school student want to become a street lord?"

"Vianca doesn't usually take one's desires into consideration."

He stood up and perched at the edge of his desk, much like Reymond had when she'd first met them both. Even so, Jonas didn't remind her of Reymond at all. Reymond had collected information by sniffing out lies and breaking bones, but Jonas's office was cluttered and full in the way Reymond's had been bare. File cabinets lined the walls, their drawers pulled out and stuffed with folders. Jonas might've had a report on every citizen of New Reynes tucked away in this room.

"I have no doubt you're doing this for Vianca," Jonas murmured, "but that didn't mean you had to excel at it. You *want* this."

Enne *did* excel at this, which was why she knew better than to be flattered. She gestured around the room. "I've made you rich, yes, but I don't believe you when you say it's about volts. You inherited this position from Eight Fingers, and it's like you said—you didn't *have* to excel at it." She stood up and inspected the closest filing cabinet. The folders were meticulously organized in alphabetical order. "So is it knowledge just for the sake of it? Or something else?" Enne brushed her fingers across the folders, as though strumming an instrument. "Maybe you're desperately trying to conceal your own secrets. Or trying to find a particular someone else's."

He hopped off the desk and slid the drawer she perused closed. He had a playful gleam in his eyes. "I'll tell you my truth if you tell me yours."

"Tempting," she said, "but I'm more curious about other things."

Jonas laughed, as though even he acknowledged that he wasn't the most interesting thing in this room. He had a strangely relaxed laugh.

"What do you know about Harrison Augustine?" she asked.

He stiffened. "Are you just trying to test my knowledge?"

"My only ulterior motive is curiosity," she told him simply, repeating his own words back at him.

"You probably want to know why Harrison hates Vianca," Jonas guessed. "I can't tell you the answer to that, but I do know something. During the Great Street War, Veil kidnapped the children of several influential people and held them for ransom. Harrison was one of those children. Before that, he was every bit an Augustine prince. After, well..."

Enne wondered what Levi would make of this connection between his favorite New Reynes legend and his secret ally.

"That was a simple question," Jonas told her. "I think you could ask a better one."

Enne had come here for business, but now her curiosity really was getting the better of her. Maybe Jonas wasn't as slimy as she'd once thought.

"Do you know who Vianca's third…" Her voice died in her throat. She couldn't say the word *omerta*, not without the omerta fighting back.

Jonas pursed his lips. "That *is* a better one. I have no idea. But I would pay you for the information, should you happen to find out."

She could've stopped there, but already a third question—a far more dangerous question—came to mind. "Do you know the names of any members of the Phoenix Club?"

She held her breath all through the Scar Lord's silence, wondering if her curiosity had revealed too much.

"Besides our newest chancellor? Only one." Jonas brushed past her and opened one of the cabinets. He removed a file marked "Owain, Aldrich" and handed it to Enne.

Her heart thundered as she flipped through the documents. A photograph was paper-clipped to the top, and Enne instantly recognized his face. She'd replayed the memory of that night so often in her mind that she would have recognized any of them. He looked old and frail, but his appearance was no indication of his true age, thanks to his immortality talent. According to the papers, he owned the media conglomerate that ran *The Crimes & The Times* and several famous radio networks.

Enne finally had a name. This man had helped murder her mother—he had almost murdered *her*—and now Enne had his name.

"That's a dangerous look you have right now," Jonas commented.

Enne handed him back the papers before she squeezed them so hard they tore. "I should get going." She fished an orb out of her purse and placed it on his desk. "For the memory fixer. Should I bring the client here tonight?"

"Bring him whenever you'd like. My door is always open." Jonas collapsed back into his chair and opened her own file, his eyes drifting between the documents and her. "You can tell me more about your plans for the Phoenix Club."

"And you can tell me more about that person you're looking for."

At first, he frowned, and then he chuckled to himself. "You were wasted in finishing school."

Two hours later, Enne danced the Skipstep with a young man named Whitacker Blake. Whitacker wore a linen suit with white polka dots and a matching vanilla cravat. His blond hair was slicked to both sides, leaving a harsh part that accentuated his large forehead. Despite this, he wasn't unattractive—if anything, he was far more interesting to look at than most of the other young men in the room, even those Poppy Prescott had so enthusiastically introduced her to.

"So how long will you be staying on Guillory Street?" Whitacker asked Enne.

"I'm not sure yet," she answered.

"It's a terrible time to be here. The election is a dreadful business," he said. "Especially, I'm sure, for a lady such as yourself."

She furrowed her eyebrows. "How so?"

"Politics is entirely improper for women—they shouldn't have to get their hands so dirty. I'm sure the campaigns are spoiling your summer vacation." Enne squeezed his shoulder a bit harder—not enough to hurt him, but enough to prevent her from biting back.

"Plus the campaigns have been all twisted by the North Side," Whitacker continued, shaking his head. "The Chancellor's death, Sedric Torren's, this street war... Be very glad you're south of the river."

"How could I not be glad?" she asked, tight-lipped. "When the South Side men are so charming?"

His smile made it obvious he hadn't understood her dig.

"But this is Worner Prescott's party—are you not here for political reasons?" she asked.

"My father is," he answered. "We'd normally never dream of voting against the First Party, but one North Side candidate replaced by another? It doesn't matter that Harrison Augustine has been gone for so long—that North Side smell never really goes away."

"I know what you mean," Enne said, nodding solemnly. "It smells acidic...like old wine."

He gave her an odd, unsteady look. "That's very specific."

"And hardly to be masked by Regalliere cologne." She slid her fingers beneath his collar, manicured nails grazing across skin. He stiffened as she exposed his collarbone, and on it, a telltale stain of red lipstick. "It's terribly difficult to get a Sweetie Street mark out, isn't it?" Enne said, pouting her lips. Then she quickly drew away. "I'd finish the dance, but I wouldn't want to get my hands dirty."

Whitacker gaped at her, but just as his expression began to warp into anger, she turned on her heels and sped away. Poppy, who'd been watching while sipping a Hotsy-Totsy, laughed. "What did you say to him? He's gone scarlet!"

"I don't mean to be picky," Enne breathed, "but these men aren't nearly as charming as you'd led me to believe."

Poppy leaned forward with a serious look. "Never, ever apologize for being picky. As if I'd want a friend so easy to please." She scanned the remaining suitors at the party. "I wish I knew what you *did* like, though. You've exhausted the three men with the best cheekbones, the two disgustingly rich ones, the one with the cute butt, *and* you don't seem interested in the girls."

"I didn't hate the one with the cute butt," Enne pointed out. Grace would've probably liked him even more, but until the business with Roy was resolved tonight, Grace needed to stay with the Spirits. Enne almost envied her. If not for Poppy, Enne wouldn't even like going to these salons anymore. They were exactly the sort of gatherings she'd longed to attend in Bellamy, but she hadn't belonged at them then, and she certainly didn't belong here now.

"'Not hating' wasn't exactly the romantic spark I was looking for," Poppy said drily. Her eyes widened, and she squeezed Enne's hand. "There's someone else then, I bet. Back in Bellamy."

Enne snorted. "Why would you think that?"

"You hardly talk about yourself." Poppy smiled mischievously. "I bet you have secrets."

Enne had little intention of revealing anything about herself to Poppy, but she didn't like lying, so she steered the conversation away. "Could we go to the powder room? I'd like to reapply my lipstick."

Several moments later, Poppy bent over the sink, straightening her false eyelashes, and Enne rifled through her purse.

"So what did Whitacker say that had you storming off?" Poppy asked.

"He mentioned something about how women shouldn't dirty their hands with politics."

Poppy barked out a laugh. "Our chancellor is a woman. And as of late, all our male politicians keep getting killed by one."

Enne jolted, smearing pink lipstick across her chin. She quickly closed her purse to hide the white gloves of the Spirits tucked inside.

"I know," Poppy said with a sigh, seeing Enne's reaction. "That's a horribly distasteful thing to say, coming from the daughter of a politician." For a brief moment, the look on her face changed from cheerfulness to worry. "I never thought he'd win, you know. But his campaign advisors are saying he might."

Enne put a hand on her shoulder. "I don't think you need to worry about your father." Not with Vianca watching over him, anyway.

"He announced his candidacy over six months ago, but lately…" Poppy shivered. "It's felt different at these parties. I no longer recognize all the faces. I don't trust anyone here."

"Why not?" Enne asked.

"I just have a terrible feeling. Superstition is outdated, I know, but still." Poppy smoothed out her hair. "I'm dreading the debate more than anything. I've heard it's a huge event, and all the South Side shows up for it. He gets terrible stage fright, and—"

"The debate?" Enne echoed. "It draws that many attendees?"

"Absolutely. It's like showing up to a music hall or a tennis tournament. Everyone pretends to be interested in the show, but they're really just there to get their pictures taken. It's not until the end of September, which is still over a month away, but he's mentioned it multiple times already. He's excited. Like he actually stands a chance of outtalking Harrison Augustine."

If the event truly garnered that level of attention, then Aldrich Owain would likely attend. And Vianca might have Enne attend, as well. She clutched at the edge of her skirts, tracing the outline of her gun.

It was a perfect opportunity.

"I need to go," Enne said quickly.

"You're already running off?" Poppy asked. "Where do you always disappear to?" Before Enne could answer, Poppy's face split into a knowing grin. "Maybe I was wrong about the Bellamy boy. Maybe it's a North Side boy, and you're worried about scandalizing me."

Enne let out a strained laugh. "You're imagining my life to be far more interesting than it is."

Nevertheless, Poppy blew her a kiss. "Tell the North Side boy he hogs too much of your time."

As Enne tried to slip out of the party, a hand grabbed her wrist, and Enne let out a gasp of surprise. "You don't even say hello to me anymore?" Vianca yanked Enne around to face her.

"I... I thought you weren't coming today," Enne stammered. In fact, as Vianca's only confidante, Enne had advised her not to. Vianca insisted these appearances made her look in control, but really, she seemed obsessive. Especially with all the rumors the tabloids reported about what might've happened between her and her son.

Vianca ignored her question. "Did Poppy tell you anything interesting? You have a job to do at these parties, don't forget."

Enne ripped her hand away. "We both know that's not why you want me here, or why you call me ten times a day."

"You think this election is breaking me. Everyone seems to think that." Vianca peered over her shoulder, making several eavesdroppers blanch and turn away. "If I were a man, all the talk would be about my financial interests in this election. Instead, it's *personal*."

Enne didn't believe that to be entirely true, but she also agreed it wasn't false, either.

The donna tucked a loose hair back into her fraying bun. "You'd think the women at least would understand, but look around—who are the ones craning their necks to get a glimpse of the heartless casino owner?" Enne did so, and sure enough, it was mostly women staring. "Well?" she snapped. "What's your opinion on this?"

Enne sighed. Vianca never listened to her advice, anyway. "I think it takes more strength to be vulnerable than it does to appear invincible."

Vianca squeezed Enne's shoulder. She'd already spent so long leaning on it for emotional support that Enne was surprised it wasn't bruised.

"That's it, then?" Vianca snarled. "I should cry motherly tears on a radio station? I should give them what they all want?"

This was what she always did, twisting Enne's honest words into something wrong. For someone convinced she had something to prove to all the men in her life, Vianca would prefer to be regarded as just another man than as a woman successful in her own right, and that made her as narrow-minded as the rest of them.

"Do you hate Harrison?" Enne asked, deeply tired.

"Of course I do. My grandfather, my father, my brother, my son. I hate them all." Her voice grew weaker as her words grew more vicious. "But this was never about the men. This has always been about me."

Enne would never admit to identifying with Vianca Augustine, but she understood the frustration of other people's assumptions. She was either "wasted at finishing school" or "corrupted by the North Side." In reality, she wasn't any particular *type* of girl. She was simply practical, dedicated, and clever.

Maybe Enne had cried over a boy who didn't deserve it. Maybe she could be called silly or naïve. But if she truly believed tears and vulnerability meant weakness, then she wouldn't merely understand Vianca Augustine—she would respect her.

"Then beat them," Enne told the donna, and Vianca's lips curled into a satisfied smile.

The words might've suited Vianca's ruthless vision for herself, but they were too pretty, too simple. But since the donna disdained women for the same reasons, Vianca wouldn't know the difference.

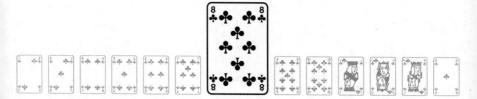

"The most romantic legend of the North Side is Innocence and
Iris. They were rival street lords, and so they hid
their relationship for years.

"Until they were both apprehended.

"Legend says Iris stayed alive for two days until Innocence
was hanged next to her. That she lingered that whole time
on the gallows, waiting for her lover to join her."

—*A legend of the North Side*

LEVI

His six weeks were over.

Levi shivered as he walked down the gaudy opulence of the hallway that led to Vianca's office. He'd worn his best for this meeting, appropriate for one of the richest men in the North Side. The Irons operated in eighty percent of all the casinos in the city. He'd even been offered the chance to *buy* a casino.

It was enough, he assured himself.

It was enough.

It was enough.

He prayed Vianca saw reason, that this wasn't just another one of her games to torment him. She ran an empire herself; she recognized when business sense forced you to set aside personal whims.

Nevertheless, Levi braced himself as he entered the elevator to Vianca's private residence, preparing for everything he cared about to be stripped away.

The elevator doors creaked closed, and he sensed Vianca's aura seeping in through the cracks, grazing the skin against

AMANDA FOODY

his cheek. It positively filled the casino—every expensive cologne and designer hand soap was laced with her odor of vinegar, the purest of white walls or marble stained faintly green.

Levi walked into Vianca's sitting room to find it empty and
eerily still. It was identical to when he'd last seen it, except
for one striking detail—the portrait of the Augustine Family now had a tear across it, forcibly removing Harrison from
the picture.

If Vianca discovered Levi was working for her son, she
would do much worse to him. So he swallowed and put on
his best poker face.

"'Lo?" he called. His voice sounded stifled in the apartment's
stillness. He jolted as a floorboard creaked beneath his loafer.

"We're in here."

When Levi had received this summons, he'd assumed Vianca would be alone. Apparently that wasn't the case. He followed the sound of her voice into a dining room, where the
donna was seated at the end of a dramatically long table with
a full spread of food across it, as though she planned to host a
dinner party. His eyes roamed over the dishes—seafood spe-
cialties of New Reynes, heavy pork roasts and potatoes, stru-
dels and cinnamon tarts, cheeses he didn't recognize. The
room smelled of so many different foods his stomach hurt.

Enne sat on Vianca's left, nearly concealed from view by a
tower of rosemary pastries. Levi felt an acute mixture of relief and guilt to find her here. After all, it was Levi's fault that
she'd fallen victim to Vianca's omerta in the first place.

But he was also grateful not to be alone.

He and Enne had only interacted in person a handful of
times since initially selling shares on Sweetie Street, but the
ache of seeing her never seemed to ease. She wore some glitzy
South Side dress, and her hair—normally tied up in a ballerina bun—draped over her shoulders. It was hard not to stare.

He cleared his throat and turned away before he betrayed himself. "Expecting more company?" he asked the donna, gesturing to the assortment on the table.

"We're sampling," Vianca answered. She nodded at the seat to her right. "Come join us. We've been waiting." As soon as Levi did so, she stood and made a slow, predatory circle around the table. "I hope you've both come hungry. I've had food brought to us from all the best restaurants in the city." There was a sharp edge to her voice that gave Levi the troubling impression he was being stuffed for slaughter.

He eyed Enne carefully. Her lips were pursed in a nervous line, much like his own.

"Maybe we're even celebrating," Vianca mused. As she spoke, she swiped a finger across the meringue cream on a pie, streaking its perfect swirl design, and popped it into her mouth. The dessert looked delicious, but Vianca made a face as though it tasted of ash. "I've been so impressed with you both. What you've accomplished is quite remarkable." She narrowed her eyes at Levi. "Don't hold your breath like that, like you're in a panic. I thought you'd be pleased. You've more than won our little bet."

The omerta forced all the air out of him in a rush, the least satisfying sigh of relief Levi had ever had.

Vianca paused over the plate of cheese and cured meats. She lifted the platter and began serving each of them, rattling off the specific names of the pecorinos and burratas. Soon both Enne's and Levi's plates were loaded with nearly a dozen varieties, mounted with olives, pickled vegetables, and crackers.

In all the time Levi had known Vianca, he didn't recall her ever feeding him. Paid him, choked him, applauded him, drugged him...certainly. He knew better than to trust anything she offered.

"All it took was a little motivation," Vianca purred, "and

now you're both some of the richest people in the North Side." Her gaze moved over them as though *they* were a dish she could sample. She slid her hand down Enne's head, getting a touch of grease in Enne's hair. *"Eat,"* she commanded.

Enne nervously bit into a stack of bread and cheese. Levi picked through his own plate, his fingers quickly growing slick with olive oil. The food tasted as delicious as it looked, but it was also rich. He began to grow full before he'd made it even halfway through his plate.

Vianca returned to her seat, and for several minutes, spoke of nothing more than the cheeses. She made a point to identify everything they ate.

"What do you think of the camembert?" she asked him.

Levi swallowed past his fullness. "It's…very good. It's all good. But I don't know why you're asking me—I don't know anything about fine food." He couldn't tell the difference between a half-and ten-volt bottle of bourbon, and he considered that a good thing. He wasn't hard to please. "And you didn't invite us over just to sample overpriced hors d'oeuvres."

Vianca never made such grand gestures unless she wanted something. It was her way of pretending they were more than her prisoners. But no matter how many delicacies she offered them, whatever she wanted, she could—and would—simply take.

She pouted. "I thought we could enjoy each other's company for a while."

"We were called here without warning. We're both missing appointments, I'm sure." Levi had nothing on his agenda that evening other than to discuss Fitz Oliver's offer with Tock, but he could think of a thousand places he'd rather be than Vianca's dining room.

"So impatient," Vianca chided. "I've left you both much to your own independence these past few weeks, though I initially hoped you'd be more like partners. I admit to missing that little idea."

She cleared the empty plates in front of them and began setting out new, larger ones. Levi's stomach gave a painful clench. "Do you think Levi would make a good business partner, Enne?" Vianca asked. "He can be so self-centered." Levi gripped his fork so hard his knuckles whitened. "And touchy," Vianca added.

"He'd be adequate," Enne answered steadily.

Levi thought he deserved more than that. Maybe not a month ago, when everything had fallen apart between them, but they'd moved past that. He didn't want Vianca's unnerving fantasies to cause a rift between them all over again—or worse, to kindle fantasies of his own.

But then Enne's foot found his under the table. It wasn't a kick, but a brief touch, probably meant to reassure him. It did, but it also made him dizzy.

Three more months, he told himself. Three more months until the election, until Harrison killed Vianca, until Levi's promise to Jac finally expired. But amid all his hope and gratitude for Jac's work lurked a seed of resentment. The promise was meant to last until the end of Jac's assignment, but Jac had seen to it that his assignment would never end.

Levi quickly jerked his foot away. He was trying to be a better person than the one who'd stolen from the Irons and killed Chez. But he was starting to doubt that goodness was in his nature, if the right thing felt like a battle and the wrong thing felt like surrender.

"And what about you?" Vianca asked him. "Enne would probably be a hard partner to work with. She takes everything so personally. No separation between business and pleasure." While Vianca piled roast pork on Enne's plate, Levi tried not to let his thoughts trip over her last word. "You should see her at the salons we attend. Always dancing, drinking, eating. It's a wonder she's not spilling her secrets into the ear of any of the young men who ask her to waltz."

Enne cast the donna a scathing look. After all, her efforts were entirely transparent, as though Enne and Levi really were her dolls. And as much as he hated to play into her games, it was too easy for Levi to fall into this trap.

An intrusive picture of Enne in the arms of a South Side boy entered his mind, and the worst part of it wasn't that Enne would do better with a South Sider—it was that she *wouldn't*. If she was going to dance with anyone, it should be with him. If she was going to be with anyone, she should be with him. Their secrets, their troubles, their destinies were intertwined, and no matter what lengths Levi took to avoid her, it wouldn't matter. It would always be her. It would always be him.

Levi wanted to be better about keeping his promises, he really did. But he was also bitter, and for the past few weeks— the past few *years*—he'd been scared that bitterness was all he'd ever feel. Maybe he couldn't help himself, and he'd never stop wanting. Or maybe everything he had seemed insignificant because he didn't have her.

"Why don't you tell him about the parties?" Vianca asked Enne, whose gaze was fixed on her heaping plate.

"It hardly seems important," she breathed.

"It looks like it's important to Levi."

Enne's gaze whipped toward him, and Levi's face burned. It would've only taken a single look from her to shatter his resolve entirely, but her face was unreadable.

"Whatever you're about to ask us," Levi told Vianca, "please just do so." *So we can leave.* He needed some fresh air. Away from Enne. Away from here.

"We haven't made it through the entrées yet," Vianca responded. "And I really do need your help with this."

"With what?" Enne asked coolly.

Vianca crossed her arms as if to say, *Fine.* "Election Day is on November ninth, and that night St. Morse will be hosting a white-tie affair for when the results are announced. I expect nearly everyone of influence in attendance, here to celebrate as a monarchist candidate finally gets elected to the Republic's Senate. I've waited my entire career for this moment, and I want the event to be extravagant."

Levi's heart skipped on the word *extravagant,* and he knew what Vianca was about to ask before she asked it.

"I'll need fifty thousand volts."

There it was. His stomach clenched—that was a fortune.

"From each of you."

He should've known the moment he walked in this room that Vianca would ask for voltage. All this talk about achievements and potential—she obviously wanted a piece of their success. But he wouldn't steal from the Irons again. Fulfilling her demand would mean letting the casino opportunity pass him by, but at least his conscience would be clear.

"You can't be serious," Enne said, gaping. "By when?"

"As soon as possible. There are decorations to buy, meals to plan." She waved her hand over the table. "Business has been down, thanks to my son's theatrics."

"One hundred thousand volts is still far more than extravagant," Levi gritted between his teeth. "That's probably the value of this whole casino."

Vianca didn't respond to that. Perhaps because this was more than a party to Vianca. If it was the night the election results were announced, then both candidates would be there. Levi wondered when Harrison Augustine had last come home.

The thought of Harrison made his already queasy stomach take a turn for the worse. Now that his wager with Vianca was finished, how many times would she summon him back to St. Morse? How many poker faces could he wear until she learned the truth?

"I'll expect both of you to attend, of course," Vianca said. "And I must say, you would look quite handsome as a set."

"We're not dolls," Enne said flatly.

"Of course not," Vianca answered. "Dolls would never be so stubborn. But that's really the fun." She took a pastry off the tower and held it to Enne's lips. "Eat. Tell me what you think."

"I think I'd like to leave." She slid her seat back, knocking it into Vianca's side.

Vianca scowled. "I could make you stay."

"But you won't."

And to Levi's utter shock, Enne walked out the door, and Vianca didn't try to stop her.

The donna collapsed in her seat, her expression strangely haggard. She gave Levi a dark look. "You'll go, too, will you?" There was only fact in her voice, no accusation.

She'd never given Levi a choice. But if it was sympathy or affection she sought after, they were far beyond the possibility of those. Levi would never forget how she'd laughed at him about Reymond's death. How he'd nearly died performing her scheme. How she'd dressed Enne up exactly to Sedric Torren's tastes.

Vianca Augustine was a monster, and a monster who learned remorse was a monster still. Her hands were too stained to wipe clean.

"You'll have your volts," Levi said, though he knew that wasn't what the donna wanted to hear. Then he left his napkin on the table and followed Enne out. And though it was from no effect of the omerta, he didn't breathe again until he saw Enne waiting at the elevator, holding the door open for him.

ENNE

♥ ♠ ♦ ♣

Enne was uncomfortably full during the elevator ride—her diet had been mostly bonbons and cookies for weeks, so the heaviness of Vianca's chosen fare made her feel bloated and tired. She had every urge to slip away to her room in the finishing school and sleep off her discomfort, but her mind was racing too quickly for any hope of sleep.

The donna was manipulative, jealous, and cruel, and no amount of weakness on Vianca's part would change that fact. If anything, the more Enne understood about Vianca, the more she hated her.

Levi cleared his throat, but said nothing. Enne could hardly bear to look at him after all the things Vianca had said. Less because of embarrassment, more because of pride. The way he had looked at her earlier...

Her heart would not be cut in the same place twice.

"I assume Vianca sent a motorcar to bring you here, as well," he said.

"Yes, but I doubt we can expect the same treatment going

home." Something heavy hung in those words. She had her home, and he had his. And there were miles in between.

"You walked out on Vianca," he murmured. "I could never do that. I've always waited to be dismissed. It was brave."

"I knew she wouldn't force me."

"How?"

"Because it wasn't her son's leaving that changed Vianca," she told him. "It was that he came back." It occurred to her that Harrison might very well be present at this event Vianca planned, and she loathed to think of the donna in the same room as her son. Enne didn't have the time or care to piece together the shards of Vianca Augustine after she fell apart.

"Are you afraid she'll find out?"

"I'm always afraid of Vianca. I was before you told me about your deal, and I still am now." She met his gaze fiercely. "But I'm glad we don't keep secrets."

"Me, too," he answered.

But there were still secrets, and this time, it was Enne who kept them. She'd never told Levi, Lola, or anyone else that she wanted to destroy the Phoenix Club. Now, after weeks of grasping for power, Enne finally had her first name. She had a time and a place. She had her gun.

There was another secret, too. One Enne didn't want to admit, not because it made her appear ruthless, but because it made her appear weak. It burned in her now as she stood beside him—the way they leaned close, but not too close. They'd hurt each other, and now they were afraid of each other, of giving or taking too much and repeating the same pain all over again.

But Enne's secret—the one she'd been running from for months, the blade that could pierce her not once, or twice, but over and over—was that no amount of giving or taking would ever be enough. Her life before New Reynes had been safe, but it had been lonely. Even if Enne's story had begun with her mother's death, it had also begun with Levi. And no matter how much she tried to convince herself otherwise, it would always lead to him, as well.

The elevator doors opened, and both of their breaths hitched. For a moment, neither moved.

"I guess we're both walking, then," Levi said awkwardly.

"Walking where?" she asked.

"It doesn't have to be home."

"No," she breathed. "It doesn't."

They walked through the hallway and into a back alley behind St. Morse. It was raining. Levi opened his umbrella and kept it low to conceal their faces. They could've been any couple walking down Tropps Street in an evening storm—almost.

"Last night, I was offered a chance to purchase a casino on the new boardwalk," Levi told her.

"That's incredible," Enne said, and she meant it. It was exactly the sort of flashy, clever aspiration that suited him.

"It would've taken me months to scrounge up the volts, but with Vianca's party, there's no way I can afford it now." He shook his head. "It was a thick idea, anyway."

"You don't mean that."

"I do. Things have finally been going well for the Irons, and I don't want to push my luck."

"Not so long ago, you told me that if I wanted something, I should let myself have it," she said, and instantly regretted it. Those words hadn't been about shopping sprees or excess treats; they'd been about him. She pressed forward, as though she'd forgotten that detail. "You don't follow your own advice?"

"Obviously not," he said slowly, looking at her. She flushed and turned away. It would be easier to convince herself to stop wanting him if he didn't look at her like that.

Around them, the flashing lights of Tropps Street were muted and dim. The rain provided a thin, hazy curtain, separating them from the rest of the world.

"We should get out of the rain," Levi murmured.

Enne examined the various taverns and storefronts. "Anywhere that doesn't serve food."

A few minutes later, they slipped inside a quiet music den. A small band played onstage, and the tables, despite the evening hour, were mostly empty. The pair crept into one in the corner, both their backs to the wall so they could keep a careful scope of the place.

When a server approached, Enne ordered for both of them—Levi kept his head down and didn't say anything, in case he might be recognized. The server didn't pay them much attention anyway.

"A Hotsy-Totsy?" Levi asked, clutching his heart. "I should've known."

"Yes, you should've. It's not easy playing politics at those parties with Vianca hovering over me." She neatly folded a napkin over her lap. "And it actually tastes good, unlike what you drink."

"North Side drinks aren't supposed to taste good. They're supposed to burn, and you're supposed to like it." The server set both their drinks down, and Levi shook his head at Enne's, all fizzy and pink. "And I don't know... Vianca didn't make those South Side parties seem that bad." He scowled as he took a sip of his Gambler's Ruin, another gesture Enne tried not to dwell on.

"Maybe not." She forced herself to shrug. "But it does get tiresome, pretending to be something I'm not."

"I would've thought you'd fit right in below the river."

"Would you?"

Levi swirled around the contents of his drink. "Well, maybe

when we first met, but no, not anymore." He almost sounded remorseful, like it was his fault she'd lost herself.

"I'm done mourning my old life," she told him seriously. "If you have something worth fighting for in New Reynes, then you need to be prepared to fight dirty. Maybe that makes me a Sinner, but at least I care about something. And at least I'm not alone."

Something in Levi's expression changed when she said those words. He leaned forward and took her hand.

"I know I made mistakes," he murmured. "I hurt you trying to protect someone else, and I'll never stop being sorry. But I want to make it right."

Her heart pounded. This was dangerous, familiar ground, taking them right back to the place where they'd fallen apart, to the same place Enne thought about every night when she wished she wouldn't—to the same place she desperately wanted to go.

"*You* are the only thing that feels right," he told her.

All her life, Enne had used words to wind herself back together. After the Shadow Game, and when the weight of losing her mother crashed upon her, Enne might've used these words to mend her wounds. But in the months they'd spent apart, she'd learned to cherish the broken parts of herself. So as she clung to his words now, she did so to treasure them, not to use them as a crutch.

"I know you don't believe in destiny," he continued. His skin was hot beneath hers; he was embarrassed. But Enne made no effort to stop him. "I know you think I've gotten everything I've always wanted, but none of it has felt right. And I think that's because, somewhere before, I made a wrong turn. I should never have made that promise to Jac. I should never have let you walk away that night at the Catacombs. And I should never have let you walk away every single night after."

AMANDA FOODY

She squeezed his hand tightly, on the off chance her heart might rupture. "Do you really believe in destiny like that?"

"I want to," he answered. "And I think that's what matters."

Enne liked those words, and so she leaned closer and pressed her forehead against his. Neither of them spoke for several moments, and when Enne closed her eyes, she swore she *could* feel a force pulling her toward him. A force far greater than desire.

She wanted to believe in their story, too.

"Are you going to say anything?" he breathed.

"Is that what you want to do right now?" she asked, opening her eyes and smiling. "Talk?"

He licked his lips. "No. No, that's not what I want."

Then the doors to the den blasted open, and a gunshot cut through the music.

Enne and Levi sprang apart, their hands still locked together. At the opposite end of the hall, several whiteboots stormed inside. Enne immediately pulled Levi down into a crouch behind their table.

"You have got," Levi growled, "to be mucking kidding me."

No one else in the hall moved—breathed, even—as one of the whiteboots jumped onto the stage. He pushed the singer aside and spat into the microphone. "The North Side is now under curfew, starting at seven o'clock. After you all show us your identification, you have twenty minutes to crawl back to your gutters. This whole city is going on lockdown."

Enne's breath caught. This situation was dangerous for her, but deadly for Levi. The door to Tropps Street filed the hall with the wails of sirens. Even if they escaped, what awaited them outside?

Enne pulled her revolver out from her pocket, and though the whiteboot didn't see her, she pointed it at him, prepared to play dirty once more.

Levi squeezed her shoulder. "You could hit one of the musicians."

"I won't miss," she said firmly. They needed a distraction so they could run.

"Then aim for the lights."

Enne directed the revolver to the lights above the stage. No one would get hurt, but even so, she wasn't sure it would be enough.

"Everyone up!" the whiteboot barked. "Your time is already running out."

Chairs scraped across floorboards. The owner of the establishment ran out of his office, complaining about the new closing time and lost business.

The whiteboot laughed, jumped off the stage, and grabbed a bottle of ale from the first table. The customers seated there let him take it. "Breaking curfew is now worth a week in prison. I don't think anyone here wants to be an example." His eyes scanned the room, and to Enne's horror, landed on them. He squinted. "'Lo! What is—"

Enne fired. Half the lights in the room flickered, then blackened, and everyone screamed at the sounds of bullets and shattering glass.

Levi yanked Enne forward, and the two sprinted toward the kitchen. Gunfire followed them, and a glass bottle along the bar's shelves exploded. But they were already pushing open the doors, stumbling away.

Whiteboots charged after them, but they didn't make it outside until Enne and Levi were already halfway down the alley. The Casino District looked darker than usual—it was typically bright no matter the hour, even during a storm, but its many neon lights had been switched off. The sirens blared so loudly, Enne needed to resist covering her ears. The wind whipped the rain sideways.

"Do you know where you're going?" Enne asked as Levi turned them down the first alley they came across.

"We're not far from Olde Town."

"Harrison's bribe can't stop *this*, Levi. It won't be any better there."

"The museum is a fortress. It's the safest place to go."

But getting there wasn't so straightforward. White motorcars blocked several streets, and both of their shadows constantly danced amid blue and red lights. Soon Enne realized that Levi didn't know where he was going as well as he'd claimed. They found themselves standing side by side in an alley, their backs pressed against the white stone wall, their clothes soaked, their guns raised.

"Are we lost?" she hissed. Lightning tore through the clouds overhead, followed by a tremendous crack of thunder. If they died tonight, at least their end would make a good story.

"What's important," he said, "is that we're not dead."

Enne grimaced and dug into her pocket. Then she tied Séance's black mask across her face.

"Is that smart?" Levi asked.

"If they recognize you, then my face will be compromised just for being with you," she told him. "This is protection."

The rain fell more fiercely, making it difficult to see or hear very far in front of them. They inched toward the edge of the alley, but as soon as they peeked around the corner, they heard a shout.

"'Lo! Who is that?" called a voice. The sound of footsteps approached.

"Muck," Levi breathed, grabbing Enne's hand and yanking her away. But before they could turn, the whiteboot caught up behind them. He was young, and his eyes widened when he saw them. He shakily raised a gun.

But Enne fired first.

The whiteboot crumpled with a thud and a splash. The water on the pavement ran red.

Levi shuddered and lowered his gun. "You needed to do that." He said it like he was convincing himself.

"I know," Enne replied. Still, she didn't look at the whiteboot. "It was him or us."

A mile still stretched between them and the Irons' hideout. There was no question that they would keep running, that Enne would still shoot when it meant "us or them," but that didn't mean they would make it.

So, before she could talk herself out of it, Enne grabbed a fistful of Levi's collar, pulled him down toward her, and pressed her lips against his. He tasted like New Reynes's polluted rain, and though his clothes were soaked through and freezing, his skin burned at her touch. She felt his mouth open to hers—either in surprise or want, she wasn't sure. His free hand reached around her waist, but before he could close the space between them, Enne lurched away.

"That's in case we die," she said.

Levi's chest heaved in shaky gasps as he wiped the rainwater out of his eyes. "We aren't dying," he breathed, "until we can do that again."

Enne's face heated with a mixture of pleasure and embarrassment. "Then let's make it home."

And so they ran.

JAC

♥ ♠ ♦ ♣

That evening, Jac paid a visit to the next Rapture den alone. It'd been Sophia's idea, an important solo assignment to prove that she trusted him. But rather than reassure him, it only made Jac feel lousy, like he was so insecure that everyone around him had to cater to his moods.

If you disagreed with him, you didn't trust him. If you tried to please him, he was a burden. Jac didn't know why he couldn't just be happy.

"I thought Sophia would be here tonight," the den manager told him. She kept a clean office tucked on the second story of the warehouse, with sheets on the walls meant to suppress the noise of music from below. This was the largest Rapture location on the North Side, a club big enough for three thousand delirious, sweaty bodies, crammed inside a metal building like New Reynes cod.

"I'm Todd Walsh, her partner," Jac told her. Sophia might've claimed that being partners made them equal, but Sophia's name still carried more influence than his.

"Should we reschedule?"

"I don't think that's necessary," he answered, trying not to sound bitter. Jac opened his briefcase and slid out a packet of papers. "Now, we know that Charles is giving you thirty percent. We can offer you—"

"There's nothing you can offer me." She slid the papers back toward him. "How old are you? Sixteen?"

"I'm eighteen."

"You don't realize what you're up against. Delia had the upper hand, didn't she? Then Charles put eight holes in her head." The woman leaned forward. "You're trying to play a game of strategy, but that's not what this is about. It doesn't matter. He doesn't even *care*. He probably loves this, waiting you out. You think you're winning, but you're just giving him his fun."

Jac resisted the urge to reach for his Creed. Their meeting with Charles was tomorrow afternoon, and Jac was growing more and more convinced that, when they entered Luckluster Casino, they'd never walk out of it.

"*You're* giving him what he wants," Jac countered. "There are more weapons than fear."

"Charles is past fear. Do you know what he did to me for betraying him and siding with Delia?" She rolled up her sleeve to reveal a gruesome series of scars, as though fishhooks had been embedded in her skin and ripped free. What remained was gnarled and uneven, rippled colors of still-red wounds.

"I—I'm sorry," Jac said.

"I'd leave the business entirely, but he'd kill me for that." The matter-of-fact tone in her voice made his skin crawl. "I'm not sure he'd take kindly to this meeting, either."

"You agreed to it," Jac reminded her. "And your support would mean—"

"No, I think it's best you leave." She hastily tugged down her sleeve, as if she'd shown him too much.

"Should we reschedule?" he tried. "I'll bring Sophia next time."

"I'm sorry. I wish you the best of luck, I really do."

Within moments, she'd shooed him out of his seat and out the door.

Jac paused at the top of the metal staircase, sighing in disappointment. The warehouse pulsed with fast-paced music, and the air reeked of the acidic smell of Rapture. Neon streamers dangled from the ceiling and writhed from the winds blowing in across the rafters. With the band's music so loud, it was easy to forget a storm raged outside, the pounding of rain swallowed by the bass.

He ran his hands through his hair and cursed. Sophia had given him one assignment—an important one—and he'd managed to muck it up in only a few minutes.

Jac climbed down the steps and dodged the dancers on his walk to the door. Outside, the rain splatters danced on the pavement, and the wind was too strong for an umbrella. He flipped his hood and trudged down the street.

Sirens called faintly in the distance.

Probably South Side, Jac told himself. After all, the white-boots hadn't made it past the Brint in over a month. But the river was over a mile away, and the storm would overpower all but the closest sounds. These sirens were close.

Jac quickened his pace. He'd planned to take the Mole back to Liver Shot, but escaping would be difficult if the white-boots somehow shut it down. Still, it was a thirty-minute walk home.

The sirens grew closer.

He ran.

The rain pelted him, and the wind whipped his hood back.

He could only go so fast without tripping, with water dripping down in his eyes.

Soon he realized the sirens weren't only in front of him, but also behind him, to the east, to the west.

It only could've meant one thing: the North Side had fallen.

And he wasn't the only one running. Doors to pubs and cabarets burst open, patrons spilling out and scattering like rats. Jac collided with one of them, so hard he slammed to the ground and dislocated his shoulder with an agonizing *pop*.

"*Muck!*" he cursed, clutching his arm. He tried to run forward, but each of his steps sent a quake of pain through him. He was in trouble.

Figures appeared at the edge of the street, murky from the rain. They ran toward the crowds, and Jac realized they were whiteboots. Each clutched a baton in one hand and a wooden shield in the other, as if they intended to ram and beat passersby.

If the whiteboots caught him, then Jac would hang.

"Muck," he shouted again, and he sped off in the opposite direction, adrenaline dulling his pain. He ducked down an offshooting alley and mentally mapped out the route back to Liver Shot. In his condition, he doubted he would make it, and Olde Town was even farther away.

He was trapped in the heart of the Factory District...and he was alone.

Other panicked North Siders pushed and sprinted past him. Some knocked frantically on doors or threw things at windows. Jac turned around, to see if there was another cause for the chaos, but then he heard gunshots, and he no longer dared to see what chased him.

The devil themself, it felt like.

He ran with everything he had. The metal traffic poles swung from the force of the wind, and after several minutes of fleeing, Jac grabbed one desperately to steady himself. With his good arm, he reached for his Creed. He knew a sinner's prayers were worthless, but he still prayed for mercy. If he could survive the night, he would never cheat anyone ever again. He would never hurt or steal or lie. He would throw the stash of cigarettes Sophia didn't know about down a sewer. If he could just survive the night.

Then, as if in answer to his prayer, he saw it.

He crossed the street toward the church with one arm raised to protect his eyes. Even through the rain, he faintly smelled smoke. Lights in the surrounding buildings flickered from the storm, and he could almost swear that this was the night the world would end.

Jac threw open the wooden church doors and collapsed onto the damp floorboards. Immediately, strong arms hoisted him up, causing him to scream out from the pain in his shoulder.

"Asylum!" he screamed. "I seek asylum!"

But the young man, he discovered, was not a priest. Though a Creed dangled from his neck, he wore regular street clothes, soaked through from the rain.

And he held a gun to Jac's head.

Jac raised his hands, wincing as he did so. "Don't shoot!"

"Are you a whiteboot?" he demanded.

"Do I look like a whiteboot?"

The man inspected his face with narrowed eyes. "You look familiar."

That probably had to do with his wanted poster. "You don't."

"You're Jac Mardlin," he breathed, and Jac braced himself for a bullet. After all, Jac was wanted dead or alive. But the man lowered his gun and laughed. "I'm Harvey Gabbiano."

Jac recognized the name. Despite their mutual friends, he didn't relax. Harvey was a Chainer—a bit like Vianca, only he could bind you to a place rather than a person. Jac knew better than to trust him.

Harvey gestured to the main church area, where a number of others huddled in pews as a priest distributed blankets. "Looks like we have a crowd for the night."

Jac didn't intend to stay more than a few hours, until the madness passed. "Do you know what's going on out there?"

"The whiteboots brought in the Republic's guard to institute a curfew. The North Side is now officially on lockdown until morning." Harvey shook his head. "They came storming into the variety show where I was, asking for paperwork and everything. The Senate had that vote this morning—the one about the talent registrations. Guess it was about more than they let the public know."

Jac had been trying to keep up with the news, but his work with Sophia took nearly all his focus. He hadn't realized the world had turned so bleak.

"Do you think the whiteboots will break into a church?" Jac asked. After all, if they were acting like it was the Revolution all over again, then their next step would be closing down all the churches of the Faithful—for good.

"They might come here," Harvey said darkly. "But I think they'd go for the gangs first, wouldn't you?"

"I guess so," Jac answered. He still didn't anticipate getting much sleep tonight.

Jac crept back into the main hall of the church. Paintings filled each wall, depicting stories that were included in the scriptures. The Faith was a collection of stories, of lessons and superstitions, each one adding more texture to the Faith's overall fabric.

The largest painting on the back wall was from a recent story—the martyrdom of a Mizer princess who credited the Revolution to the work of a malison, a Faith term for someone with an unholy talent. The painting illustrated her last moments of life, her head bent low with a noose slipped around her neck. It'd taken place in New Reynes, in Liberty Square—the same place crime lords were executed now.

A number of blue votive candles burned in rows beneath her, and Jac treaded carefully toward the display. A votive candle symbolized a prayer offering, a wish.

He wondered if he would die like she did—the death of a gangster. All for an oath he'd made to Levi on a drunken night five years ago. Jac had agreed to this assignment because he'd been prepared to face the worst for his friend, but he wondered if Levi even flinched at the thought of such a death for himself. It was a fitting ending for a lord. For a king.

Jac reached forward and lit a votive candle for Levi.

Maybe Jac would die at the hand of Charles Torren. At least then it would be because of his own decision, his own choices, but he couldn't imagine a more gruesome end. The rumors he'd heard about Charles were frightening enough to paint and frame on one of the walls of this church.

Jac lit a candle for Sophia. Because of all the rumors he'd heard, he still suspected her tales were the worst.

Lastly, he lit a candle for himself, and prayed that if he did die, that he'd do so unburdened and unafraid.

"I don't meet many gangsters who are Faithful," Harvey said behind him, causing Jac to startle and knock his candle on the floor. The glass shattered, and the flame flickered out. "Muck. I'm sorry. Let me—"

"No. *No*," Jac told him sharply. He didn't want a favor from Harvey—a favor from a Chainer meant a debt that demanded something in return. But then pain radiated out from his shoulder, and he let out a groan.

"What did you do to yourself?" Harvey asked.

"I dislocated my shoulder," Jac grumbled. "I've had worse."
He realized he said that phrase a lot.

"Give me five volts, and I'll fix it."

Jac narrowed his eyes. "Like I'd let you help me."

"It's not a favor if you pay me." Harvey also spoke those
words like he said them a lot. "Or sit around and moan to
yourself and play martyr, if that's what you'd like. As if I'd try
to trick you in a church."

Jac glanced at Harvey's Creed, the one that shared a chain
with an antique gold key. Reluctantly, he paid Harvey his five
volts and let him fix his shoulder. This time, he was ready for
the pain, and he didn't make a sound.

"You're made of sturdy stuff," Harvey told him, clearly
impressed.

Jac cleaned up the broken bits of glass and wax and deposited them in an empty bowl of holy water. He slipped into a
pew beside Harvey.

"It's funny I ended up in a church," Harvey murmured.
"It's been a while."

Jac also hadn't visited a church for several months. "It hasn't
exactly been an easy year."

"No, but that's when you make the time for it, as my parents
used to say. They're real Faithful people. They'd probably tell
me I don't deserve to step foot in here, not even for asylum."

His words reminded Jac of the priest he'd met at the hospital, the night he'd overdosed and Levi had saved his life. The
priest who told him a sinner's prayers wouldn't go answered.
Looking around the quiet church full of trembling North Siders, Jac was feeling more repentant than usual.

He should've just apologized to Sophia about the boxing.
He still wished she'd be honest with him, but the last thing he
wanted to be was a burden. Not with the way he felt about her.

"Do you believe in demons?" Jac asked Harvey quietly.

"Strictly speaking—by the Faith, I mean—demons exist, whether you believe in them or not. They're just called something else." Harvey peered up at the painting behind them, featuring a red-eyed malison with a dozen shadows meant to be shades. Shades were curses malisons placed on the souls of sinners, according to more esoteric stories.

Maybe Jac was too gullible, or maybe it was the sounds of the storm rumbling through the quiet reverence of the church, but he could almost believe in that moment that Charles Torren was as unholy as any story Jac had ever heard.

"Can you unlove someone?" Harvey asked Jac suddenly, pulling Jac's thoughts from his own problems.

Jac cleared his throat awkwardly. He didn't know Harvey well enough to give advice. "I don't think so, not really," he answered. "But you can love someone differently."

Harvey sighed. "That won't be enough."

A menacing crack of thunder boomed overhead. Both boys jolted as though it'd been meant for them.

ENNE

♥ ♠ ♦ ♣

By the time they reached the museum, Enne's clothes were soaked through from the storm, her wet shoe leather had blistered her heels, and her gun was out of bullets. Still, she pointed it ahead of her, taking comfort in its steady weight in her hand. The lockdown had begun nearly forty minutes ago, and the rain continued to pour. Water rushed in streams below the street curbs, and the wind at times whipped hard enough to send Enne skidding sideways.

Levi ran to the wrought iron gates of the museum's grounds. He shook them, and chains rattled. "Who's on watch?" he called.

"It's Stella," someone answered through the darkness. "Who's that?"

"It's Levi." Lightning flashed between tree branches and church spires.

A figure stepped out from behind the trees. "*Pup.* You're back. We didn't know—" Stella stopped as she approached, taking them both in. "What *happened* to you?"

"We've been running in circles dodging whiteboots. Half the streets in Olde Town are blockaded, and the other half are flooded."

Stella unlocked the gate and opened it for them. They slipped inside, and Enne felt a rush of relief to have something separating her and the rest of the North Side.

"We're missing a few others," Stella told him. "Hwan and Liddy."

Levi's face darkened. "Is Tock here?"

"Yes."

"We'll go see her now."

Stella looked nervously at Enne. "And… Séance?" Last time Enne had entered the museum, she hadn't been wearing her mask. Now, she looked like a rival lord.

Enne cleared her throat. "Are the phone lines working?"

"The storm took them all down."

She wouldn't be able to contact the Spirits until morning. She'd told Grace to take Roy to Jonas's contact, but she hoped that Grace had the good sense to stay inside.

The three of them retreated into the museum. The Irons slouched over card tables, playing Tropps in the dim candlelight. Enne recognized a few faces from the Catacombs and the party, but even with some missing, the Irons' numbers had grown—maybe even doubled—since she'd last seen them. The building itself had changed, as well. A black carpet draped down its magnificent grand staircase, and flowing curtains now concealed the boarded windows.

Tock appeared around the corner. Her eyes widened, and she threw her arms around Levi. "I thought the sirens meant you'd been caught."

"You think I'm worth all this commotion?"

He smirked, and she punched him in the arm. "Hwan and Liddy are still missing. They were both at shifts at the Sauterelle." Her expression turned serious. "We need to send searches out."

As Levi launched into a heated discussion with his third, the other Irons peered at Enne curiously, taking in the sight of her soaked South Side dress and the gun by her side. Her hands trembled. They'd nearly died tonight. She'd *killed* tonight. But instead of feeling scared or horrified, she only felt numb.

She wanted to convince herself that the worst was over, but she had no idea what this "lockdown" would mean. They should've expected this level of retaliation. For the past month, the North Side had been theirs, and Enne wondered how many people had died tonight for the wigheads to take it back.

"We can't leave them out there," Tock growled.

"We have to. We all have death warrants on our heads. The streets are crawling with whiteboots. *No one else is leaving here tonight*," Levi commanded. "They're smart. We need to believe they found some place to wait out the night."

"Do you believe that?" she challenged.

"No one knows Olde Town better than us," he answered. "Keep the watches out, but don't leave the grounds."

Tock gritted her teeth. "Fine. We'll wait until morning."

"Good. Now, unless there's an emergency, please don't disturb us. We've been shot at for the last hour." Levi's voice remained impressively nonchalant as he started up the steps and motioned for Enne to follow.

Her heart was still racing from earlier, and she almost didn't have it in her to be embarrassed. *Almost.* And though no one snickered, Levi's steady voice didn't fool Tock, who shot Enne a lewd smirk before she turned away.

Enne nearly ran up the steps, eager to escape their stares. But that left her and Levi alone in the empty hallway, and the quietness made her breath hitch. Every sound—his breathing, the rain's drumming on the roof, the click of the door sliding open—made her stomach loop in uncomfortable, delirious knots. She'd faced far scarier predicaments tonight than a room alone with Levi Glaisyer, but her heart seemed to believe otherwise.

"Are you worried about the missing Irons?" she asked. Though subtle, she could see the angry force in his movements as he jammed his keys in the lock and threw open the door.

"Of course I'm worried," he said, stalking into the room. Enne followed him, but could make out nothing in the dark.

Levi flipped the light switch, then muttered something under his breath about the storm and snapped his fingers, igniting several candles along his bureau. Like his old bedroom at St. Morse, everything here was impeccably clean, and his headboard looked like it had been made from Olde Town iron.

In the shifting darkness, she could just make out Levi's furrowed eyebrows and pained expression. "But I can't send anyone out, right?" he asked her. "Would you?"

"It's the right decision," she agreed. Then, because it seemed far easier than staring at him, she turned around and opened the drawers of his dresser. She pulled out a shirt several sizes too large for her, but blessedly dry.

"I think so, too... What are you doing?" Levi asked.

She peeked over her shoulder. "Finding myself dry clothes."

He opened his mouth, then promptly shut it. "Probably a good idea." Though his voice seemed to hint that he'd had other ideas.

They each turned around so the other could dress. "I nearly lost Tommy last night, and now this?" Levi said. "It doesn't matter how rich we are now. If anyone gets caught, I can't bail them out without getting arrested myself."

Enne turned around, feeling swallowed by his shirt—it hung nearly to her knees. And though she was far warmer than she had been, she shivered from the way he looked at her in that moment. He'd changed into a sweater, old and clearly worn many nights before. He looked particularly boyish in it.

"You're already making plans for every terrible scenario," she told him. "I can see it in your face."

"I can't help it—I like to be prepared. I *need* to be prepared." Even as he spoke, he made for the papers organized with tabs and clips all over his desk, like he could find his answers hidden in the numbers. "When I had problems before, I'd go to Reymond. And you know what Reymond would say if he were here?"

"That he was proud of you?" Enne guessed.

"That I'm in over my head." He collapsed into the desk chair.

When Enne felt that way, she found an isolated corner of the finishing school and fired bullets into the wallpaper. But joking about that felt wrong after everything that had happened tonight.

"Do you ever feel like it's all our fault?" Enne asked.

"The lockdown?"

"The street war. The Orphan Guild. All of it." Enne swallowed down a painful lump in her throat. "Ever since the Shadow Game, since you killed—"

"Do you regret saving me?" Levi asked.

She gaped. "What? No, of course not—"

"Do you wish I hadn't killed Semper?"

Enne remembered the *thump* his body had made when it hit the table, how the blood had seeped across the cards. Lourdes had died at that same table, at his hand.

"Never," Enne whispered. "Do you?"

"I should, but I don't." Levi looked to the window as a crack of lightning flashed across the sky. "Even after the worst does happen, I can't bring myself to stop, and I don't want to. I want to be legendary. I want my mark on this world to stain."

Enne looked out at the storm and thought of all the night remaining between now and morning. If a violent end awaited them at sunrise, then she wanted the hours until then to be infinite.

She walked until she stood in front of him. It was hard to think of their kiss earlier without also remembering the white-boot she'd killed, but she hadn't survived this night only to fill it with regrets.

Levi watched her, his breath hitched and silent, as Enne lowered herself onto his lap. No sooner had she slipped her arms behind his neck did his mouth find hers.

Even with the sirens fading miles away, kissing Levi still felt like waiting for the axe to fall. She couldn't touch him without remembering the bruises that had once painted his skin. She couldn't taste him without recalling the blood as it mixed with summer rain. They both understood what each kiss was worth in secrets and volts and sins, and so they did not spend them carelessly. They were slow and savored, like the last meal of those condemned.

Her wet hair had dampened both their shirts, and the coldness left chills across her neck. Levi's hand slid beneath the fabric and up her spine, burning against her bare skin, pulling her closer to him until her chest and stomach felt crushed against his. His other hand crept up her thigh, teasing the hem of her skirt higher. She shuddered, and he smiled against her lips.

When his fingers reached her hips, when there was no more space to close between them, Levi stood up, her legs wrapped around his waist, and carried her to the bed.

After laying her down, he took a step back, as though simply to admire the image of her there. A flush crept up her face, and a memory stirred in her of the vision from the Lovers card during the Shadow Game, of her and Levi in a position much like this one. How many doors in that hallway led to this night? Or did all of them, eventually, even if they'd tried to avoid it?

As he climbed onto the bed, his lips trailed the slopes of her until they returned to hers. Enne's hands roamed over him, finding the places and doors left unexplored, and she drew her name from him like a dying breath.

"We should stop," he whispered, even as his arm snaked beneath her back and raised her toward him. She protested, lifting her head to resume their kiss. "This isn't our last night."

"You don't know that," she murmured.

He pulled away. "I've been thinking like that for too long. I don't want that here, with us." He lay back, and Enne rested her head against his shoulder.

She interlaced his fingers with hers. "But it will always feel that way," she said softly. "Even if we pretend otherwise."

Levi sighed. "I know."

The sirens outside had faded out. Every few moments, thunder rumbled overhead, the only reminder that this night was not infinite. The storm would pass, and dawn would come.

And a different North Side would await them when it did.

JAC

♥   ♠   ♦   ♣

Jac had worn his good suit for their lunch with Charles Torren, because it was his only piece of clothing that he'd be willing to die in. When Sophia answered her apartment door, dressed in her usual red clothes and thigh-high boots, she gasped, swung the door wider, and threw her arms around him.

"You didn't come back last night. I thought after the lock-down, you might've—"

"I had to spend the night in a church." Jac stretched out his shoulders. "But other than being a bit stiff, I'm fine."

She took a step back and looked him over. Jac expected her to ask him how his meeting with the den manager had gone, but instead she asked, "Did you bring me a corsage or something?"

So they were back to this place. At least empty banter was preferable to fighting.

"I thought I'd dress to impress. Isn't that what you're supposed to do when you meet the family?"

"Not my family," she said.

They took the Mole the few stops to the casino. The passengers who shared their train car were unusually quiet for a commuter's morning, unwilling to meet anyone's eyes. When they emerged onto Tropps Street, Jac noticed the gambling taverns had already opened their doors in a pitiful attempt to attract business before the new curfew. Whiteboots and troopers directed traffic with assault rifles slung over their shoulders.

A concierge greeted Jac and Sophia at the front doors of Luckluster. Jac had never actually been inside the casino before, and its black-and-red decor made him feel like he was walking into a haunted fun house, everything striped and glossy as though candy coated.

Sophia's eyes roamed over every detail of the place, from the flowers carved into the crown molding to the dark candlesticks arranged on a center table, like the pipes of an unholy organ. She ran her fingers over everything, as though deciding which piece to ignite first.

"I was never allowed down here," Sophia murmured, making him startle. "I was so young. My family has a private entrance to the floor."

Jac didn't trust himself to answer her—otherwise he'd probably snap. This offering was a tiny fraction of her truth, a piece of the distorted puzzle that made up her past.

"It's uglier than I imagined," she said.

"You've never been? In all this time?"

"I didn't want to come unless it was to burn it." She curled her hand into a fist. "This comes close enough."

They followed the concierge down a maze of curving hallways to a private elevator, much like the one in St. Morse that led to Vianca's personal suite.

When the doors closed, Jac felt for the pistol in his pocket, to reassure himself it was still there.

"I don't want to kill him today," Sophia murmured. "I need to face him first. It's time he learns I'm not the child I once was."

"You act as though we *could* kill him," Jac said.

"He's only human." She spoke those words like she was still trying to convince herself. "When he looks us in the eyes and knows that he's lost, then we'll kill him."

"And if he tries to kill us?"

She took a deep breath and pulled a small handgun from her pocket to match his own. "It's two against one."

When the doors opened, Charles Torren stood before them, his hands clasped behind his back. He was tall and broad-shouldered, his shirt stretched tight over his large frame. Unlike Sedric, who'd carried a ruby-encrusted knife and worn his hair slicker than his smile, Charles had a serious look to him. His shirt was buttoned up to the collar, almost like his late sister's medical jacket. The pleats in his pants were perfectly straight, his expression as cool and sharp as a surgical knife. A silver stopwatch hung from his breast pocket, wedged beside a row of pens and a miniature black leather journal.

"Hello, Sophia," he said. There was a nasal quality to his voice, awkward and uncomfortable. "Look at you." He clapped his hands as though with glee. "That's a nice trick, isn't it? How did you afford a skin-stitcher? That's what you did, right? I saw the pictures and thought there was some mistake, but I know that look. It's still you, blonde and blue-eyed and all."

Jac frowned. Was he shatz? Sophia had brown hair and green eyes. But he remembered the strange reflection in Delia's glasses when she'd looked at Sophia. That reflection had been blonde, too. Was it possible they saw her as a different person?

She only gave him a nod. "Hello, Charlie."

If the nickname bothered him, he didn't show it. He turned his attention to Jac. "You must be Todd." Charles held out his hand to shake, and Jac obliged. His skin was icy. "Or do you prefer your real name?"

"Call me Jac," he answered, smiling with tight lips.

Charles didn't smile back.

Jac tried to imagine how this man could've been Sedric Torren's closest friend. Sedric had always been fond of parties, the more wicked the better. But Charles seemed to take his pleasures served cold—*dead* cold.

"Thank you for accepting my invitation," Charles said. "I didn't think you would."

"I won't be scared away," Sophia said firmly. "Not anymore."

"Are you still scared of the dark?"

She stiffened. "No."

But Jac knew that was a lie. In the tunnels beneath the Mistress parlor, she'd clutched him in the dark. Another secret.

"Why did you invite us here?" Sophia asked.

"Because I wanted to see you. You're the only family I have left." He smiled, but it was false and sinuous. "Uncle Garth always used to talk about the importance of family."

"If you've missed me at all, you've only missed torturing me. Terrifying me." Sophia took a threatening step forward. "Every day since we left, I've dreamed of killing you."

Charles licked his lips, like he could say the same. "Is that what you've come for?"

"No. Not until I take every last den in this empire. Until I convince everyone you're even worse than the monster they say you are."

"Monsters aren't real, Sophia. You took our stories too much to heart."

"Only because you carved them into mine." She glared at him. "So that's the only reason you invited us here? To reminisce?"

"Of course not. I wanted to make you an offer."

Sophia narrowed her eyes.

"I'd give it to you," Charles told her. "All of it."

Sophia paused. "What do you mean?"

"The casino. The dens. They could be all yours to burn."

Charles reached into his jacket and removed two envelopes. He handed the first to Sophia. "As long as you're willing to play a little game."

Sophia grimaced and, with no hesitation, tore the envelope in two and let the pieces flutter to the floor. She pulled Jac closer toward the elevator, but Jac refused to turn his back to Charles, in case he later found a knife in it. "Clearly nothing has changed," Sophia growled. "Go muck yourself, Char—"

"And one for your partner." Charles held out the second one for Jac. "You have as much stake in this feud as she does."

Jac halted, his heart pounding. "What game?" He couldn't help but ask, even when Sophia shot him a furious look. He should turn away like she did, a united front. But it wasn't like she'd ever kept them on the same page.

"The greatest one." Charles took several steps forward, close enough that Jac could smell him. He reeked of disinfectant. "Life and death."

Unlike the last envelope, Jac recognized his true name written across the front.

"I'm not taking that," he growled, remembering the Lullaby in his last one.

"This is no trick," Charles said. "It's an invitation."

Jac suspected he might know the game Charles meant—it was a legend. A game where the invited players always lost. And even if Levi and Enne had survived the Shadow Game, Jac knew better than to accept such an invitation willingly.

"It's not the invitation you're thinking of," Charles urged. "Card games aren't really your style, are they? *This* is more suited to your preferences." Charles's gaze fell on Jac's lip, inspecting the scar there.

So, Jac guessed, Charles's game was a fight. And if it was anything like the Shadow Game, then it would be a fight to the death.

If he won, then Charles would be gone, and Jac could watch this entire empire go up in smoke.

If Jac lost, then he would die.

Still, he grabbed the envelope. As he did, Charles's cold hand slid around his wrist and gripped it tightly. He pulled his pocket watch out from his shirt as he held him. Jac tried to yank his arm away, but even with the help of his strength talent, Charles managed to hold fast.

"One hundred and twelve," Charles murmured, his voice making goose bumps prickle across Jac's skin. "Oh, you're very scared." He leaned forward and lowered his voice to a whisper. "I'd hurry. You don't want that invitation to expire. Or she'll pay the price for it." His gaze flickered to Sophia. "I bet I've made her scream louder than you."

Jac shoved him with his other hand and tore himself away. "You're twisted."

This time, when Charles smiled, it was genuine. And much like his late cousin's, it was wolflike.

"Let's go," Sophia said sharply. Jac nodded and followed her. Charles smiled as the doors of the elevator closed.

And even though Jac knew he shouldn't accept anything from such a man, he slipped the invitation into his pocket.

The pair didn't speak for most of their journey down Tropps Street. Sweating in the August heat, Jac removed his suit jacket and draped it over his shoulder. His heart still pounded, and he craved a cigarette.

Sophia followed him down his street, though she lived several more blocks down.

"Walking me to my door?" Jac asked. Even though his words were joking, he sounded terse. He didn't want another fight. "Looking for a kiss goodbye?"

Sophia managed a half-hearted smile. "I thought I'd invite myself inside."

"That's forward of you." Jac climbed the stoop to the door and blocked it from her. He didn't want her inside. All the meeting with Charles had proven to him was that Sophia's secrets would always create distance between them. Jac had always known Charles to be a monster, but she could've prepared him. She could've—for once—actually treated him like a partner.

Sophia's hand slipped around his waist, making him tense. Then he realized she was reaching for the invitation in his pocket.

Jac grabbed her by the wrist and yanked it out of her hand.

"You don't know Charles like I do," she growled at him, tearing herself away. "He gets into your head."

"You're right. I don't know anything, but that's on you. I'm done. I have an offer to finish this alone, and so I'm taking it." He turned his back to her and twisted the handle.

Sophia pulled him by his shoulders, but he didn't budge. "You can't do this."

"Of course I can."

"I won't let you."

"And how will you do that?" He slid inside and turned around, prepared to shut the door in her face.

She slid her foot between the door and the frame, stopping him from closing it. "Whatever it takes."

"You know what it would take."

"I…" She bit her lip, and Jac hated the way it made him stare.

When the pause lasted a second too long, he pulled away and let her stumble inside. He wasn't going to resort to kicking her foot out of the way. So instead, he did the mature thing: he ran up the stairs and locked his apartment door behind him.

Much like his last one, Jac's apartment was cramped and empty of nearly all belongings. His bed stood across from a small gas stove, and a clothesline spanned from the kitchen table to the closet.

"Todd!" Sophia pounded on his door. He ignored her and fumbled around his drawers for a pack of cigarettes. "Please." Her voice cracked. She'd never been good at begging.

Jac found his secret pack hidden inside what looked like a deck of cards. He lit one and collapsed onto his unmade bed.

"I haven't told you these things because you'll look at me differently," Sophia said through the door. "And I know that isn't fair to you. I know it's not."

She paused, as though waiting for Jac to let her inside. But she hadn't actually told him any answers yet, only more meaningless, pretty words. So he didn't move, and let her continue.

"Delia, Charles, and I are all half siblings. We all have different mothers, and so we all each have different split talents. Delia was a split-Apothecary. Charles comes from a Dorner family, just like you. But his split talent manifested differently than yours. He can give pain, rather than take it."

Jac had met others with the same surname before. It was uncommon, but not unheard of. He didn't know his parents, but he preferred to assume he and Charles weren't actually related.

A talent for giving pain certainly explained Charles's reputation. The memory of his words when he shook Jac's hand made him shiver. *I bet I've made her scream louder than you.* Jac recalled the scars on the den manager's arms—wounds he hadn't actually needed to inflict with his talent, when all it took to give pain was a touch.

The sound of Sophia's voice dropped lower, like she'd slid down to the floor.

"I know Charles's invitation is for a fight," she said. "You won't be able to outmatch him, even though you're stronger. Not with his talents."

"How does he know who I am?" Jac asked. "About my past?"

"Hospital records, probably. He can get access to those things."

Eventually, Jac decided to sit by the door, where it was easier to listen. It would've been even easier if he let her inside, but he wasn't ready for that yet. He'd meant it when he told her all or nothing.

"I explained to you how good and bad deeds can manipulate luck. I carry charms. Uncle Garth used to be all about charities. But our father had other methods. As you might know from the Faith, there's more than one type of penance. Charles, Sedric, and Delia all preferred the physical variety."

Jac's stomach turned. There *were* Faith stories that included that, but he'd never known anyone to practice them.

"I remember the scars Sedric had on his back, like grooves," Sophia whispered. "My father started Delia and Charles on it young—too young—but he coddled me. Charles always had to sneak behind his back if he wanted to torment me. He used to hurt himself just so he could give the pain to someone else. He loved to play with people's fears—or give them new ones."

Jac realized, for all the secrets he demanded of her, he didn't want to hear about this, so he quickly asked, "Why do Charles and Delia see another face when they look at you? I saw that picture of you as a child. You only look older, not different. But they see someone else." He'd never heard of a skin-stitcher who could do that. They were usually hired by rich people to adjust their noses or jawlines. The procedures were long, painful, and permanent.

"This is the part where you stop believing me," Sophia murmured.

"Try me."

Jac could almost sense her stiffen on the other side of the door. If there'd been nothing between them, he might've reached for her hand, given her some sort of assurance that he was grateful for this information. But he was also protecting himself. He hadn't forgotten where they were, and how small his apartment was beyond his bed. He hadn't forgotten the way she'd looked at him and touched him at Liver Shot. How he'd liked it.

All or nothing was as much a demand from her as it was a promise to himself.

"Do you believe in demons?"

Jac shuddered and repeated Harvey's words about malisons from last night. "Strictly speaking, according to the Faith, demons exist whether you believe in them or not."

"And what about the Bargainer?"

That story didn't come from the Faith—it came from a legend, one of the oldest and most ludicrous of the North Side. The subject of it had many names—the Bargainer, the Devil. In the stories, you could bargain with them for anything... even your own soul.

"Not every street legend is true," Jac answered.

"This one is."

An icy dread filled his chest that even the nicotine couldn't send away.

"After my father died, I ran away," she said. "I can't remember if I went looking for her, or if she found me. And I swear, it was just like those Faith stories. I remember her red eyes. I remember I asked for her to make me unrecognizable to my siblings, even if I stood right in front of them. To Delia and Charles, I'm a different person entirely—different face, different voice. It was incredible, the first time I tested it."

But if the Bargainer did exist and really was like Faith's stories, then what she'd given Sophia wasn't a gift—it was a curse, a shade. And no doubt it came with a price.

"What did she take in return?" Jac asked, chills creeping across his skin.

"My split talent. I don't know why—I don't remember it. She carved it out and all my memories of it, too. It's like I'm nothing but a Torren." Her voice shook, and Jac realized she was crying. He hurriedly stubbed out his cigarette and stood up. "I told you I'd sacrificed for this, and I meant it. Destroying Luckluster is all I have left. I'm nothing without that."

He opened the door, making her jolt and fall back. She scrambled to her feet and wiped at her eyes. It took a moment for Jac to realize what he'd done by letting her in.

All or nothing, he'd promised himself.

Jac had always wanted what was no good for him, but wanting Sophia felt different. Jac had used Lullaby to fill himself whole, if only for a few hours. To make him forget how he felt trapped and lousy and worthless, only to make him feel twice as awful when he woke.

This wanting felt like the opposite. Like each step toward her led to a destination instead of an escape.

Sophia wordlessly closed the door behind her.

Jac had never had a girl in his own apartment before, and a flush crept up his face as she examined it, messy and bare. Suddenly, it was him who felt exposed. She'd been worried he'd think she was shatz. Now she was probably wondering why he lived like this, like he was barely living at all.

"I don't...own many things," he said awkwardly. "I lost it all when they put the bounty on my head." But even before then, he'd never had much.

"I don't either, since I ran away," Sophia told him, her back pressed against the door. They had both left pieces of their lives behind, for better or for worse.

Still, Jac resisted the urge to pick up discarded clothes off the floor. "I thought this would be temporary."

"I know," she answered.

"I mean, I could've gotten a new place, but I—"

"Jac," she said, and he stopped. She rarely called him by his actual name, as though everything about their relationship was a game. But it had never felt like one to him.

"Stop looking at me like that," she told him.

Jac tried to mold his face into something unreadable, but it was difficult. She'd somehow managed to reapply her cherry lipstick in between tears. He liked how it looked a little smudged.

"Like what?" he asked.

"Like I'm dangerous. It's very hot."

Jac laughed as he walked toward her. She *was* dangerous. Already, the burden of her secrets weighed down on him, as though nestled in the space between his bones. But as he leaned forward and pressed his mouth to hers, he knew he would never take any of it back.

Her lipstick even tasted like cherries.

Jac had kissed—and more than kissed—several girls before. But never in his own apartment, never with so much shared past and future between them.

He'd always thought of what he'd overcome as the broken pieces of himself, but even damaged as they were, he could still build something good upon them. With every kiss, he felt a little closer to collapsing. But with every kiss, he also felt more secure. The weight of her burdens supported his own.

Sophia stumbled as she kicked off her boots. Once she did, they stood at eye level. It made it easier to brush her hair to the side and kiss a trail down her neck. She sighed as she leaned into him, and her fingers dug into his back. She pulled him closer to her, so that there was no space between them—not for secrets, not for second guesses. Every moment of empty flirting and teasing, moments that had originally seemed like a game between them, now felt like promises, waiting to be collected.

Sophia pulled clumsily at the buttons of his shirt, but it was hard to undress him when he was already focused on undressing her. The breeze from his open window sent goose bumps prickling across bare skin. Jac shivered, but not from the cold. Then she pulled him into the bed and climbed on top of him, so she could make him shiver some more.

Her dark hair draped over the both of them, and while he soon discovered how much he liked to run his hands through it, it nearly made his heart stop dead to watch her do it. She might've been dangerous and cursed, but he still smiled against her lips when he said, "Do that again."

Those words, however satisfying to say, proved far more so to hear from her.

"Do that again," she commanded several minutes later, clutching at his wrist as his fingers wandered upwards. Jac obliged and trailed back down.

All or nothing, it turned out, did not mean one thing or the other. It meant whatever could be contained with the grasp of a single night. It meant giving now what the future could take away.

Many hours later, Jac carefully crawled out of bed so as not to disturb Sophia sleeping beside him. He had a lot of practice with that, but this time, he didn't intend to sneak out.

Jac reached into his discarded jacket and pulled the invitation out of the pocket. He held it up to the moonlight and squinted as he attempted to make out the words. His eyes skipped over the letters to a date scribbled on the bottom.

11/8/25

Three months. That gave him time.

Jac needed to find Levi, to ask him for help—even advice. And, if it came down to it, he needed to play.

LEVI

"Two weeks?" Levi barked angrily into the phone. "The Irons already missed their shifts yesterday. They have more tonight. We need those papers now."

"Pup, you know how much I love doing business with you," Jonas said, and his voice sounded slimy even through the receiver. "But I'm still making calls. You're not the only one in the North Side suddenly scrambling for new identification papers."

Levi slammed his fist on his desk. Since Enne had left this morning, his phone had rung every other minute with another concerned casino manager trying to cancel their contracts due to the lockdown on the North Side. The talent registration period would begin in three days' time, and until the "violent crime lords were apprehended and brought to justice," all those with either a blood or split Talent of Mysteries were required to be home by nine o'clock. All others, ten o'clock.

This is only a temporary situation, Levi had repeated over and over this morning. *We'll have it under control soon.* But, of course, he'd been lying through his teeth. The wigheads had sent a military force to patrol the North Side, and the only thing the lords could do was wait until the tension died down.

"We can't work without those papers," Levi grunted.

"You're supposed to be rich now, aren't you? Surely you can get by for two weeks."

Two weeks, sure. But if all the casinos pulled out, how would they get by after?

"And you're supposed to be the most connected person in the city," Levi countered. "I don't see why—"

"You think you're the only one with these problems?" Jonas shouted. "Scrap Market has been permanently shut down—the Scarhands are scattered across the city. I'm sitting in a basement closet with fourteen different phone lines, all ringing with calls from my clients and suppliers, but you know which one rings the most? *Yours.* So maybe you could try solving some of my problems before you expect me to solve yours."

Levi pressed his head against the desk. He didn't have any clever ideas. Not this time.

Sure enough, Levi made out the ringing of another phone in the background. "Do you really think I'm taking custom orders right now?" he heard Jonas bark to some other client.

"Well, smart-ass?" Jonas snapped, once again on Levi's line. "You got a solution for me?"

"We're all mucked!" Levi growled and slammed the receiver back down.

As soon as he did, his phone rang again. He ripped the cord out of the wall and collapsed onto his bed. It was hard to believe he and Enne had lain here only two nights before, talking as if the rest of the world didn't exist, when really, the rest of the world was ending.

In his dream, Levi's footsteps echoed down the alternating black-and-white tiles of the hallway. He approached a white door, hoping it held the answers he needed, but all it contained was a nightmare.

Levi's father had a regal face, with wide, square features, a strong jaw, and brown skin like Levi's own. He wore the same linen tunic whenever he worked as an orb-maker, the one with gold embroidery along the collar—finer than anything else they owned. Their family home was just a collection of cheap furniture and hidden treasures. It'd also felt empty since his mother died. Levi still slept in the bedroom across the hall from his father, but no one had truly lived in this place for over a year.

"So when will you leave?" his father asked him, startling Levi from the book he read. Levi quickly concealed his surprise—and his guilt—and molded his face into something expressionless. He'd gotten good at doing that. "That's what you're planning to do, right? To leave?"

"No," Levi lied.

"Don't lie to me." His father ripped the book out of Levi's hands. Levi carefully sat up from his seat, in case he'd need to run. "You think you can go anywhere? There are restrictions on this family, even if you might pretend you're not part of it."

Levi wasn't pretending. He was rejecting. He'd spent years listening to his father's stories about the Revolution, about the tragic events that had led them to this miserable house on a cliff so far from their original home. He'd listened, and he rejected it. He rejected his father's victimized apologies for the plates, the windows, the bones he'd broken. He rejected his father's claims that the Mizers had been fair rulers, when history told otherwise. He rejected the idea that he was trapped here, bound to this same house, to this same tragedy.

"I'm going to New Reynes," he said quietly.

His father started toward him, but Levi had already stood up and backed into the parlor.

"You know what they did to all the orb-makers who served the queen in Reynes?" his father asked. "They hanged them."

That had been twenty years ago. Another tragedy Levi refused to claim.

His father reached for the book Levi had left on the cushions. It was thick, with sharp leather edges and a real weight to it.

As freeing as it'd seemed to reject the Glaisyer name, it hadn't felt so simple to leave. That night, he cried out of guilt the entire train ride to New Reynes, his ticket bought by one of his father's treasures that he'd stolen and sold. He cried because its new owner wouldn't understand what it meant. They wouldn't know that Levi's grandfather's head had been hanged like an ornament from the palace walls before they'd burned. They wouldn't know that Levi's father had smuggled the treasure in his shoes when he fled the city. They wouldn't know the story because it was tragic, and no one wanted to hear a tragic story, Levi least of anyone.

That was why his new life wouldn't begin with tragedy. In the legend he planned on writing for himself, he had come from nothing. He whispered it under his breath so often that, by the time his train pulled to a stop in the City of Sin's North Side, he'd even begun to believe it.

Levi woke from his unpleasant nap to find Jac standing over him. He jolted and sat up. "What are you doing here? How did you get in?" He shook out the grogginess in his head and looked out the window. It was still daylight, so he couldn't have slept for long.

"Nice to see you, too," Jac said, a strange edge to his voice.

Of course, Jac was allowed to be on edge—as anyone would be, with all this curfew business—but that didn't stop Levi from examining him. He checked the circles under his eyes— dark, but not too dark. He stared at Jac's pupils, undilated. At his fingers, untrembling. Those were all good signs, but he still had a vicious cut across his lip from fighting. Altogether though, Jac probably looked better than he did.

"All done?" Jac gritted through his teeth. Levi cleared his throat. He wasn't trying to be rude—he was trying to be a good friend. "I've been wanting to talk."

"So have I," Levi said. "I'm glad you came."

But then a terrible thought occurred to him, sitting in this bed. Enne's aura still clung to one of the pillows, making his sheets smell faintly of coffee. Levi changed places for his desk.

"You don't look glad," Jac said.

Levi had rehearsed his words to his friend over the past few days. *I'm sorry I broke my promise*, he'd say. *But I'm sorry I made it. I know I asked—*

"I need your help," Jac told him.

Levi glanced at the stacks of ledgers in front of him. He wasn't sure he was in a condition to help anyone. "My help? With what?"

"I think Charles is going to kill Sophia."

Levi should probably have considered his words before he spoke them. And he might have, had he had another seven hours of sleep. "Hasn't that been a concern from the start?"

"Of course," Jac snapped. "But we met with him yesterday for the first time, and—"

"You *what*? Why would you—"

"Because we needed to know what we were up against. I never met Sedric, but I swear, this one is worse." Jac shivered. "Sophia is—"

"Sophia knew the risks, and so did you." Levi tidied up his papers just to have something to do with his hands, tossing nearly all of it into the waste bin. He didn't mean to be so frustrated, but the past two days had been far from easy. "Harrison is depending on this. If the deal is compro—"

"It's about more than the deal, Levi," Jac growled, now pacing around his bedroom. Levi winced as Jac leaned against the exact spot on the wall where he and Enne had kissed. "This isn't just business."

"Of course it isn't just business!" Levi said, then cleared his throat. He shouldn't raise his voice. "You need to get out before you get hurt."

"What about the election? What about the deal?" Jac asked.

"My biggest priority is making sure that you're all right."

"Since when?" Jac asked, making Levi wince. "This has *always* been about your freedom. You don't get to pretend like this is suddenly about keeping me safe."

Levi's mouth went dry. Was that what his friend really thought of him? "I never should've asked you to do this, but I never asked you to stay there. This hasn't been about me for a long time. It's been about you and her."

"Am I supposed to just not care? You know what the Torrens did to me. Are you upset that it isn't all about you?"

"I'm upset because I don't want to see them destroy you all over again!"

Levi stood up. He didn't want to have this argument with Jac. He was too frustrated about the volts for Vianca's party, about the Irons, about the city. He was holding so much together that Jac's words threatened to make Levi say something he didn't mean—or worse, something he did.

So Levi walked toward his door, trying to come up with an excuse to speak to Tock or the other Irons, but then he stopped and turned around.

"What help did you need?" he asked, his voice strained.

Jac crossed his arms. "I need volts—and men."

"What about the volts Harrison gave you?"

"I don't think outplaying Charles is the best strategy anymore. The only way to end this is to kill him. Sophia doesn't agree with me, but she wouldn't need to be involved. It would only take—"

"So you're acting alone now? Are you shatz?"

"I'm doing what needs to be done."

Levi didn't even know what to say to that. Since when did his Creed-clutching friend talk so casually about murder? "The city's on curfew. You think the Irons are making voltage now? I can't help you. And Harrison *won't* help you. What would you have me do?"

I sound like Jonas, he realized, hating himself a bit.

"I'd have you care," Jac growled, as though Levi didn't. As though those papers in his waste bin meant nothing to him. Not his friends, not his dreams.

"I care about *you,* but I think you should leave."

"What about Enne? Isn't she one of the richest people in the North Side now?"

"Not anymore, with…" Levi squeezed his hand into a fist. "You'd ask *her?* You'd ask her after the promise you made me swear?"

Jac stiffened. "I only asked because of Vianca. It's Enne's freedom on the line, too."

"Vianca is *our* problem. You overheard one conversation and pretend like you understand. It isn't that simple, and these past few weeks have been awful because of it." Levi took a deep breath. When he'd practiced saying this, he hadn't imagined it would be here, in this room. He didn't want to taint his good memories with an added layer of guilt. "Jac, I… I broke the promise I made to you. I tried not to for a long time, but—"

"I'm not surprised, Levi," he said brusquely. "And it's fine. I don't care. If anything, I get it—"

"You're not surprised? You don't care?" Levi bit back the urge to shout. He'd spent months trying to be better about keeping his promises, and his best friend was telling him he'd known all along that his effort was useless? That it hadn't mattered to him anyway?

"I didn't mean it like that," Jac said quickly. "Just that knowing you both…it was going to happen. And no, I don't know everything about Vianca, but I know it would've been better for you and Enne to wait."

"How can you say that you don't care?" Levi snapped. "I've been beating myself up for *months* about this. I made her cry. I've been so unhappy, and just… You don't care?"

"Unhappy? You've gotten everything, Levi. You got the gang. You have more volts than you could ever need. Everything you've ever wanted fell right into your lap. Just like it always does."

"Like it always does?" Levi kicked over his waste bin, sending crumbled paper scattering across the floor. "Like that time Chez nearly killed me? Or Vianca trapped me? Or I was invited to the Shadow Game? Meanwhile, I've been so worried that sending you on this assignment would be a mistake—would be terrible for you. Now I realize I sent you away to have the time of your life. What was I worried about?"

"You told me you trusted me," Jac said sternly. "Did you lie about that?"

"Of course I lied," Levi hissed. His voice was rising—he wanted to scream—but he restrained himself. It was a habit with Jac.

"You still won't yell at me." Jac shook his head. "I can't believe this. I shouldn't have come. I didn't even think you'd have it in you to last this long."

Levi winced. He was used to taking blows from Jac—he'd said far worse years ago when he'd been desperate for his next lull. But that had been then. And while he knew Jac wasn't coming from the same place, whenever his friend grew harsh with him, it left a bad taste in his mouth. Like worry and helplessness.

As Jac headed for the door, Levi followed. "You don't get to claim the high ground when you're taking the same risks—

worse, even! You don't get to ask for help when you should be leaving the Torren business behind!" Jac stopped, his shoulders tensed. "Are you happy? I'm yelling now!"

Jac whirled around, and Levi took a step back. Jac looked angry enough to punch him. "When *you* take risks, it's part of the game. When *I* do it, I'm self-destructive." He curled his hands into fists. "When *I* ask for help, you make a business decision. When *you* ask for help, there is no decision. I'm constantly trying to make it up to you, keeping my cool so you don't get worried, not wanting to weigh you down."

"You've never weighed me down," Levi said, quickly sobering. "I just want to understand why you're doing this. I never asked you to take it this far. Is it just for her?"

Jac took a slow, steady breath, and that was when Levi knew he'd lost him. "You still don't get it. I'm doing this for me." Then he turned around, opened the door, and left.

Levi froze in shock. That was his best friend walking away.

But Levi didn't know what words to say that wouldn't be lies. He wouldn't apologize, because he wasn't sorry.

Everything you've ever wanted fell right into your lap. Just like it always does.

He sighed and bent down to clean up the mess. The waste bin overflowed with schedules and invoices that no longer mattered, thanks to the lockdown.

For weeks, the lords had lived like kings. And now he feared they might die like kings, too.

Levi plugged his phone back into the wall.

Moments later, it rang.

He kept the receiver several inches from his ear as the casino manager yelled. "This is only a temporary situation," Levi said reassuringly. When the yelling continued, he forced a tired lie. "Believe me, I understand. But you know me. I came from nothing, and here I am. I'll have it under control soon."

JAC

♥ ♠ ♦ ♣

Jac fell asleep on the bench outside his old One-Way House, and he woke to an unpleasant jabbing on his forehead. He swatted it away, expecting it to be a pigeon or a seagull, but then Lola grunted, "Did you ask me here to tell me you're homeless now?"

Jac groaned and sat up. He hadn't meant to take a nap while he waited for Lola, but he hadn't slept well last night, dwelling on Charles's threat, and his argument with Levi had drained him down to empty.

"You look terrible," Lola told him.

"And did *you* come here just to insult me?"

"I came because you sounded desperate." She sat beside him on the bench. "But I don't have forever. I'm meeting a date later."

Jac furrowed his eyebrows. Lola's hair, as always, was tangled and unkempt. She'd donned the same pleated men's clothes she wore every day, in varying shades of beige, as well as his stolen watch. "Lucky them," he said sarcastically.

"I could leave, Polka Dots."

Jac admittedly hadn't called Lola to fight. He needed advice, and though Lola Sanguick was far from a sage, she was a keen listener. So he launched into the story from the beginning, filling in the pieces of what Lola had already heard from the radio and from Enne, all the way through his fight with Levi.

"Of course Levi didn't give you volts. According to Grace, the Irons are about to go dead broke," Lola said. Levi had told him as much, but it did little to lessen Jac's anger.

"It's not about the volts. It's about the fact that he can't see why I want this."

"Why *do* you want this?"

"Because this is my story. It's not Levi's or Enne's or Vianca's. It's mine. But the whole city revolves around them. He can barely sneeze without making the front page."

"So it's about your ego," Lola prodded.

"So what if it is? Don't I get one?" He squeezed the iron arm of the bench in his fist, hard enough to make it bend.

She smacked him. "Stop destroying property with your toxic masculinity."

Jac frowned and put his hands in his lap. "What am I supposed to do? I can't protect Sophia, not from Charles. And I know it's not just about me. It's her fight, too. But I don't think she realizes—"

"If this was also her fight, you'd be talking to her right now, not to me."

He cleared his throat. "I haven't seen her since last night. And...you know..."

Lola crinkled her nose. "Gross."

"I didn't want to ruin it by being like this." He'd left his cigarettes in his apartment because he hadn't wanted Sophia to see him grab them. He hadn't told her he was going to speak with Levi because he didn't want her to suspect that he was planning something. It'd barely been twelve hours, and he was already being weak and dishonest and avoiding her, and it would all crumble, just like everything in his life always did. "I'm sorry. I didn't mean to drag you into this. These are my problems."

She smacked him again. "Do you think I came out here thinking we were going to a taffy store? I came out because I knew we would sit here, on this bench, and you would cry to me about your problems and you wouldn't ask me about mine. But that's okay, because I want to be here. Because I'm your friend. I want to help you, not hear you apologize to me."

It hadn't even occurred to Jac to ask about Lola's problems. "Thanks. Now I feel like an asshole twice over."

"It's not my fault you don't know how to have a healthy conversation. I'm not trying to make you feel lousy. I'm trying to help you decide how to make yourself feel better."

Jac narrowed his eyes and begrudgingly continued. "I still stand by what I told Levi. I think Charles needs to be taken down." *Before he has the chance to take us down.*

"You told me his deadline isn't until November."

"He didn't seem like the sort of guy who cares much about deadlines." Jac resisted the urge to squeeze the arm of the bench and for Lola to scold him again. "He wants some sort of brawl, and I refuse to give him that. But I don't have the resources I'd need to take him down otherwise."

"What would Sophia say?" Lola asked.

"She'd say that it's only been one night, and we have months to figure out a new plan." Jac normally wasn't the man with the plan—that was Levi. But now Jac was alone in this. "What would you say?"

"I'd say it's only been one night, and you have months to figure out a new plan."

Jac scowled. "And what if he kills her between now and then?"

"She decided to do this as much as you did. She knows the consequences, probably better than you do, even." Lola gave him an awkward, reassuring pat on the shoulder. "You're convinced something terrible is going to happen because a lot of terrible things have happened to you. I mean, of all the places in the North Side, you wanted to meet *here* again. The sad origin story of sad Jac Mardlin. So if something terrible does happen, you can turn around, you can point to this, and you can have an excuse."

Jac winced. Lola didn't need to carry any of those daggers when she could throw around words like that. "You're the one who used to always say, 'This story will end badly.'"

"We're psychoanalyzing you right now, not me," she snapped. "All I'm saying is that, however much of a monster Charles Torren is, he's gotten into your head. And when you let something get into your head, you don't tell anyone about it. You avoid your girlfriend. You get in an argument with your best friend. And when every single one of them gives you the same advice, you ignore them."

Jac stood up. "I really do that, don't I? I'm..." He rubbed his temples and cursed himself for craving a cigarette. Everything Lola told him was absolutely true. He was a muck partner, a muck friend, and an all-around muck person. And not because he was rotten, but because he sat around and let himself rot and claimed he didn't know how to stop it.

Lola stood up, too. "Don't walk away. I'm not done. You don't get to leave yet." She placed a hand on his shoulder and turned him around. She glared down at him until he returned to their bench, and Jac swore that tall women would be the death of him.

"When we last spoke months ago, you were anxious and

resentful. You were convinced this assignment was going to kill you, and you talked about it like, when Levi asked, you didn't even have a choice. But you don't talk like that anymore. You're more confident. You're less twitchy. You're *better.*"

Lola had a way with words that made you want to believe her. Probably because she was an honest person who had been unwillingly dragged into all of this. But it wasn't like that for her, either. Not anymore. She'd chosen this, just like he had.

"You're better, too," he told her.

Lola crossed her arms, but she didn't quite manage to hold back her smile. "This isn't about me, though."

"It could be. I'm very curious about this date. Do you like them?"

She flushed. "Stop it."

"I bet I can guess who it is. I remember, that night at—"

"You've never met her. She's not from here. She's from, um, far away. She won't even be here long, because she's just visiting. She doesn't read the papers or know who any of you are. She—"

"So when's our double date?"

Lola had an awfully serious face that didn't handle embarrassment well. Nor did she lie well, but Jac could forgive her for that...for now.

"She'd...she'd hate you," she stammered.

Jac placed a hand on his heart. "And yet you'd keep her?"

Lola apparently decided she'd suffered enough humiliation, because she spun around and walked away.

"Don't do anything I wouldn't do!" he called after her.

She held up a rude hand gesture.

"Thank you!" he added, no longer joking. Lola didn't have to drop everything and travel across town for someone she'd barely spoken to in weeks, but she had. And Jac might've preferred gentle comfort to her particular brand of tough love, but he'd needed to hear it. He was still far too angry at Levi right now to walk back to Olde Town and apologize, but he knew Levi still cared about him, and so he'd listen to everyone's advice. He'd wait.

Lola turned back for a moment, hands stuffed in her pockets, and gave him a smile.

"Next time we'll talk about your problems!" Jac called. "Like why you're far too private with your personal life when I already know—"

"Good*bye*, Jac!" Then she swiveled away, quickened her pace, and waited for the pedestrian light to flash.

Once she'd disappeared from sight, Jac turned to stare at his One-Way House, and he decided that chapter of his life would finally end here. He had a far grander story to write.

He took Charles's invitation from his pocket, shredded it, and tossed it away.

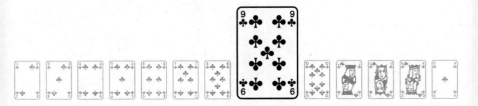

"Eight Fingers didn't create the Scarhands on his own, you know. There was someone else. Not just his second—he was his partner.

"But that's not how oaths work. There can only be one lord, and without oaths, there's no loyalty.

"They were good friends, I heard. That's why gangsters don't have friends. Because one day, you might have to put a bullet in their head."

—*A legend of the North Side*

ENNE

♥ ♠ ♦ ♣

Morning meals at Enne's finishing school had always been extravagant affairs, with frittatas in scallion cream and teas mixed with flower petals. In the Spirits, each of the girls washed down stale bread with spiked coffee, their dark under-eye circles hidden beneath the day's copies of *The Crimes & The Times*.

"Did any of you feed Roy yet?" Enne asked.

"Why can't we just get rid of him? He barely eats his food, and he still refuses to talk," Grace grumbled. Her eyes—like Enne's—were only half-open, and she slid her plate away to lay her head against the table. The lockdown had cost the Spirits thousands of volts in a matter of weeks, and both Grace and Enne had stayed awake through the night discussing possible solutions. Without success.

"Because until the occupation of the North Side is lifted, Jonas suspended our meeting indefinitely." Enne poured herself a mug of sugar with a side of coffee. She desperately needed caffeine, but she couldn't tolerate the drink's bitterness any other way. "Marcy, why don't you take something up for him to eat?"

Marcy's face had been permanently flushed since Roy arrived, and Enne's suggestion made her choke on her toast. "Me?"

"He only eats if Grace brings him his meals," Charlotte said.

Enne furrowed her eyebrows. "Why?"

Grace stabbed her butter knife into the table. "He has a death wish, probably."

In the hall outside the dining room, there was a giggle. All of the girls looked up groggily, eyes squinting at who could possibly be in such a good mood at this hour. Enne counted heads and noticed one was missing.

A figure darted past the archway, but not fast enough for Enne to miss the bluntly cut black hair and a pair of leather combat boots...and someone who looked an awful lot like Tock. Lola turned the corner into the dining room wearing a lopsided grin. She stopped abruptly when she saw them all. "You're all up early."

"It's not that early," Enne pointed out.

"Oh, well..." She cleared her throat and sat down in the last empty seat at the table.

Grace shot Lola a coy glance. "Aren't you always complaining about the Iron boys?"

Lola poured herself a cup of coffee, very carefully avoiding their stares. "The *boys*, yes." She smirked as she took a sip, and her comment was met by several snickers. Then she examined Enne and Grace with narrowed eyes. "You both look terrible."

Enne downed her coffee and forced a half smile. "We've never been better—"

"You're both going upstairs and taking the day off," Lola declared. "Charlotte can handle the numbers today."

Charlotte's eyes widened. "So can Marcy."

"Either way," Lola grunted, "you're both useless like this. Go sleep."

Grace needed little encouragement. She staggered up and wordlessly left the room, her eyes fluttering closed as though she were already drifting off.

Enne, however, hesitated. If they were communicating with other lords or with investors, she needed to be available.

"Go," Lola told her sharply, and Enne, both defeated and grateful, climbed up the stairs and collapsed into her bed.

Enne roamed the black-and-white hallway in her dreams, and the first door she opened led into a classroom. Unlike those at Madame Fausting's, these girls carried schoolbooks rather than firearms.

The teacher at the front of the classroom read down the roster. "Erienne Salta?" she asked. Her neatly plucked eyebrows furrowed at the name, and she looked up, scanning the students with confusion. Her gaze fell on an empty desk in the back of the room.

"Who?" one of the girls asked. The others around her shrugged in equal bewilderment.

The teacher crossed off the name and moved on.

Enne closed the door with an acute feeling of distance. Only one summer had passed since she'd last seen those girls, but a scene that would've once brought her to tears now only left her empty. Erienne Salta no longer existed.

The next door proved far more painful—it was always painful to look at Lourdes Alfero, especially in New Reynes. Whether or not the visions of the hallway could be believed, this was the side of her mother Enne had never known, that Lourdes had purposefully concealed from her.

It was daytime. Lourdes perched on a couch in a parlor

that, judging from the lavish decorations, was located in the South Side.

Sitting across from her was Josephine Fenice. Unlike Malcolm Semper, who'd started his career as a famous revolutionary, Fenice had a law degree from one of the most esteemed universities in the world. Amid all the articles and radio shows Enne followed about the new talent registrations and curfews, the senator-turned-chancellor made few statements and no appearances. But it was she who'd initiated the street war, she who'd signed the order for the lockdown of the North Side, she—Enne suspected—who pulled the strings of the First Party.

She was also a member of the Phoenix Club.

"When will it be?" Lourdes asked.

"Tonight," Fenice answered. Her voice had an eerie flatness. "But it wouldn't have to be, if you gave it up."

Lourdes crossed her arms with an expression of indifference. "He'll have to kill me."

"You really are that cold."

"I just know the truth of it. More of it than you do, even. Because you think that the story is over."

Fenice frowned. "All these years, you dug up these secrets. But even if you know the story, you've done nothing to change it. You are inconsequential. And come midnight, you will be dead."

It'd been several months since her mother's death, but still the words dug into Enne. She recalled the scene of Lourdes at the Shadow Game, another vision from the hallway. She'd worn these same clothes.

This was the day she died.

The scene changed around her. The walls of the parlor fell away, revealing a crowded public square and a wooden platform raised at its center. A woman walked upon it. She wore tattered clothes, so torn they barely covered her, and her body looked bruised and scarred even from a distance. Her eyes burned violet.

Enne stood on her tiptoes to peer over the crowd. It was too far, and she could hear nothing over the disjointed chatter and chanting. Until she heard the slam of the axe.

The scene changed. It was another face, another set of violet eyes.

Another axe.

Enne pushed her way to the front of the crowd, so close to the platform that the cobblestones had flooded red. It was a gruesome display. Of nakedness. Of bodies that had already suffered enough. Of the young and the old, made a spectacle for an increasingly boisterous audience.

Soon the executioner was replaced with a noose. Enne winced at the sound of every snapped neck. Even though she understood the tyranny of these kings, she also knew that not every person was a king. Some were guilty by association. Guilty by birth. And when Enne looked into their eyes, she saw her own staring back.

Years flew by as she stood witness to death after death. A man approached the gallows, this one with a mask covering his face. It wasn't until he reached the platform that Enne realized it was actually layers of black gauze wrapped tightly around his head, exposing not even a stray hair. He was hauntingly faceless, as though he could've been anyone.

But Enne knew who he was. He was Veil, the most notorious street lord of New Reynes history. And he was about to die.

At the snap of the rope, she was transported once more. Her own weight creaked on the wooden platform, and her wrists were bound behind her back, blistered and raw. She winced as the whiteboot pushed her forward, but she didn't stumble.

Not even when he slipped a noose around her neck.

★ ★ ★

Later that evening, Enne awoke gasping and clawing at sweat-soaked sheets. She could still hear her mother in her head, discussing secrets that Enne would never understand. She could still feel the roughness of the noose around her throat.

She held back a sob and instead took the glass of water on her nightstand and smashed it on the floor. It shattered like the Shadow Game's timer. The water seeped across the carpet like Semper's blood.

Before the lockdown, the Spirits had made Enne one of the richest people in the North Side. For months, she'd claimed she wanted power, and she'd *had* it.

But now it was gone, and she'd spent so many weeks kissing Levi and dreaming of destiny that she hadn't noticed. Not until she woke with her rage rekindled and burning inside her, a reminder that—like before—everything in her life could be taken away.

Fallen or not, she was done waiting.

Enne stormed out of her bedroom and down the hallway, then threw open Grace's door. Both Grace and Roy jolted awake—Grace in her bed, a knife jutting out from beneath her pillow, and Roy on the floor handcuffed to the radiator.

Enne pressed her gun to his head and clicked off the safety.

"In less than a month, Aldrich Owain will attend the election's first debate," she told Roy. "You're going to tell me how to kill him."

Grace flung off her covers. "What are you doing?" she hissed.

Enne barely recognized the growl in her voice when she answered, "I'm finally doing something."

"By threatening to kill him?" Roy shot Grace an appreciative glance, which Grace didn't return. "Don't look so grateful, whiteboot. If I had my way, you would've been dead weeks ago. You think I like hearing you snore all night?"

"You talk in your sleep," he muttered.

Grace's eyes widened. "You haven't said a word since the night you got here, and *now* you decide to talk?" Grace kicked the radiator he was handcuffed to. "You don't smile. You don't frown. You knock on the floor when you need to piss, like I'm not even worth your words, and *now* you speak?"

Roy turned his head to the side and didn't say anything.

Grace scowled, grabbed Enne by the arm, and dragged her to the other side of the room. "Who is Aldrich Owain?"

Enne hadn't told anyone about her plan, because she wasn't going to be talked out of it. She knew revenge would do nothing to heal the painful hole in her heart, but she didn't care. It would still feel good to put a hole in his.

And so she answered, "He's one of the people who killed my mother."

Grace eyed Enne carefully. "There are times for blood, but this isn't one of them."

"He deserves to die," Enne snapped.

"I'm not talking about Owain—I'm talking about *him*, and whatever it is you stormed in here to do." Grace gestured to the whiteboot, who glared at them. "Tell me why you need him."

Enne's eyes widened in surprise. She hadn't expected Grace's support—she hadn't expected anyone's.

"There will be whiteboots guarding the debate," Enne answered, "and Roy was a whiteboot. He'll know what sort of weapons they'd carry, how many they'd station."

"But why there? You'll be more at risk for getting caught."

Because Enne wasn't Ivory. She wouldn't kill Aldrich Owain in the quiet seclusion of his home, leaving his body and a murderer's calling card for a neighbor to find. She didn't want to send the Phoenix Club that blatant a message—not yet.

She wanted to make them look over their shoulders. She

wanted them to fear the creak of floorboards in the middle of the night, to mistake the shadows in their bedroom for doom. She wanted them to know, deep in their cruel, eternal hearts, that death was coming for them. She wanted them paranoid. She wanted them weak.

And so she'd decided that her first murder would look like an accident.

Owain, a newspaper mogul, would undoubtedly attend the upcoming debate. And if he was shot amid the chaos of a crowd turned violent, no one would suspect foul play.

But rather than explaining all that, Enne only answered, "Because it feels right. It has to be there."

Grace narrowed her eyes and paused. "Fine. Then I'll talk to him."

"But—"

"Put your gun away. I can do this."

Roy hadn't cooperated with them since he'd arrived, so Enne had no idea why Grace thought she could convince him. In her nightdress and without her eyeliner, she was far less fearsome than usual. But still, Enne trusted her third, so she did as she was told.

Grace sat down in front of Roy. "I just want to talk," she said. "Do you know why I used to work as an assassin?"

Roy said nothing.

"I did it for the volts. I bet you hate that, right? A lot of whiteboots just want to wave their guns around, but not you. You're the noble type. I can tell." Grace lay down and propped her head on her elbow. "I probably could've been a Dove, but creepy cults aren't really my style. So I let Séance make an honest woman out of me."

Roy snorted, but still said nothing.

"What's so funny?" she asked. "Go on. You've been watching me so closely these past few days—I see you looking. I bet you have a lot to say."

He pursed his lips. "Nothing about what you all do here is honest."

Grace grinned. "You like it? It was my idea."

Enne crossed her arms. She realized she couldn't paint Owain's murder as noble if she tortured Roy to make it happen. But at least torture would've been quicker.

"You know what else isn't honest?" Grace reached up and grabbed his badge off her bureau. "Don't they take your badge after you're fired? But you *were* fired, otherwise people would've come looking for you a long time ago. Did you steal this?"

"I didn't steal it," he gritted through his teeth.

"You didn't steal this, but you're also not a whiteboot." Grace leaned against the wall beside him, pondering this. He inched away from her, as though disturbed at the thought of them touching. "I know you are who you say you are. I've seen your picture in the papers. You led the attack on the Orphan Guild. You killed a nine-year-old, you know. He wasn't a Guildworker. He was just somebody's brother."

Roy stiffened, but remained silent.

"So why is the golden boy of Humphrey Yard no longer a sergeant? Why didn't you go back to give them your badge? That's procedure, and you're all about procedure." She tossed his badge across the floor. "Because you couldn't. You're *running* from them. Captain Hector wants you dead."

Roy still said nothing.

"Because it wasn't the whiteboots who attacked the Orphan Guild. They've been telling a lie on every radio station for weeks, and you just can't live with it."

Roy's eyes widened. "How did you know that?"

Grace gave him a wicked grin. "I didn't. But now I do."

Enne's mind reeled. The whiteboots had claimed credit for the attack. If they didn't do it, who did?

Roy glared at the floor as he spoke. "The captain thought it would be better for the city if everyone believed we'd done it. And when I wanted to find out who was really responsible, the captain forbade me from following the case. I did anyway. I left after my partner tried to kill me, probably on Hector's orders, but if I find out the truth... I can expose them. I can go back."

"So you think *I* did it?" Enne blurted, horrified.

Roy startled, as though he'd forgotten Enne was there. "No. I think the Guildmaster or one of his associates planned it, but when I saw you leave that day, I knew it was an opportunity. So I followed you."

"Bryce would never hurt the Guild. And Rebecca and Harvey are too loyal to him to do so, either," Enne said. "Why do you even suspect them?"

"Because of how quickly they moved, how few people were hurt. It was like they knew it was coming. Like they tried to limit casualties."

"That's not evidence," Grace pointed out. "That's coincidence."

"At the time, only the Families had those sort of weapons," he admitted. "But I still trust my instincts."

"I trust logic," she countered.

"You asked, and I'm telling the truth. But I'm not helping you kill a man."

"He's not an *innocent* man. He killed her mother. Think of it this way—you would be helping bring him to justice. You love justice."

"Stop doing that. Stop talking about me like I'm some comic strip character."

"I can't help it when you look like one. I bet you'd look great in tights."

He flushed and inched as far away from her as his handcuffs would allow. "If my precinct knew that the headquarters of the Spirits was like *this*... The whole damn building smells of nail polish. There are *cats* everywhere named after *murderers*. And all you eat are sweets."

"Roy," Grace cooed, and Roy scowled at the raspy, provocative way she said his name. Enne suspected she knew why Roy insisted on staying with Grace, and it was far from a death wish. "Who *does* have a motive for starting a street war? Who *does* want to see the North Side fall?"

When Roy didn't speak, Enne took it upon herself to answer. "The Phoenix Club."

"The Phoenix Club hasn't been active since the Revolution," he said.

"Troops in the North Side. Talent registrations. Curfews. It's starting to feel an awful lot like the Revolution repeating itself." Enne got up and walked closer to Roy. This was the first time he'd actually looked at her—not at Grace or at the floor—since she'd entered the room, and his eyes widened as she approached.

"Yes, it is," he croaked. "You're a Mizer."

Enne realized that she wasn't wearing her contacts.

"Oh, good," Grace said cheerily. "Now we *have* to kill him."

Enne wouldn't panic. Not yet. After all, Roy had already been a captive who knew too much information. "I guess now we're all being honest." She knelt in front of him. "If my mother hadn't protected me, the Phoenix Club would've killed me when I was born, eight years after the Revolution, and called it justice. My mother wasn't a Mizer, yet they called it justice when they killed her. You were going to tell the truth, and so Hector tried to kill you. If you want justice in this city, you have to take it." She held out her hand to shake Roy's free one. "I think we could help each other."

Roy's glare slowly faded into reluctance. "You could've tortured me."

Grace shrugged. "That would've been easier, since you already hate me. But I realized, for you, the alternative would be worse."

Roy grimaced as he reached for Enne's hand to shake. "I have one condition."

Grace frowned and opened her mouth to argue, but Enne quickly answered, "Sure."

"I want to sleep in a different room." He shot Grace a nervous glance. She bared her teeth.

"We'll get you your own room," Enne told him. After they added bars to the windows and padlocks to the doors.

Grace scowled, as though still disappointed they hadn't killed him, but Enne was about to get exactly what she came for.

She reached into Grace's nightstand drawer and grabbed the key to Roy's handcuffs. She dangled them in front of his eyes. "Now tell me what I need to know."

Vianca Augustine entered the tea shop wearing a dress black enough for a funeral. It was a pleasant spot, with outdoor seating and pots of flowers lining the patio. Enne gave the donna a small wave to indicate where she was sitting, and Vianca made her way over, servers darting anxiously out of her path.

"Where did you find a place like this?" she asked with pursed lips. The decor was very trendy, the wallpaper filled with geometric patterns rather than art nouveau swirls.

"We're only two blocks from St. Morse," Enne pointed out.

"Yes, but why are we *here*?"

Because Enne was about to do something very dangerous—she was going to manipulate Vianca Augustine. And what else would sweeten Vianca's mood better than a tea shop?

"I wanted to talk to you about something important," Enne told her. "And it's a beautiful day."

"Yes, if you can ignore the sight of armed soldiers parading the streets," Vianca responded coolly. "My husband was a soldier, you know."

"I didn't," Enne said. Vianca never discussed her husband. The only men she liked to discuss were those who had betrayed her. "How did you meet?"

"At an execution."

Enne was saved from having to respond by the waiter, who placed a complimentary basket of tea cookies on the table. Enne politely ordered a pot of their rose hip brew.

Vianca squinted at the menu of over three hundred choices. "I'll try the gunpowder green. Something different." As the server hurried off, the donna helped herself to a cookie. "I've never seen such a long list." She examined the decor with a new admiration. "What is it you wished to ask me about?"

Enne had hoped to devise her plans for the debate on her own. But the Spirits, though clever, were few in number and narrow in skill set. In order to sway the crowds, she needed more gangsters at her disposal.

"I'm worried about the debate later this month," Enne said, her words careful and practiced. "Prescott has been pushing ahead in the polls you asked us to run, even though the wigheads are keeping that quiet. What sort of personal protection does Prescott have?"

Vianca rolled her eyes. "Whatever I provide. He pays no attention." She ate ungraciously, chewing loudly and licking her fingers afterward. "Why the concern? Did my son—"

"It was something Poppy mentioned to me," Enne told her.

"I think it would be wise to increase his guards." She hoped saying so wasn't too presumptuous of her, but she was saved, once again, by the waiter, who came bearing two kettles of tea.

"Prescott will make a fool of himself at this debate, no doubt. Harrison is a clever little snake. It will be a disaster." Vianca downed her steaming cup in one furious gulp. "My father and grandfather would be turning over in their graves if they knew Harrison was running for the First Party. That the Augustine legacy was just fodder for gossip columns in tabloids." She refilled her cup. "Not that anything I did prompted him to such extremes."

"It's not about you," Enne said consolingly, her lies leaving a bitter taste on her tongue. "It's about greed. You could've given him everything, but he still wanted more."

Vianca lowered her tea cup and narrowed her eyes. "I see what you're doing. You're not usually so…in agreement with me."

Enne nervously poured most of the sugar bowl into her mug. "What do you mean?"

"You're hiding something you don't want me to know." Vianca smiled wickedly. "Neither of you really could keep it from me. It was painfully obvious from the start. I don't normally work with girls, but Levi had never brought me a girl before, either."

Enne took a deep breath. If she was going to sway Vianca, then she needed to rise to a status that she had never before reached.

She needed to become Vianca's favorite.

Levi might've attained the title by resisting her, but Enne understood Vianca. All her life, she'd been trying to measure up to men who'd already deemed her unworthy, and so Enne could give her something she'd never had: solidarity.

"I told him you'd find out eventually," Enne told her, praying her honesty would pay off.

Vianca let out a horrifying cackle and took another sip of her tea. "I always do. Levi will try to convince you otherwise, but he knows more old world history and manners than half the South Side."

The thought of sitting here and gossiping about Levi made even Enne's sweetened rose hip tea taste sour.

"With the curfew, the Irons are losing all their business. Levi says the North Side won't last. It's affecting people's lives. It won't be long before they riot."

Vianca's green eyes lit up. "A riot? Is that what Levi wants?"

Enne swallowed down her conscience. She knew she was crossing a line, but she needed the Irons, and Levi would never agree to her plans otherwise. They were together in a lot of things, but not in this. "Perhaps. How much longer can these conditions last?"

"The monarchists would typically be blamed for a riot, but not if it occurs at the debate. After all, both sides are present. The whole South Side will be there. And if the Irons are running out of business, then surely they're looking for something to do." Vianca reached over the table and patted Enne's hand. "He hates it when I try to help him, but it'll sound much sweeter coming from you."

Enne couldn't believe she'd done it. All it had taken was pretty words to convince the donna it was all her idea. And Vianca would never know that the riot would end with a murder.

"I'll tell him," Enne said, biting down a smile to conceal her victory.

Vianca patted Enne on the hand. "We should have appointments like this more often." Then she gave the tea shop a strangely girlish smile.

LEVI

♥   ♠   ♦   ♣

Levi popped the collar of his black trench coat and snuck down
the museum's stairs, hoping to avoid the Irons so he didn't have
to admit what he was doing. Because it was silly, and because
he couldn't afford it, and because even if he could, he didn't
deserve it. But he'd been so on edge since his argument with
Jac three weeks ago that he'd needed a distraction. So in a
moment of weakness, he'd made the phone call.

Levi opened the front door, and to his horror, Tock sat on
the stoop outside.

"You're not subtle," she told him.

He scowled. "I have an appointment."

"I know your schedule, and that's a bold-faced lie, but sure,
you have an appointment." She waved her hand dismissively.
"There are only whiteboots on every other street corner. What
could go wrong?"

"You know, it was just a few months ago that you were
looking for a job with danger."

"It's not me I worry about," she grumbled. As Levi slipped

past her down the steps, she called after him, "I hope your ego is worth it!"

Levi sighed. As always, Tock knew *exactly* what he was up to, but all he gave her was a nod before he disappeared down the Street of the Holy Tombs.

Enne's Houssen was parked on the corner. Since the lockdown began, they'd spent every day clinging to the cliff's edge of ruin. But they'd carved out a place for themselves there, however teetering, and built something good upon it.

Levi slid into the passenger seat and gave Enne a quick kiss. "Thank you for joining me for my appointment with destiny."

"Funny," she said. "My guidebook doesn't show 'destiny' on the map."

"That's because it's still being built."

She raised her eyebrows. "You told me this meeting was important."

"Come on…we've hardly seen each other these past few weeks, thanks to the curfew. And you're always running off to South Side parties—" his eyes wandered over her uppity dress "—wearing far too much periwinkle when you could be wearing…" He stopped, laughing at his own joke, knowing she probably wouldn't.

"What were you going to say?" Enne prodded.

He bit his lip to hold back his grin. "Nothing."

She looked confused for a moment, then her eyes widened and she pushed him away, smirking. "And you wear far too much silver. You look ridiculous."

"You should take some off me, then."

She rolled her eyes and shifted the car into drive.

Fitz Oliver waited for them as they got out of the motorcar. He wore a red-and-white-striped suit, like peppermint candy, and his own motorcar was cherry red to match. He lifted his arms up as they approached, gesturing to the entire board-walk behind him. A ferris wheel imposed on the skyline, the clouds behind it as idyllic as candy floss. The air smelled of sea and freshly poured concrete—like opportunity.

"Levi!" he exclaimed. "I was ecstatic to get your call. And you brought company." He kissed Enne's hand, as though they were meeting at a party rather than behind a construction site. "Your boyfriend is about to make the best business decision of his life."

Enne gave Fitz a startled but polite smile. "And what exactly *is* the best business decision of his life?"

"After today's tour, he's going to agree to purchase the largest casino on the boardwalk." Fitz beamed and looked up at the sky, unfazed by the blinding sun. "I have a lot of interested buyers—in far better criminal standing, I might add. The deal wouldn't be public, of course. But a mystery buyer?" He tipped his hat at Levi. "I know the value of a rumor. And what they say about you? Priceless."

Levi was easily swayed by flattery, even if it came from a man with expensive taste in hideous things. "Lead the way, then," he said.

But Enne was harder to convince. "The North Side has been on lockdown for three weeks, but you're still interested in selling it to a gangster?"

Levi shot Enne an annoyed look, but Fitz seemed hardly perturbed by her comment. "The boardwalk opens next summer. Do you really think the city will still be in lockdown by then? The curfew has everyone losing volts. No, in a few months, my firm believes New Reynes will look entirely different."

Levi was beginning to like Fitz more and more. He wrapped his arm around Enne's shoulder as they followed Fitz across the parking lot.

"This is the casino you mentioned last month?" Enne whispered to Levi. "Where are you finding the volts for this?"

"I just…" He sighed. "I just wanted to see it."

Fitz stopped and pointed at an unpainted, half-finished structure. It was magnificently large, with spiraling towers and grand windows that overlooked the ocean.

As Levi breathed in the smells of sea and construction, he felt a wistful pang in his chest. He wanted this terribly, but standing here, looking at it, he knew he couldn't have it. Not just because of the volts, but because he already had everything. Wasn't that what Jac had told him? That Levi was selfish and incapable of self-restraint?

"Well," Fitz said, beaming, "let's give it a peek, shall we?"

They followed Fitz inside, Enne pulling Levi ahead even as he froze in front of the threshold. Marble tiles glistened along the floor of the lobby, alternating black and white. Those same colors were everywhere he looked—on the wood of the attendant desks, on the columns, on the doors. It felt like walking into an optical illusion.

Or a dream.

Levi and Enne halted abruptly past the doors, and chills broke out across his neck.

"Is this what you call destiny?" she whispered.

This was the opposite of what he considered destiny. Levi hoped and wanted for things so much that he could see destiny in anything—in the numbers on a pair of dice, in the graffiti on a corner of Olde Town. But he always saw destiny as positive, a force guiding him toward something great.

If this was his destiny, it felt like something darker. Something cursed.

"This is what I call coincidence," he answered carefully.

Fitz turned around, his arms lifted up once again. "Tremendous, isn't it?" He shot them an ear-to-ear smile. "And we're only just getting started!"

Fitz toured them through the rest of the casino. Each room, indeed, seemed more tremendous than the next. But even if it wasn't exactly identical to the hallway, Levi still held his breath each time Fitz opened a new door, expecting to find a nightmare waiting behind it.

"So what do you think?" Fitz asked finally, once they returned to the atrium.

Levi looked at Enne. She hadn't said anything the entire tour, only nodded politely at Fitz's many comments. She gave Levi a thin smile.

"I'll have to think about it," Levi answered.

"Think about it? But this is a dream!" Fitz said, and Levi cleared his throat at the word choice. "The boardwalk's grand opening seems far away, but the contractors can't wait for a buyer much longer."

No matter how many times Levi had dreamed of the hallway, it was still only a dream. He shouldn't let superstition sway him from a once-in-a-lifetime opportunity.

Not that he could take it, anyway.

"How much is the down payment?" Levi asked, keeping up the charade.

"Same as before—fifteen thousand volts down."

Levi cringed inwardly. Between Vianca's request and the lockdown, he was far from one of the richest men in the North Side anymore.

"Can I talk to Levi in private for a moment?" Enne asked, and Levi numbly let her pull him away to the other side of the room. "I think you should take it."

Levi gaped. "With what voltage? You were just saying earlier that it was impossible—"

"Just *look* at this place. We never talk about it, but I know you see the same thing I do."

"Zula called it a shade. That isn't anything *good*, Enne." And he worried that dwelling on it would send their one good thing over that cliff's edge.

"That's just Jac rubbing off on you," she pushed. "You *want* this. I know you do."

"I want everything!" The desires he'd once admitted freely now felt tainted with his friend's disdain. Because if Levi got this, he would go on to wanting bigger, better things. He might have the Irons, and Enne, and the reputation he'd always wanted, but the problem with ambition was that it was never satiated. "Besides, it's impossible."

Enne slipped her arms around his waist, a touch that would normally make him relax, but the dangerous glint in her eyes did quite the opposite.

"There *is* a way," she whispered. "There has always been another option."

The last time she'd suggested this, Levi had immediately declined. Making volts was dangerous—even criminals needed an explanation for their fortunes. But the two of them were far from the nobodies they'd been only a few months ago. Every breath they took was already accompanied by danger.

But the more he thought about it, the more the image of his father lingered in his mind. Levi had built a life for himself that had nothing to do with the bloody history of his family, and he was proud of that. How could he rationalize all the years cursing his father if he carried on his legacy after all?

"Enne…" He smiled apologetically and squeezed her hand. "It's not worth it."

She bit her lip, like she was considering pushing more. Instead, she only nodded. "It's your decision."

The two returned to Fitz. "I'm sorry," Levi said, with what

he truly felt was a heavy heart. "I can't accept. But I really appreciate your offer."

Fitz's smile fell. "Well, if you change your minds, you know how to reach me." He handed them both fresh copies of his business card. "Can I trust you to show yourselves out? I have another appointment in a few minutes for a taffy shop." Then he waved his goodbyes and left.

For several moments, the two of them stood there in silence.

Levi shook his head bitterly and wandered into the card rooms. No matter how unsettling the decor, he liked how little this place resembled St. Morse. Inside that casino, he always felt trapped beneath Vianca's shadow.

He leaned against a white card table—they, too, alternated colors—and tried to imagine himself owning it.

"Jac would probably hate this place," he said.

Enne wrapped her arms around his shoulders. "You can't keep punishing yourself for what happened. You've been friends for years. You'll get through this."

But Levi thought of the words flung between them that day, and he wasn't so sure. Lately, he wasn't sure of anything—not his instincts, not his survival, not his destiny.

"A long time ago, before I came to New Reynes," Levi said, "someone in my life taught me to believe that I needed to be punished for every mistake." He'd never talked to Enne about his father before, and he almost felt silly bringing it up now. It was a lifetime ago—sometimes, he even forgot his father's voice. But he'd never forgotten his father's lessons. "I thought I had unlearned all of that since then, but I guess you never really do."

Enne pressed her head against his chest. "I'm sorry."

"It was a long time ago."

She took his hand and interlaced their fingers. He liked the gesture, how it reminded him that they were in this together. Enne was by far the most dangerous of all the things he wanted, but truthfully, even if the whole cliff collapsed, it would feel so sweet to fall.

With his other hand, he pulled her into him. Someone could happen upon them, but he didn't care.

"I have something I need to tell you," Enne said warily, lifting her head to look at him. "Vianca is giving us another assignment."

Levi groaned. "Are we not paying her enough already?"

"She doesn't trust Worner to face off against Harrison. She wants us to stop the debate at the end of the month. With a… demonstration."

"A demonstration," he repeated.

"Like a small riot."

"A *small* riot." As if Levi wasn't already dealing with enough. As if the South Side needed another reason to send more soldiers across the Brint.

Enne gave him a weak smile. "No one innocent will get hurt."

"The Irons could get hurt."

"Not if we plan it right," she assured him.

He sighed and lowered his arms, but she didn't pull away. Instead, she pushed him back against the table. Her hands fiddled with the top button of his shirt, and Levi's heart sped up.

"You don't even sound angry," he said. "Do you agree with Vianca, or something?"

"Of course not, but I trust us." Her hand slid behind his neck, pulling him toward her. "Don't you?"

It wasn't Enne he didn't trust, but it was hard to think when she pressed herself against him. The violet storms of her aura made him dizzy.

She pressed her lips to his, and everything about the way he kissed her was full of want. He wanted what she said to be true. He wanted to own this casino. He wanted her in this place beside him.

Enne smiled against his lips. "Did you know I have one pistol and four knives hidden on me right now?"

Levi turned her around so that she took his place on the table. He braced one hand against the felt to steady himself, and with his other, he traced up the stocking on the inside of her calf. Her fingers undid the rest of his shirt buttons, and a thrill stirred in his stomach. He liked how she looked, with her pearl necklace crooked, her chest pressed against his, smiling up at him.

It was fitting that this place resembled a dream—a dream he couldn't let himself have.

Not yet, his ambitions whispered, rising—despite himself—at Enne's touch.

Levi's hand found something secured at her mid-thigh, but even as he traced over the grooves of the metal, he found himself far more interested in the lace around it. Still, he slid the knife out from its holster and tossed it on the table.

"There's one."

ENNE

♥ ♠ ♦ ♣

It was a beautiful day, all things considered.

The Park District of the South Side was still lushly green even in late September, and a tent had been erected among the trees. At precisely noon, Enne held out her identification papers for whiteboot inspection and entered the tent. She searched the throngs of reporters and campaign assistants for Poppy and found her seated on a fold-out chair, a romance novel Enne had recommended in her hands.

Poppy's face brightened as Enne approached. "Thank you so much for coming—I'm so glad you're here. Father's making me introduce him today, and I hate speaking in front of crowds."

"But you're a performer," Enne said. One of these days, Enne assured herself, she would go see one of Poppy's ballets. She might've only attended the South Side salons on Vianca's orders, but her friendship with Worner Prescott's daughter wasn't a farce—she genuinely liked spending time with Poppy.

"Elegance, not eloquence." Poppy ran her hands down her conservative, stiff dress. "I don't even feel like myself."

"You'll be fine," Enne assured her. *Because if everything goes to plan, you'll be quickly interrupted.*

"Well, I'm no more nervous than Father is," Poppy told her. "He's been in a tizzy all morning. I covered his face with powder because it's so red." She nodded toward him, seated across the tent, fumbling with a set of speech cards. "I'm just so anxious for all this to be over. Did you hear that Vianca Augustine is throwing a party the night the results are announced? Her son agreed to go, and now everyone has to be there to watch and gossip." Poppy smiled conspiratorially. "I hope it's dramatic."

"I'm sure it will be," Enne replied carefully. She didn't like discussing Vianca with Poppy—Enne was always afraid she'd reveal more than she meant to about how well she knew the donna.

"You're dressed nice. Is today when I get to meet this lover you've told me nothing about?"

Enne laughed. "You've been reading too many of those books."

"I read mysteries, too, you know." She tapped her fingernails on the paperback's glossy cover. "I'm collecting clues. I almost have your North Side boy figured out."

"You're still stuck on your North Side fantasy?" Enne also wanted to avoid talking about Levi and remembering the lies she'd spun this past week in preparation for this day. He'd be furious when he found out, yet even though the Phoenix Club had tried to kill Levi, he didn't still hear the timer ticking down in his mind. He didn't still tremble at the thought of facing them once more.

But the Phoenix Club had taken more from Enne than she could ever forgive.

Before Poppy could respond, Worner appeared behind them and rested a hand on his daughter's shoulder. "The manager wants us to stand together and prepare to go outside." He nodded to the tent's entrance, where Enne spotted Harrison Augustine in a navy suit that matched his eyepatch. Enne's stomach churned. Estranged or not, he looked every bit as intimidating as his mother.

Enne reminded herself of the Irons and Spirits stationed all around the stage area to keep watch, but there were still so many ways today could go wrong. She wouldn't forgive herself if anyone she cared about got hurt.

Poppy gave Enne a final smile. "Let's celebrate tonight when this is over," she said. Enne nodded politely, but her mind was already on murder, and whether she truly could kill a man in cold blood.

She could, she decided. From the moment she'd lost her mother, she could.

After the father-daughter pair went outside, amid cheers throughout the park, Enne slipped out herself and made for the building she and Grace had scouted earlier. Using the crowds as a distraction, she turned into the alley unnoticed, hiked up her skirts, and climbed the fire escape, up two floors, four, six.

Once at the top, she examined the rest of the climb between her and the roof with unease.

No worse than a trapeze, she told herself. Besides, she'd made the same leap last night to plant her supplies.

Enne hoisted herself over the metal railing of the stairs and reached, carefully, for the closest window. Then she clung to the bricks and climbed the rest of the way up to the roof.

To her surprise, she found Grace waiting for her, dressed in her usual all black, though her pale skin was pink from sunburn.

Enne huffed and wiped the sweat off her forehead. "How did you get up here? Shouldn't you be with the others?"

"I've been here for hours." Grace marked her place in her novel and set the book on the ground. "I decided someone needs to keep an eye on you."

"Why is that?" Enne asked, stepping around Grace to the duffle bag she'd stashed last night. She unfastened it and revealed a sniper rifle—a token of good luck from Jonas.

"Because I'm your friend."

"You're going to try to talk me out of it." Enne turned around and scowled. "Why would you let me come this far if that's what you wanted?"

"Because I think there's something to be said about coming this far, about knowing you *could*." Grace grabbed Enne by the shoulder and led her to the edge of the roof. Enne's eyes immediately swept over the park to a VIP box beside the stage. It wasn't very crowded, as most of the reporters had moved to stand closer to the podium. Aldrich Owain sat alone in a gray suit, his legs crossed. Two whiteboots stood watch behind him.

"Consider this," Grace said. "You could shoot him right now. All it would take is pulling the trigger."

If it was that easy, then Enne should do it. She'd manipulated Vianca. She'd lied to Levi. She'd put so many people in danger—all for this. It was far too late to back down now.

"He deserves to die," Enne told her.

"I'm not disagreeing."

But Enne could tell from the heaviness in Grace's voice that she wanted to stop her all the same.

She tore Grace's hand off her shoulder. "Aren't you proud?"

"Should I be?" Grace asked flatly.

"You *are* the one who taught me this." Enne brushed past her and turned back to the duffle bag.

Grace seized Enne's wrist as she reached for the rifle. "I came here to support you, but don't accuse me of teaching you *this*."

"That's ironic, coming from a killer." Enne yanked her hand away.

"Do you think I wanted to be a killer?" Grace demanded.

"I did it because I was alone and desperate. Because it was easy. And it was only easy because, up until I met you and Lola, I didn't care about anyone enough to realize what I was doing was wrong."

Because Grace was her friend, Enne refrained from shouting. A wind tore across the rooftop, and Enne tied her hair away from her face, staring at her shoes even as she felt Grace's eyes on her.

"Don't I get a response?" Grace demanded.

"You can't tell me killing is wrong right after you said Owain deserves to die. You can't help me every step of the way only to try to stop me now."

"I helped you before I knew this wasn't just between you and me and Roy." As she spoke, Enne set up her rifle. Harrison's associate had already taken the stage in the park below to introduce his candidate. "But now you have the Spirits and the Irons out there. Other people could get hurt."

"I've done as much as I could to stop that from—"

Grace grabbed Enne by her coat sleeve and yanked her up. "I'm too smart for you to lie to me."

"Thank you all so much for being here," Enne heard Poppy say below. The microphone screeched as Poppy adjusted it slightly.

Enne gritted her teeth. She didn't have time to argue with Grace—the debate would start soon. "What do you want me to say to you, Grace? My life isn't just dresses and tea cakes and Sadie Knightley novels! So unless you plan to fight me—"

"The only reason I *won't* fight you is because we both know I would win." Grace let go of Enne's sleeve. "But I've given you the chance now to back down. So take the shot. I won't stop you."

Enne wanted to argue more, but if she did, she might miss her cue. She set the rifle on the roof's edge and lined up her shot.

Poppy continued, "I couldn't be prouder or more honored to introduce my father, Worner Prescott—"

"The North Side has been under curfew for weeks!" some-one—a Spirit—shouted from the crowd. It was one of the lines Enne and Levi had written. "How can we be expected to get to the polls when we need to go home immediately after work?" Several other voices echoed the question.

Enne adjusted the scope and peered through it, toward Owain's balding head.

"You're holding it too low. It'll jerk when you fire," Grace told her. "I'm just saying, *I* didn't teach you that."

Enne swallowed down an angry retort and adjusted her left hand.

Poppy cleared her throat into her microphone, despite the commotion in the crowd. "During the Revolution, my father served under the esteemed Admiral Karga, and was respon-sible for relocating noble families to—"

"My business is closed down because of the curfew! How am I supposed to eat?" an Iron called out.

Enne took a deep breath. She could fire at any moment. She could kill one of the men who'd murdered her mother.

"Are you factoring in the wind?" Grace asked.

"Stop it," Enne snapped.

The microphone amplified Poppy's hitched breath. "The questions portion of the debate will take place later—"

"—The Talent Tax is archaic—"

"—The North Side depends on the gangs—"

"—yet the Families are fine. The Families get to run for office—"

"Please," Poppy rasped.

"Are you planning on telling your boyfriend about your murder spree?" Grace asked.

"Stop," Enne hissed again, all the voices breaking her focus. "The Phoenix Club won't know, and neither will..."

Enne swallowed down the rest of her words along with a scorching lump of fury. She couldn't let Grace distract her— she'd lose her chance. But as her finger continued to trace along the edge of the trigger, Levi's face came, unbidden, to her mind, and Enne's heart clenched. She thought how defeated he'd sounded when they toured that casino. When he thought of how his power affected the city, he really thought of something better that this.

But those were his dreams, not hers. Enne didn't *have* dreams—they were fantasies for the childish or disillusioned, and hers had been stolen away the moment she'd come to New Reynes. She could spend her days in the palace she claimed for herself; she could spend her nights in the arms of a boy she cared about. But it wouldn't matter, because when she woke up, she would still be afraid.

"I might tell Levi," Grace said, "if you don't."

Enne's heart clenched. "You wouldn't."

"Because he'd hate you?" Grace asked. "Or because you'd hate me?"

Enne hesitated. She didn't think Grace had been lying when she said that before Enne and Lola, she'd been alone. Enne hadn't grown up with friends, either. And so she understood the weight of Grace's threat, that she'd sacrifice friendship if it meant saving her. And wasn't that what Grace *was* doing? Saving Enne from herself?

If Enne fired, she would kill a man who deserved it. But Levi would hate her for it. Grace and Lola and every person she'd manipulated would see the ugliness and fear inside of her, and they would hate her, too.

And if Enne fired, if she pushed them away, she would hate herself.

As the demands from the crowd grew louder, Worner took the microphone, his face red despite all of Poppy's powder. "All of your questions can be addressed later during the public forum—"

Grace drummed her fingers on the roof's ledge. "I don't get what you're waiting for—"

Enne cursed and pulled back her rifle. She could kill in self-defense. She could manipulate and lie and steal, but she couldn't do this.

She stood up, defeated. She turned to Grace and shoved the rifle into her arms, and Grace smiled smugly. "Fine," Enne seethed. "*Take it.* Are you happy now—"

Boom!

A gun had fired, but it wasn't hers.

The crowd erupted into a scream. Whiteboots lunged to surround the candidates and their companions, while other officers immediately made for the crowd, batons raised.

Grace grabbed Enne by the shoulders and hauled her to her feet. "Who was that? What's happening?"

But Enne was too shocked to speak. She and Levi had planned for commotion, not chaos.

Several more gunshots rang out. The people in the crowd pushed each other in their efforts to flee the park, knocking over chairs and tables. Enne squinted to search the masses for familiar faces—for any of the Spirits or the Irons—but there were too many people, and they moved too fast.

"We need to find the others," Enne breathed.

The two girls took the inside stairs down. Rioters had thrown a rock through the window of the ground floor cafe, raining shattered glass onto the tables and along the sidewalk.

Enne and Grace threw open the door to the street. Motorcars were halted all around, horns blaring. Several inflamed passersby pounded on their hoods, making the passengers duck and scream. Whiteboot sirens wailed in the distance.

Something shimmered around her, strangely beautiful amid the chaos. It was a string thinner than a piece of hair, pale and iridescent, like those she'd seen during the Shadow Game. She didn't know what it was, only that it bound the players of the game together, like a spindle spinning a thread, like an instrument playing a song.

Enne reached for it, but her hand only grasped at air. It was a trick of the light.

"Come on!" Grace urged, pulling Enne down the closest alley. "Where are the others? Where was Levi supposed to be?"

"In a motorcar, parked at 84th and Amaranth." That was on the opposite side of the park from where they stood now. Enne watched, dazed, as a man knocked over a trash can and dropped a lit match on its contents. The sparks crackled and spread to engulf the campaign flyers, and even from a distance, she smelled the smoke. "Did we cause this, Grace?"

"You could have," Grace grunted. "But you didn't fire those shots."

A woman knocked shoulders with them as she carried her crying child out of the crowds. Enne winced. This panic had been her design, but even in the worst of her rage, she hadn't imagined this.

Now she knew what power felt like.

And she hated it.

She and Grace followed the rush of the crowd along the sidewalk until they reached the rendezvous point.

As Enne searched the vehicles for Levi's white Amberlite, she felt something strong tug on her shoulder. She whipped around and faced a man trying to grab her purse. Its contents were minimal—her two tokens, her white Spirit gloves and her black Séance mask—but she wasn't keen to lose any of it.

"Let go!" she shouted. When he wouldn't obey, Enne kneed him in the groin. He doubled over onto the ground, releasing his grip.

"Not bad," Grace said, smirking.

"Does that mean you forgive me?" she asked.

As the thief scrambled away, Grace shrugged. "I'm not sure. You might need to kick a few more men in the—"

A motorcar honked repeatedly, and though it was only one of many, Enne and Grace looked toward it. Lola leaned out the window, motioning frantically for them. Enne and Grace sprinted across traffic and leaped into the back seat. As soon as Lola sped off, dodging pedestrians and whiteboots at Tock's panicked *look outs*, Enne felt Levi's hands on her shoulders.

"Are you hurt?" he asked.

"I'm fine," she said, but her voice cracked. "Is everyone all right?"

"We're fine, but we haven't been able to find anyone else. This wasn't what we planned." Levi slammed his fist against the side door.

Enne pulled away from him, tears streaming down her face. "Yes, it was," she said hoarsely. "This was exactly what I planned."

He frowned even as he tried to wipe the tears off her cheeks. "What are you talking about?"

She could've lied—she'd gotten good at lying, even to him. But *he* was the reason she hadn't killed Owain. Because of him, she wanted to be better than that.

"This wasn't Vianca's idea—it was mine. Owain is a member of the Phoenix Club. I... I thought that if I killed him..." Enne looked away from him. It ached to see his expression change, from confusion to concern to shock.

During the drive home, Enne told him everything—about questioning Roy, manipulating Vianca, lying to him. The

Shadow Game didn't haunt Levi the way it did her, but at least he, more than anyone, might be able to understand.

Enne didn't finish her story until after they'd reached the Ruins District. The others got out of the car, but Enne and Levi remained behind. It wasn't until Levi slammed the door closed again that she noticed a muscle straining as he clenched his jaw.

"You manipulated Vianca so she could make me do what you wanted," he murmured, and Enne's breath hitched. His voice was unrecognizably cold. "You used her to use me. How am I supposed to forgive you for that?"

Each of his words sent a blade through her heart.

He made her sound despicable.

And he was right.

Enne bit her lip and blinked back tears. "You're not."

Levi took a shaky breath, his eyes closed. "I've done a lot of things I never thought I would, but not to you." His voice cracked, and Enne resisted the urge to comfort him. She no longer felt like she had the right to.

"I don't think I know you anymore," he said.

Enne hugged her arms to herself and put as much distance between them as possible. It was strange to think that many months ago, when they'd first met, he'd laughed at how naïve she'd been.

"Do you wish you'd killed him?" he asked her.

She'd originally thought the price of killing Owain would be her soul, but now she knew the sacrifice had been far greater. The moment she'd used Vianca against Levi...*that* was when she'd paid her price.

And now she had nothing to show for it.

"I don't know," she murmured truthfully.

Levi shook his head and, without a goodbye, opened the door and walked away.

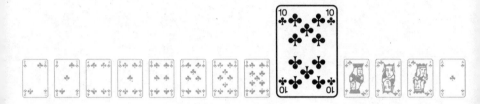

"These stories aren't just *legends*. There are too many things in the North Side you can't explain. Oaths? Shadow Cards? They have to be talents, don't they? I've been thinking a lot about it lately, and I think they do. You might say legends are superstition. I say they're a pattern.

"Maybe it's not Families or street lords or wigheads who own New Reynes. Maybe it's one person. Maybe all these legends are the same story."

—*A legend of the North Side*

JAC

♥ ♠ ♦ ♣

Most tourists flocked to New Reynes in the summer for the warm weather and the beaches, but Jac had always preferred the City of Sin in the fall. The pubs served spiced cider in copper mugs, and the trees wore every color from saffron to gold. This year, however, it'd been hard to focus on usual fall festivities with all the chaos surrounding the election. Now, only days away, you couldn't even turn on the radio anymore without hearing about it.

"Turn that off," Jac grumbled to Sophia, who switched off the news station from where she perched on the desk.

"Don't you want to hear it?" she asked.

He took a deep breath. The First Party controlled all the media outlets, but lately, even their cheerful optimism about Harrison's victory had lost some of its usual confidence. Levi had told Jac that Harrison needed the Torren empire for his victory, so what happened if Jac couldn't give it to him?

"I don't," Jac answered, turning his attention back to the map of the Casino District mounted on the wall of Liver Shot's back office. Even with all the dens the two of them now controlled, they'd still chosen this one as their primary base. It had a central location and familiar faces.

"You are not a failure," Sophia told him, standing up and resting a reassuring hand on his shoulder.

He grasped it with a weak smile. "But I will be."

"Even if we can't give Harrison the votes," she murmured, "we'll still win."

Like the news, Sophia, too, had lost some of her confidence. The endless curfew had hit them exactly where it hurt most: their bottom lines, and now their war with Charles had devolved into a waiting game of seeing who would bleed out of voltage first.

At this rate, it would be them.

"Are you and I looking at the same ledgers, or…?"

"All that matters is that Charles is hurting, too," she said.

Jac laughed mirthlessly. "Can he hurt?"

Sophia grimaced and dug her coin out of her pocket. She flipped heads. "Twenty-seven." She pulled out a collection of knotted necklaces from under her shirt and examined the dull beads, checking to see if there was any luck left in them.

"Twenty-seven?" Jac echoed. "What happened to your one-hundred-flip streak?"

"Until we set this all aflame, we're still selling drugs, and I'll never feel good about that." She sighed. "And without trying to cut off any of Charles's monopoly on Lullaby, we won't, well…"

Jac stiffened. "Three seconds ago you were telling me we'd win. Now you're saying it's hopeless unless we start to sell Lullaby?" He didn't care how desperate they were; he refused to stoop to such lows.

Sophia took both of his hands in hers and turned him away from the map to face her. He didn't like the look on her face.

"I'm saying..." She bit her lip. "We need a plan in case we lose."

He dropped her hands. No, no. They hadn't come this far to make contingencies.

The scar on his arms gave a phantom itch, and he craved a cigarette. But he'd already had one this morning, and he'd been trying to limit himself to one per day.

"We could go somewhere else," Sophia said. "It would be starting over—"

"You gave up everything for this," he breathed.

Her green eyes welled with tears, and she blinked them away and hugged her arms to herself. "Yes, well, Charles won't let this end peacefully. And before, I never had to consider losing you." She sniffled and laughed. "You've made me soft, and it's disgusting."

He snorted and wrapped his arms around her. "You aren't losing me." But despite his words and how much he cared about her, too, he struggled to imagine leaving New Reynes. Leaving Levi.

You haven't spoken in two months, he reminded himself. But that didn't stop Jac from thinking about Levi every time he tallied their profits, every time he saw the Iron tattoos on his arms. Levi had saved him countless times, but he couldn't save Jac from this.

But there was another option. Another deadline that drew closer.

Just because Jac had torn up Charles's invitation didn't mean he'd forgotten it. Tomorrow was Jac's last day before the deadline expired, and he dreaded to think how the war would change when Charles stopped playing nice.

Sophia buried her face in his shoulder. "Don't worry—I haven't given up. Not—"

Suddenly, the lights went out, and the room fell into blackness. Sophia's breath hitched, and she squeezed his arm tight enough to hurt. "What's going on?" she hissed.

He shushed her, his heart hammering. It could've been coincidence, but Jac didn't believe in coincidences.

Sedric Torren had once killed Eight Fingers to send Levi a warning.

Maybe Charles had tired of playing nice.

"Are we the only ones here?" Jac whispered. Few employees but them came to Liver Shot this early.

"I think Ken left…"

Faintly, a sound murmured in the darkness. It was eerie and high-pitched, like some sort of flute.

Sophia clutched at him tighter and cursed under her breath.

The music gradually came closer.

"A match," Jac rasped. "Strike a match."

He could hear footsteps approaching the den, the creaking of floorboards, the melody of the flute. Jac fumbled in his pocket for his pistol while Sophia dug out a match from his stash in the desk. He aimed his gun in the direction of the door.

The music stopped, plunging everything into silence.

Sophia struck the match.

They both screamed at the sight of the stranger standing directly in front of them, close enough to stare down the barrel of Jac's gun. In the dim matchlight, Jac made out the freckled face of a young man, and greasy hair dyed white.

Jac fired, but the Dove had already ducked. Sophia shrieked and pressed herself against the wall while Jac lunged for the man, intending to tackle him to the floor. He grabbed him by the arm, spinning the Dove around. There was a flash of silver.

"Jac, watch out for—"

But then the match burned out, and the room slipped back into darkness. Jac grunted as he threw their assailant against the closest wall. Books tumbled off the adjacent shelf, thumping on wooden floorboards and the edge of the carpet. Jac stumbled on one as he pinned the man down. He was bluntly built but skinny, his elbow jamming painfully into Jac's stomach as he struggled to break free.

Jac let out a groan, but quickly collected himself. The man landed a hard punch at Jac's face, and Jac took it, using the opportunity to bury his pistol in the Dove's gut.

"Don't move," Jac panted.

Sophia struck a second match and edged closer. She held it up to the young man's face, and his pale green eyes narrowed at her inspection.

"Kill me," he spat.

"Who sent you?" Sophia demanded.

He said nothing. There was something feral about his face and the way he pressed himself harder against Jac's gun. Jac squeezed tighter on his shoulder, keeping him pinned to the wall. He didn't want to kill if he could help it.

"Did Charles Torren send you to kill us?" Jac asked.

"I doubt it," Sophia answered. "Charles killed Delia himself."

But Jac wasn't so sure.

He'd overpowered this Dove now, but how many more Doves would it take? One for every day that passed after the deadline? Two? Three? Jac didn't think Charles could afford that, but he couldn't be certain.

Jac twisted the gun into his stomach. "Well, you can tell Charles—"

"I'm not a messenger." The Dove squirmed so that the gun moved closer to his heart. "Do it."

Jac faltered.

"Do it," he repeated.

Then Sophia grabbed a lamp off the shelf and slammed it

hard against his head. The man crumpled to the carpet. Jac took several steps back and leaned against the wall to steady himself, trying to make sense of this.

He'd promised Lola that he'd listen to Levi and Sophia when they'd told him not to take Charles's offer. But Levi was gone, and Sophia was already planning contingencies.

She could've died.

Which was why Jac couldn't wait for Charles to make a second move. He couldn't wait until tomorrow, couldn't wait for Sophia to come up with any more final, desperate options.

The thought of facing Charles terrified him more than anything, but if he was going to save both Sophia *and* Levi, he needed to face his fears.

Tonight, Jac Mardlin would play a game of his own.

LEVI

As Vianca Augustine poured herself a cup of tea, Levi pictured all the ways she might die.

The cold November weather had made the air in her office dry, and each of his breaths scratched at his throat. For months, Levi had counted down the weeks until he achieved his freedom. Until Vianca Augustine was dead. And now the election was only two days away.

But the Spirits ran new polls every few days, and according to Lola, the results looked bleak. Despite Fenice's mass deregistration and voter suppression, the North Siders held unwavering support for the monarchists.

No word from Harrison. No word from Jac. No contact with Enne. After months of following every news story and debate, their hope was waning. Levi had done everything to give Harrison this victory, but apparently everything wasn't enough.

And the last place Levi wanted to be when mourning his losses was St. Morse Casino.

"Levi," Vianca purred, and every hair on his neck stood on end. "Please take a seat."

She poured him a cup of tea, spiking it with whiskey cream. He raised his eyebrows as he accepted the drink. Levi never willingly consumed anything she offered him, but he could admittedly use something strong.

Vianca unlocked one of her desk drawers to reveal a sparkling orb.

"You and Miss Salta have, once again, exceeded my expectations," she said.

Levi tried not to stiffen at the mention of Enne. He'd avoided thinking about their last conversation for weeks, but it'd been very hard to avoid thinking about *her*. He'd thought it would grow easier, but hearing Vianca say her name only made his stomach clench. Enne knew the horrors of Vianca Augustine as well as he did. So he'd never understand how she could've taken the one thing he hated and feared most and used it against him.

Vianca clearly didn't notice his distress, because she didn't mention it. She usually did, when given the chance.

"I've been dwelling on this conversation for a long time," she said. "Surely you must realize what I'm going to say to you."

Levi straightened in his seat, trying to decide whether or not that was a threat. "I have no idea."

"What does this city say about me?"

Witch. Shatz. Pathetic. Terrifying. Ruthless. Monster. The list was endless. Vianca was the villain of every fairy tale, leading helpless North Side children to ruin with a line of breadcrumbs and poker chips.

"Um," Levi started. "That Worner Prescott is barely more than a puppet, and if he wins the election, you'll be the one truly in power."

The corner of her lips turned into a smile. "That's correct, but that isn't what I meant. St. Morse Casino isn't run by *me*. It's run by the Augustine Family. But look around..." She gestured around the office. "I have no family left. When I die, there will be no cousins feuding for my throne. My son will have nothing to do with this place, or with me. If my legacy lives on, it will do so by one of my inept employees, all of whom have only a child's understanding of how this empire operates."

Levi took a long sip of his drink to cool his nerves. He wasn't sure where this was headed.

"I have no heirs," Vianca continued. "I only have the three of you."

"Three?" he repeated. He knew she was referring to her omertas, and he'd always suspected there was a third. Over the summer, Zula Slyk had confirmed those suspicions. *I've always wanted to meet her other boy.*

"Surely you've guessed the third by now," she said with amusement. "I would've thought it obvious."

"It's Prescott, isn't it?" The world already called him Vianca's puppet.

"No—though it's probably better you don't know. I don't want you doing something reckless and interfering. He's useful—but he's difficult. Anyway, after the debate, I decided he won't be a problem much longer."

Levi's heart quickened. He knew Vianca well enough to recognize the cold flippancy in her voice. Vianca was going to kill him, whoever he was. If it was happening before their own plans were carried out, then Levi would be powerless to stop it. He might not know who the third was, but death at Vianca's hand was a fate he'd imagined for himself dozens of times. If he could uncover the boy's identity, he could try to save him.

"Oh, don't look at me like that," Vianca snapped. "He's *far* from innocent. And I'm one of the only ones who knows his secret."

"Have I met him?" Levi asked.

"We're not playing that game," Vianca said sharply. "The only person in New Reynes who truly understands how this empire works is my son, but he'll do everything in his power to burn it down. I've worked too hard to be where I am to have my legacy destroyed. So, for the very first time, Levi, I am offering you a choice."

She slid the emerald ring off her fourth finger and set it in front of him.

"The Augustine Family owns one of the largest empires in New Reynes. And I'm offering it to you."

Levi's initial reaction was shock, quickly overshadowed by abhorrence. When he imagined himself walking these halls, portraits of dead Mizers watching him, he could think of nothing but Vianca. In this office, he thought of nothing but Vianca. In the card rooms, the theater, the suites... The donna's so-called legacy was only torment.

But once those emotions settled, his ambition stirred. Levi had come to New Reynes to write his own story, and rising from nothing to become a don had an attractive sound to it. It wouldn't be the first time in his life he'd made a decision with his own legacy in mind. His relationship with Narinder, his dangerous promises to the other lords... Levi had gotten to where he was by seizing opportunities when they came his way. He wasn't sure he wanted Vianca's empire, but he couldn't simply dismiss her offer, either.

"I'm not interested in the narcotics trade," Levi said. "That's what this casino is built on, isn't it? Mortar and Mistress?"

Vianca pursed her lips. "The Apothecary families are keeping this Family in business, yes."

"But once, it was just a casino," Levi countered. "The Irons run all their operations on gambling. It could be done, if I wore both crowns." The Irons and St. Morse. It made an impressive palace for an impressive empire.

"Is that an acceptance?" she asked.

Levi thought of the casino on the boardwalk, of the opportunity that had passed him by. But now he couldn't imagine that casino without also remembering Enne in it.

"What about Enne?" he asked, his voice choked.

"You've always been my favorite," Vianca said, and it was strange to hear those words from her. For so long, those words had been used by others to cut him. Vianca's favorite. Vianca's bitch. "But I have faith in the both of you. I know that by offering it to you, I'm also offering it to her." Vianca gave him a crooked smile and tapped her fingertips together. "You really are *quite* the pair. I hope you're both grateful for all I've given you."

This time, the pain on his face must have been obvious, because Vianca leaned forward and licked her lips.

"Is something the matter?" she asked.

"Nothing," he said quickly.

She pouted her lips. "This won't do, Levi. I had really hoped for the set."

Levi recoiled in disgust. "Forcing us together seems like a new low, even for you."

A glimmer of something passed through Vianca's eyes. He'd hardly imagined he'd insulted her—nothing he said ever seemed to wound her. But then she shivered, and Levi realized what that look was. A memory.

She folded her hands neatly on her desk. "Very well. My offer stands, and it's for you alone."

Alone.

He swallowed down the painful lump in his chest.

"I'm wanted for treason and murder," Levi said. "How can you want my association?"

Vianca shook her head. "Once Worner wins the election, you'll be pardoned. All of the gangsters will be. The plans are already in motion."

Levi had been so focused on Harrison winning the election and giving him this freedom, he'd never considered that maybe, just maybe, this scenario could be a win-win. Harrison had supported Levi and Jac when they needed it, so Levi didn't like the idea of betraying him. But now, Harrison's promise was a sinking ship.

Still, could Levi really abandon all his efforts these past few months for... Vianca?

There was far more at play in this decision than just Levi's destiny—there was politics, and blood. Every gangster, every Mistress-dazed vedette, every citizen of the North Side could be affected by his decision, and that was an incredible weight on his shoulders.

It'd been far easier to hate Vianca when there had been no choice at all.

He'd resented Enne for using Vianca against him, yet now, he'd consider Vianca's offer? He knew it was hypocritical, and if he and Enne were still together, he would've immediately declined. But now Harrison was losing, the Irons were going broke, the North Side was falling. Both Enne and Jac were gone.

It'd been far easier to want to be good when he'd had someone to be good for.

"I need to sleep on it," he told her.

Vianca reached into her desk and handed him a key. "Sleep on it in your old suite. I hope you come to the right decision."

JAC

♥ ♠ ♦ ♣

The lights of Luckluster Casino strobed down Tropps Street, beckoning patrons with the offer of discounted rooms, for nights spent at card tables and on king-size beds to pass the time from curfew until dawn. Jac hadn't seen the Casino District so bright in several weeks, hadn't seen crowds this size in longer. Music blared with an erratic pulse, and those around him murmured in excitement.

As Jac slipped past the doors into the casino, stepping on discarded flyers for all-night theatrics and drink specials, he felt with cool certainty that the grandiosity of the night was meant for him.

"Do you want me to come with you?" Sophia had asked when he told her he planned to oversee a drop-off.

"I'll be fine," he'd told her.

She didn't know his words had been a promise.

As Jac wove through the entrance hall, dancers beckoning to him from shadowy alcoves, servers passing him with trays of glittering Snake Eyes, he knew there was a very good chance he was walking toward his death. There were a lot of things he wanted to do before he died, that he'd never be able to do if he failed tonight. He wanted to tell Levi that he was sorry, that trying to protect him had seemed noble at first, but really the request had come from all the worst parts of Jac—the ones that obsessed and worried and itched—and all he'd done was make his friend miserable. He wanted to apologize to Enne, who hadn't deserved any of the mess he'd made for them.

Most of all, he wanted to kiss Sophia in front of a smoldering Luckluster Casino once they burned it down.

But no matter what happened tonight, Jac had accomplished the one thing he'd always wanted—to be a story worth telling. And maybe he would still turn into a cautionary tale, but even if North Side kids whispered about this night with terror in their eyes, at least they would know that Jac Mardlin had finally faced his fears.

He'd earned his story.

Jac approached the concierge desk and told the man he had an appointment with Charles. The man nodded, as though he'd been expecting him, and motioned for Jac to follow.

They climbed the casino's wrought-iron spiral staircase, one Jac had always assumed was just for show. It looked like something out of Olde Town, black and sharp and gothic. Red ribbons circled around the rods like sticks of candy, and lipstick marks stained several of the widest spikes. The stairs curved up three floors and ended on the fourth, and the landing wrapped around the entire lobby, so you could lean over the railing and look down upon the entrance hall, merely a shadow among the ceiling's scarlet lights.

The man opened an impressive set of double doors, and Jac walked into a dark room. Though he couldn't see, he felt the floor change from carpet to wood, and the room was large enough to make his footsteps echo. He reached to the wall, fumbling for a moment, and then switched on the light.

It was a banquet hall, the chairs folded in one corner, the tables deconstructed and stacked to the side. Mirrors covered each of the walls, stretching Jac's reflection infinitely in all directions.

This was no fighting pit.

"I wasn't expecting you until tomorrow," a nasaly voice said behind him. Jac whipped around to see Charles standing at the threshold. He wore a white blazer long enough to be a medical jacket, and his eyes were bloodshot.

"You sent a Dove after us," Jac said. "Were you expecting me at all?"

"It was all for fun. A good scare." He licked his lips at that last word and took a few steps closer. Jac stood his ground, even if he preferred to keep several feet between him and Charles. He took the opportunity to examine Charles for any weak spots, ones he might've missed last time. But Charles was several pounds and inches greater than Jac, and though Jac was stronger, he knew that Charles's split talent would work against him. With a touch, skin to skin, he could give pain. Jac had planned for this by wrapping most of his skin in gauze, but he didn't know if that would be enough. He could only guess at Charles's limits and hope he was right.

"I don't want to talk," Jac said brazenly. "Let's start this."

Charles drew a coin and flipped it. "Two hundred and six," he murmured, a smile sliding across his features. Jac stiffened. He'd never heard Sophia reach anywhere close to that high.

Then Charles removed his blazer, his button-up, and even his undershirt. Layers of white clothing piled on the floor, and each new piece was a little more stained. Jac's eyes widened as he saw the painful red lashings covering Charles's skin. Sophia had told Jac that her half siblings used physical penance to raise their luck, and now Jac understood the disgust in her voice. They paid for their misdeeds in blood. The skin across Charles's chest and shoulders was rippled and uneven from years of whipping, and some of his wounds were so fresh, they still shone with a wet sheen. Charles was clearly practiced, because anyone else would've struggled to stand in such pain.

"Not very pretty, I know," Charles murmured. "But it's well worth it, to see the fear in people's eyes. Just like in yours."

Jac gritted his teeth. "I'm revolted, not afraid."

As Charles walked closer, Jac crinkled his nose at the smell of him—of blood and antiseptic. "Hasn't Sophia told you what I can do?" Charles asked.

When Jac took on pain, it needed to come from somewhere. He imagined that was also true of when Charles gave it. If so, Charles had walked into this fight heavily armed.

Jac stripped down to his undershirt, which was several sizes too large to conceal more of his skin. The tape and gauze he always wore around his knuckles extended up his forearms. Only a few inches were exposed below his sleeve, pale skin covered in various tattoos. His inner elbow itched slightly underneath his bandages, but he ignored it. He could push past his fear.

Charles never bothered to close the doors, so the music from downstairs pulsed in here, and some of the red lights danced across the floor.

"There's no audience," Charles said. "Before, during, and after your death, the party will continue in this casino. No one will know who you were or what happened to you, or that you existed at all."

"I said I didn't want to talk," Jac spat. Really, he didn't want Charles to see how his words had disturbed him.

Charles grinned. "Then hit me."

Jac approached, his fists raised. First he aimed for Charles's chest, then his face, his sides. Charles blocked most of his blows, but he did nothing to counter them. It was difficult for Jac to lose himself in this fight, like he always did. There was no sound of an audience cheering or whistles blowing. The reflections in the mirrors played tricks on his vision and balance, but Jac still fought with everything he had, and before long, he'd backed Charles into the wall beside the door.

Every time he hit Charles, the man smiled. His teeth were red with blood.

"Keep hitting me, Jac," he said, his voice edged and manic. "Keep hitting me. Keep hitting me." And Jac did, even as Charles repeated himself over and over. He should be winning—no matter his talent, Charles should be collapsing from the pain of it all—but somehow, Charles remained standing. He watched Jac with reddened eyes, and then he spit at him, landing bloody saliva on Jac's cheek. "Keep hitting me, why don't you?"

Jac shoved him against the mirror, and Charles's head thumped hard against the glass, leaving a web of cracks. Still, Charles laughed. Jac held his forearm against Charles's neck, pinning his wrists behind him. He pressed down hard, choking him.

"You're still afraid," Charles rasped with the little breath he had.

"You're shatz," Jac growled. When he'd imagined this fight, it wasn't like this. It had felt more satisfying. Even if Charles died tonight, Jac would still hear his laugh in his nightmares. In that way, Charles would still have won.

"You're afraid of killing me," Charles rasped. His eyes fixed on the Creed Jac wore around his neck. "You've never killed anyone before."

"I *want* to kill you." It was both the truth and a lie. Taking an innocent life was an unforgivable sin in the Faith, but Charles was far from innocent.

"You don't. You don't you don't you don't." Charles gasped as Jac pushed on his throat harder. "Maybe... I...can help you...want."

Then he turned his head just enough to lick the exposed skin of Jac's arm.

It hurt.

It hurt where Charles had touched him. It hurt afterward, when Jac wrenched his arm away, where his skin was still wet from Charles's tongue. It hurt all over him, like a fire lit within his veins. Jac staggered back and clutched at his stomach as the pain washed over him.

Charles straightened and cracked his neck. The smile fell from his face, his expression turning serious. "It's finally time to play."

While Jac caught his breath and lurched forward, desperately aiming to strike, Charles's hand found the light switch. The room turned dark, and the doors suddenly closed. Charles caught Jac's punch by the wrist and wrenched his arm up. Jac kneed him hard—hard enough to hear one of his ribs crack—but Charles's grip barely even loosened. His tongue found Jac's skin again, tracing down his underarm where his sleeve had slipped. Jac screamed, and his knees buckled.

Charles held him there as he rode out agony's wave. Up close, he smelled vaguely acidic—an odor Jac recognized immediately as Rapture. The drug was probably the only thing keeping Charles from passing out.

Charles's finger traced up Jac's stomach beneath his shirt. Jac grabbed his arm to push him away, but he was weak from the pain of it all. Even the fabric of his shirt burned him, as though *his* skin had been lashed. Charles found Jac's bruises from old fights and played them as though they were piano keys.

"Keep hitting me, Jac," Charles said. He punched Jac hard in the stomach, skin hitting skin, knuckles hitting bone. "Keep hitting me, Jac. Keep hitting me, Jac." Blow after blow, and Charles's grip on his left arm was the only thing keeping Jac from collapsing on the floor. The contents of his stomach spun, and Jac barely had enough control left to keep them down. To keep himself breathing.

Charles snapped his fingers in front of Jac's face. "Stay with me. No fainting."

He let go of him, and Jac hit the floor hard enough to knock the wind out of him. His mind urged his body to scramble up, to run, but everything ached. He was helpless as Charles grabbed his leg and dragged him toward the back of the room, like an alligator pulling its victim into the deep. Jac arched his neck only enough to see the crack of red light beneath the door. It was a glimpse of hope, and it was growing farther away.

Jac had walked into Luckluster knowing this could be his fate, and no matter what Charles did to him, he didn't want to break enough to regret his decision. He'd come here to save Sophia and Levi. He'd come here to destroy the empire that had nearly destroyed him.

But it hurt. So much.

His skin, his bruises, his bones, his stomach, his head. Everything hurt. And every time a wave of pain began to fade, Charles seemed to sense it. As he dragged Jac across the floor, his pointer finger found its way under Jac's sock, twisting beneath the cotton, stroking the smooth parts of the skin below his ankle. Jac tried to stifle his screams, but it seemed like everything only hurt more, then. He could see nothing but the red light, feel and hear and smell nothing but Charles. He didn't even have enough lucidity in him to form a useless sinner's prayer.

Charles dropped his leg. Jac managed to prop himself up on his elbows, but Charles's shoe found his breastbone and pushed him down. He grabbed Charles's calf to push him off, but he could only sputter, only gasp.

"I've been thinking of our game for months now. I wanted one I've never played before."

Charles lifted his foot and knelt beside him. As Jac tried to push himself away, Charles grabbed him by the wrist and wrenched his arm closer. Slowly, he unraveled the gauze. Jac felt something cold and wet swab over the inside of his elbow. It smelled sterile.

"No," Jac moaned, panic making his voice crack. He tried to kick his legs at Charles, but he missed.

Pop. Something opened. And even if it was too dark to see, Jac knew what it was. Though Charles was still preparing, Jac could already feel the needle against his skin, like an itch, like a nightmare. The liquid inside would be clear and familiar. It wouldn't be enough for an overdose—on the contrary, it would be just enough to take all the pain away. Just enough so that Charles could continue to *play* with him. To draw out the game as long as he liked.

"Don't," Jac whispered hoarsely. He'd prepared himself for everything…except that.

"Have we already reached the part where you beg?"

Charles traced his finger down Jac's neck, and Jac choked as he burned. Every breath was fire.

"It would feel better. You know it would. All of the pain will stop."

Then Jac *did* feel the needle against his arm, teasing circles over his skin.

"Killing can grow boring after a while," Charles said. "I forget the faces half the time. So I like to experiment. I like to make sure I learn something. And I always knew what

I would ask you, once we reached this point." The needle pressed into Jac's skin. The pinch was almost unnoticeable compared to the rest of it, but that tiny prick made Jac's chest heave. "Would you plead for me to keep hurting you? Or would you beg me for this?"

Jac didn't recall the last time he'd cried, though he could feel tears streaking down his face now. He didn't remember anything outside of this room—nothing except a promise…a promise he'd made to Sophia that he'd be okay.

Jac mustered all the breath he could. "Keep hitting me, Charlie."

The red light behind him grew brighter. The door swung open, and a long shadow stretched across the floor. Their game was no longer private.

The lights switched on, and though Jac couldn't see who'd entered, he could see Charles. He could see the Raptured redness of his eyes now, the oozing lashes on his chest, the syringe he pressed into Jac's arm. But something about the brightness, the *seeing*, made him less afraid.

Charles claimed he forgot the faces of those he killed, but with the darkness lifted, he wouldn't forget Jac's. He would remember this moment, the one he'd been waiting for. And he would remember that Jac had said no.

"Sophia," Charles purred, licking his lips. "I don't remember inviting you."

Jac should've felt relieved, but he didn't have any illusions about being saved. If anything, Sophia had only damned them both.

"Back away from him," she commanded. Jac made out the shape of a gun in her shadow.

"My sister tried a gun, too," Charles said. "Are you lucky enough to hit me? She wasn't."

"I was lucky enough to find this room." There was the *click* of a safety pulling off. "If you give him that, I'll kill you."

Jac felt the needle sliding out of his arm, and he choked out a sob of relief.

"Give him that? He asked me not to." The syringe clattered on the wooden floor. "I admit, I hadn't expected that."

"Stand up," Sophia snapped.

"You won't hit me. All those lucky charms, all this bad luck I've been accruing on him… You still won't have enough to kill me." Charles stood up and walked closer to her. "But we could play. How many bullets do you have? How many chances? If you were sure, if you were lucky enough, I could turn out the lights, and you could try to shoot me through the heart."

Jac struggled to catch his breath, and he rolled himself over so that he could see them. Charles walked toward Sophia, in a direct line toward her gun. Her hand trembled as she aimed it. Her eyes flickered to Jac's, and it was painfully obvious that she was afraid. She hadn't walked into Luckluster prepared to die, like he had, but she'd come for him all the same.

She fired. The bullet shattered the mirror across the room. The sound of it stung Jac's ears, pounded around his skull. He cringed and pulled himself to his knees. He'd never felt so weak. He knew it was temporary, knew he would recover until Charles touched him again, but he couldn't heal fast enough. He needed to stand. He needed to help.

"You could keep firing," Charles told her. "Keep pressing your luck until you run out of it altogether. You know what might happen then. You know the two of you can't beat me."

She fired again. The bullet buried itself in the plaster where the mirror had once been.

Jac cursed and stood, even if it ached to do so. Their game wasn't over yet.

"Or you could take one step back, and let me close that door," Charles cooed. "Then he and I can finish what we were doing."

Sophia's green eyes flickered to Jac's one last time. Jac had a plan, but he didn't have the voice to tell her. He tried to mouth it to her, but she shook her head. Jac knew she'd misunderstood. He hadn't told her to run.

He'd told her to move.

With all the energy he could muster, he charged at Charles. The man neared the door's threshold, focused on the pistol Sophia had pointed at him, just a few feet away. In the mirror, Jac glimpsed Charles's smile when Sophia stepped back. For a moment, Charles had thought he'd won. He was already reaching for the door to close it, already licking his lips in anticipation.

Then Jac knocked into him with all the force he had. He dug his shoulder into Charles's back and pushed, and pushed, and pushed. They stumbled onto the carpet, into the lights, and collided with the railing.

Charles slipped, and the momentum made him flip over. As he fell, a look of bewilderment crossed his face.

Charles's luck had finally run out.

Screams erupted from the party below. Heaving for breath, Jac looked over the railing to see that Charles had fallen onto the casino's spiral staircase, several of the wrought iron stakes protruding from his stomach. His bare chest, already laced with lashes and old scars, seeped over with red. His arms dangled limply beneath him, his mouth hung slightly ajar.

His bloodshot eyes were dead.

Sophia's hands found Jac's shoulders, pulling him away and into her. Jac buried his face in her shoulder and leaned against her to keep his balance.

"I'm sorry," he croaked. "I'm sorry I didn't tell you. You were right—"

"Don't be sorry." She rubbed her hand down his hair. Jac took deep breaths to steady himself, and he kept his gaze locked on the banquet hall, on the floor where he'd lain only moments before. He wanted to remember it like this—bright and empty.

"The Dove had escaped, and so I went to find you, just in case. But you were already gone." She squeezed him tighter. "I wish I was angry with you."

"You should be."

She shook her head. "It's over now. We'll call Harrison and we'll tell him that it's finally done."

Jac reached for the scar on his arm, but realized it no longer itched. So he rubbed his Creed instead. With each passing moment, the residual burning from Charles's touch faded. The nightmare had finally reached its end.

Of all the pain he'd experienced tonight, he'd expected killing to hurt more than this—or at least to hurt at all.

Maybe your soul didn't break like a bone. Maybe it broke like a promise.

LEVI

Levi caught his breath and knocked on Harrison's door in the Kipling's Hotel.

Last night, Vianca had put Levi up in his old room at St. Morse, as though his former apartment held any nostalgia for him. He'd lain restlessly on the familiar sheets, wondering if he could truly make a palace out of a prison, and realized that if he was going to accept this crown, he needed to know why the last prince had rejected it. He needed the truth.

"Levi," Harrison greeted him as he swung the door open. He wore a satin robe and leather, fur-lined slippers. "Have you come to kill me?"

"Wh-what?" Levi stammered, panting. "Why would I be coming to kill you?"

"Because you're pounding on my door at six in the morning, and because it's the sort of thing my mother would probably send you to do." Harrison looked him over with a crinkled nose. "And you're sweating."

"I took the stairs," Levi explained.

"It's the sixty-third floor."

"Well, I couldn't just walk in the front door like last time," he snapped, bracing himself against the doorframe. "I'm alone, and there's ten thousand volts on my head."

"So dramatic," Harrison muttered. He motioned for Levi to follow him inside, and Levi nearly collapsed onto the carpet. The room, like before, was covered in a disorganized mess of papers, telephones, and campaign buttons.

"I'm actually surprised my mother hasn't sent anyone to assassinate me," Harrison said, pouring Levi a glass of water. "Last night, I received word that Prescott's eight-point lead in the polls is gone, and it's all thanks to you."

Levi opened his mouth to say, "Come again?" but quickly collected himself. He had no clue what'd given Harrison such a lead, but he was very willing to accept the credit. "Yes… yes, that's why I'm here."

Harrison cocked an eyebrow in disbelief. "Of course," he said, smirking. He ushered Levi to the couch and handed him the glass. "Now that Charles Torren is dead, it will only be a matter of days until both casinos will be nothing but rubble, and I can grind my heels in the ashes."

Levi choked on his drink. It might've been a hairbreadth away from the election, but Jac and Sophia had pulled it off. Just like Jac promised he would.

His triumph was quickly replaced by guilt. This entire time, he'd been betting against his friend.

Harrison checked his watch. "I have an event in two hours. Because I'm grateful, I'll give you fifteen minutes for whatever you actually came here for."

Levi had come loaded with questions, far too many to squeeze into such a short meeting. So he started with the most important. "Are you certain you'll win?"

He licked his lips. "Unfortunately, you can't ever be certain. My team thinks the Torren votes will leave us evenly matched. The results could go either way, which is why it's even more crucial that I win, if I want to kill my mother. Despite the curfew and all the new regulations, the Capitol wants this election to *seem* fair. My mother's murder would, unfortunately, give the wrong impression."

Levi's heart—already hammering—now pulsed with nerves. If Prescott won, Vianca claimed Levi would be pardoned—and made heir to the Augustine empire. But if Harrison won, then Levi remained a criminal, the Irons stayed broke, and nothing in the North Side changed. But at least Vianca would be dead.

"Do you know the identity of Vianca's other... Her other...?" Levi asked, unable to utter the last word.

"I know about Séance, and I suspect the other," Harrison answered, but Levi couldn't guess how he'd learned that. "I suppose I'll be doing all three of you a favor. It doesn't matter much to me. There have been nearly a hundred of you coming and going for as long as I've known about my mother's practices."

"Not *your* practices?" Levi asked. Harrison and his mother shared a blood talent.

"It's not exactly to my taste."

Levi wanted to press more on how he'd learned about Enne, but he was running low on time. And so he asked what he'd come here for: "What happened between you and your mother?"

Although such a question would've unraveled Vianca, Harrison didn't hesitate. He even chuckled. "You really don't know? I thought everyone knew the sorry story of what happened to me. The tabloids aren't all wrong about it." He inspected Levi closely. "I was about your age."

"I know about how Veil kidnapped you, if that's what you mean." Enne had once told him as much.

"Yes, Veil and his psychotic attempts to undermine anyone else with power in the North Side. I was abducted from my bed at university and smuggled out of the city. We were kept in an attic, Leah and I."

"You mean Leah Torren?" Levi asked. "Sedric's older sister?"

"Yes. It was a brilliant move on Veil's part. The Families only care about two things: volts, and their legacies." Something dark swam in Harrison's eye. "Five months spent in that attic, it was only me and her. We were both seventeen. We were heirs to rival Families in New Reynes. The story practically tells itself." And if the details didn't, then the sharpness in Harrison's voice certainly did. Love always carved the deepest wounds. "When I returned, my mother grew even more obsessed with the future of the Family. Which was why she was far from pleased when I told her of my own naïve hopes—that our empires could be stronger together." Harrison laughed bitterly. "I should've left with Leah and never came back. I tried to, but my mother got to her first."

Levi filled in the rest with what he already knew of street history. Leah Torren was murdered shortly after her return. Sedric had been a child at the time.

"I imagine the real reason you're here is because you think my mother has offered you some kind of choice," Harrison said, and Levi stiffened. He hadn't wanted to give that away. "But once someone knows what matters most to you, they own you. The omerta binds your life, but if she manages it, she'll also bind your heart."

Vianca had killed the person Harrison loved in order to control him, and her plan had backfired. And as Levi thought of Vianca's suggestive comments over the past few months, he realized Vianca had since tried to engineer the opposite. She'd bound Levi and Enne together through her. She'd devised ways for their partnership to continue. She'd played with their chains like puppet strings, twisting and intertwining them until she got the end she wanted. Until she rewrote the mistakes she'd made with her son.

She hadn't picked Enne because of her finishing school manners or because of Sedric Torren—she'd picked Enne as bait. For him.

"I have a last favor to ask of you." Harrison nodded to a cigar box on the coffee table. The box was an antique, its woodwork covered in rose petals and faded paint. It looked so delicate, Levi was almost afraid to touch it. Gingerly, he opened it.

Inside was a gun.

Levi sucked in his breath. "Who is this meant for?"

"This election has become another game of fifty-fifty chances for you, hasn't it?" Harrison asked. "But this doesn't have to be a gamble. Whatever else you need to convince you—a pardon, riches, anything—I can give it to you. You can take matters into your own hands—choose your throne rather than betting on one. You need only name your price."

Once again, Harrison was handing Levi his destiny.

All it would take was a single shot. He couldn't take out Vianca, but he could kill Prescott. The turmoil would tip the election in Harrison's favor.

But the blame would have to fall on someone, and Levi's gambler's instincts told him it would fall on him.

Levi could, at this very moment, shoot Harrison between the eyes. A different choice. He wouldn't even need Harrison's weapon and all it symbolized to do it—he had a perfectly good pistol in his pocket. He could accept Vianca's offer. He would still remain a prisoner, but at least he'd wear a crown.

But there was a third option. There had always been a third option.

All this time, Levi had focused on those who could give him power. He'd wagered with Harrison. He'd wagered with Vianca. But all of those bets had required sacrifices—sacrifices he should've never been willing to make.

Now a new plan formed in his mind.

"Someone else will accept my offer, if you don't," he said smoothly, and the deep green of his eye had never so perfectly matched his mother's.

But Levi was already making his way toward the door. "I wish you luck with tomorrow's election and your other plans. But I'm going to claim my own throne."

A knot tightened in Levi's stomach as he entered Luckluster Casino. The last time he'd stepped foot here, he'd received a death sentence. And even with its signature red lights dimmed and its lobby empty, he still saw the ghost of Sedric Torren stalking him from the corner, smiling wolfishly and clutching a deadly invitation.

Levi couldn't simply go up to the concierge and ask for Jac Mardlin, a wanted criminal. He knew Jac had been using an alias, but he had no idea what it was. So instead he cleared his throat and asked for Sophia.

"She's not here right now," the concierge replied.

"Then I'd like to see her partner."

This request was understood, and the concierge led Levi to an office much like Vianca's. Jac sat on a leather chair beside a fireplace, grinding a barely smoked cigarette into an ashtray. His gray aura wafted throughout the room, cooling and familiar and steady.

He looked up as Levi entered and shot to his feet.

"Levi," he let out.

"It's good to see you," Levi managed. Out of habit, he inspected his friend's appearance for any signs of Lullaby, but thankfully found none. Instead, he noticed other changes. Jac seemed to stand taller, and there was a faint scar on his lip that he wore well.

Levi swallowed. "I heard Charles Torren is dead."

"He is," he answered darkly. "And just in time for you, isn't it?"

Levi couldn't tell if that was an insult, but he still winced. "I ended my arrangement with Harrison." When Jac's eyes widened, Levi blurted, "I'm sorry for all the things I said. For the way I acted. I trusted you with everything except yourself, and I didn't consider what you wanted."

Levi held his breath as time passed in silence. It was only seconds, but he felt the weight of these past months inside them—months of looking over his shoulder for whiteboots, of leaking voltage, of reassuring everyone he had the situation under control. But he didn't. And without Jac, without Enne, he had struggled alone.

When Jac didn't respond, Levi made his way toward the door and sighed, defeated. "Well, I said what I came to say."

"Wait," Jac said, and Levi stopped. "I'm the one who's sorry. I was never doing this for you—I was doing it for me—so I shouldn't have asked you anything in return. It was unfair. And pretty mucking low."

Levi's shoulders sagged with relief. That sounded like forgiveness.

He stepped forward and wrapped his arms around Jac, and his friend squeezed back.

Levi wanted to unload everything from these past few weeks, about Vianca and Harrison and Enne. But instead, he sat on the opposite armchair, swallowed down his own problems, and said, "Tell me the story."

Jac grinned. "The exciting version, or the truth?"

"Whichever one you'd rather tell."

And so Levi learned what had happened since he'd last spoken to Jac. How Charles had toyed with them before attempting to have them killed. How Sophia had used every volt they had to try to push him out. How Charles had arrived at the match bloody and wounded. How Jac had finally finished him.

Jac, Levi realized, was very good at telling stories. He always had been. He had a story after every fight. He knew Faith legends; he knew street ones. Levi had spent so many years listening to Jac tell stories that he'd never realized his friend, too, wanted to become one.

"So are you and Sophia…?" Levi asked, because it seemed the only part of the story missing.

Jac flushed. "Um—"

"Are we what?" Sophia asked from the doorway. She wore all black, as though in mourning for the half brother she'd despised, and she carried a large clothing bag. "Dating?" She kissed Jac on the top of his head, making him flush deeper. "Nah. We're cohorting."

"What do you have there?" Jac asked her.

"Harrison invited us to the party at St. Morse tomorrow night." She unzipped the bag and revealed something shiny and burgundy. "I already got your tux."

Levi cleared his throat. "You might not want to attend."

"Why is that?" Sophia asked.

He hesitated.

"It's Irons business," he said uncertainly.

Jac stiffened. "I see how it is, then. Tock is your second now?"

Levi held his breath. He would give just about anything to have Jac back. Even though Levi was lord, Jac was the one who'd really started the gang on the day he swore. But he didn't know if Jac even missed the Irons. He didn't think he'd want to come back.

"No one has ever called her anything but my third," Levi answered. He hoped it sounded like an offer. But after a few moments bracing himself for rejection, he worked up his courage to actually say the words. "I want you to come back, but I understand if you won't. Either way, you're still my best friend."

Jac's face broke out into a smile. "Of course I'll come back."

Levi was so relieved he stumbled over his words. "We don't pay much. It's been tough since the lockdown. Not great at all, if I'm being honest. But you've always been my partner. And we could use—"

"I said I'm coming back, didn't I?" Jac said, smirking. "And I like the sound of that. Partner."

Levi smiled his first real smile in a long time. He didn't have a chance to continue on about how he was lousy and selfish and had made a mess of things in his friend's absence, because Jac leaned forward with a serious look in his eyes.

"So what did you mean by Irons business?"

Levi cleared his throat. He'd worked out his plan on the way here, and already, Tock was making calls to the other lords.

"Well, as you know, the winner of the election will be announced at Vianca's party at St. Morse Casino." He grinned mischievously. "And the North Side is going to crash it."

ENNE

♥　　♠　　♦　　♣

Vianca Augustine poured herself a glass of bourbon, and when she sipped it, disgust evident on her face, it was clear she had no taste for the drink. But still, she poured more. She offered none to Enne, despite having a full bottle of it on her desk. Enne saw through the cracks in Vianca's velvet office curtains that it was close to sunset, and therefore, close to curfew. Her heart dropped. She didn't relish the thought of spending the night in St. Morse.

"Did Levi tell you what we spoke about yesterday?" Vianca asked. She traced a fingertip around the edge of her drink, her nail scratching the grooves in the glass.

Enne hadn't spoken to Levi in weeks, but she'd heard from Tock this afternoon. All five gangs would be meeting tomorrow morning to prepare for the events Levi had planned, and after being summoned to St. Morse, Enne spent most of her drive here imagining how she'd face Levi again after what she'd done. She'd never get Lourdes back, but she might someday earn his forgiveness, even if meant abandoning her plans for revenge.

"He didn't," Enne answered nervously. She didn't like the flatness of Vianca's tone. Though her voice could hardly ever be called lively, there was something unmistakably dead in it at this moment.

"I suppose not. I heard about your little falling out."

Enne's heart quickened. Had she forced the details out of Levi? Did she know how Enne had manipulated her? "What did you and Levi talk about?"

"I offered him the chance to become my successor. It wasn't an offer I made lightly." Vianca pulled herself to her feet and swept past Enne toward the door. As Enne stood to follow her and express her surprise, Vianca chirped, "Oh, no, my dear. Keep your seat."

The door *clicked* as it locked.

"I knew from the second I saw you," Vianca continued. She walked in front of Enne and wrenched her face up by her chin, hard enough to hurt. Enne winced as the donna's eyes roamed over her. Vianca hadn't touched her like this since the first day they met. "Levi had never introduced anyone to me before, and I never really believed he owed a favor to your father, like you told me." Vianca leaned forward, her breath hot on Enne's face. "Where is your father, dear? Nobody who comes asking something of me ever has anyone waiting for them."

Enne knew Vianca well enough to understand none of her questions begged answers. Even if she *could* speak, her voice was buried somewhere deep inside of her. When she opened her mouth, not even air came out. She choked, her windpipe suddenly as small as a sipping straw, and panic seized in her chest.

The entire time the omerta toyed with her, Vianca didn't

let go. She gripped Enne tighter as she squirmed. Her body was rooted to the chair.

"You were so lost," Vianca said, just as Enne's eyes welled with tears. Though she *was* afraid, she hated giving Vianca the satisfaction of showing it. But the longer she failed to draw breath, the more her body betrayed her. When she coughed, Vianca wiped the saliva away with her thumb, smearing it across Enne's chin with a streak of pink lipstick. "But I saw the potential in you. The potential in *him*."

She pulled Enne forward so violently that Enne needed to squeeze her armrests to keep from falling over. "How long have you known?" the donna spat.

Enne shook her head. The omerta's grip around her lungs squeezed tighter. There were dozens of things Vianca could've been referencing, and if Enne said the wrong one, she'd only make her situation worse. It didn't matter how much she'd accomplished, how fearsome she'd become: when it came to Vianca, Enne was helpless. She was still the same schoolgirl who'd arrived in New Reynes, lost and alone, just as Vianca had described.

"How long have you known Levi was working with my son?" she demanded.

So of all the secrets it could've been, it was the worst one.

"I...didn't," Enne sputtered.

"Liar," Vianca sneered. She pushed Enne so that her back slammed against the chair, with a surprising amount of force for an old woman. The omerta's grip lifted, and Enne doubled over, gasping for breath.

"At every party in the South Side, were you toasting to my downfall? Every time we met for tea, were you plotting my ruin?" Vianca slammed her fists on her desktop. "When you fucked each other, did you both laugh at my ignorance? Without me, you would be working a corner on Sweetie Street, because your finishing school education is worth nothing in this city. Without me, Levi would be dead at the hands of some better street lord, or glassy-eyed over Lullaby just like his friend. You would both be *nothing!*"

Vianca reached over and finished the rest of her bourbon. Enne was absolutely frozen in her seat—from the terror or the omerta, she wasn't sure. Her thoughts collided together like a car wreck. She needed to warn Levi. She needed to find a way to survive this.

"I'm sorry, Madame," Enne said quietly.

"You're. Not. Sorry!"

Vianca threw her empty glass across the room, and it shattered on the portrait of the last Mizer royal family. Enne jolted at the sound and shivered down to her bones. She had seen Vianca furious, broken, and vulnerable. Now she was seeing her as all three, witnessing what she guessed very few had seen who'd also lived to tell the tale.

"I could kill you," Vianca swore, her voice rasping and shaking. "I could kill *all* of you."

When Enne didn't respond, Vianca let out a devastated cry, then pressed her hand to her mouth. She was truly unraveling. "I trusted *you*. I never trusted *them*, but I trusted you. My girl. And this morning... I've been waiting here, expecting a phone call. A chance to rewrite my wrongs from years ago. And instead, who is it? Not Levi. It's an attendant at the Kipling's Hotel, informing me of the words spoken at a meeting between Levi and my son." Her voice became shrill. "You think my son is honest? You think you can simply kill me? If I die, then so will you! To plot my destruction is to plot your own."

Enne's stomach clenched in horror. No. That couldn't be true. She didn't want to believe it was true. If so, then Levi's bargain had been empty from the start. Everything they'd worked and sacrificed for was meaningless.

They would never be free.

"No, no, that won't be enough," Vianca murmured to herself, as though Enne was no longer even there.

"Madame," Enne cut in, in the gentle voice she'd grown accustomed to using around Vianca, "I'm sorry for not—"

"You may *not* speak!" Vianca shrieked, and Enne felt her jaw snap closed, so hard she bit her tongue. Her mouth filled with the taste of blood.

Vianca leaned forward over the desk's corner, unwittingly knocking papers and baubles aside onto the carpet. "I could slit your pale little throat, just like I did Leah Torren's. It would be poetic, wouldn't it? History repeating itself."

Enne had never stopped despising Vianca, but somewhere along the line, she'd stopped fearing her. Now that would be her downfall. Vianca was like a wounded animal, cornered and desperate, and unlike the heroine of a fairy tale, Enne had no means of escape. She was utterly at the witch's mercy.

This is how I die, she thought, attempting but failing to squirm out of her seat. Her wrists were tethered to her chair by invisible constraints. Her head even leaned back of its own accord, exposing her throat to Vianca. Enne's heart beat so fiercely she felt its pulsing all over her skin.

"I could kill you both, and Levi would still be devastated, wouldn't he?" she mused, and Enne wondered who else Vianca was referring to. "He'd be alone. He could spend his life at my card tables. And I could find new pretty dolls and watch him try to save them. How many dolls would it take for him to break?"

For a brief, desperate moment, Enne considered telling Vianca the truth about herself. Her true identity was the only card left up her sleeve. The Augustines were a family of Mizer sympathizers, and surely, if Vianca knew, she wouldn't kill Enne. It would buy her time.

But then Vianca would own her. Completely. This was the only secret Enne had left.

Before Enne could make a decision, Vianca continued. "No. I've been betrayed. Now I know that all this time, Levi has hated me. Anything *I* do would only burn his hate brighter. It won't be enough." Her gaze fell on Enne. "It will come from *you*."

"What?" Enne gasped.

"*You* will do it." Vianca took several steps closer to Enne so that she loomed over her. She dug her finger into Enne's breastbone. "You will be the one to break him."

Dread seeped into her. "I don't understand. We're not... We're not together. Not anymore."

Vianca laughed, high and sharp. "Leaving him—that's all your creativity can come up with? I know there's darkness hidden beneath that pretty face. *Think. Harder.*" She leaned back onto the desk and twisted her family's ring around her finger. "Tell him what he wants to hear—anything. Repair whatever you managed to break. And then, you will do it. I don't want the first method you think of, but the way that will hurt the most." She purred out her last words.

"I won't do it," Enne said firmly.

"You're just as guilty as he is. Would you like me to kill him instead? I know you don't believe I could, but I've. Done. *Worse*," Vianca seethed, snapping forward like something rabid. Bits of white hair slipped out of her bun, clinging to her flushed skin. She grabbed the liquor bottle and cradled it in her lap. "Apparently the most dangerous position to be in is within my affections."

And then the donna cried.

Enne imagined Vianca Augustine must've hated to cry.

After all, Vianca was a woman. She'd been tossed aside and ignored her entire life because of it. And she despised herself for it. Enne didn't pretend to know her full story, or the circumstances around her family and her husband's death, and how it must've felt to live the life of a mother, a wife, a crime boss, an activist, and a monster.

But she would *never* disregard that last title.

Monster.

The world had once led Enne to believe that to cry—to be *weak*—was to be a woman. Vianca certainly still believed that. And maybe that was why Vianca had always surrounded herself with men, why she sought the favor of political parties ruled by men, why—until now—Levi could always fight against her and she'd still welcome him back with fondness.

Maybe she had turned herself into a monster because the only other option was to be a woman.

Enne swallowed down her own sob. "People betray you because you don't love them. You own them. And you revel in it."

Vianca's face twisted into something ugly, something truly monstrous. "You will stay here tonight. You won't breathe a word of this conversation to anyone. You will pretend like nothing has happened." Then the donna smiled so brightly it reached her eyes. "Tomorrow, you will break his heart. And then you will die."

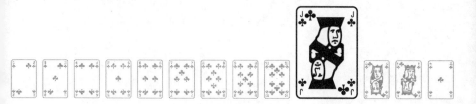

"A buddy of mine used to go around Olde Town robbing graves.
Not a *close* buddy. Just someone I knew, all right?
But he told me this story. He opened up a coffin—it belonged to
a woman, died only a few months before. He wanted
to steal jewelry. But he found *two* bodies inside.

"That's not even the spooky part. The spooky part is that both of
the women had the same face. Same *exact* face.

"And the woman whose grave it was?
She didn't have a twin sister."

—*A legend of the North Side*

LEVI

The Irons filled every seat in the Catacombs, dressed in the swankiest clothes they'd managed to steal. Politicians, celebrities, lobbyists, and paparazzi would fill the streets outside St. Morse tonight, and in order to crash a white-tie affair, the Irons would need to blend into the crowds. However, there was something definitely not South Sider about their outfits: heels measured an inch too high, hair combed a bit too slick, and pockets and purses bulged with the unmistakable shapes of guns.

Beside him, Jac fiddled with an unlit cigarette. "Have you heard from her yet?"

Fear blossomed in Levi's stomach. "No."

Last night, Lola had called to tell him that Enne hadn't returned to the finishing school before curfew. Levi had struggled to focus on his plan while he spent hours with his ear to the radio, anxious for news about whether she'd somehow been apprehended. She'd probably found somewhere to wait out the night, or so Tock had tried to assure him. But morning had arrived and, still, there'd been no call.

"I'm sure there's a good reason," Jac said nervously. He reached for his Creed, his classic tell.

"Liar," Levi snapped. Even after what Enne had done, he still cared. Probably too much.

Tock approached their booth wearing a glittering silver dress. She'd been speaking with Narinder upstairs, who—unsurprisingly, given his hatred of gangsters—had refused to join them.

"Looking sharp, boys," Tock said, even though Levi was fairly certain he looked like muck. "All of the Irons are here," she added, her eyes falling on Jac. "Even the prodigal second."

Jac examined the clusters of Irons sitting around the club. "I haven't seen the Irons looking this good in a long time."

Levi might've felt nauseous with nerves, but he still gave his friend an appreciative smile. Only four months ago, the Irons had been half-starved, squatting across abandoned places in Olde Town, scrounging for volts while Levi fed their earnings into Vianca's investment scheme. He wasn't sure any amount of amends would make up for what he did to Chez Phillips and the rest of his gang, but it felt good to know that, no matter what happened today, he'd done this much right.

The front doors to the Catacombs opened, and several new faces filtered inside. Levi recognized a few of them as Spirits. He sighed with relief...until he noticed that Enne wasn't among them.

Lola broke away from the group and hurried over. She wore a full tux, red lipstick, and a nervous knot between her brows. "I thought Enne would be with you," she hissed.

"We thought she'd be with *you*." Levi stood up, his heart racing. "We need to look for her."

"Where?" Lola snapped. "She could be anywhere." Her

voice cracked, and Levi couldn't tell if she was scolding him or volunteering to join him.

Tock pushed herself between them and squeezed both their shoulders. "Listen. She already knows her role today at St. Morse. She's deadlier than you—" she looked at Lola "—and smarter than *you*." She looked at Levi. "We should trust her."

Levi had always thought Reymond was invincible. He wasn't about to make that mistake again with another person he cared about. "The party doesn't start for another hour." St. Morse was thirty minutes uptown, but that still gave him time to do *something*. Anything.

Jac cleared his throat. "Tock, are *you* still prepared for what you need to do today?"

"I'm always prepared to blow things up," Tock answered smoothly.

Several eyes around the room watched them, and Levi took a reluctant seat. Tock was right. He needed to trust in Enne— she already knew her part in the plan, and if the worst *had* happened, then Grace or Lola would step in.

He'd planned for everything, even destruction.

Within the next ten minutes, Jonas, Ivory, Bryce, and Harvey arrived, as well. Jonas brought all the Scarhands, who each looked as though they'd purchased their clothes second-and thirdhand from Scrap Market. It wasn't until all the Scarhands were gathered in one room that Levi realized how *large* his gang was, maybe twice the size as when Reymond had been alive.

Then his eyes fell on one of the Scarhands, on a face he recognized but hadn't seen in months. Mansi. His heart gave a painful clench. *Why am I surprised?* he asked himself. Mansi had left him, and her oath had broken. Even if she'd given it to someone he despised, it was nothing that Levi didn't deserve.

He hoped, at least, that she saw something different when she looked at the Irons now. Something better.

The Doves, though not as few in number as the Spirits, were still smaller than Levi expected. He counted fourteen of them, including Ivory and Scythe. Each wore a haunted look in their eyes and had hair bleached white.

The Orphan Guild was the scrappiest lot. Their formal attire was ragged and old-fashioned, as though they'd been dug up out of graves. Bryce, with dark circles under his bloodshot eyes and wearing a dress shirt several sizes too large, looked the most ragged of them all.

"I brought what you asked for," Jonas told Levi. He reached into his pocket and produced a large pack of counterfeit silver Shadow Cards. He flipped several over to reveal that each face was the Fool.

This was the brilliance of Levi's plan: he would leverage an old legend to write a new one. Every Sinner who held that card knew it meant a death sentence, and tonight, every partygoer in St. Morse would receive one.

"You think an ultimatum will end this street war," Ivory sneered, "but you're wrong."

Lola, Tock, and Jac gaped at Ivory as though they'd never seen her before, and Levi remembered, of course, that only the lords had seen her face.

The entire club fell silent. They were in the presence of a legend.

Without warning, she drew her ivory knife and pressed it against Harvey's throat.

Everyone around her froze, but no one made a move to stop her. Harvey looked around and paled.

"Anything I asked you right now, Harvey—would you do it?" She spoke her words against his ear, then ran a hand through his head of curls. There was something strangely possessive about her touch. Ivory was old enough to be Harvey's mother.

"Obviously," Harvey said darkly.

"And, Bryce, what about you? Would you do anything right now?" If possible, Harvey stiffened more.

"Obviously," Bryce echoed, glaring at her.

"If you did what I asked, and then I backed down," Ivory told Harvey, "you'd come for me the second my back was turned." Her gaze met Levi's. "You'll give the wigheads the Shadow Cards. You'll fill them with fear. You'll make them swear to end the war. But whatever promises they make in this position are worthless. And worse, it'll only show them that we're desperate." She pressed the knife harder against Harvey and spoke into his ear. "Killing you is a better promise. The only promise you cannot break."

"Murdering the entire party won't end the war, either," Levi said hotly.

Ivory lowered her knife and laughed. "All of you! So tense." She flicked Harvey underneath his nose, and he scowled. "I'm merely proving a point."

"You act as though we aren't prepared to follow through on our threats," Jonas told her. "Those Shadow Cards will be a promise—whoever strikes against the North Side will die."

Levi didn't like the idea of murder, but Jonas was right—they were playing with legends, and every legend needed a shred of truth.

Their truth would be blood.

Levi couldn't have been more on edge when his car arrived at St. Morse. Through dark-tinted windows, he watched the guests waiting in a queue in front of the building. White-boots were swarming everywhere, and Levi's heart jumped nervously at the thought of them spotting him. Of course,

his name would be on Vianca's secret guest list, and every
employee at the casino would know to let him inside, but he
still needed to make it to the entrance. And amid the mostly
fair skin of the other attendees, his darker coloring would call
more attention.

The valet opened the door, and Levi slid out of the motorcar. Like always, he wore all black except for the bits of silver on his clothes. The real Fool card peeked out of his breast
pocket.

Levi paid the valet, keeping his head down. As he slipped
inconspicuously into the queue, he noticed someone familiar
in the car behind his.

When Harrison Augustine stepped onto the sidewalk, every
head in the crowd turned toward him—not because he was
one of the candidates and thus a man of this occasion, but because everyone knew about the bad blood between him and
his mother. For the first time in eighteen years, Harrison Augustine was returning home.

He spotted Levi and gestured for him to join him. Levi
froze; if he wasn't Harrison's ally, did that make him his
enemy? Lately the friends and foes in Levi's life had grown
harder to differentiate. But none of the whiteboots parading
up and down Tropps Street with assault rifles strapped over
their shoulders would dare give him trouble if he looked like
Harrison's companion. So Levi strode over and flashed his
best smile.

"How are you feeling about the results being announced?"
Levi asked him.

"I feel great," Harrison answered smoothly. He studied the
revolving doors of the casino, a ghost in the edges of his one
eye. "The story finally ends tonight."

Levi's skin broke out in goose bumps as he remembered
the words Zula Slyk had spoken months ago.

This story will end badly.

He chalked up his nerves to Enne's disappearance. He needed to find her, but he, too, had a role to play tonight. Almost three hundred gangsters awaited his signal, divided between two nearby Tropps Street buildings Bryce and the Orphan Guild had secured. That was three hundred people who were depending on Levi, but he was beginning to realize how much he depended on Enne.

"Did you take my mother up on her offer?" Harrison asked.

"You told me yesterday that you want to grind this casino beneath your heels," Levi said. "I know better than to bet against you."

Harrison raised his eyebrows. "So no offer ended up being good enough for the Iron Lord."

With the staff checking names for the guests just a few feet in front of them, Levi lowered his voice. "Just because we're no longer partners doesn't mean we're working against each other. There's a lot of ground between friends and enemies."

Harrison absentmindedly handed the attendant his paperwork. "That's a pretty thought."

And then he walked inside, leaving Levi with an unpleasant taste in his mouth.

The inside of the casino was more crowded than he'd ever seen, and with the volts from Levi and Enne, Vianca had spared no expense. Servers carried crystal buckets of sparkling wine and every sort of North and South Side cocktail. Live music played in every room. The ceiling, usually covered in faux chandeliers, glowed from hundreds of twinkling lights, like the night-time New Reynes skyline.

This was the part of the plan when Levi was supposed to head to the ballroom, but Enne's absence still made everything feel wrong. He searched the faces around him, weaving his way between shoulders, tripping over the trains of gowns.

"I'm sorry—"

"Watch where you're—"

"Excuse me—"

Levi helplessly pushed his way through the casino. She could be here, lost amid the crowds and drinks and laughter, and he would never find her. She could be in a cell. In the trunk of a car. In the trash clogged at the bottom of the Brint.

He fought the urge to be sick.

An invisible force pulled him toward the Tropps Room, and though he'd like to call it destiny, it was purely habit. Anxious and heart racing, he was walking toward the most familiar place, even if that place had once been his cage.

"Don't you look dashing," a voice purred behind him, and Levi whipped around to face Vianca. She wore a floor-length emerald gown that matched her eyes, the eyes she and her son shared. She kissed him on both cheeks, as though he were truly a beloved guest. Then she gestured to the casino around her. "St. Morse has never looked so grand."

It should, Levi thought bitterly, *considering how much it cost us.*

"I'd love to stay and talk," he lied, "but I can't—"

"It's such a shame you rejected my offer," she told him.

His mouth went dry. He hadn't spoken to Vianca since their last meeting. How did she know he'd made his decision? "What makes you think that?"

"Because you don't take this much time to decide things. We both know how you are—when an opportunity comes, you seize it. This would've been your night. But now it is *mine*." When she leaned closer to him, her long earrings shook and clacked like rattlesnakes. "Where's your date?"

There was something insidious in Vianca's voice. The donna might've known Levi well, but he also knew her, and she delighted in being cruel. She'd given him a choice, and he should've realized his choice would have consequences.

Enne.

"What did you do?" he seethed.

She smiled. "Oh, it's not what I did to her that you should worry about."

Even though he couldn't hurt the donna, Levi took a threatening step closer. He smelled the alcohol on her breath.

"If something happened to her," he hissed. "I'll never forgive you."

Vianca looked around the room, at the grandeur bought with the volts and lives she'd stolen, as though she watched it all from far, far away.

"Neither did he," she murmured.

Levi cursed and pushed past her, frantically searching the faces in every room of the casino.

Tick. Tick. Tick.

Another game had begun.

And this time, he would save her.

ENNE

Enne had spent an anxious morning trapped within the St. Morse Spa, under the sadistic care of Vianca Augustine.

You will not contact anyone, the donna had hissed as her assistant scrubbed Enne's skin scarlet and raw. *You won't speak of my instructions.* Enne gasped as the dress—several sizes too small—crushed her chest like a corset of iron. *You won't leave this casino.* Not ever again.

But because Vianca didn't know of the plot the street lords had devised for tonight, she hadn't known to forbid Enne from acting out her part in it. So as the gangsters waited outside the casino to set that plan in motion, Enne slipped her mask and her revolver into the pink satin of her dress, and concocted a plan of her own.

"Hurry up," Vianca's assistant snapped, tapping her heels. "The guests are already arriving, and I still need to speak with the caterers."

Enne applied her black lipstick and puckered her lips in the mirror. She needed to match her wanted poster. "You could always leave me be."

"No, Madame wanted me to watch you until you arrived at the party." She checked her watch. "Which was supposed to be ten minutes ago!"

Fear crept over Enne's heart like ice as she followed the assistant down several stories to the ground floor. The lobby was already crowded with people, and Enne recognized many faces she had encountered during her parties on the South Side.

Her eyes scanned the crowds for Lola or Grace. The three girls had been assigned an important piece of Levi's plan, and Enne would see it through.

Even if it was the last thing she ever did.

While searching for the Spirits, she instead found another familiar face. Poppy Prescott entered the casino on her father's arm. Her white dress shimmered with beads like sugar crystals, and she wore black satin gloves up to her elbows, cinched with ruffles and pearls. She waved at Enne from across the room and hurried over to her.

Enne swallowed. She didn't have time to spend with Poppy tonight.

Poppy gave her a hug and admired the dress Viana had chosen for her, a dress meant for a doll. "You look stunning." Then she studied Enne's face. "But you're practically shaking. Are you okay?"

"I feel fine." Though of course, she didn't. Across the room, Vianca Augustine watched from the entrance to the Tropps Room, and she smiled at Enne knowingly. The fear of the past night swept over her, and Enne unconsciously held a hand to her throat.

You will break his heart, and then you will die.

Poppy snatched her hand down. "You don't look fine. Did something happen?"

Enne shook her head. "No, don't worry about me. What about you?"

"I'm just thrilled this will all be over soon. This night couldn't have come fast enough." She examined the opulent decor of the casino. "I've never been this far up the North Side."

Enne let out a laugh. There was still much of the Casino District and Ruins District above them. But of course, Poppy would have no reason to come here. Enne had spent the past four months sneaking into Poppy's world, but what would Poppy say if she learned that this was Enne's? For all that she might tease Enne about her supposed North Side boy, Enne was sure their friendship would collapse under the weight of her real secrets.

"My father can't go anywhere without his bodyguards trailing after him. They're like gnats," Poppy complained. "I don't see why we needed to bring them here. Half the city's whiteboots are outside."

"Are they?" Enne said shakily. They'd been expecting as much, but it still worried her to hear it.

Tick. Tick. Tick.

Enne tried to steady herself. The Shadow Game had ended months ago, and no matter how much the sound of the timer still haunted her, what mattered was that she had destroyed it. She closed her eyes and pictured its clockwork exploding apart, the moment the ticking stopped, the way the gun felt in her hand.

Even so, she could still hear it. She didn't know what it was counting down to. To the moment the gangsters shut down the casino? To the moment she broke Levi's heart?

Or to when her own terrible plan succeeded?

The dread in her mouth tasted sharp and metallic.

"Enne," Poppy said, waving a hand in front of her face. "You're worrying me. Whatever it is, you can tell me."

Then two girls entered the party. The first was dressed in a tux, cut formfitting and slender, her red hair curled and pinned to one side. The second wore a scandalously tight gown of black lace. When they both met Enne's eyes, their shoulders sagged with relief, and they rushed over.

"Not a *word* we've heard from you since last night," Lola snapped, throwing her arms around Enne. "What's going on? Are you hurt?"

"Nothing. I'm fine," Enne assured them, the omerta drawing the lie from her lips.

"Oh, it's been ages, hasn't it?" Poppy said, extending her hand. Lola and Grace turned to her and blinked, as though they hadn't realized she was there.

Rather than greeting her, they smiled faintly and pulled Enne aside.

"Every gangster in the North Side is out there waiting for our signal," Lola hissed in her ear.

Behind them, Poppy frowned and disappeared back into the crowd. Enne tried not to feel guilty about ignoring her when she'd been trying to help.

"Have you spoken to Levi?" Enne asked.

"He's been trying to find you. Worried himself sick over it," Lola told her. "He'll be here soon. He's with Jac right now."

Enne's heart clenched in a sad sort of relief. Levi had been torn up for weeks after his fight with Jac, and he would need his best friend now. Whatever happened to Enne, whatever Vianca forced her to do to him, at least Jac would be there to pick up the pieces.

The thought of him needing to made her ill.

If only Enne could tell Lola to warn him. Because more than death or discovery, the one thing that could ruin her plan was to encounter him. Under no circumstances could she see Levi tonight.

Not even to say goodbye.

"We need to hurry," Grace urged. "They're all waiting for our signal."

The girls slipped down a vacant hallway, one Enne had once used to go to her acrobatics rehearsals. Grace handed each of them sleeping darts, and the weapons felt steady in Enne's hands. She took a deep breath—she'd trained for this. The others outside were depending on her—*Levi* was depending on her—and so she would not fail.

They spotted a trio of whiteboots smoking cigars by the door.

"What are you doing here?" one of them said gruffly as the girls approached. He eyed Enne in confusion, then shook his head. "The party is behind you."

Enne clutched Grace's shoulders. "My friend doesn't feel well and needs to lie down in her room. We were headed toward the elevators, but…" She flashed him a smile. "We're a bit lost."

One of the other whiteboots grinned and walked toward them. He steered them around, his arm on the small of Enne's back. As he bent down to her level, she grimaced from the stench of his breath. "It's that way," he said, pointing. "Pass the next two turns, then make a right."

Before he could turn back, Enne slammed the dart into his outstretched arm, and he crumpled to the floor.

The others reacted immediately, stepping back and reaching for their guns. But the girls moved faster. Quickly, the whiteboots fell in a heap at their high heels.

Grace crinkled her nose at the one with the bad breath.

"Not exactly up to Roy's standards, are they?" Lola asked, smirking.

After helping Enne conceive her plans for the riot, Roy had become an honorary Spirit, as all the girls liked to say. All the girls except Grace, who still complained regularly about when

Jonas could muddle his memories and get rid of him. A little *too* regularly to be believed, in Enne's opinion.

"Oh, shut up," Grace muttered, slightly pink.

Together, the girls dragged the bodies into the closest supply closet, bound and gagged each of them, and locked the door.

"We're leaving now to give Tock the signal," Lola told Enne. "You wait here. Once the other lords arrive, you'll be needed on the stage in the ballroom."

Enne swallowed, resisting the urge to pull both her friends into a hug. This could be the last time she ever saw Lola and Grace again. After Enne was gone, she liked to think they would both move on. That Lola would enroll in university like she'd clearly always wanted. That Grace would find an ever after softer and frillier than any of Sadie Knightley's novels.

But the omerta forbid her from letting on that something was wrong, so she said, "Good luck," when she really meant to say, "Goodbye."

They each gave her a nod and disappeared out the door, leaving Enne alone to guard the hallway—or so they believed.

But her piece of Levi's plan was over, and it was time for her own plan to begin.

She repeated her mother's words to herself—something she hadn't needed to do in a long while.

Never allow yourself to be lost.

Never let them see your fear.

They steadied her heart, as they always had, and when Enne strode down the hallway, her chin lifted, she looked powerful.

If she was going to die, it would be on her own terms.

As she approached the lobby, where dozens of staff members and whiteboots watched the entrance, Enne reached for her mask and tied it, trembling, over her eyes.

It was the only way to stop Vianca. Because even if this was her casino and her party, this was not her city. Séance had a warrant for execution on her head, and in a choice between a death in Vianca's office or a death at the gallows, it was a simple decision.

Séance was recognizable, but at a party like this, her mask might be mistaken for a costume. For Enne's plan to work, she needed the whiteboots to be *sure* it was her.

So she reached for her gun.

She trembled as she raised it, aiming for the ceiling and its hundreds of glittering lights.

The only way left to win, she told herself, tears blurring her vision, *is to lose.*

But before she could fire, Enne felt arms wrap around her, pulling her back. And she let them. She was ready to be apprehended, ready to leave this casino once and for all, even if it was in the back of a whiteboot car.

But when the person gripping her spun her around, she realized he wasn't a whiteboot, and her heart sank with despair.

"You're alive," Levi choked out, wrapping himself around her and pushing her face into his chest. Enne froze at his touch, something that would normally fill her with relief, but now only filled her with dread. She could feel his heart pounding beneath her ear, but all she could hear was *tick, tick, tick.*

She had been so close, but he'd found her.

And he had damned them both.

"What did she do to you?" he whispered, fingers unlacing her mask. Wearing it was supposed to be her death sentence, but she felt twice as vulnerable with it removed.

Enne pulled away to tell him to leave her, to focus on his own plan for saving the North Side, but she couldn't. Even as panic rose in her throat, the omerta forced her lips into a smile.

JAC

♥ ♠ ♦ ♣

"I told all of you to *Shut. The muck. Up!*" Jac hollered. The gangsters behind him—over a hundred in total, a mixture from all the gangs—immediately stopped their chattering.

Jac shouldn't have felt surprised at his own authority. With Levi in the casino and Tock cutting off the party's power, Jac was the only leader of the Irons present. But he didn't think that was the reason.

Even now, he heard their hushed whispers of how he'd pushed Charles Torren to his death. That was his story. His legend.

He and Sophia stood at the window, peeking out at the front entrance of St. Morse. All of the gangsters had been divided into two groups, and theirs was stationed at the top floor of a pub, one that had closed down from the financial pressures of the curfew. Scythe and Rebecca, sitting in a booth across the room, were also here to supervise the Doves and members of the Orphan Guild.

Down below, the last of Vianca's guests were arriving, and Tropps Street—once congested with expensive motorcars—

was emptying for the curfew. Any minute now, Tock's explosion would light up the Casino District brighter than any of its neon signs.

And that would be their cue.

There were a thousand ways for this plan fail. But it was Levi's plan, and Levi had a way of pulling off anything. Still, Jac's fingers fiddled with his Creed. He craved a cigarette, but he hadn't smoked one all day yesterday, and maybe that could become a new normal. He hoped so.

Footsteps thundered up the stairs, and Lola appeared. "The back entrance is clear." She hurried to Jac and Sophia. "Grace went to tell the other group, and... Where's Tock?"

"She's not done yet. She'll be back soon."

Lola stared up at the roof of St. Morse Casino, her expression pale. "Did she go alone? I told her not to. She always does—"

"She took another Iron with her. Tommy's a dealer, but he has a speed talent. He's good for more than tricks."

Lola swallowed and nodded.

"I don't think Tock hates me," Jac told her.

"What? Why would Tock hate you?"

He grinned. It wasn't the time for jokes, but he couldn't help himself. "You told me your date would hate me."

The memory dawned on her, and she scowled. "It's not your business."

Jac bit his lip, initially wounded. He liked to think that, by now, they were friends.

But then she grumbled, "It's been a few months. And yeah, I like her. She doesn't get hung up on nonsense, like all of you." Then Lola crossed her arms, and Jac knew that was all he would likely get out of her. Her lip curved slightly into a smile, but it quickly disappeared. "Enne is inside."

"She is? Is she—?"

"She's fine, but... I have a bad feeling."

"Have you ever had a bad feeling that's come true?" he

asked nervously, because if there was ever a time for superstition, it was tonight. Levi was playing with legends, and
just because Jac thought this plan was clever didn't mean he
thought it was smart.

"Once or twice." Lola stuffed her hands into her pockets.
"Enough times that I don't ignore them."

From his other side, Sophia flipped her coin, and it landed
heads. "Eighty-four," she said, her mouth full with a piece
of taffy.

"That's just *your* luck," Jac told her.

"I'm willing to share it." She handed Lola the coin and
curled her fingers around it. Jac doubted that her talent actually worked like that, but he supposed it was a supportive
gesture. "Besides, my brother and sister used coins. I'd like to
try something different." Sophia reached into her pocket and
pulled out a pair of dice. She rolled them on the dusty window ledge. Two sixes.

"What does that mean?" Jac asked.

"That means we're getting lucky."

Lola crinkled her nose. "Gross."

Jac ignored her and pulled Sophia closer to him. Her dress
was Luckluster red, with sleeves that draped off her shoulders
and exposed the delicate curves of her collarbone and the
sparse freckles on her arms.

Sophia cast him a smile. "What are you thinking about?"

Jac grinned impishly. "Tomorrow, we get to burn Luckluster to the ground. And then you and I—"

Boom.

Sophia jolted, and Lola let out a stifled scream. It was the
sound they'd been waiting for, but it was quieter than they'd
expected. The rest of the gangsters scrambled to their feet,
brandishing knives and pistols. Jac squinted up at the roof of
St. Morse—there'd been no light, no visible explosion.

"What's happening?" Sophia whispered, pressing her hand against the glass.

"I'm not sure..." Lola whispered. There was no need to whisper, of course, but the room had fallen dead silent. Everyone held their breaths. Scythe and Rebecca immediately bolted out of their seats and joined them at the window.

"That didn't sound like an explosion," Scythe said darkly. "Where did it come from?"

"There!" Jac said, pointing toward the far corner of the roof. Though distant, he could make out the figures of Tock and Tommy as they sprinted across the rooftop of St. Morse Casino.

"Did they do it?" Sophia asked. "Why are they running?"

"She has to run to lay the line," Lola explained.

"But we already heard something." Jac looked up into the sky, but there was no smoke.

The door burst open. It was Grace, followed by the Scarhands' second, a young woman Jac only recognized from the Catacombs. He was surprised to see her and not the Scar Lord, who was supposed to be commanding the other group.

"That was no explosion!" Grace shouted, panting, one arm braced against the doorframe. "That was a gunshot."

Boom.

This time, the sound was no louder, but it rang in Jac's ears, roared inside his ribs.

One of the silhouettes atop the casino fell.

The body hit the ledge and toppled over. It seemed to take ages to fall all twenty stories. It was time enough for Lola to scream. For several of the Irons to curse and make for the door. For Jac to register what it meant—that one of them had been shot, that someone had gotten wind of their plan, and that everything was about to go to muck.

The body fell onto the sidewalk of Tropps Street. Jac looked at the gore only long enough to determine who it was, and his heart clenched.

Tommy.

Lola let out a strangled sigh of relief, but it was short-lived for two reasons. Jac wasn't even sure which of those happened first.

An explosion tore across the rooftop of St. Morse, far larger and louder than he expected, its angry black smoke reaching claws into the sky. The lights of the casino all went out.

Either before it, or after, or simultaneously, bullets fired from across the street, shattering the windows of the pub. Every person inside fell to the ground while glass rained through the air. Jac landed hard on his side, and his first instinct was to cover Sophia's head with his arms, the same way Scythe protectively braced Rebecca. Behind them, an Iron he recognized as a runner clutched the blood pouring out of her shoulder and let out a wail.

"What is this?" Lola called, her back pressed against the wall, her head ducked down between her legs.

"Who knew?" Jac shouted. "Who knew who isn't here?" He looked wildly to the Scarhands' second, who crouched by the door.

"Scavenger's inside!" she shouted.

"Why would he be inside?" Rebecca hissed.

"I… I don't know. He just told me where he was going." The second cast a doubtful look to the other Scarhands in the room, and that was all the confirmation Jac needed. The Irons never would've doubted Levi; the Spirits never would've doubted Enne. If Scavenger didn't have the trust of his gang, there must be a reason. "Ivory is gone, too," she added. "Along with the other half of the Doves."

The Doves in the room made no expressions, but each of them reached for their weapons.

And Jac understood.

Scavenger and Ivory had betrayed them all.

The power in St. Morse was out, which meant Levi and Enne were waiting for them to barge through the open exit.

But Scavenger and Ivory might've already alerted the white-boots that the Iron Lord and Séance were inside—maybe they'd done it in exchange for their own pardons. Whatever reason, the plan ended here, before it'd even begun.

"I need to warn them," Jac gritted through his teeth. He refused to see any more friends die tonight. "And I need to hurry—before all the doors are locked."

Sophia squeezed his hand. "You can't go out alone."

"You said we were lucky."

"Not lucky enough for you to sprint into gunfire!"

"There are whiteboots coming!" Lola shouted, peeking out through the window. "Nearly thirty of them—probably more."

They couldn't stay here. They'd be fish in a barrel.

"Everybody out!" Jac called. He didn't have Levi's way with words, but he still had some show in him. "The lights are cut. The others are waiting. And the whiteboots are asking for a fight." He raised his pistol high enough for the room to see. "When I call it, we charge." It would mean a battle, but it would also give him an opportunity to get to that door. To change the plan. To shut it down.

He crawled up beside Lola and pressed his back to the wall. Carefully, he peeked out the window as well, to see what she'd seen. His eyes widened at the whiteboots approaching the pub's front door. They were nearly upon them.

It would be a shame if his legend ended here.

He undid the safety on his gun.

"Three!" he called.

The others hurried and gathered around the stairs, weapons raised.

"Two!"

Sophia blew him a kiss. He liked to think it was for good luck.

"One!"

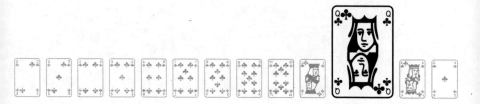

"Oaths, omertas, Chainers—there's a reason so many in the North Side favor such weapons. New Reynes killed the queen on the very day she hoped to negotiate peace. The City of Sin was built on duplicity."

—*A legend of the North Side*

ENNE

♥ ♠ ♦ ♣

Enne held her breath, waiting for the grip of the omerta. She could feel the ghost of it, as though a caress of Vianca's jagged fingernail traced from her navel to her throat.

You will break his heart, and then you will die.

"What are you talking about? I'm fine," Enne told Levi.

"Where have you *been*?" His voice cracked. "You didn't go home last night. You didn't call. You—"

"I couldn't make it home before curfew, so I had to stay here. And Vianca's kept me here all day, complaining about the party and the polling turnouts and everything. I couldn't escape." The omerta drew the lie from her easily, even as the truth ate at her from inside out. "I'm sorry I worried you."

"Worried me?" He squeezed her shoulders hard enough for her to wince. "We're infiltrating the largest party of the year, threatening some of the most powerful members of government, and committing treason. But I..."

He swallowed.

But he was preoccupied with his worries over her, Enne

realized. Only a day before, the thought would've filled her with hope. Now it only burdened her with dread.

Repair whatever you've broken, Vianca had commanded her.

Enne tucked the revolver back into her dress, and the apology she'd long practiced was pried from her lips. "I'm sorry," Enne sputtered. "I'm so, so sorry. I was so focused on fixing myself that I was hurting the people around me. And I—"

Levi's expression flickered with surprise, as though he'd forgotten he was supposed to be despising her. He shook his head and squeezed Séance's mask in his fist. "What is this? This wasn't in the plan."

Her lips trembled. She didn't know if she should feel relieved he'd interrupted her apologies or wounded that he hadn't listened. They were still her words, even if Vianca had turned them into weapons.

The omerta forced Enne to shake her head. She felt like a puppet. She felt sick. "It's not what you think—"

"I saw Vianca. I know she's done something to you, and she's forbidden you from telling me what it is."

Enne had no way of indicating to him that he was right, not when the omerta, once again, stretched her lips into a reassuring smile.

He met her smile with a hopeless look in his eyes, and she could almost see the weight of the entire night on his shoulders. Of the cleverness of his plan and fearing it would fail. Of saving her. Of the destiny and throne he'd sacrificed everything to claim.

Now that Levi had found her, Vianca's cruel assignment would inevitably be fulfilled, and she braced herself for the omerta's orders. Enne didn't know what the omerta would conceive. She could spew hateful words about how he was selfish and inconsiderate and egotistical. She could turn and run back to the whiteboots and betray everything they'd ever worked for.

The omerta gave her no direction.

But Enne wasn't foolish enough to believe they were safe. This only meant something worse was still to come.

"Then there's only one option, since I don't know the truth, and you can't tell me," Levi said lowly. He tucked her mask into his jacket and clasped her hand. "I won't let you out of my sight."

Enne wanted to tell him that it was useless and that none of his clever plans could save them, but she remained forcibly silent except for a single sob. The omerta let her cry. Maybe it liked her like this, playing the damsel to Levi's knight.

Levi wiped away a tear on her cheek, and she flinched as he touched her. She both craved it and hated it.

"Tock will be finished soon. We need to man our stations." Levi took her hand and pulled her into the ballroom. The mirrored wall behind them bore two banners: a blue one, to represent Harrison and the First Party, and purple, for Prescott and the monarchists.

A member of the St. Morse staff handed out balloons, jewelry, and various accessories to guests. As she passed them, she slipped a strand of beads around Enne's neck and placed a silver plastic crown on Levi's head.

A few feet from them, Worner Prescott danced with Poppy. It was a sweet image of a father-daughter dance, one the media present at the party was certainly capturing. Enne looked away from the flashes of cameras. In the newspapers tomorrow, if the reader looked closely enough, they might glimpse two notorious street lords in the corner. Perhaps they'd chalk it up to a blur in the photography. Or perhaps that would be part of the legend.

"Dance with me," Levi said. It didn't sound like a request.

It sounded like a plea. "We only have moments left until the lights go out. Vianca doesn't know about our plan, does she?"

"She doesn't," Enne answered softly. That truth she could share.

"Then we haven't lost yet." He pulled her toward him, held her in the same way he'd held her before. But as much as Enne wanted his forgiveness, she'd never wanted it like this. Vianca had taken the broken pieces of their relationship and crafted them into blades, and every time Levi touched her, it felt like a cut.

"I can't believe you," Levi murmured, and the edge to his voice filled her with equal hope and equal dismay. He didn't forgive her.

Repair what you've broken.

"I'm sorry. You know I'm—"

"Is sacrificing yourself really the best plan you have?" Levi snapped, startling her. He no longer sounded broken. He sounded furious. "That stunt with your mask wasn't for Vianca, or you would have been relieved that I stopped you. I won't let you be a martyr for me."

Tears spilled from Enne's eyes, but she couldn't tell if they were her own doing or the omerta's coercion.

Levi's face softened. "I'm asking you to trust me, Enne. Whatever is coming that you're so afraid of, I can take it. You saved me before, and I could do nothing but watch." He pressed his forehead against hers. "I'm begging you—this time, let me play. This time, trust in *me*. Let me be the one to save *you*."

Enne's heart crumbled at his words. If she *knew* the answer to Vianca's twisted, cryptic demand, then it would be easier to trust he could outsmart it.

Did she trust him more than she feared Vianca?

It didn't matter. The omerta still forced the wrong words

from her lips, still intertwined her fingers with his when all she wanted to do was run.

"You haven't said it yet," she whispered.

He shivered at her breath on his lips. "I haven't said what?"

"That you've forgiven me."

"I…" He swallowed. "I've made the most desperate wager of my life tonight, but I'd still throw it all away. What's the point of saving the city if I can't save you?"

Enne fought against the omerta. She was breathless and gasping as its power pressed her lips to his. It was Vianca's work. It was wrong. But that didn't stop Enne's heart from swelling. It didn't make the words either of them had spoken any less true.

She wanted this, even if it spelled ruin for both of them.

Enne kissed him like it was the last chance she'd ever have, breathed in his sigh like it was the last breath she'd ever take. The music around them was ending, playing its final chord, and even though Enne was the one with a heart full of tragedy, it was Levi who lifted her higher, who shuddered as her tongue ran across his lips, who clung to her like at any moment she would disappear beneath him. Maybe, somehow, he also knew what this was.

A surrender.

She let out the faintest sob against him. "I love you," she whispered. Enne hoped it was her own will that said it, because she meant it. "I trust you."

Boom!

The entire casino rattled—crystal chandeliers clacking, guests screaming, dancers stumbling. Enne held on to Levi so as not to fall.

The ballroom was thrown into darkness. This only caused the guests to scream louder. The noise of it pierced through Enne's ears, but the sound was sweet. This meant the plan was still unfolding. There was still hope. She clung to that, and to Levi, in the dark. Tock had managed it.

I love you. I trust you.

Maybe that really would be enough.

Bang!

A woman's scream rang out, followed by a chorus around the room.

Someone had been shot.

It was impossible to make out the victim in the darkness, but Enne spotted a figure only feet away, wearing a dark mask with a hooked bird's beak, like a vulture. They held something in their outstretched hand, and it gleamed through the dim light of the stars through the window.

"Holy muck," Levi breathed. "Is that—"

But then someone slammed into them, knocking the wind out of Enne. Their hands broke apart, and Enne was pulled away in the stampede of bodies toward the exit.

"Enne!" Levi called, pushing toward her, but there were too many people between them.

Everyone kicked and shoved to reach the door, though the shooter had only fired once. Enne, smaller than so many of them, was wedged painfully between several panicked couples.

Now that she was separated from Levi, she had her chance. She could turn herself in. She could claim *she'd* been the assailant. Enne had told Levi that she'd trust him, but Levi's plan had been violently disrupted. They hadn't planned for a murder, and with such high-profile attendees at this party, the whiteboots and private bodyguards would quickly secure all the doors, to ensure the assailant didn't escape.

And that the others outside couldn't get in.

Enne made a split-second decision, pushed through the crowds, and wove through the maze of hallways in the darkness. Then she found the door where Lola and Grace had left her earlier and sighed with relief. It was still unmanned. The plan hadn't failed yet.

The door swung open, and Jac stumbled inside, his tuxedo covered in dust, his black hair windswept and tangled from running. Through the open doorway behind him, Enne heard the unmistakable sound of gunfire. Her stomach lurched—what was happening outside?

Jac took several deep breaths, his hands on his knees, then he looked up. His eyes widened with relief when he saw her. "You're okay," he breathed. "What happened? Is Levi here?"

Something sinister planted itself in Enne's mind. She didn't know where the thought came from, but she felt a sudden tightening in her lungs. And then she knew.

The omerta.

"We've been betrayed," he rasped, taking a step toward her and letting the door close. "You need to find Levi. Tell him it's all over. If we don't escape, it'll be a massacre."

As Jac spoke, Enne's fingers reached for the slit of her dress, but it was not of her own doing. Her heart clenched as she struggled against the omerta's power. But of course, she couldn't fight it.

"What's wrong? Did something happen?" Jac laid a consoling hand on her shoulder. "Just tell Levi—"

She cupped a hand over her mouth and choked on a sob.

Jac's eyes widened when he saw what she held, but he didn't react in time. He moved only enough to let her go.

You will break his heart, and then you will die.

Enne raised the gun and pulled the trigger.

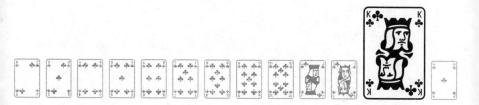

"Legend says the Bargainer can take anything from you.
A name, a face, a memory. I wonder what they do with
all of them. They only approach the desperate, they say,
but everyone is desperate. They must want something,
don'tcha think? They must have a goal."

—*A legend of the North Side*

LEVI

♥ ♠ ♦ ♣

Levi tried to chase after Enne the moment they were pushed apart, but the crowds quickly consumed her, and he could barely make out anything in the darkness.

Panic seized at him. His plan was already collapsing, but he didn't know how to save her and save the night, too.

He knew the omerta had twisted a lot of what she'd told him, but he had to believe that those last words had been her own. That she loved him. That she trusted him. If she could have faith in him, then *he* had to believe she wouldn't immediately surrender herself. Whatever Vianca had planned, they could escape it.

His sights fell on another figure in the crowds, the same one he'd spotted earlier, with a feathered mask like a hooked beak. He was the one who'd fired the gunshot. He was the one who'd derailed Levi's plans.

But Levi didn't run after him for what he'd done.

Levi ran after him for who he was.

Feathers had always been Scavenger's calling card, but Jonas wasn't supposed to be here. Not yet. Not right when the power went out. The other lords had agreed to wait outside with the gangsters, so if Jonas was here, something was wrong. If Jonas had betrayed them, then everything he'd planned might truly fall apart.

Jonas fled through the door to the theater, and Levi followed, apologizing as he pushed his way through the crowds. With all the chaos, Jonas didn't notice Levi was following him. That he was probably thinking he'd gotten away with it.

Levi slipped through the theater door and immediately collided with Jonas. He grabbed a fistful of Jonas's shirt and slammed him against the wall of the ticket booth. Cursing, Jonas fought against him, until Levi snapped his fingers and lit a flame, illuminating both their faces.

"Pup?" Jonas spat. The stench of him made Levi's nose wrinkle.

"Why are you here?" Levi demanded. Then he looked down and noticed the gun gleaming in Jonas's pocket. It was an antique—far flashier and more expensive than anything the Scar Lord would typically carry. As the weapons provider to the North Side, Jonas usually only carried guns he could sell—easy marketing.

Levi recognized that gun.

"Harrison Augustine made you an offer," he said flatly. "Is that why you betrayed us?"

"Betrayed you?" His eyebrows furrowed. "This has nothing to do with you."

"You're supposed to be outside!"

"My second is there. My *gang* is there," he growled. "I haven't betrayed anyone."

"They're going to lock the doors to find the culprit, which means no one will be able to get in or out." He slammed Jonas against the wall again for good measure. "You've ruined the plan, and you might've killed every gangster already inside."

"Then leave with me."

"Séance is still here."

"Then it will be your own fault if you die tonight," Jonas spat. "How did you even know about Harrison, anyway?" When Levi didn't answer, Jonas smiled. "I knew you couldn't be that clever. He's been helping you all this time. That's why no one likes the Irons—you want to believe they're really winning, but all of it's a cheat."

"Cheating or not, we were *all* going to win tonight. Was his offer really worth it?" Levi was so angry that his skin began to heat. It could've been a repeat of his fight with Chez Phillips all over again, the only difference being that he had never been Jonas's friend.

"Wow, you really must have some sort of complex," Jonas sneered. "It takes something special to work for mother *and* son. You're not even worth being called a cheat. You're just an Augustine bitch."

Levi punched Jonas in the face, knocking his head against the ticket window.

Jonas took a swing at him, but Levi dodged it. As soon as he did, the lights in the theater flickered on, and with a heart-stopping jolt, Levi realized they weren't alone.

Someone watched from the stage, standing beneath a single spotlight. Her hair was white.

"Ivory?" Jonas called hesitantly.

Ivory raised a rifle. It was an automatic, similar to the ones the troopers and Families carried. Levi and Jonas instantly raised their hands in the air, and both, at the exact same moment, let out a muffled *"Muck"* under their breaths.

"Come here," she commanded.

Levi and Jonas shared a meaningful look. Only moments

ago, they'd been close to killing each other, but neither of them hated the other so much to die over this. Suddenly, they were on the same side. And though the numbers might've been two-to-one, that weapon would've been terrifying in anyone's hands, let alone the most notorious killer in the City of Sin.

"Don't say anything that will irritate her," Jonas growled at Levi under his breath. "You know what? Don't say anything at all."

"As if I'd leave my life in your hands."

"You're talking. And you're irritating me."

They walked down the theater's aisle toward the stage, keeping their arms raised. Levi's heart quickened with every step. Was Ivory acting alone, or had the Doves betrayed them, too? His plan to end the war between the North and the South Sides was already crumbling, but if the gangs also turned against one another, then all hope was lost. He'd be lucky to leave this encounter alive.

"There was blood too soon," Ivory said. "It wasn't yours to take. Who is responsible?"

"Are you threatening us?" Jonas asked coolly. Levi had personally found the assault rifle to be a strong indicator of a threat, but Jonas had always had a brain smaller than a lead bullet.

"One of you two killed Worner Prescott," Ivory said. "Now all our plans have to change. They could be *ruined*."

Levi cleared his throat. "Why would I have ruined my own plan?"

Ivory let out a laugh so choked it sounded like a cough. "*Your* plan? You mean your pathetic ultimatum? Something much bigger is going to happen tonight. We failed at the riot, but we *will* succeed this time."

There was far too much in that statement to process. When the debate had gone out of control too fast—had that been

Ivory's doing? Who else was she working with? What did she have planned?

Jonas cleared his throat, and when he spoke, he did so under his breath, so only Levi could hear. "I saved your second. You still owe me a favor," he murmured. "See that I don't die here."

If Jonas had done anything less than save Jac's life all those months ago, Levi would've left Jonas to die. As far as he was concerned, Jonas had still betrayed all of them, whether or not he'd actually sold them out. But so had Ivory, apparently, and Levi wasn't thick enough to have a go at both of them. Not by himself.

"Don't do it," Levi told her carefully. "You'd be making a mistake."

"Then don't make me kill you, orb-maker. You're still a required piece."

Levi's mouth went dry. He didn't know that meant, other than that it was a threat. He and Jonas weren't getting out of this without a fight.

He glanced at Jonas and saw his fingers were twitching, signaling him. On his left hand, Jonas counted down.

Three. Two. One.

In a heartbeat, Levi had his gun in his hand. He crouched and aimed at the stage above.

But Ivory was gone.

Jonas whipped around wildly. "Where did she—?"

A hand grabbed Levi from behind, throwing him down with the force of a strength talent. The breath was knocked out of him, and his pistol flew from his hands and slid across the carpet.

Ivory stood over him. When he rolled over to reach for his gun, she stepped onto his side, her bare foot digging painfully into him. She pointed her rifle at Jonas as he straightened, his own gun raised.

"This one will fire first, as I'm sure you know." Ivory sneered at Jonas and patted the top of her weapon.

"I thought you only killed with your namesake," Jonas said.

"I wasn't planning on killing tonight." Beneath her, Levi struggled to reach for his gun, but it was too far away. His heart pounded. Neither he nor Jonas could best Ivory in a fight—not even together.

Jonas seemed to realize the same thing, because his eyes flickered to Levi with a look that said, *I won't die for you*. Levi instantly regretted holding true to his debt for when Jonas had saved Jac. There was no point in acting honest among the crooked, and now that mistake might cost him his life.

Then Jonas surprised him. He cracked his neck and put a second hand on his gun, clutching it decidedly with both hands.

"You know what Reymond used to always say about you?" Jonas asked Ivory. "That everything about you was a lie."

"Are you trying to scare me?" she asked.

Jonas circled around the theater aisle, and with every step, Ivory jammed her heel harder into Levi's side. Levi gasped, but he didn't resist.

"A lot of talents come in threes," Jonas continued. "The Augustine talent comes in threes. Chaining comes in threes. And—"

"Don't," Ivory warned. She lowered her gun from Jonas and aimed it directly at Levi's face. Levi cringed and pressed his cheek to the floor. There were countless ways his story could end, but if death had to be one of them, he'd prefer it not to be shot at point-blank range.

"That's why Reymond and I were such a good team," Jonas told her. "Because he found the lies and I found the truths. And it's taken me years, but I know almost all of yours. So if you're going to kill anyone, you might as well kill me."

Levi hadn't known Jonas had one noble bone in his body. He also had no idea what they were talking about, but judging by Jonas's face, Levi didn't think he was bluffing.

"I hope Pup is worth your loyalty," Ivory said.

"Reymond is still worth my loyalty," Jonas countered. Then he lunged to the side, making Ivory quickly point her rifle at him. But even as she fired—an ear-deafening *Pop! Pop! Pop!*—she failed to notice that Jonas's move hadn't just been a dodge.

Levi's gun skidded across the floor toward him.

He grabbed it, raised it, and fired.

Ivory fell back, clutching her right shoulder. Blood coated her clothes—some even dribbled down her lips. Levi pushed her off him and scrambled away before she could reposition her rifle.

"Time to run," Levi panted once he reached Jonas.

They sprinted up the aisle, and Ivory's gunfire roared after them. They reached the back of the theater and rushed toward the doors, only to find several others waiting there. Levi counted seven faces blocking each of the exits. They had matching white hair and each held a different weapon: a spear, a rope, a saber, a flail, a carbine, a flamethrower, a scythe.

Jonas and Levi skidded to a halt.

"Muck," Jonas breathed, in a way that sounded like defeat.

"Split up," Levi told him, shoving him to the right. They didn't have any chance two against seven, especially when the seven were Doves. But he wasn't willing to surrender—not here, not yet.

And so the two of them took off down opposite aisles. Levi mapped out his escape route in his mind. He would climb up on the stage, burst through the dressing rooms, and flee out the back hallway. He would find Enne somewhere in the chaos, and he'd tell her to abandon all their plans. He'd tell her to run.

But just as he made it past the curtain, something wrapped around his legs and dragged him down. He crashed onto the wooden floor, the rope from one of the Doves tangled around his feet. He kicked it off as the Dove stood over him, two others flanked behind her. He eyed their scythe and saber with dread.

"We were told not to kill you, but you shot Ivory," Scythe said. His voice betrayed no emotion, only a cool matter-of-factness. Levi tried to peek at where Ivory had been in the seats, but the stage curtain blocked his view. "I don't know why she insisted on keeping you alive. You're not a lord; you're a show."

Scythe leaned down and removed something from Levi's front pocket: the Fool card. He flipped it over so the art faced Levi, and Levi flinched just seeing it. "You want to distribute fakes tonight, but you're too afraid of your own story."

Across the theater, Jonas screamed. Levi couldn't see him, couldn't get to him, couldn't save him. He wasn't even sure he could save himself.

Scythe straightened, his weapon poised against Levi's throat. "I'll kill you for this."

Levi swallowed. "If Ivory *insisted* I stay alive, I think you ought to listen to her."

Scythe grabbed Levi by his tuxedo collar and yanked him to his feet. "Who would spew the wishes of the person they almost killed?" He dropped his scythe to the ground with a clatter. "Your death could've been honorable, if you'd deserved that. But you don't."

While Levi tried to wrestle out of his grip, Scythe threw him to the floor—with surprising force for an older man. Levi gasped as the wind was knocked out of him, as his head knocked painfully against the wood. Before he could collect himself to fight, Scythe held Levi's feet together, reached for a rope from the stage floor, and tied it around Levi's ankles. Behind him, one of his companions pulled the lever of a crank. It spun.

Tick. Tick. Tick.

Levi cursed as he was jerked forward. The rope was connected to a piece of machinery that controlled the stage curtains, a short, heavy contraption of gears nailed into the floor. Even as Levi grasped at the ground, the force of the pulley spinning dragged him forward, like a fishing line reeling in its catch. Once he reached those gears, the metal would crush his legs.

"The theatre is soundproof. That means no one will hear you scream," Scythe said before turning with the others and disappearing into the dressing rooms.

"Wait!" Levi called after them, his voice high and strangled. He struggled to untie the knot, to kick out his feet, but it was impossible while the rope dragged him on his back. He wouldn't be able to stop himself in time. His death would be painful, and it wouldn't be quick. He would bleed out on the stage floor.

"Help!" he shouted. His shoes reached close enough to kick at the metal contraption, and he locked his legs, his back still braced against the ground, fighting against the force of it. His muscles burned, trembled. "Someone! Help!"

Levi's last thought before his feet slipped was that he always knew he would die in this casino.

LEVI

With his eyes squeezed shut, bracing himself for the agony of
bones being crushed, Levi didn't see the person lunge behind
him to pull down the lever—he only heard the gears shudder
to a stop. He sputtered and rolled over, his own relief making him dizzy.

"You're lucky I saved you when I did," a voice said from
beside him.

Levi blinked at his companion, his vision slowly coming
into focus as Harvey Gabbiano sat cross-legged beside him.
His face was painted with concern, but not so much at Levi's
physical state as at the time on his watch.

"*You* saved me?" Levi rasped, fingers shaking as he unknot-
ted the rope around his ankles.

"Of course I did. Of course…" Harvey's voice trailed off,
as though his words were meant to convince himself. He
didn't meet Levi's eyes. "I needed to find you. I have something to give you."

Harvey slipped his hand into his tuxedo jacket and pulled

out an envelope. Levi didn't reach for it. He was grateful someone had saved him, but he would've preferred it be anyone else
in this casino. The Gabbiano family were Chainers, and even
if Harvey claimed he didn't use his blood talent, Levi trusted
Harvey and his crew about as far as he could throw them.

"You don't have to look at me like that. The favor is free."

"Nothing is free," Levi responded flatly.

"Would you rather I left you to die?" He flashed Levi a
smile, and even if that smile didn't meet his eyes, something
about it was reassuring. Trustworthy. But Levi knew that was
just Harvey's talent playing tricks on his mind. He didn't know
Harvey well, but he suspected those effects were involuntary.
He couldn't help but charm.

And so Levi couldn't help but distrust him.

Harvey pushed the envelope closer. "Take it. It's not a favor
for you. It's a favor for someone else."

Levi hesitantly accepted it. He tore open the envelope and
pulled out a Shadow Card. His heart dropped as soon as he
saw the silver foil, though to his mixed surprise and relief, it
wasn't the Fool.

It was the Emperor.

"You're invited to join him in the ballroom," Harvey said.
He climbed to his feet and held out his hand to help Levi up.
Once again, Levi didn't accept the favor.

He shakily stood on his own. "Join who? What is this?"

"Haven't you been wondering where your friends are?"

Levi's stomach knotted. Jonas was gone—probably as good
as dead. If the backup generator had been turned on, then a
fair amount of time had passed since the lights originally went
out. Jac and the others should've already infiltrated the casino, but they'd never made it inside. Something was wrong.

Harvey checked his watch. "You're running late—"

Levi reached forward and grabbed a fistful of Harvey's jacket. "Do you know what happened to them?" Levi growled.

For the first time, Harvey truly *looked* at him. He wore a pained, apologetic expression, which, for all Levi knew, could be a trick, as well.

"You already know—Ivory betrayed them," Harvey answered. "Now the casino is on lockdown. No one comes in. No one goes out."

"Ivory betrayed *us*, you mean," Levi countered. "You and Bryce were part of this, too." Levi was in no condition to fight, but he would—if only to punch that slimy, panicked frown off Harvey's face.

"It had to be tonight. He didn't have a choice," Harvey snapped at him. "She plans to kill him tonight."

"Ivory?" Levi asked.

Harvey gave a bitter laugh. "Didn't she already tell you? I thought you were her favorite." He wrenched Levi's hand off him and stepped away. "You're needed in the ballroom. I have other Cards to deliver."

He walked off toward the dressing rooms.

"Harvey! Wait!" Levi called, rushing after him, but Harvey ignored him and disappeared out the exit.

Levi cursed. He didn't care about what Harvey's words had meant. He just needed to find Enne, and they needed to leave.

Levi returned to the lobby and found it hauntingly still. The guests huddled together in groups, whispering in panicked voices. St. Morse staff stood in a barricade by the front door, and Levi hurried toward them.

"I'd like to leave," he said flatly.

"There's been an incident outside, sir. I'm afraid we cannot allow anyone to leave…for your own safety." The man's face grew flushed as he spoke.

"What sort of incident?"

"We don't want to alarm you, but there's been some gang violence—"

"I'd still like to leave." He pushed past the man, hard enough for the man to stumble. His heart was racing with panicked questions. What sort of violence? Who had been hurt?

The man grabbed at his jacket, but Levi shrugged him off. "No, sir, you can't—"

"If you don't let go of me," Levi growled, snapping his fingers to ignite a flame, "I'll burn you so badly you'll never make it out of here, either."

The man let go.

Levi turned and shoved at the revolving door. It was locked. He whipped around. "Unlock it," he hissed. The fire in his hand grew brighter.

"I can't," the man said, his voice hitched. "We didn't lock them."

Levi tried several more times, but still the door wouldn't budge.

No one comes in. No one goes out.

Dread seeped into him, and he jammed harder at the door. An unwanted memory entered his mind, of the power of the Shadow Game as it drained his life.

He pulled the Emperor card from his pocket and stared at it.

Another invitation. Another game.

He brushed past the attendant again and made his way toward the ballroom. He'd had a similar feeling in his stomach when he'd climbed the stairs in the House of Shadows. It was a hollow feeling, a stirring of something inside him, pulling him somewhere he was meant to be.

He'd been wrong about destiny. It wasn't found within a handsome smile on a wanted poster, in the touch of Enne's fingers intertwined with his, in an opportunity meant only for him. All of that had merely been desires, fantasies.

The true feeling of destiny was dread.

Music began to play in the ballroom when Levi entered it, a band of musicians nervously continuing onstage. Standing in front of them was Vianca Augustine, a microphone clutched in her white-knuckled hand.

"What has happened tonight…" She swallowed. "It is a tragedy, but the culprit has been apprehended. And until the authorities alert us that the incident outside has been resolved, it's safest to remain inside the building."

Levi frowned. If the St. Morse staff was guarding the doors to prevent the guests from learning the truth—that the entire casino was mysteriously locked—Vianca had to know, as well. Indeed, she looked paler than usual—almost ghostly. She'd staked everything she had on Worner Prescott, and he'd been killed right beneath her nose. She had played the game, and she had lost.

"The music is still playing, the drinks are still being served," she said. Levi grimaced. Continuing the party seemed in bad taste after a man had been murdered. Since none of the guests around him moved toward the bar, he assumed they agreed with him.

Vianca's eyes scanned the crowds, and then, to Levi's horror, they fell on him. She faltered for a moment, though he'd never known her to be at a loss for words.

"You," she growled. Her words sounded so sharp that the entire room stiffened.

Levi swallowed under everyone's gaze. Somewhere behind him, he heard his name. There were whispers, gasps. Vianca was going to expose him. He nervously loosened his tie. He'd already been hanged once tonight.

Vianca's mouth twisted into an unnatural smile, and her aura coiled away from her, reaching for him. "Did you think I wouldn't know?"

Then Levi realized this wasn't just about rejecting her offer. She knew about Harrison.

His first thought wasn't for himself, though it should've been—Vianca sounded furious enough to kill him. Instead, he thought of Enne. This was why she'd been so scared. What else had Vianca planned?

"Answer me!" Vianca shouted. The microphone screeched at the change in volume.

There was a gasp, the undeniable sound of an omerta squeezing the life from its victim.

Levi reached for his throat, but the sound hadn't come from him.

Because Vianca wasn't looking at Levi—she hadn't been this whole time. Her gaze was focused on someone behind him.

Before Levi could turn around to see who that person was, a shot rang out from across the room.

Bang!

Scarlet blossomed across Vianca's chest, and blood seeped between her fingers as she clutched at her heart. Her mouth hung open as she looked between the three people in the room still standing.

Harrison Augustine lowered his pistol. He didn't sigh or smile or whimper. He didn't make any expression at all.

Levi felt the omerta snap inside him, with a sound like a bone breaking. He took a deep breath, deeper than any breath he'd taken in four years, as Vianca Augustine's body slumped to the floor.

The donna was dead.

As triumph coursed through him, his first thought was of Enne. He scanned the room for her, but she was nowhere. With the casino on lockdown, she had to still be in the building. He needed to find her. Whatever terrible plan Vianca had devised for the night had been foiled. At last, the two of them were finally free.

Behind him, someone let out a loud, strangled laugh. There was a coppery taste to the air, and black crept into the corner's of Levi's vision, an aura like smoke.

Didn't she already tell you? Harvey had asked him. *I thought you were her favorite.*

In Levi's shock at Vianca's death, he'd forgotten that there'd been a third person left standing. That more than Levi and Enne had been freed. That there had always been a third.

The doors of the ballroom slammed closed.

Levi finally turned around.

Bryce Balfour clutched at his throat as he took the stage, and his eyes were the color red.

ENNE

♥ ♠ ♦ ♣

Jac jolted back from being shot at such close range. Blood
blossomed across his white shirt, and he fell, clutching his
lower abdomen. His heavy breaths punctured the silence in
the hallway.

Enne cried into her hand. The omerta continued to urge
her forward, choking her like a clamp locking around her
throat. Her finger trembled against the trigger as she resisted,
and she didn't even have enough breath to utter an apology
or to call for help.

Again, the omerta urged. *Again.*

Jac looked up at her weakly, and Enne waited for him to
curse her, to blame her the way she blamed herself.

Again, the omerta commanded as Enne let out a sob and
dark spots bled over her vision. She could feel Vianca's bony
hand tightening around her chest, breaking her own heart
along with Levi's. *Again.*

Jac coughed up a mouthful of blood. When he spoke, he

didn't clutch at his stomach. He clutched at his Creed. "It's all right," he managed. "I've beaten worse."

Bang!

Enne gasped for breath as Jac's head slumped to the side, crimson pooling from his chest, and the omerta released her.

"No, no, no, no," Enne moaned, and she scrambled toward Jac's body. She felt for a pulse, but didn't find it.

I killed him. A wave of nausea passed over her, and Enne hugged her arms to herself. She'd never felt more helpless—not during the Shadow Game, not during any time spent with Vianca. Jac was Levi's best friend. He was *her* friend. And no amount of tears or apologies would bring him back.

Enne had no idea if Harrison would succeed in his plot to kill his mother—tonight, or ever. But if he did, Enne hoped Vianca suffered. That it was slow. That every wicked thing she'd ever done was magnified on herself tenfold. And when the donna did die, Enne's only regret would be that she hadn't been able to do it herself.

Enne was still shaking when she realized she wasn't alone.

Harvey Gabbiano took in the image of her and the revolver and Jac's body, and for a moment, Enne came truly close to being sick. She slid the gun across the floor, away from her.

"I didn't... I..." The words died in her throat because, of course, she had.

"What happened here?" he asked sharply. In his hand, he held two envelopes.

"I couldn't—" The omerta squeezed at her throat. "I can't explain." She didn't dare look Harvey in the eyes. Even if this was Vianca's doing, Enne had pulled the trigger.

Harvey knelt beside Jac, and his fingers brushed Jac's Creed. "I'll move him for you. I'm one of the only ones who can go in and out of this place."

Enne cringed. *She* should be the one to move him, to stay

with him, but even the thought of touching him again made her stomach quake.

"What do you mean?" Enne asked.

Harvey nodded at the door. "Try it."

She narrowed her eyes as she did. But no matter how hard she pushed, the door wouldn't budge.

"What is this?" Enne asked, her voice hitched. "Why won't it open?" She tried again and again, panic rising in her until tears flooded her eyes. She sank to the floor, her knees against her chest. The world felt broken.

Harvey crawled to her side and placed one of the two envelopes in her hand. "You're needed in the ballroom," he told her.

"I'm staying here," she snapped, even if she hated to.

"You can't," he murmured. He placed his hand over hers, and she flinched, as though her shame was a grime he could feel against her skin. Then he sighed and let her be, and something about the gentle way Harvey tucked the other envelope in Jac's pocket made her trust him.

"Okay," she whispered. She didn't care about whatever debt she might owe to Harvey, only that he would take the body away. Take away what she had done.

As Harvey lifted Jac and pushed open the door, Enne moved out of his path, her eyes fixed on the puddle of blood left behind.

"There's a loophole to killing her, you know, which I'm sure she didn't tell you. It's family," Harvey said, and a dark look crossed his face. "Levi isn't the only one who made a desperate deal with Harrison Augustine."

He gave her a weary smile. Unlike any of his previous ones, it didn't appear to be a trick. "I'm sorry about all this," he said, and then he let the door close behind him.

As Enne tried to blink away her tears and pick apart what he meant, she slid out the contents of her envelope.

A Shadow Card. The Empress.

The taste of bile filled her mouth. She couldn't play the game again. Not tonight. Not ever.

Trembling, she turned the envelope over and read the writing scribbled on the front. *Erienne Salta.* In all the time she'd known Harvey, she'd never given him a name other than Séance. And the Empress figure on the card unnerved her—they might've addressed the envelope to Erienne "Salta," but was there something more sinister the card implied?

For several moments, she froze there, her cries quiet and broken. She'd killed Jac. The gangs outside were compromised. But a dreadful feeling inside her warned that worse was coming.

I need to find Levi, she told herself. She needed to tell him. She needed to save him. And if they lived through tonight, there would be time later to fall apart.

Enne pocketed her gun once more and followed Harvey's summons to the ballroom. A crowd barricaded the door, but she pushed through, tripping over her own gown, the Empress card crushed in her fist.

It was when she emerged at the front, tears blurring her vision, that she felt the gunshot.

For a moment, she thought *she* had been the one shot. She startled at the jolt in her chest, and she looked down at the layers of satin, searching for red. Something snapped within her, piercing, relieving. She took a deep breath as a heaviness lifted off her shoulders, one that had been there for months.

She realized what had happened before she saw the body, yet still the image shocked her. Vianca Augustine lay facedown, blood seeping out around her, soaking confetti and joining the spilled champagne on the stage floor.

Yet neither Enne nor Levi were dead.

She should've felt joy. Even relief. But the longer she stared at Vianca, the only emotion she felt was rage. Jac had died minutes before her. Had Enne fled somewhere other than that hallway, had she fought the omerta harder, had she done *anything* differently, then maybe Jac would still be alive. Maybe none of this would've happened.

Behind her, the ballroom doors slammed closed.

"Some other players have arrived," a voice said into a microphone, and Enne tore her gaze away to see Bryce Balfour bent over, examining the body. Levi and Harrison were the only others in the room left standing. Everyone else crouched on the floor, many with their eyes squeezed shut in fear.

"Why don't you come up here?" Bryce asked Enne, motioning her forward. "I have a few more safe cards to distribute."

But Enne felt far away as she studied the scene around her, as though watching from a distance. Too much tonight didn't make sense. Harrison had killed his mother, ensuring that the carriers of her three omertas survived, but he'd also done it in a crowded room. He still held his gun, in fact. Yet no one moved against him. None of the guests even spoke at all.

She opened her mouth to ask, "What's going on?" but she didn't know if the words came out. She didn't trust her own senses.

She must've spoken, though, because Bryce responded, "This is a game. *My* game. And tonight, everyone in this casino is going to play." He licked his lips as he turned back to the crowd. "If everyone would reach into your pockets, you should all have a card."

Hesitantly, every person searched themselves, and Enne watched numbly as the guests each pulled out a plain, typical playing card.

"Would those with the Shadow Cards please join me up

here?" Bryce asked impatiently, meeting Enne's gaze. With a start, Enne realized that his eyes were scarlet, like a story plucked from one of Grace's legends.

She felt foolish now for never suspecting. Bryce's eyes, Enne recalled, had always looked bloodshot. He'd been wearing contacts, just like her.

The Balfour family doesn't have a talent, Lola had once told her, but even then, of course, Enne had known that couldn't be true. When she and Bryce had shaken hands for the first time, she'd felt a power in him, the same power of the Shadow Game. But, like all things that reminded her of that night, she'd locked the memory away, buried it beneath anger and ambition, all—so she told herself—to make herself stronger.

She'd been a fool.

Enne climbed onto the stage and stood at Levi's side, Harrison behind them. The relief in Levi's eyes when he looked at her was nearly enough to make her break down again. He reached for her hand, but she wrapped her arms around herself.

"What happened?" Levi asked her.

But Bryce's next actions drew her attention away. He reached into his jacket and pulled out a long red cloth, then unfolded it and threw it into the air. As the cloth billowed and drifted down, it rested around the shape of something large and circular, though there'd been nothing there before.

Bryce smiled. "And the game begins."

He tore away the cloth to reveal a lottery wheel, alternating red and black like a game of roulette. The crowd gasped— a few people even clapped, as though this were some sort of show, as though Vianca's bleeding body didn't lie at Bryce's feet.

"Don't do this," Harrison said, stepping forward. He laid a protective, almost paternal hand on Bryce's shoulder. "I know what you're doing, and you can't—"

Bryce swatted him away. "I *can*. And if you do know, then you also know you can't stop me."

Bryce turned back to the crowd. "In my game, there's only one rule—survival," he told the room. The clapping abruptly died. "This roulette wheel contains a number for every card from two to ace. You'd better hope it doesn't fall on yours."

He spun the wheel, and the metal pegs on the table whirled. *Tick. Tick. Tick.*

Enne saw the glimmer of strings in the air, and she frantically grasped for Levi's hand, despite herself. For a moment, she was back at that card table, facing those who had killed her mother. The strings hummed around them as the board spun, plucking an eerie song as though playing a harp. The hairs on Enne's neck standing on end.

The wheel stopped on the number ten.

A dozen people across the room crumpled to the floor. At first, it only seemed like a trick, and it wasn't until the guests around them began to scream that Enne realized those people were dead.

She watched in shock as many of the guests rose and fled for the doors, only to find them locked. They pounded on them, threw themselves against them. But still, they remained closed.

The rules of the world had broken, and with that realization, Enne regained the last shreds of her composure. She didn't know this game, but as she clutched Levi's hand beside her, she knew she still had things to lose. And so she couldn't afford to break, too.

This night had already claimed too many lives.

She reached into her dress and pulled out her gun. Her hand trembled as she clutched it—it was the same gun that had killed Jac. But still, she aimed it at Bryce's chest.

"Stop this," Enne growled. Beside her, Levi squeezed her

other hand, but made no move to stop her. Many of the guests, too, had stopped their escape attempts to watch.

"Why so angry?" Bryce asked her. He kicked Vianca's body in the side, and Enne winced. No matter how wretched Vianca had been, there was something unsettling about how carelessly he wounded her corpse. "The three of us should be celebrating."

The three of us. Enne's hand shook, though she made no move to lower her gun. *Bryce* had been Vianca's third omerta? But of course it made sense. Vianca was the one who'd suggested Enne visit him—she'd even referred to Bryce as "dear." And then there was the way Bryce had always spat out the name of this casino.

"You didn't know?" Bryce asked, letting out a strangled laugh. "How do you think she knew about the words spoken at our meetings?"

Bryce took a step closer to them, and even if he claimed to be their ally, Enne and Levi both backed away. The crimson glint in his eyes matched the blood he had spilled.

"Shoot him!" somebody shouted from the other side of the room. Enne whipped her head toward the crowd, at the terror in their faces. Several men had tried to climb the stage, but an invisible barrier stopped them. They cursed and pounded on what looked like air.

Enne avoided their stares, her hand quivering. It'd been easier to kill the two whiteboots, to kill Sedric Torren. She'd hated Sedric, and she hadn't known the whiteboots. But Bryce, as cruel and twisted as he might've been, had once felt close to being her friend. And worse, she understood his anger. She and Levi understood it better than anyone.

Bryce ignored the crowd, just like he ignored the aim of Enne's gun. "Jonas was right to wonder how the whiteboots ever got the rifles in time," he continued. "But the Families have them, don't they? Just like he said. You see, it was never the whiteboots who ambushed the Orphan Guild. It was *me*. Vianca gave me the weapons and told me to start a war."

His gaze darted wildly between them. "But she never asked you to kill your friends, did she? Not her favorite. Not her girl."

Enne's heart clenched. What Bryce and Levi didn't know was that she already had.

"She was going to kill me tonight. She told me over tea. I would be forced to attend this party, and Worner's victory would be announced, and then my use to her would be finished." Bryce's shoulders heaved. "If Harrison hadn't stopped her, I'd already be dead."

Harrison stiffened. "I didn't save you for *this*." He gestured at the anguish around the room. So many people shouted that Enne could no longer make out their words.

"Even so, it's thanks to you that I'm alive," Bryce told him. "And that I now get to save someone else."

Bryce spun the roulette wheel again before Enne could decide what to do.

Tick. Tick. Tick.

"It won't work," Harrison warned her, but she didn't listen. She could break rules, too. She could shoot the wheel, just like she'd shot the timer.

She pulled the trigger.

The bullet whizzed through it as though it were made of smoke. It blew a hole in the wooden stage floor, and still the wheel spun.

Tick. Tick. Tick.

The peg stopped on the two.

A dozen more people in the room dropped—one moment standing, the next dead. Those remaining resumed pounding on the ballroom doors, screaming at anyone outside to help them escape.

"That's impossible," Enne murmured, staring at the splintered floor.

"The Shadow Game wasn't," Levi said, and Harrison gave him a weary nod.

But Enne wasn't convinced. She'd cheated the Shadow Game, and so she could cheat this, too. She would save these people, like she couldn't save Jac.

She trained her gun on Bryce.

"I'll shoot you," she threatened.

"Just like you shot Owain at the debate?" Bryce said, cocking an eyebrow. "I was there, too. Vianca told me about what you planned, of course. She loved to talk to me about you two. But I knew there was more on your mind than just the riot. And I knew you wouldn't go through with it."

Enne winced. She hadn't been weak. She'd been right to back down.

Then Levi's eyes widened. "*You're* the one who fired the shots that day."

"Yes, Vianca was furious with me about that. Furious enough to kill me, so it seems." Bryce gave her body a smug look. "She'd hoped for something more organized, but I don't know... I think I preferred the chaos."

Something about the way he said that last word made Enne shiver.

Bryce took a menacing stride closer to her and Levi. "You think the whole city revolves around the two of you, but this isn't your story—it has always been *mine*. Who do you think sent you that letter?"

Enne reached for the empty envelope Harvey had given her with confusion. Bryce smiled wickedly, stalked away, and spun the wheel a third time.

Tick. Tick. Tick.

Enne fired, her gun aimed at Bryce's heart.

Like before, the bullet lodged itself in the floor. Bryce winked at her, unharmed, and Enne nearly dropped the revolver in shock. No matter what she did, this was one game she could not win.

"What *are* you?" Levi asked Bryce, though of course, Enne felt they all now knew the answer. In the City of Sin, all of the legends were true.

"I am the secret of the House of Shadows," he answered.

The peg stopped on the nine, and several others in the crowd dropped dead.

Amid the screams, something in the room shifted in that moment, as though the air had grown sparser, the temperature colder. The strings around them, all at once, pulled taut.

Bryce let out a triumphant howl of laughter and snapped his fingers. The roulette table vanished, and from where it had stood, hundreds of silver Shadow Cards rained down, sweeping across the stage floor. They were Jonas's counterfeits—the key props to Levi's plans for tonight. The Fool.

Bryce tossed a final card on top of them, and unlike the others, its foil shined gold. It fluttered as it fell and landed face-up. The Magician.

"There's a price to keep the devil away," he murmured, echoing the lines someone else had once uttered to Enne before the Shadow Game. Another villain. Another monster. "Unless you'd prefer they'd come to play."

And with those words, Bryce disappeared like a wisp of smoke.

"My mother was superstitious. Shatz, really. Whenever she got
attached to something, she would throw it away.
She said that's how shades find victims—they bind
to pieces of you. They need a connection.

"She told me, 'Evil isn't random—that's what makes it
the opposite of goodness. Evil is designed.'"

—*A legend of the North Side*

LEVI

♥   ♠   ♦   ♣

For the first time in his life, Levi lost his faith in destiny.

The Irons and the other gangs outside had failed. Jonas had been apprehended. Levi himself had nearly died. He'd watched countless others die in front of him, in this ballroom, at the hands of an impossible villain who had disappeared before their very eyes.

This was not glory.

This was not greatness.

He grabbed Enne by the wrist and pulled her toward him. "Down the hallways, past Vianca's office, through the back entrance," he hissed, because fleeing was their only option left.

Enne didn't move. "We couldn't save any of them." Her voice was hoarse, and Levi didn't like the hopeless look in her eyes as she scanned the dead in the room. It wasn't a look he recognized on her.

"No, we couldn't," Levi breathed. Bryce being Vianca's third omerta felt painfully obvious now. He'd run into Bryce for the first time outside of St. Morse after all. And there'd always been a certain spite in Bryce's voice when he spoke of the donna—the same spite in Levi's own.

But he couldn't dwell on that now. After tonight, the fate of the city dangled by the thinnest of threads.

The ballots were still being counted.

One of the candidates was dead.

The other had openly murdered his mother in public.

And if Levi and Enne didn't escape before the whiteboots swarmed this casino, then each of them would face the gallows.

"Let's go," Levi urged, once again pulling Enne forward. Now that Bryce and his power was gone, the guests had burst through the ballroom's doors and raced for the exits. Harrison had also slipped out and disappeared within the crowd.

Before he and Enne moved to join them, Levi took one last look at the ballroom. Dozens of bodies littered the floor, discarded like the party favors and the Fool cards. Vianca's body stared at the violence around her with eyes wide open.

This had always been her legacy—blood and betrayal.

Hands linked, the pair made their way through the hall to one of the back exits. It was the same one Levi had fled through after the Shadow Game, when he'd first seen his wanted poster, when the events of this war began.

Enne pulled at his hand, slowing them down. "Levi, *wait*."

"We don't have time to wait," he answered. "We need to get back to Olde Town."

"But—"

They turned the corner, and a puddle of red glistened beside the doors. Levi frowned, but before he could inspect it, Enne twisted him around to face her and her bloodshot eyes. Her hand trembled as she let go of his.

"I need to tell you something," she said, her voice barely above a whisper.

"Then tell me," he snapped. He didn't mean to sound impatient, but they couldn't afford this now. They couldn't slow down. And she was starting to scare him, the way she shrugged him away when he reached for her, the way her gaze remained fixed on the blood.

"Vianca found out about you and Harrison," Enne whispered.

"It's fine," Levi assured her hurriedly. "She's dead." He was already planning their escape route in his mind. They would find the others. They would barricade themselves in the museum...

"She told me to... I didn't want to." She placed her hand on her forehead to steady herself, and Levi almost didn't catch her next words through the strain in her voice. "I couldn't tell you about it. I couldn't stop it."

Amid a thousand horrifying possibilities, Levi's mind settled on his darkest thought. On the worst-case scenario. The fear felt like a stone on his chest.

"Jac's dead," she choked out. "I killed him."

"What?" Levi asked, even though she'd spoken clearly.

"She..." Enne swallowed. "She ordered me to fix it, to fix *us*. Then she told me to break your heart."

New Reynes was loud with sirens as Levi threw open the back doors and vomited onto the pavement. His mind had gone quiet, numb, but something about that wailing still made him sick.

Enne apologized, over and over. He didn't hear her over the sirens. He didn't hear her at all.

As they wove through the streets of the Casino District, all Levi's memories of the past day with Jac seemed meaningless. His heart kept returning to that one day—the day they'd fought. Jac had been right. Levi was selfish, shortsighted, and arrogant. And Levi had willingly taken all of those insults, apologized for them. But it didn't matter. In the end, Jac was the one who'd taken the bullet.

Only as St. Morse fell farther behind them did Levi remember that he was finally free of Vianca, free of that casino.

But as he listened to the sirens, Levi couldn't believe he'd ever called the ache in his chest destiny. No desire was as precious as what he'd already had.

When they returned to the museum, Tock and Lola were leaning against the hood of Lola's motorcar. They still wore the same clothes from earlier, but Tock's skin was covered in soot, her dress torn. Lola clutched her keys in her fist like a weapon. Blood was smeared on her cheek, and she held a leather notebook open in her hand.

When Levi and Enne approached, equally as worse for wear, Lola choked out a sob, tossed the notebook down, and threw her arms around Enne.

"We thought you were gone," she said.

"Almost," Enne whispered.

While the two of them hugged, Levi made his way over to Tock. He felt so exhausted that it was a struggle to stand. Exhausted and nothing else.

He waited for Tock to perform some sort of grand gesture, to wrap her arms around him and cry as though they all had something to be thankful for.

"Tell me," Tock said instead, gently.

"I can't. Not here." His voice shook. He peeked at Enne over his shoulder, and something ached inside him to look at her. All he could see was that pool of blood.

"Tommy was shot beside me. I couldn't save him," Tock murmured. "It was an ambush. Ivory hadn't brought all the Doves to the Catacombs, because there were at least another thirty of them waiting for us at St. Morse. It was a massacre.

Not just Tommy—we lost Linton, Melika, Anna, and Eric. The Scarhands' second died. Scavenger is gone. The Spirits made it out without casualties, but several of them were wounded."

Levi's knees shook, and he leaned against the hood of the car for support. He'd intended to end the war tonight.

But the war would continue on, and with Bryce and Ivory now their enemies, the North Side would turn bloodier than ever before.

"I mucked up," Levi choked out. "This was all my plan." He took a shaky breath and held his fist to his mouth. He knew Tock too well to be ashamed, but still, he looked away as his chest heaved. "I can't believe…"

"This isn't on you," Tock told him. "We all agreed. You couldn't have known—"

"I should've known!" There was so much that Levi had ignored. The legends of New Reynes weren't dreams to aspire to—they were nightmares. He'd adopted what he wanted from those stories and abandoned the pieces that didn't suit his own ambitions. All this time, he'd tried to convince himself that he was different from the other lords—different means, different ends. But the past few months had proven him to be just as cruel, just as selfish.

He had chosen this story for himself, knowing all of these stories ended the same way.

Lola stepped away from Enne. "Where's Jac? I thought he'd be with you. He went inside St. Morse right before the doors locked." She fiddled with her watch.

Levi's gaze flickered to Enne's. He didn't recognize his own voice as he snapped, "Why don't you tell them?"

Something passed over Enne's face, something Levi suspected to be hurt. But as Enne danced around her story, from Vianca's orders to every moment that led to the hallway, to the puddle of blood, Levi couldn't listen anymore. It all sounded like an excuse.

"He's dead," he interrupted. "He's dead. And it's Vianca's fault."

But it was also his.

A horrified silence fell over the group—Lola, Levi noticed, looked particularly stricken. But as he turned away and walked back to the museum alone, an insidious thought crept into his mind.

If Vianca hadn't explicitly told Enne to kill Jac, then where, exactly, did Enne get the idea?

A few hours later, with many still to pass until sunrise, seven people gathered around a radio. A bottle of whiskey rested on the table, half drunk and abandoned. It was one of the museum's common rooms, but everyone else had gone to bed, leaving it quiet and empty.

"What happened tonight was a tragedy unlike anything this city has seen in a generation," Chancellor Fenice spoke through the radio. She had an eerily flat voice, just as Levi remembered from the House of Shadows. "With over one hundred confirmed casualties, it's become starkly clear that this wasn't only an attack on the event at St. Morse Casino, but on our entire democracy. The monarchist agenda has spread like a disease throughout the North Side. Our chief concern has always been the safety of our citizens, but the displays of talents tonight prove the threat that unregistered Talents of Mysteries pose. And the gangs of the North Side provide refuge for the most dangerous who hide among us."

Levi leaned back in his seat and rubbed his temples. He struggled to keep his eyes open, but all night the radio had released statements regarding what had happened tonight at

St. Morse. This had been his plan, and so he needed to hear the consequences.

"Bryce is exactly the excuse they've always needed," Lola said from beside him. She'd been flipping expertly between the radio stations all night. "By next week, not a single church in New Reynes will be left standing."

Grace groaned from the couch, where she was spread out with her feet shoved awkwardly into the side of some young man Levi didn't recognize, someone the Spirits called Roy. These past few hours, he'd said very little, but he sat rigidly beside her, watching everyone with narrowed eyes.

"They won't make any decisions tonight," Grace said. "It's too soon. There's no point waiting up for—"

Lola ignored her and turned the radio up louder. Tock, who'd been sleeping on her shoulder, startled awake for a moment, looked wearily around the room, and fell back asleep.

"The eyewitness accounts have been erratic and unreliable," the Chancellor continued. "But it is our understanding that the death of Worner Prescott can be attributed to Jonas Maccabees, also known as Scavenger. He is a twenty-nine-year-old male running the largest gang of the North Side, called the Scarhands. He has been taken into custody and awaits execution in the morning. Until—"

"We have to save him," Enne said seriously. She sat at the last seat at the table, her hands knotted together, her eyes bloodshot from crying and from wearing her contacts for so long. Every so often, she reached forward to touch him, but then she wrenched back—wise enough to think better of it.

"We can't save him," Levi told her coolly. "He's going to be killed in less than six hours." And Levi was done coming up with plans. Saving Jonas wouldn't save the rest of them.

"He's our ally," she pushed.

"Our allies are limited to the people in this room," he said.

He'd made the mistake of trusting the wrong people before, and he wouldn't do it again.

"But we need him if Bryce and Ivory—"

"You don't even know if Ivory is still alive," Tock pointed out groggily, her eyes still closed. "Levi did shoot her."

Grace let out a muffled snort from the couch. "As if Pup could've killed her."

Lola scowled and turned the radio up louder. At this volume, they would wake half the museum.

"—Captain Hector believes that all of the other deaths within St. Morse Casino, including Vianca Augustine, can be attributed to Bryce Balfour. The suspect is a twenty-three-year-old male—"

"But Harrison killed Vianca!" Lola snapped, shaking the radio. "The whole room saw it! This is a blatant lie. They're going to use St. Morse as an excuse to do everything that—"

Levi shushed her so they could hear Fenice.

"After the tragedy and treason that occurred tonight, it is vital that I end this message with a statement of hope. Despite the best efforts of criminals and of the monarchists, our sovereignty has prevailed. I have just received news that the election results yielded a two percent lead in favor of Harrison Augustine, the next representative of New Reynes. On behalf of the First Party, the city, and the entire Republic, I offer him sincere congratulations on this victory. We will not let such progress be overshadowed by violence. We—"

Levi swatted Lola away before she blew the radio's speakers and switched the dial off.

"There you have it," he said drily. "The new era."

The room fell into silence.

"When Bryce left, his last words were about the devil," Enne said. She held the golden Shadow Card Bryce had given her in her hand. "He said the same words Sedric once said to me. I don't think that's a coincidence."

"Malisons and shade-makers are part of the Faith," Lola told her. "But the Bargainer is a legend from New Reynes. They can't both be true."

"Of course they can," Sophia said. She was the last one in the room, and she lay on the other couch. This was the first Levi had heard her speak since Lola told her about Jac. Since then, all she'd done was burn a series of matches and watch them snuff out.

She stood up abruptly, making everyone in the room blink and wake up. She stomped over to the table and threw down something with shining gold foil. A Shadow Card.

"How did you get this?" Levi asked. "You weren't inside the casino with us."

"I found it in my pocket when I got here." Levi was about to respond that that was impossible, but of course, he'd learned better by now. "Check yours."

The others nervously rummaged around in their own clothes. Roy was the first to find his, tucked away within his shirt. "That wasn't there earlier," he murmured, paling. He pushed away Grace's feet, as though it was her touch that had caused this trick. Then he turned it around, revealing the Justice card.

Levi and Enne revealed the Shadow Cards they already possessed: the Emperor and the Empress. Then Lola found the Hermit folded within her boot, Tock brandished the Chariot from the front of her dress, and Grace pulled the High Priestess from a slit in her skirt. Sophia reached out and flipped over her own card: the Wheel of Fortune.

"Every legend about this city is true," Sophia said.

Tick. Tick. Tick.

Whether it was the countdown of a timer or the spin of a

roulette wheel, Levi had escaped one game only to fall victim to another. But he no longer had a taste for destiny. New Reynes could take his throne and bury it beside his best friend.

For so long, Levi had wanted to be better than the other lords; he'd thought he would take his kingdom but keep his conscience. But now he didn't see the point in being better if he couldn't protect the people he cared about.

He didn't need to be *better*. He needed to be smarter.

He didn't need to be righteous. He needed to be ruthless.

For several moments, none of them spoke. Not until Enne pointed at Levi and said, her voice strained, "There's one more. In your front pocket."

Levi looked down, and his shoulders relaxed. He pulled it out. "This one is always there. It's the Fool…" But he frowned when he saw the writing scribbled across the Fool's face in red ink.

You have been invited to play…

ENNE

♥ ♠ ♦ ♣

Today a gangster would hang, and half the city had gathered in Liberty Square for the occasion.

Enne wrapped her coat tighter around herself and leaned into Levi. She was hyperaware of the number of whiteboots present, standing watch at every corner.

As much as it pained her, Levi was right. They couldn't save Jonas.

But they could stand witness…and say goodbye.

Not that Enne had any particular attachment to the Scar Lord. He'd helped her once, and she appreciated that. The City of Sin was full of villains, but she was starting to believe that maybe he wasn't one of them.

Not that it mattered now.

"Who's that?" Levi asked, nodding to the stage, where a young woman ascended the steps.

Enne almost didn't recognize Poppy, dressed all in black, her eyes downcast and bloodshot. She looked as though she'd come straight from her father's funeral.

"That's Prescott's daughter," Enne answered quietly.

There was an obvious shift in the crowd upon her arrival, from chatter to whispers. The image of a grief-stricken daughter could move the heart of anyone, even those who'd disagreed with Worner's politics. Harrison Augustine was being sworn into office across the city, but Enne was willing to bet far more spectators had come here.

"I bet they won't let him fall," Levi said darkly. "I bet they'll let him choke."

Grace and Roy had returned to the Ruins District with the rest of the Spirits to recover in their own home. Sophia had retreated back to Luckluster. Lola and Tock were elsewhere. Which left Enne and Levi to attend the execution.

"I hope you're wrong," Enne whispered. They'd both seen far too much death last night for such a gruesome display today.

"I'm not."

Unfortunately, Enne agreed with him. The city hadn't come to watch a clean death, and the wigheads would want make a spectacle of this. Last time New Reynes went to war, each of the lords had hanged. This wasn't just a sentence—it was a promise.

Enne hadn't only attended for Jonas's sake—this was a promise to herself, too. Considering the haunting message Bryce had left them and the dangerous rhetoric on the radio, Liberty Square seemed a likely fate for them, too. So she would watch Jonas die. She would surround herself with hateful stares and morbid anticipation.

And she would make a promise to herself that her story wouldn't end here. Not hers, not Levi's, not anyone's she cared about.

"Did you mean it?" Levi asked suddenly. "Did you mean anything you said yesterday at St. Morse?"

Enne's breath hitched. "I meant... I meant *everything*—"

"But Vianca told you to fix things between us." His voice was frighteningly cold.

"She did," she answered softly.

"Then..." His expression darkened. "I guess we'll never know, will we?"

Enne gaped at him. She knew he was grieving, but she had seen him grieve Reymond. He hadn't sounded like this.

"I'm telling you I meant them," she said, fighting to keep her voice steady. "Don't you believe me?"

She reached for him with trembling fingers, but Levi stiffened and turned away.

"Vianca told you to break me. But she didn't tell you how," Levi said. "You almost murdered in cold blood before. Killing Jac... The thought came from *somewhere*."

Enne was so horrified that she could think of nothing to say in her defense. Was that what he truly thought of her? That she was a monster? That she'd devised this?

"You don't mean that," she said quickly.

"I keep wondering... Do you wish you'd killed Owain that day? That Bryce hadn't fired first?"

Enne didn't like the coldness in Levi's voice. It didn't sound defeated, like it had last night when she'd told him about Jac. It sounded heavy and resolute, like he'd already made up his mind. As if she didn't already relive Jac's death every moment she closed her eyes. As if she hadn't spent all night awake with guilt.

"Now that I know you'd hate me either way," Enne said softly, "I guess I do."

Levi was prevented from responding when Jonas was brought to the stage, a dark hood over his head. Enne's breath hitched at the sight of him. He was limping, and though most of his skin was covered, violet bruises peeked out below his sleeve. When they pulled off his hood, Enne felt her blood run cold as the crowd sneered. He'd been beaten until he was almost unrecognizable, and someone had carved "Scar Lord" into his forehead with a blade. The skin around the words was oozing and raw.

"Jonas made his choice when he killed Worner Prescott," Levi said. Even so, Enne found his fate difficult to stomach, and all the more so when she considered how her and Levi's ends could be the same.

Jonas looked up through swollen eyes and scanned the crowd. Enne swallowed as his gaze fell on them. Jonas mouthed something to them that she couldn't make out.

"Do you know what he's trying to say?" Enne asked. She had to force the words out, force herself to speak to Levi. If he truly felt as he'd told her, that she'd conceived the idea to kill Jac herself, then how could he bear to stand beside her?

"I think he said, 'I'm sorry,'" Levi answered. "I don't like this. We shouldn't have come." But Enne stayed rooted where she stood. She needed to watch, no matter how much it hurt. Maybe Levi thought otherwise, but she was *not* heartless.

The judge climbed onto the stage as the executioner secured the noose around Jonas's neck. "The accused is found guilty of the crimes of murder and treason. His sentence is death."

Jonas grimaced and continued searching through the crowd. Enne's stomach tightened. He was waiting for help, she realized, but they had no plan this time.

"The accused is given an opportunity to confess or bring forward names in an attempt to lighten their sentence." The judge cleared his throat. "I've been told you intend to bring forward information. Is that correct?"

Jonas nodded.

A dreadful feeling settled into Enne's stomach.

There's no information in New Reynes that I don't already know, Jonas had told her the day she visited him. *Or that I can't find out.*

"Speak your confession for the crowd," the judge told him.

"I know the identity of Séance," he said. Though his voice was hoarse, Enne heard him perfectly, and her blood ran cold in her veins.

Once the city knew her name, it wouldn't be long before they knew her face. And she would never walk freely again.

Levi gripped her shoulder tightly in warning, but Enne's fingers were already reaching for her gun. Jonas hadn't damned her, not yet.

Levi wrenched her arm down before she could aim, his expression livid.

Maybe it really was instinct. Maybe she really was a monster.

But he didn't scold her for that. "You'll be telling the whole crowd you're here," he hissed. She would've preferred him to curse at her with hatred, not *this*. This cold, unfeeling logic.

"So what do we do?"

"We do nothing."

She shouldn't push him—his best friend was dead. He wasn't himself. So Enne swallowed down her nerves and turned her attention back to the stage, where Jonas was working himself up to speak again.

"Her name is Enne Salta," Jonas declared.

A murmur passed through the crowd, and Enne winced at the sound of it. She could no longer hide behind a mask. She had come close to considering Jonas an ally, but with five words, he was leading her into ruin.

My only ulterior motive is curiosity, he'd lied.

"Come on," Levi hissed, sliding his hand into hers and shoving through the crowd, and Enne was too dazed to think anything of his touch. Soon, the wigheads would search her records. They would dig up her life in Bellamy. Her old classmates would stare at her face on the front page of their newspapers and not remember who she was. Her home would be searched, her belongings looted. Everything about her life would be on public display.

"The sentence stands," the judge said, taking a step back to join the executioner.

"Wait," Jonas rasped. Enne was no longer looking at the stage—she was pushing, ducking, stumbling her way toward the edge of Liberty Square, her one hand in Levi's, her other still squeezing her gun. "There's more."

Enne cursed Jonas's desperation. There was nothing he could say that would save him—the wigheads were determined to have a victory today. He was only committing more betrayals, and any remorse she'd felt over his death had long vanished.

"Enne Salta isn't her true name," Jonas said. "And I'm not sure what is."

Do you have other secrets I should know about?

Her heart leaped into her throat. She made a split-second decision to break away from Levi, lunging for the closest bench and climbing on top of it. Although she stood behind the crowd, the whiteboots and civilians focused on the gallows, she was still in plain sight. She could be seen.

But the other option was worse.

"Then it's no help to us," the judge said gruffly. The executioner reached for the lever, and Enne aimed her gun, hoping the executioner would pull first.

"No—I'm not done. I don't know her name, but I know her talent," Jonas gasped.

Enne fired, but a moment too late. The crowd screamed, but not before Enne made out Jonas Maccabees's last words.

"She's a Mizer."

The bullet hit him between the eyes, and he slumped over into the noose. Even so, the executioner pulled the lever, dropping the trapdoor below him, so that his already dead body fell, jolted, and then hung limply from the gallows.

A spectacle.

Enne had made a promise—a pointless, pathetic promise—not to die here, and so, as the eyes in the crowd turned to find the Scar Lord's killer, she jumped off the bench and raced to the street corner, where Levi stood waiting, his gun also raised.

But it didn't matter how fast she ran—they'd seen her.

It didn't matter how precisely she'd shot—her secret was known.

It didn't matter that she'd escape today—from now on, she'd always have to run.

The City of Sin had asked Enne to play another game, and this time, she wouldn't have her mask or a false name from an old life to hide behind. And after facing countless villains and repeated betrayals, the only thing Enne knew for certain about the game was that there were infinite ways to lose.

But even broken and exposed, this was not the end.

Her gang was out of volts—she would make more.

The North Side was a kingdom conquered—she would take it back.

The Families and the Scarhands had fallen—she would rise.

If Levi believed the city had stolen Enne's conscience, then so be it. For the first time since she'd come to New Reynes, Enne wasn't merely playing to survive. She was playing to win.

And in order to do that, she needed to become what history feared most.

She needed to become queen.

EPILOGUE

♥   ♠   ♦   ♣

Harrison Augustine was sworn into office with one hand on the Republic's constitution, and the other over his heart—or, more specifically, over the pistol concealed in his breast pocket.

Hours later, he sipped a Snake Eyes and stared out his window at the City of Sin. It was late evening, and of course, like any compassionate politician, he'd canceled his victory party in light of the despicable and shocking assassination of his opponent.

It was unfortunate that Jonas Maccabees had been caught and hanged. There was no way to pardon the North Side now, as he'd planned. Harrison still had appearances to keep up after all.

Black smoke smothered the skyline of the North Side, and Harrison knew the city well enough to pinpoint the exact location of the fire: Luckluster Casino.

Harrison smiled to himself. He and Sophia had both gotten what they'd wanted. Vianca Augustine and Charles Torren were dead. Luckluster burned, and soon St. Morse would, too. Harrison had even won the election fairly, but slimly enough that he didn't regret the fact that Worner Prescott now lay in a mausoleum, dead from Harrison's own gun.

He didn't like close calls.

But as much as Harrison wanted to celebrate, he wasn't drinking this Snake Eyes to reward himself. He was drinking because he needed to think, and thinking about the House of Shadows was best done at least partially inebriated.

The bell on his door rang. Harrison startled—he wasn't expecting anyone tonight. He downed the rest of his drink and answered it, raising his eyebrows when he saw who was waiting for him.

"I'm surprised you're here," Harrison told her. "I thought we were done with each other."

"Not quite," Sophia Torren answered, unrolling a piece of saltwater taffy.

"I was just admiring your work across the river." He moved to let her in, and she took a seat on his living room sofa. She smelled of smoke and candy. "Where's your partner?"

Something dark passed across her face. "You should lock the door," she said flatly. Harrison pursed his lips, but he did as instructed. "I'm going to get right to the point—Luckluster is burning, and I have new plans." She popped the taffy in her mouth.

"Not even going to congratulate me?" he asked.

"Does that really work on you? Flattery?" She met his gaze coolly.

"It depends on your request."

Sophia leaned forward, and there was something about her eyes in that moment that made him uncomfortable. They looked familiar. "I know you're more like your mother than you care to admit."

"You must be feeling awfully lucky to walk into my home and say those words to me." He smiled tightly. "I'm not even sure what you mean."

"I'm assuming you heard about the Scar Lord's last words," she said.

Harrison nodded grimly. Everyone in the Republic had probably heard by now. It was why he'd been dwelling on the House of Shadows. First, Bryce Balfour had showcased his talent in a violent spectacle at St. Morse, and now one of the most notorious street lords of the North Side had been revealed as a Mizer.

His first day as a senator had been nothing short of disastrous.

"I know her," she said. "I know Pup, their seconds...all of them. I could be a useful tool to have at your disposal."

She studied him carefully, knowingly. Harrison had gone to great lengths to keep his secret. He'd burned and discarded every piece of his birthright.

Except one.

"I'm surprised Pup never noticed, after all that time spent with Scavenger," she said. "I realized it at the execution. I was there, too. Jonas was waiting for you to help him."

Harrison had learned from his mother's mistakes not to get too attached. Jonas's death inconvenienced him more than it upset him, even if Jonas had held out hope that he'd be saved. But Harrison had sent him to St. Morse to die.

"Clever," he said quietly. "So what exactly do you want?"

"At least one of your omertas is now vacant, and I'm willing to make a trade." Sophia stood up and held out her hand, but it wasn't to shake. "I'll be your chess piece."

Never had Harrison seen someone offer themselves to him before. No one volunteered to be a victim. But now it had happened twice in three days, and the coincidence of it all made him suspicious.

He narrowed his eye. "And in exchange?"

Sophia tossed a golden Shadow Card on the table—the Lovers. Harrison recognized it immediately from the night before, but he couldn't imagine how Sophia had obtained it. It wasn't her card.

It was his.

"I want a key to the House of Shadows."

★ ★ ★ ★ ★

ACKNOWLEDGMENTS

♥   ♠   ♦   ♣

My "girl gang" book, as I've grown to call it over the years, would not have been possible without the support of so many talented and wonderful people—many badass women included.

Thank you to Christine Lynn Herman—if I ever found myself wanted and on the run with two bodies in the trunk of my car, you are the person I'd want riding beside me.

To my agent, Brianne Johnson, who fought for me every step of this process, I am in awe of your savviness and grateful to count you in my crew.

To my editor, Lauren Smulski, who never batted an eyelash when I told her how long and complicated this book would be. Thank you for your faith in me.

To Meg Kohlmann, kissing scene editor extraordinaire. To Amanda Haas, fellow accounting mastermind. To Katy Rose Pool, tireless champion. And to all the other amazing women in the Cult: Melody Simpson, Akshaya Raman, Janella Angeles, Kat Cho, Claribel Ortega, Mara Fitzgerald, Erin Bay,

Alexis Castellanos, and Tara Sim. You all inspire me as a creator and a person.

To Kaitlyn Sage Patterson, who has often felt like a partner in crime during this journey.

To Laura Gianino, Jennifer Abbots, Evan Brown, and the entire team at Inkyard for their work in making this series a success.

To the many other wonderful minds who have traveled with me into the world of New Reynes, including Zoe Sivak, Jena DeBois, Sarah Hudson, and Audrey Fae Dion.

To the OwlCrate team for placing *Ace of Shades* into the hands of such a vibrant, enthusiastic community of readers.

A special thank-you to the #ShadowGang for your incredible efforts to share this series with the world.

To my family and friends for always supporting my creative endeavors. To Jelly Bean, who contributed countless typos to this manuscript while walking across my keyboard. And to Ben, who patiently listens to me ramble about all my ideas, no matter the hour—I suppose I'll finally let you read the book now.

Turn the page for a sneak peek at Amanda Foody's
Queen of Volts, *the thrilling conclusion to*
The Shadow Game trilogy...

HARVEY

♥ ♠ ♦ ♣

It was early morning when Harvey Gabbiano dug the grave.

Harvey didn't like the cemeteries in the Deadman District, precisely because they *were* cemeteries. Most people didn't know it, but there was a difference between a cemetery and a graveyard—graveyards were connected to a church. But the only place to find devotion in this neighborhood was at the bottom of a bottle.

This cemetery was a bleak, soulless plot of land, made bleaker by the drizzle that had soaked through Harvey's clothes. Rusted industrial plaques marked each of the graves. There were no flowers anywhere, not even weeds, and the unkept grass grew patchy and brown.

"It would've been easier if you'd burned it," Bryce told him. He'd watched Harvey work all morning, but not once had he offered to help...or even to share his umbrella. Bryce didn't see the point in helping with tasks he disapproved of, even if this task was important to Harvey.

"It's holier to bury him," Harvey repeated yet again. Even

though Harvey was Faithful, he wouldn't have gone to all this trouble had the deceased not been wearing a Creed of his own. He didn't know many others who practiced the Faith anymore—it had been banned for so long now. "You don't have to stay."

"I'm staying. You're funny, you and those superstitions of yours. I could use a laugh."

Harvey didn't know how Bryce could find humor in the situation. The November weather was cold. The cemetery was irreverent and depressing. The dead had not deserved to die.

But Bryce had come with him, and so, no matter the circumstances, Harvey couldn't help but feel a little bit pleased.

"I'm not doing this to be funny," Harvey responded, forcing his voice into a grumble. He pressed his bulky leather boot against the step of the shovel. The mud he lifted glinted with green shards of broken bottles.

"My mistake," Bryce said drily. "You're doing this to be decent."

Harvey absolutely was doing it to be decent. To be *good*. Because Harvey might not have been the person who killed this man or any of the other hundred who'd perished two nights ago at the party in St. Morse Casino, but as long as he remained hopelessly in love with Bryce Balfour, he would always have blood on his hands.

It was hard not to glance at his friend as he worked. Harvey hated to look at him. But he didn't need to—he had long ago memorized every agonizing detail of his face, his figure, his posture. Bryce could be absent and still be Harvey's distraction.

Harvey hated himself for it.

The body made a *thump* when he pushed it into the hole.

Harvey straightened, his back aching from the exertion, his fingers blistered even through his gloves. The hours of rain had made the dried blood on the body and clothes run again, and the flattened brown grass it had been lying on moments before now flooded with red. Harvey watched as the puddles washed the blood away, and he murmured a silent prayer that the rain would do the same for his immortal soul.

"Harvey," Bryce said sharply.

Harvey's gaze shot toward him, and he flinched. Bryce hadn't worn his brown colored contacts since that night at St. Morse, when he revealed himself to be a malison, someone with the talent to create curses known as shades, a talent the world feared but hadn't believed to exist. And despite always knowing what Bryce truly was, Harvey wasn't used to this adjustment.

Bryce's malison scarlet eyes were a reminder of how low Harvey had fallen.

But Harvey's gaze didn't stop there—of course it didn't. It traveled across Bryce's face, down concave cheekbones and lips chapped from kissing someone who wasn't him. Down bony shoulders and a tall, skinny frame, over threadbare clothes and a black wool coat that draped shapelessly over him. Harvey lingered on the places *he* had kissed, on slender fingers and narrow hips and the smooth pale skin between. Those memories haunted him.

Bryce didn't pay Harvey's staring any attention. He never did. His concentration was focused on the card in his hand. He ran his thumb over its foiled gold back.

It was a Shadow Card, one of the cursed cards the Phoenix Club used to play the Shadow Game. Except it wasn't. Shadow Cards were silver. This one belonged to a different game, one Bryce and his girlfriend, Rebecca, had devised themselves, one they had set in motion at St. Morse two nights prior. Harvey had helped them deliver golden cards to every designated "player" across New Reynes, and now all that remained was to wait for the star player to make a move.

"They're here. I can feel it," Bryce said hoarsely, squeezing the card so hard it bent.

By "they," he meant the Bargainer. The City of Sin treated all of its legends with a hallowed reverence, and this one was the oldest, most famous of them all: the wandering Devil who would bargain for anything. Bryce had been obsessed with the tale for years, ever since Rebecca had fallen sick. Despite every effort—ethical or otherwise—Rebecca wasn't improving, and Bryce had convinced himself her last hope for a cure was the Bargainer's power. It was why he'd murdered all those people at St. Morse—a desperate, ruthless attempt for the Bargainer's attention.

I'll sell my soul, if that's what it takes, Bryce had once told Harvey, back when his smiles weren't so much like sneers, when he looked more like the boy Harvey used to love—the kinder version of himself, the one Harvey couldn't manage to let go of. Though Harvey had never voiced his opinion, Bryce had lost his soul the moment he'd formulated this horrible plan.

They all had.

Harvey tried to ignore Bryce's words. In the legend, the Bargainer approached people of their own choosing. The only way to summon them directly was through chaos.

Surely Bryce wouldn't attempt such evil, Harvey had once told himself.

But he had, and since that night at St. Morse, all of New Reynes seemed ablaze. The Scarhands, the largest gang in the seedy North Side, had crumbled, their lord executed. Séance, the notorious assassin of Chancellor Malcolm Semper, had been unmasked as both the last surviving Mizer and, to the city's shock, a seventeen-year-old girl from finishing school. Mafia donna Vianca Augustine had been shot dead, and her son had won his election. Luckluster Casino had burned, and the Torren Family empire along with it.

Thanks to Bryce, the City of Sin was in a state worse than chaos—it was in hell.

And now the Devil had returned home.

Even though Harvey was an accomplice in Bryce's plans, the thought of all that had transpired—and all that was still left to unfold—filled him with dread. He tried to focus on the shovel and the dirt and the grave, on this *one good thing*, but his sins weighed heavy on his soul.

"Harvey," Bryce snapped again. He never tolerated being ignored.

Harvey sighed. "How can you be certain the Bargainer *is* in New Reynes now?"

"I told you. I can feel it."

At that moment, the rain began to fall harder, shifting from a drizzle into a downpour. Harvey's brown corkscrew curls stuck against his fair skin, and he wiped the water from his eyes.

"Why haven't they come to me yet?" Bryce rasped, his hands trembling while he clutched his umbrella. "I'm the one who summoned them. I deserve my bargain."

"The legends never mentioned whether the Bargainer was prompt," Harvey pointed out. He dumped another pile of mud into the hole.

Bryce's lips formed a thin line. He trudged over to the grave. The body was now entirely covered with earth, but the plot was only half-filled. "That's good enough. We should go back."

"You can go. I'll finish," Harvey told him.

Bryce nodded and fiddled with his card anxiously. It was moments like these, when he looked so young and vulnerable, that made Harvey weak. Because even if Bryce Balfour had lost his soul, Harvey still kindled a hope that it could be found. That *he* could be the one to find it.

"Never mind," Harvey murmured. "I'll go with you."

Harvey heaved his shovel over his shoulder, said a final prayer for Jac Mardlin and his unfinished, unmarked grave, and followed his friend home.